Howard Blackett

Life of Giuseppe Garibaldi

Italian hero and patriot

Howard Blackett

Life of Giuseppe Garibaldi
Italian hero and patriot

ISBN/EAN: 9783337131487

Printed in Europe, USA, Canada, Australia, Japan

Cover: Foto ©Raphael Reischuk / pixelio.de

More available books at **www.hansebooks.com**

G. Garibaldi

ITALIA
LIBERATA
GARIBALDI
HIS LIFE AND
TIMES

LIFE OF GIUSEPPE

GARIBALDI,

Italian Hero and Patriot.

BY

HOWARD BLACKETT.

———◆———

LONDON:
WALTER SCOTT, 24 WARWICK LANE
PATERNOSTER ROW.
1888.

PREFACE.

A T the time we write this, men's hearts are moved at the passing away from amongst them of the veteran GARIBALDI; and the following pages aim at giving, in an appreciative spirit, the ways and words and doings of this wonderful man.

That a Life of Garibaldi ought to be written, no one who knows anything of the scope of its far-reaching influence will deny. Italian unity, though the fruit of the labours of three other mighty men—Mazzini, Cavour, and Victor Emmanuel—was certainly hastened on to completion more by the sword of Garibaldi than by the pens and diplomacy of the others. With a deep love for his dismembered and tyrant-ridden country, he set out with a firm faith that Italy could again become united and free. To all but an elect few this appeared as quixotic as the faith that would remove mountains, but Garibaldi believed in it, fought for it, and attained it. "Heart of Gold" he was called from his purity of purpose, his high-souled bravery and daring, and for the utter unselfish way he gave himself up to be spent for the good of his country; and there are golden lessons to be learned by all from his life.

For the youth of our times there is no character of modern days so worthy of admiration. Giving himself up to a noble end, it mattered not what dangers and difficulties he encountered—what kings, or statesmen, or nations said of him—he went forward in the path of Duty, fighting his way victoriously and gloriously. Full of adventure and deeds of daring, the story of his life will be read by the youth of future ages, even as they now read the old half-mythical stories of Tell and Wallace.

To lovers of Liberty his name will ever be a watchword, and his memory will be held in loving remembrance. The world, looking on at him in his rash expeditions, called him enthusiast, revolutionary adventurer, and conspirator, but now that the dust of his battles is laid, and the results of his fighting seen, he stands out clear in all men's view as "the one great heroic figure in the nineteenth century, which in purity and nobility of character, in loftiness of aim, in simplicity of motive, in courage and endurance, and in splendour of achievement, is hardly to be surpassed by any other with which the world has made acquaintance."

H. B

20th June 1882.

iv
er
hi
w
dc
yc
m

ar
w
er
nc
hi
"
w
ai
in
ar

CONTENTS.

CONTENTS.

CHAPTER VII.

CHAPTER VIII.

CHAPTER IX.

CHAPTER X.

CHAPTER XI.

CHAPTER XII.

CHAPTER XIII.

LIST OF ILLUSTRATIONS.

THE LIFE OF GARIBALDI.

CHAPTER I.

INTRODUCTION.

"Take him for all in all,
We shall not look upon his like again."
—SHAKESPEARE.

THE key-note of GARIBALDI'S life is his enthusiasm for liberty. Without this he might have been an honest, brave, and illustrious citizen; with it, the world recognises in him such a hero as one does not frequently meet with in the long annals of human history. In him the zeal for that sacred ideal which he had enshrined in his soul consumed all earthly ties and affections which might have marred the perfectness of his service; and he has been, throughout his life, not the mere devotee, but the chief apostle and champion of freedom. This may be admitted even by those who would set Mazzini, in one sense, above him. Mazzini was the prophet where Garibaldi was the king. Mazzini was the man of thought, Garibaldi the man of action. Mazzini was the interpreter and the lawgiver of Liberty, during the long years of Italy's passage through the wilderness; but it was Garibaldi who led his countrymen into the promised land. Italy reveres Mazzini as her teacher and guide; she loves and venerates Garibaldi as her deliverer.

The Cincinnatus of modern Rome, the man to whom no honour is greater than the simple discharge of his duty, to whom no reward is acceptable beyond the triumph of his sacred cause, in whose eyes emoluments and dignities are worthless; who retired, more than contented, from the salvation of his country to the cultivation of his farm— this man, whom Italy may justly rank as amongst the very noblest of all her sons, is yet, in the widest and most general sense, the champion of universal liberty. Not in Italy alone, but wherever he has found tyranny and oppression and cruelty, he has hated them with an implacable hatred, and has thrown himself, heart and hand, into the unequal contest. No cause, however hopeless, so long as it commended itself to him as the cause of right against might, has appealed to him in vain. Perhaps his noblest deeds of heroism and self-devotion were those which distinguished his champion-ship of the South American Republics. In Europe his sympathies have ever been on the side of those who, at whatever odds, were struggling for the rights of freemen. The Hungarians, the Poles, the victims of Ottoman mis-rule, have received the most hearty encouragement from his mouth, as they might have commanded the most unhesitat-ing assistance from his sword. His generous impulses have no doubt occasionally misled him, but he would not be the man he is, nor have won the triumphs he has won, without that very lack of calculating prudence and hesitation which is part and parcel of an enthusiast's nature.

The liberation and unification of Italy demanded a man of Garibaldi's stamp; and glorious as are the records of a hundred of his constant companions and followers, it is hard to see who, in the absence of this one hero, could have led the disheartened and discordant nation to victory. The task was a difficult one. Dismembered as Italy was, parcelled out under the sway of half-a-dozen petty tyrants, enslaved in mind by the oppressions and cruelty of a corrupt Papacy, and physically enslaved both by the harsh rule of her own kings and princes and by the ruthless severities of a foreign yoke, she was still more desperately divided in the counsels followed by those who most ardently yearned for her deliverance. Italian patriots were distracted by the multitude of their would-be leaders. Their jealousies and indecisions, the sure fruit of a life-long servitude, for many weary years rendered union impracticable, and successful resistance impossible. Mazzini himself more than once attempted to lead them against their oppressors; but they continually shrank back and failed in the very crisis of the enterprise. It was but the old story over again. Slaves by force of circumstances become slaves by force of habit; and when once the manliness of spirit has been cowed and beaten out of an oppressed community, it becomes next to impossible for any one man to restore it again.

If Garibaldi succeeded in this apparently hopeless task, it was because his unique character was precisely the one which was specially calculated to succeed. Simple and straightforward, like the Republicans of ancient Rome, he was absolutely untainted by the degrading influences to which the mass of his fellow-countrymen had been subjected. Where they had learned the sad lesson of suspicion and jealousy, he had inherited and cultivated the independence of a thoroughly honest and transparent mind. In all but the plain dictates of duty, he was as gentle and pliable as a child. In all but the severity of his hatred of tyranny, he was as soft and amiable as a woman. His life, even from early boyhood, was a life of self-devotion and heroic philanthropy. Self never entered into his calculation when there was a friend to assist or a fellow-creature to serve. His purity, his sympathy, his benevolence, his endurance, his prowess, and his invincible determination, charmed and fascinated all who came across him. There was an indescribable attraction in his very look, which did more to cement a friendship and to gain a follower than years of acquaintance could do with other men. His first meeting with Pietrocolo Rossetti was an instance of this unusual power. "I had not the trouble of seeking him," he himself says. "We passed accidentally, we exchanged a look, and all was said. After one smile, after one pressure of the hand, Rossetti and I were brothers for life."

The liberation of his country was the dream of Garibaldi's existence; and long as was the exile which fate condemned him to pass in dreary yearnings for his native land, it was perhaps better for him and for Italy that he should have been spared the protracted apprenticeship to conspiracy and intrigue undergone by Mazzini and his friends. Our hero had not the soul of a conspirator. He could not have hung on the skirts of inaction, satisfied with a perpetual cycle of plots and projects, half-hearted insurrections and precipitate retreats. If Garibaldi had never gone to South America— never left the company of his restless and injudicious fellow-countrymen, he would in all probability have thrown himself, even single-handed, upon the swords of the Neapolitan or Austrian tyrants, and died on the battle-field or in prison, leaving his name undistinguished and his task unfulfilled. It was indeed to his participation in the earlier attempts of Mazzini's disciples that Garibaldi owed his exile; but throughout his long absence from Italy he never forgot that his country was being crushed under the heel of an oppression scarcely credible in the present day; and he never ceased to cherish the hope that a time would come when he could return to the well-beloved land, and place himself at the head of her deliverers.

There was assuredly something in this dream of Italian Unity well calculated to inflame the spirit of a patriot.

Italy had been the mistress of the world, the bulwark of civilisation, the shrine of learning and art, the home of poetry and song. To be a Roman citizen had been a title of honour: and there was no existing nation, however great and glorious, which could match its greatness and glory with those of ancient Rome. Mighty conquerors, like Scipio and Cæsar, splendid rulers, like Augustus and Constantine, orators like Cicero, historians like Livy and Tacitus, poets like Virgil and Ovid, Horace and Lucretius, had shed deathless brilliance upon their country. The mantle of the ancients had fallen upon the moderns: Dante and Petrarch, Ariosto and Alfieri, had caught and transmitted the inspiration of the golden age. Even the annals of the Christian Church, with all their shameful episodes, had added lustre to the Eternal City. No wonder the Italians are proud of their native land. No wonder their souls burned within them at the thought that she might once more be united and free, and march yet again in the van of an enlightened world. It is necessary to recall the history of Italy in order fully to appreciate the records of the past half-century; but this recalled, the rest is easily understood. The Italians are free and united to-day, because the decline of ancient Rome never absolutely involved her fall, and because the spirit of their ancestors lives in them still.

There was yet another reason for the devotion with which Italians of the past two or three generations clung to, and stedfastly laboured to realise, the idea of a regenerate Italy. They were persecuted and oppressed beyond the power of Englishmen in the present day to estimate. A perusal of the Italian records of half a century ago will no doubt furnish some conception of the wretchedness which resulted from the unscrupulous misgovernment of Naples, Modena, and the Papal States, and from the ruthless tyranny of Austria: but such a conception must fall far short of the reality, as it was experienced, day after day, by those upon whom the rod of iron fell. The worst sufferings of the Turkish rayahs are not to be compared with the miseries endured throughout a large portion of the Peninsula, between the Congress of Vienna and the assumption by Victor Emmanuel of the crown of Italy. It was a hard school through which Italian patriots had to pass, but the discipline was effectual. The re-unification of their country was not possible without great sufferings, and the sacrifice of many heroic lives ; but there is not one lover of Italy, dead or living, who would not readily admit that the final triumph was well worth the price which has been paid for it.

The brief visit of Garibaldi to England in 1864, and his reception in the provinces and in the City of London, astounded the courts of Europe, whilst it manifested the deep impression his career had made upon the hearts and minds of the people. The most illustrious of Peers, the tens of thousands of artizans, the magnates of the world's money market, vied in their homage to the illustrious hero who had evidently been raised up by Providence for the purpose of liberating his country and bringing about mighty political changes; changes puzzling to all and confounding to some, but exciting alternately the awe and admiration of mankind.

His is a memory that will be hallowed while history has any charm, or its lessons any power : for in his life is included more than romance could have imagined of adventure, and more than political philosophy could have conceived of results. The simplicity which no applause can disturb and no disaster interrupt, is a characteristic very dear to Britons, for it is the distinguishing mark of her best-loved sons, as it is also of those in ancient story who are counted worthy examples to succeeding generations.

Garibaldi stands alone in a policy-ridden age : one whom wily diplomacy could never direct or divert, but whom diplomatists were compelled to consider. Fearless when kings were in fear, calm when Europe was in a tempest, he shook the Eternal City as it had never been shaken since first cradled amongst its seven hills. Brave, when the wicked were mighty, and bold, when they dared to overstep their line, he dreaded not their power, and he scorned their pride. Too great to threaten, but great enough to do, he performed deeds that toppled crowns from the heads of tyrants by the instrument of a righteous confidence in a population despised throughout the world. A degraded, debased, and demoralised multitude, they, at his presence, were inspired with faith to follow, as he led them to an elevation rivalling that of the most cultured and the most free. At his bidding the manacles rivetted by kings and priests dropped from the captive, and a disintegrated mass of humanity became coherent. Whilst Europe, and chiefly England, was continually reiterating—as the land of dethroned glory was considered—" Can these dry bones live?" he spake, and, behold, the valley was filled with a living host, quickened, vitalised, and mighty. Epic poetry could add to its own immortality by celebrating his renown ; for Homer and Virgil have no such tale to tell in all their imaginative flights as truth could utter of his greatness, nobleness, prowess, purity, and patriotism.

CHAPTER II.

GARIBALDI'S YOUTH.

" How has kind Heaven adorn'd the happy land,
And scattered blessings with a wasteful hand !
But what avail her unexhausted stores,
Her blooming mountains, and her sunny shores,
With all the gifts their heaven and earth impart,
The smiles of nature, and the charms of art,
While proud oppression in her valleys reigns,
And tyranny usurps her happy plains ?"

—ADDISON.

ELIGHTFULLY situated under the Maritime Alps, on the border of the Mediterranean, with the citadel of Monte Abano perched on a high-pointed rock overhanging the town, with the Paglion, a mountain torrent, on the west side dividing the town proper from the English suburb, lies the well-known Nice, or, in Italian, *Nizzo*, the birthplace of Giuseppe (Joseph) Garibaldi. Not incongruous with the life of such a man is the eventful history of that town. Fortified very strongly in the middle ages, it was besieged on the land side by the French, under François I., and by the Turkish fleet under Barbarossa. These took and plundered the place, except the citadel, which held out. A hundred and fifty years passed, and again the French entered ; in fifteen years the process was repeated, and in 1774 they took it once more. Amid the general upheaval during the Great Revolution in 1791 it was annexed to the Republics and made the capital of the Alpes Maritimes ; but on the overthrow of Napoleon Bonaparte in 1814–15, Nice reverted to Sardinia, and finally, being

THE HOUSE IN WHICH GARIBALDI WAS BORN AT NICE

made the bribe whereby Count Cavour secured the concurrence of Napoleon III. in the reunification of Italy, it was,
with Savoy, ceded to France in 1859.

Garibaldi was born on the 22nd of July 1807. His
father, Domenico Garibaldi, born on the sea, followed a sea-
faring life, and at one time owned a trading vessel. His
mother, Rosa Raguindo, the daughter of a major-domo of a
noble house in the neighbourhood, is described as a singularly gentle and affectionate woman, whose cares and hopes
were centred in her home and her boy, to whom by pre-
cept and example she imparted much of her affectionate
disposition and instinctive purity. At the time Giuseppe
entered this troublesome world his father seems to have
done with wandering. He had experienced many vicissitudes, and though he still clung to the sea, he seems to have
amused himself with, rather than depended on, the labour
of a fisherman's life. To this occupation the boy was introduced very early, and in it he learned endurance, skill, and
manliness. The occupation of a sailor was not intended by
his parents to be permanent: the partiality of the mother
and the ambition of the father united in the desire that he
should enter one of the professions—the church, the law, or
medicine ; but the boy's thoughts would not run in a groove.
The freedom of the sea, its labour and its leisure in their
incessant irregularity, charmed and weaned him from the
study which is an essential qualification for a professional
career. He himself said, " I passed my first years as all
children pass them—amid smiles and tears—fonder of
pleasure than of work, of amusement than of study; and I
did not profit as I should have done, had I been more seriously inclined, by the sacrifices my parents made for me."
He attended school from obedience rather than desire, and
his dislike for books was the only cloud that overshadowed
the mutual affection of parents and child. One day he ran
away from school, utterly tired of sedentary existence, with

three of his fellow scholars, gained possession of a fishing boat in the port of Nice, and set out for Genoa, some one hundred miles distant. They were, however, pursued; for an abbé, who had seen the urchins making their preparations, communicated with the parents in time for a horseman to be sent off, who overtook and captured them at Monaco, much to their confusion. He brought them home, and Garibaldi said humorously, in after days, "An abbé had seen us start and betrayed us; whence, perhaps, arises my little sympathy for abbés." There is nothing extraordinary in these incidents of childhood, save as they shew the self-reliance, love of liberty, independence, and daring common to many boys, but in him the shadowing forth of a life dominated and characterised by such attributes. He is remembered by his school-fellows as the hero of many an eventful day.

On one occasion some of them were sailing in a pleasure-boat between Nice and Villafranca, and, a squall coming on, their lives were in danger. Giuseppe saw the danger and the duty; he swam out and saved them. A another time he was hunting with one of his cousins in the Var, and, as he was resting on the banks of a deep ditch, where the washerwomen were accustomed to wash their linen, he saw one of the women fall in. Young as he was—only eight— he threw himself into the water and saved her. Garibaldi has told this anecdote to support his contention that the rendering of aid to others is an instinct of his mind, and with a natural modesty he disclaims all merit for such actions; an argument that would strip many of us of our reputation for charity, patience, and domestic virtues.

One of his tutors, Arena, was still residing at Nice a few years ago. Between him and Garibaldi there was ever a mutual regard : from him our hero derived his much-prized acquaintance with Roman history. His general education was repressed by a fear on the part of his parents that too much learning might lead him into hazards that would bring them trouble. We may smile at the fear; but the circumstances of the time made a little knowledge a dangerous thing. Piedmont was over-run by priests. Every young man was discouraged from citizen life and exhorted to the monastic. The tyrants, Pope and King, heard strange sounds now and then, and dreaded the growth of an intelligent community that might break their bonds in sunder. Garibaldi's wit was not acquired in schools; experience was his chief tutor.

He counted himself one of the strongest swimmers in existence, and declared "that he was born amphibious, and no wonder he jumped into the water to save a fellow-creature that was not so." Gymnastics he learned by climbing among the shrouds and slipping along the ropes. The use of the sword he describes as having been acquired in defending his own head, and using his best efforts to split those of others; and as for horsemanship, he had it from the Gauchos, the best horsemen in the world.

The love of his mother never forsook him. He deemed her perfect. When, in after life, he was in direst danger, hazardous imprisonment, wounded, forsaken, the most poignant grief was the thought of the pain she would suffer if by any means she could know of his distress: and his very life of adventure, he feared, kept her in continual apprehension of his danger. On the other hand, the recollection of her was his great source of endurance. He said, "I am not superstitious, and yet I will afirm this: that in the most terrible incidents of my life, when the ocean roared under the keel of the ship, tossing us about like a cork, and when bullets were whistling around like hail, I constantly saw her praying for me; and I felt that no harm could happen when such holy prayers ascended to Heaven."

But it was now time for Garibaldi to be doing something. The boy had overmastered his father's wishes that he should adopt a professional career, and now his mother had the mournful duty of packing his first portmanteau—he must go forth, and "take his part of danger on the stormy sea." Romance filled the brain of the novice, but it was no romance to her. The ship to him was a mistress, and the crew demi-gods; the sailors' songs were to him enchanting music; the captain the boldest of mankind. His first voyage was to Odessa.

Going to Odessa is very charming in the eyes of those who have never seen anything but the surroundings of childhood: but his going to Odessa had no charm whatever for father and mother, who were to be left behind, and daily gaze upon the empty chair. His father could not bear that; when the time came for a second voyage he insisted on becoming his son's companion. The destination was Rome: and, in times when long travel was infrequent, and the leisurely visit to historic shrines the taste of few, Garibaldi was conscious of an inexpressible delight in the expectation and in the accomplishment of the project. He used his eyes well, gaining much knowledge from observation. The city, its ways and customs, the priests, the people, produced countless and ineradicable effects upon the young mind now for the first time brought in contact with them. Possessing, as he did, a natural loftiness of thought and aim, that visit made so strong an impression as to remain bright for ever. Other voyages followed, but they were chiefly coasting trips, in which the incidents were the commonplace ones of fishing and trading. These were all made in his father's society, and most probably in the interest of the household: but the journey to Rome remained vividly before him. It touched the political side of life; and Garibaldi became conscious of a latent thirst for the knowledge of every phase of Italian and Roman story, and an acquaintance with the arrangements that were or had been made for carrying on the functions of government in the Imperial City and the provinces. That thirst was not yet insatiable, and could be endured a while. He found that nobody knew anything about the subject, and also that they were afraid to inquire.

Shortly after this Garibaldi apprenticed himself, independently of his father, on board the brigantine *L'Enea*. They had been to Cagliari, and were returning in company with several other vessels, in fine weather. After two or three days, the winds which sweep the Libyan desert, and lash the Mediterranean into storm, began to blow, driving the ships out of their course. One vessel, which had seemed to be the best of the company, succumbed to the fury of the tempest, and the rest escaped. A terrible wave struck her, and in an instant they saw nothing but a few miserable wretches upon the sloping deck, holding out their hands, imploring help. A more terrible wave swept them off in an instant, and no aid could be rendered. Nine individuals of the same family perished before their eyes; and this frightful occurrence Garibaldi described as making an eternal impression upon his mind. The *Enea* returned by way of Vado and Genoa to Nice.

His next experience of life's vicissitudes was acquired in several voyages to the Levant, a part immemorially infested by pirates, by whom their ship was taken three times and plundered; but the wretches coming twice on one journey, and finding nothing on the second visit, were furious at the unnecessary trouble they had been at. Here our hero saw life divested of fear, and he caught the inspiration. Men who did not know that sensation inspired in him the same indifference; and he called to mind the doings of Nelson, who delivered Nice and other places in Sardinia out of the grasp of the French with the most inconsiderable force, and in avowed breach of the regulations of the service. He had read the history to some purpose, and consecrated himself to courage from that time forth.

During another of these Mediterranean coasting expeditions he fell sick, and was left at Constantinople. His sickness lasted longer than his money; but fortunately for him a lady, a native of Nice, received him into her house, nursed, and restored him. Much as he loved the sea, life must be maintained on land; he had to depend on the hospitality of the gentleman whose home he shared. He could not get away; for, to say nothing of the state of his exchequer, a war had broken out between Turkey and Russia, and every port was blockaded. A physician, M. Diego, saw his condition, and procured him an engagement as tutor in the house of a widow who had three sons. Here he remained several months.

His engagements in the merchant service had been a necessary qualification for the seafaring career, according to the law of his country; and as soon as the four stipulated years were ended, Garibaldi sought an opportunity of taking the command of a vessel himself. His first ship was the *Notre Dame,* of which he became captain, and subsequently commander. He also qualified himself for naval service. Thus the years passed on until he had reached his twenty-third or twenty-fourth birthday; not without many an aspiration that he might be able to perform some exploit in the interest of his country which should tend to her liberation from an augmenting thraldom, and that he might devote himself entirely to her service.

No opportunity of gathering information was permitted to pass unimproved; but the general political intelligence was clouded by ignorance and prejudice. The current of events, and the sentiments of the population, could not be accurately ascertained; but there was evidently a widening breach between rulers and people. The conduct of the first gradually tended to violent repression, and that of the others to rebellion—the monarchs becoming more absolute, the people more republican.

The French Revolution of 1830 had just been enacted, and the waves of that terrible outbreak were still uncalmed. There were other monarchs who deserved as harsh a dismissal as Charles X. of France, for the iniquity of their rule was more grievous. Men were comparing notes; questioning the titles of kings; wondering whether they were indispensable; counting up their wrongs; studying how to be avenged; growing anxious about the future of their children; inquiring why nations should be incapable of self-government; and, in the end, finding all these questions resolve themselves into one issue—their country.

Through some such course of reflection passed the mind of Garibaldi as he conversed with a French patriot whom he casually met when on a voyage to Taganrog. He was a man who knew more than any previous acquaintance of the manner in which things were going on in Italy, and the feelings of the people thereon. From him he learned for the first time that there existed a number of Italians whose chief thought and purpose was to compass the liberation of their illustrious country from the tyranny of its kings and the oppression of its priests.

Barrault, a wild enthusiast, of whom there were many in Italy at about the time of the French Revolution, and during the subsequent years, was at the head of a sect of Saint-Simonians, who aimed at the purification of religion by the negation of certain pretentions and doctrines then accepted; and it happened that among the passengers on board his vessel, bound for Constantinople, were some of these people and their leader. Garibaldi, who had found it almost impossible to obtain positive knowledge of the thoughts of his countrymen from sources he could trust, gladly put himself in the way of knowing his passenger; and, in the interviews which followed, he threw open his heart to him as a fellow patriot. Hitherto his thoughts had crystallised about his country and its wrongs; under the influence of Barrault they widened to embrace the cause of the oppressed and benighted under every circumstance. From him Garibaldi learned that the defender of his country alone is but a soldier: if, on the other hand, he be a cosmopolite, offering his aid in all struggles against tyranny, he is more—he is a hero.

"There arose in my mind strange glimmerings, by the light of which I saw in a ship no longer a mere vehicle of commercial exchange, but a winged messenger bearing the word of the Lord and the sword of the Archangel; became greedy for emotions, curious for new things; asking myself if this irresistible vocation, which I had believed to be merely as the captain of a long voyage, had not for me horizons still unperceived. Here I fancied that I saw glimpses through the vague mists of the future."

From the Saint-Simonians Garibaldi heard the name of a young man who was then rising into fame among the murmuring, brooding population, as of one that might turn out to be their deliverer, and certainly desired to be regarded as their friend. Mazzini was issuing thousands of pamphlets, addressed to the people in the provinces, first at one place and then at another, recalling to their remembrance the glorious history of their ancestors, their mighty power and influence in Europe, and the capacity they had for self-government in the times of the Italian Republics. This he contrasted with their present condition, asking the cause of the contrast, and appealing to them to be worthy of their history, and vindicate their fathers in the face of the oppressors, whose perfidy and cruelty were pictured in words of marvellous pungency and enthusiasm. It was a gospel to Garibaldi. He heard, and the vision of the seer was given to him. He felt his former inspiration return, and this time, stronger and more uncontrollable.

There had been many revolutions in the peninsula. Indeed, the people had never submitted to their bondage.

The wave of the French Revolution of 1830 had not been unfelt in Italy, and once more the patriotic element felt the pleasures of hope. They had greater grievances than any nation. Their tale of oppression was longer than that of any other people ; and much greater effort had been made by their oppressors to destroy every means of help and every helper ; and made, too, with greater success. But nothing could stamp out the love of country. That remained ; practically unmeaning, because inoperative ; but held with religious tenacity, waiting for the coming of the hour and the man, when the hope for freedom might shew some prospect worthy of the struggle and of martyrdom.

There had been great efforts toward establishing a constitution in 1820 and 1821, and the struggle had the sympathy of Englishmen. That struggle was repressed under atrocious circumstances, and Naples went on from bad to worse ; her people became more demoralised ; her rulers more ruthless and tyrannical. Now, in 1831, the cycle of history brought another prospect of revolution. It broke out in Piedmont, Lombardy, Florence, Bologna, and other places ; but the people were not ready, and kingcraft and priestcraft were. It failed. There was lacking both intellectual and practical leadership. Austria arrived promptly on the scene. She had undertaken the duty alone, at the peace of 1815, which before that had been performed by combination of France with herself. Any Italian government might rely on her instantaneous assistance *in the event of the people demanding a constitution, and also if they should create confusion by insurrection.*

Lord Byron describes in one of his letters the condition of affairs in his time. The description minutely applies to the days when Mazzini and Garibaldi were just beginning their labours. "Oh, those scoundrel sovereigns ! Let us but see them beaten, and there is yet a resurrection for Italy and hope for the world. If this country could but be

freed, what would be too great for the accomplishment of
that desire; for the extinction of that sigh of ages? Let us
hope. They have hoped a thousand years. It is no great
matter, supposing that Italy could be liberated, who or
what is sacrificed; it is a grand object, the very poetry of
politics. Only think, a free Italy! Why, there has been
nothing like it since the days of Augustus. I shall think it
by far the most interesting spectacle and moment in existence, to see the Italians send the barbarians of all nations
back to their own dens. I lived long enough among
them to feel more for them as a nation than for any other
people in existence. But they want union, and they want
principle; and I doubt their success. There are materials
in them, and a noble energy, if well directed; but who is to
direct them? No matter. Out of such times heroes spring
—out of chaos God made a world—and out of high passions
come a people."

Again: "You have no idea what a state of oppression
this country is in! They have arrested above a thousand,
high and low, throughout Romagna—banished and confined
others without trial or even accusation. It has been a
miserable sight to see the general desolation in families.
There has been thousands of these proscriptions within the
last month in the Legations. You neither know nor dream
the consequences of this war. It is a war of men with
monarchs, and will spread on the dry rank grass of the
vegetable desert."

It did spread. That work was again in hand, and the
tragedies of 1820–1 were repeated in 1831–2. Again Austrian
cannon had been planted in the market-places. The uni-
versities of Turin, Genoa, Parma, and Pavia were closed,
and the Sapienza at Rome suspended. The youth of the
country could not be trusted to assemble in the halls of
learning. Pope Pius VIII. had died; and on one of the
first days of February 1831, from Bologna nearly up to the

capital the governments fell. While Austria was using its forces in repressing this great effort, it was compelled by the remonstrant Powers to join in a diplomatic note with England, France, and Prussia, to the new Pope Gregory XVI., imploring him to improve the government, that he might have tranquillity, and at the same time tendering some practical suggestions of reform. The Pope promised "a new era;" and he was as good as his word; for he ruled so infamously that, if he had not been taken away by death, Rome and Gregory would have been hurled to destruction by a maddened nation. He excelled his predecessor, Pius, in cruelty. Provinces had been deluged with blood for years and years: but now a new scourge—afterwards denominated Pontifical Volunteers—was formed, and furnished with weapons and the Apostolic blessing! These bravos were under a vow to exterminate the Liberals, by the dagger and by fire, all over the land, and not even to spare the women and children. Red-handed rascals, the scum of the whole land, whose ordinary life had ever been robbery and murder, were consecrated by the Vicar of Jesus Christ to this bloody business as a regular occupation; and they took their commissions with alacrity, and fulfilled them with fiendish zeal.

Mazzini saw that, whatever was to be effected in the future, there must be a general preparation throughout the whole of the peninsula; and he therefore laboured to kindle and foster the spirit of agitation, that it might ripen to a universal resistance whenever the opportunity should arise. The Mazzinian literature was caught at with avidity, and although prohibited, nothing could hinder its dissemination. Mazzini had been driven to Marseilles, and from that French town he issued his journal, entitled *Young Italy.* It was here that Garibaldi, through a mutual acquaintance, was introduced to him.

Charles Albert had ascended the throne of Sardinia under

most favourable auspices. He was disposed to make his reign pacific by making his policy just, or at least more just than that of his predecessor. He professed to be willing to yield constitutional rights, and to rule according to the wishes of the people. They trusted him, and hoped that a brighter day was dawning. But in a short time the Jesuit Fathers gained an ascendancy over him, and their influence upon his policy was baneful. They advised forcible repression of revolutions, by silencing all who fomented agitation, and by keeping back from the people the knowledge for which they instinctively longed. The consequence was that the King's crown was soon tarnished with blood, which, when once drawn, created an insatiable thirst for more. Mazzini's journal gave him and his friends umbrage. They trembled before public opinion, and the King was easily led to apprehend personal danger, as well as loss of prerogative. Its circulation was prohibited in Italy; its possession a crime, and its perusal treason. A military tribunal was formed for working the decree, and the first victim, a certain Corporal Tamburelli, appeared before them, charged with having read a copy to the soldiers. Ten or fifteen others immediately followed, charged with possessing seditious or unlawful books. All were shot in the back, as being a greater degradation than the ordinary court-martial executions. One went through a long period of suffering, and left a memoir of the treatment he had received. "They commenced by taking away my books—a Bible, a collection of prayers, and some religious books; irons were put upon my legs, and I was removed to a more loathsome dungeon than the wretched place I occupied; the windows were double-barred, and the door double-locked. My neighbour, Vochieri, I could faintly see through a chink in the wall. He had irons upon his legs, and a guard on either side with drawn swords as he lay on his bed, and an armed man at the door, none daring to speak. Now and then the

Capuchins came to vex him into recantation, but that was in vain, and one day he was led out to execution." He was taken a long way round, that the route might pass his dwelling, where his wife, sister, and children lived. He smiled at their wicked craft, and said, unmoved, "They forget that there is that in the world which I love more than them, and exclaimed, "*Viva l'Italia!*" He bade them "March on," and in a short time became another of the thousands whose lives were not dear to them in comparison with their country's deliverance.

These narrations were the daily food of Garibaldi. His intercourse with Mazzini became so constant as to be almost uninterrupted, working in his mind an ineradicable conviction that his life must be spent in the career of patriotism. The communion soon passed from words to projects, but Mazzini had received a warning from the French authorities that he must quit France, as the King of Sardinia had preferred a complaint to Louis Philippe of the publications he was issuing against his government.

Mazzini left and went to Genoa. But he had excited hopes he could not satisfy. He had set on fire the enthusiasm of the people, and they would not wait. They demanded action; and action he was incapable of wisely directing. But the demand was a reasonable one, and he felt it must be met. In the conference which followed, a leader was agreed upon against Mazzini's wishes. The choice fell upon a certain Ramerino, who had been prominent in the Polish struggles, and acquired in consequence a great name. It is surprising how powerful among democrats may become the prejudice for or against a name, quite irrespective of any actual knowledge of the individual, and how eagerly the disputants will contend on a matter requiring, above all things, mutual concession, conducting the controversy to the very verge of disunion. Mazzini did not approve of this man; his followers did. They

would not yield, and in the end he gave way.   A plan
was agreed upon in September 1833, and this plan included
the co-operation of Garibaldi.   Ramerino was summoned to
Genoa, and at the next conference it was resolved that two
republican columns should march upon Piedmont, the one
by way of Savoy and the other direct from Genoa.   Mazzini's opinion of the new leader was speedily justified.   No
sooner had Ramerino received the 40,000 fr. for the
expenses incident to the expedition than he pursued a
policy of delay, so that the affair dragged languidly along
until January 1834, by which time the authorities had
gleaned sufficient knowledge to put them completely on
their defence, and to render the project abortive.   Irritated
with the procrastination, Mazzini compelled decision on the
31st January, when Ramerino met him in council of war,
with two other generals and an *aide-de-camp.*

Mazzini proposed that they should take military occupation of the village of San Juliano, and there raise their
standard.   To this Ramerino agreed.   Both columns were
to start on the same day : one from Carange, the other from
Nyon.   Ramerino took the command of that from Carange,
and a Pole, Gransby, was appointed to the other.   The
Genevese government looked suspiciously on these proceedings.   France and Piedmont might both unite in
regarding it as a breach of international courtesy, if not of
international law.   They wished to prevent the departure
of the first column, but the populace rose, and there was no
alternative open to the Genevan authorities but to allow
the column to set out.   The other departed from Nyon in
two barks, one conveying the men, the other the arms.   A
government force was instantly despatched in pursuit ; the
arms were taken and the men arrested.   With the first
column was Mazzini, ill from fever, and unfit for shouldering
muskets and making long marches.   The column that was
to come by water not arriving, Ramerino diverted the

march, taking his party by another route, not even knowing whither it led. The cold was intense, and the roads heavy; besides which, the company, being chiefly composed of Italian volunteers, who were impatient to begin and ill-disposed for this delay, were discontented. As they passed through certain Italian villages none wished them God-speed. Mazzini was in anguish; he perpetually inquired whither they were going, and could obtain no satisfactory reply. They arrived at Carra, and halted for the night; and the patriot then, fixing on Ramerino a dark and suspicious look, exclaimed in his impatience, "It is not by following this road that we can hope to meet the enemy: we ought to go where we can be put to the test. If victory be impossible, let us at least prove that we know how to die." Recriminations followed, and at the same time a sound of firing broke on their ears. It was, indeed, a false alarm; but it effectually disheartened Mazzini, whose energy here failed, and with it consciousness. He had disturbed visions of retreating companions; and before coming to himself again he was in Switzerland. Ramerino declared that all was lost, refused to go further, and beat a retreat. Another column of French Republicans set out from Grenoble, and passed the frontiers of Savoy; but on the information of the French authorities, they were attacked by Sardinians and dispersed, leaving two prisoners, who were ruthlessly shot.

Garibaldi's share in the abortive enterprise of 1834 had been allotted to him on board of the frigate *Eurydice*, where e had been busy making proselytes for the revolution. Had the movement opened well, he and his converts were to seize the vessel and hold it for the Republican service. But this part was not enough for him. He had heard of a rising that had been arranged at Genoa, where the barracks were to be seized. Leaving his companions in charge of the ship, he came by boat to Genoa, landed at the appointed hour, and hastened to the barracks.   Here he waited for an hour, but nothing happened.   The affair had become known, and the Republicans had fled, though some were arrested. He had only entered the service to help the Republican cause, and now deemed it useless to return to the ship.   He thought of escape, but found that troops were surrounding the place.   There was no time to be lost.   Hastily he entered the house of a fruiterer, which was kept by a woman, to whom he confessed his dilemma.   She did not refuse her aid.   She took him into an inner room, and provided him with the disguise of a countryman.   At about eight o'clock in the evening, with the air of one who was at ease, he left Genoa on the 5th of February 1834.   He judged it best to direct his course to the mountains.   Crossing gardens, and climbing walls, he took the road to Cassiopea, by way of the mountains of Sestre, with the design of reaching Nice, which he effected in ten days.

Wishing to avoid alarming his mother by his sudden appearance, he went to the house of his aunt in the Piazza di Vittoria, where he rested for a day.   On the following night, accompanied by two friends, he resumed his pilgrimage.   On reaching the banks of the Var, which is on the border of Nice, they found the river swollen with rains. Garibaldi took the water, and, half-wading, half-swimming, reached the opposite shore.   The two friends could not imitate his example; so, waving his hand in signal of farewell, he left them, and deeming himself safe, went straight to the French Corps de Garde of Douaniers, telling them who he was, and why he had quitted Genoa.   The Corps de Garde considered him their prisoner until further orders ; and those orders must be sent to Paris.   Making no resistance—because he felt sure of some opportunity of escape—Garibaldi allowed himself to be taken to Dragnignan, where he was lodged in a first-storey chamber, having a window some fifteen feet from the ground.   But fifteen

CITIZENS SHOT FOR READING MAZZINI'S JOURNAL.

feet was nothing to him. He sprang out, and they did not, preferring the tour of the staircase. Making for the road, he was soon lost in the seclusion of an unknown mountain. Strange places brought no disheartening : a sailor without a map has one in Italy which he always can depend upon. Garibaldi looked at the sky, from whence he had been many a time glad to learn his way. He soon made out his position, and marched off for Marseilles.

The next evening found him at a village ; he went into a hostelry, where two persons, a young woman and young man, were warming themselves previous to supper, which was being prepared. Eighteen hours had sharpened his appetite, and he also wished to eat. The supper was good, the wine pleasant, the fire was cheering, and he was revived ; on which the host began to rally him upon his appetite and cheerfulness. Candid and fearless, he answered that, as for his appetite, it was not extraordinary, eighteen hours having passed since it had been gratified ; and as for his cheerfulness, he thought himself entitled to be merry after having escaped, in his own country death, and in France imprisonment. So much of the story being told, the rest followed, for the host appeared frank, and his wine good. But to his amazement, when the recital ended, the brow of "mine host" darkened. Garibaldi said, "Well, and what's the matter with you ?" To which the other answered, "After having heard the confession you have made, I conceive it is my duty to arrest you." This did not alarm our hero. He burst into a loud laugh, pretending to deem it a joke. He did not lose heart, because, as he says, "there was not a man in the world he feared." "Very well, then, arrest me ; but it will be time enough for that when we come to the dessert. Let me finish my supper, if I have to pay double for it, for I am still hungry."

The place was a rendezvous for the village youth who came thither to drink, learn the news, and talk politics ; and gradually ten or a dozen of them assembled, and these began playing at cards. The host said nothing, but kept his eye on his visitor. Assuming carelessness, and having no luggage or other guarantee for the reckoning, Garibaldi chinked his crowns, and the sound was harmonious. One of the party had just concluded a song, amid the bravos of all, when Garibaldi rose, glass in hand, exclaiming, "It is my turn." Forthwith, in his own good tenor, he carolled forth Beranger's *Le Dieu des bonnes gens*, in a free rollicking style. Beranger is the beloved song-writer of France: his choruses are fraternal ; and after repeating some of the couplets, the company fell to mutual embracing, with vivas for Beranger, Italy, and France. There was no further question about the arrest, and the night was spent in drinking, singing, and playing. When morning broke the young fellows insisted on escorting their new acquaintance, which he permitted, provided the distance were six miles. He then trudged on to Marseilles without any accident. When he reached that place he read in the newspaper that he was condemned to death ! The notoriety was novel to him : he had never seen himself in print before. But it occurred to him that under the circumstances he had better change his name, at least for the present. So he became M. Pane, and availed himself of the hospitality of a friend until he should succeed in obtaining employment. This came at last, and he entered as mate on board the *Union*, Captain Gazar.

Here again he was fortunate enough to save the life of a fellow-creature. As he was looking listlessly from a back window, on a Sunday afternoon, he saw in the harbour a young college student amusing himself by jumping from bark to bark. All at once he missed his footing, and fell shrieking into the water. Booted and dressed as he was, Garibaldi sprang into the basin, diving twice without success : the third time the arm of the boy was seized and his head raised above water. As the brave swimmer pushed

him to the quay, the mother 'and an immense crowd gave
vent to their emotions in heartfelt thanks and in loud
huzzas. The parents also made him costly presents.

These incidents did not interrupt the most serious reflec-
tions of his mind upon the great cause to which he had
devoted himself.

Garibaldi had read in the history of his country the
various policies which leaders had assumed when acting
upon and controlling large masses of his countrymen.
These were as diverse as their number, but had they been
identical, imitation was not Garibaldi's way. If the life
before him were to be useful it must take its own free
course. As he contemplated the character of his countrymen, he saw the effects of the past injustice and tyranny;
they were suspicious, listless, morose. Of leaders they
were weary. "Who will shew us any good?" they asked
with cynical sarcasm. He determined himself to be their
leader. Italy, to be free, must free itself; and he would go
down among them, bear their troubles and misfortunes,
be charged with their crimes, accept the odium of their
degradation, be himself sometimes cheated, robbed, betrayed
by them, and see if his faith in them would create their
faith in him, and whether in the end they might cast off
their chains and claim freedom. He had heard "the
continually reiterated objection urged by those who wished
them ill, that Italians are unfit for self-government, and
should not be entrusted with it until they could use it
wisely." He would shew the world the falsehood of the
sneer. All the liberty in the world has come from the
assertion by the governed of the right to govern themselves.
He would hurl back the calumny by working until stroke
after stroke should throw down all barriers, and the world
should see whether a popular administration could not be as
just, as humane, as far-seeing, as generous, as unselfish
as that of the score of kingdoms of which Europe was

composed; and whether the behaviour of his countrymen, rude as they then were, did not favourably compare with that of their tyrants.

The ship *Union* was bound for Odessa, but on reaching that port Garibaldi resolved to return by another vessel to Marseilles. A Turkish brig, which he met with at the Gouletta, took him back. Marseilles was smitten with cholera, and the people had deserted the place. Nothing was to be seen but the signs of mourning and death; nurses were scarce; the physicians were at their wits' end to provide suitable attendants for their patients. Garibaldi and a young man from Trieste volunteered, and spent a fortnight in the common hospital of the city. The chivalry of this deed may be estimated when it is remembered that the disease was almost invariably fatal, and carried off its fifty to sixty a day. Those who were compelled to stay in the town shut themselves in the garrets of their houses-drawing up food, water, and provisions by ropes. Public places and eating-houses were closed, and half the physicians fled. Tuscany also suffered terribly at this time.

At the end of a fortnight an opportunity occurred for Garibaldi to take another engagement on board ship. A vessel from Nantes was just setting sail for Rio Janeiro, and he was offered the position of second-mate. He accepted it, and, soon after arriving at that port, had the good fortune to make an extraordinary and undying friendship with Pietrocolo Rossetti. It was a case of mutual attraction, which he thus describes: " I had not the trouble of seeking him; we stood in no need of studying each other to become acquainted. We passed accidentally, we exchanged a look, and all was said. After one smile, after one pressure of the hand, Rossetti and I were brothers for life."

The purity of this friendship was touching in the extreme. The piety, the poetry, the melancholy, the faith, the earnestness of Rossetti must have added a singular charm to the wildness of Garibaldi's chequered career. The friends spent a few months in Rio, sometimes trading, but mostly enjoying each other's society, when an accident made them acquainted with the President's secretary of Rio Grande. This Republic was then at war with Brazil, and letters of marque were being issued to those who would cruise against the latter power.

They soon ascertained that the contest was an unequal one : the stronger seeking to coerce the weaker. The course was instantly clear. They joined the weak. They obtained a thirty-ton vessel and fitted her for war, christening her the *Mazzini*, and manned her with sixteen of their companions, chiefly Italians and Maltese. With this audacious outfit they determined to attack the Empire of Brazil, and lost no time in setting to work. Their arms and ammunition were concealed under some meat, and they set sail for the Marica islands. Touching at the largest of the group, Garibaldi leaped ashore, scrambled to the most elevated spot, and, imitating an eagle, uttered a cry intended to denote freedom and possession. And then to business. His observatory soon enabled him to spy a goëlette flying the Brazilian colours in the offing. He returned on board, put to sea, and steered straight for the ship, which, being within two or three miles of the channel of Rio Janeiro, had no idea of danger. She was boarded and taken without resistance. A poor, wretched Portuguese passenger came crouching up to Garibaldi with a casket of diamonds in his hand, which he tendered on condition of his life being spared. The box was closed again, and returned with the assurance that his life was not in risk, and an intimation that perhaps he might have a more urgent occasion for his diamonds.

This kind of work was, however, too perilous, for the port could easily open fire upon them. They decided therefore to scuttle their own vessel, after shifting the cargo on to the prize. This was done, and so ended the brief glory of the bark *Mazzini.* Much to Garibaldi's delight, the vessel proved to be an Austrian, laden with coffee, bound for Europe. He felt himself instinctively at war with Austria; but in all his engagements of this nature neither himself or any of his men ever did otherwise than respect the life and fortune of passengers.

Changing the name of the new craft from *La Louise* to *Scano Pilla*—The Tatterdemalion, a compliment to his crew —they went on towards another island near the mainland, where the passengers and their property were lowered into the ship's boat, and left to go where they choose. They then departed to Rio de la Plata, casting anchor at Maldonato, in the Republic of Uruguay, where they were well received by the people. Rossetti set out for Monte Video, to dispose of some of their cargo, and turn it into cash. Lying off the entrance to that splendid harbour, they spent some eight days in idleness; but the authorities on shore were cogitating mischief. Republics are not always mutually sympathetic. Orders came from Monte Video to the chief man at Moldonato to arrest Garibaldi and sieze the vessel. Entertaining a kindly sentiment, the subordinate sent a messenger to Garibaldi with a request that he would depart immediately. A little difficulty occurred in carrying out this direction. One of the merchants there had purchased some coffee and some articles of vertu, taken from the prize, but had not paid for them; and as he probably had learned from the town gossip that the *Scano Pilla* must quit her moorings, he procrastinated when he ought to have been prompt. It was enough vexation to Garibaldi to be politely ordered away; but a bad debt was the addition of injury to insult; and, moreover, the money was wanted. He felt that future payment was a very remote contingency; and when the evening drew on for their departure, having ordered all things to be ready for sailing, he put a brace of pistols in his belt, threw his cloak over his shoulders, and took a walk in the direction of the debtor's house in the bright moonlight. The gentleman was refreshing himself in the cool of the evening at his own door, and the two recognised each other before the distance was covered. The merchant made a deprecating sign, and warned his visitor off; which sign Garibaldi pretended not to understand. He walked straight on, and putting a pistol to the other's breast, exclaimed hastily, "My money!" The merchant desired to "argue the point," but the only answer was the reiteration of "My money!" This persistence availed, and the merchant counted out his two thousand patagons. Throwing the bag over his back, and restoring his pistol to its place, Garibaldi calmy returned to the ship, and at eleven o'clock they raised anchor and entered the Rio de la Plata. But when the morning came the amazing spectacle of breakers all around met their bewildered eyes: breakers larboard and starboard, ahead and astern, and the deck covered. Springing upon the mainyard, Garibaldi soon perceived the direction in which they ought to go; and although the danger was so great as to paralyse the men, and though part of their sail was taken away by the wind, the ship yielded quietly to the helm, and in an hour was out of danger. He was much puzzled to know by what stupidity they had come upon the rocks so clearly mapped and so well known, when by the compass they should have been miles wide of them. The cause was soon ascertained. Apprehensive, when he left the ship to deal with his debtor, that there might be trouble requiring a sanguinary solution, he had ordered the guns to be brought on deck, to defend them if attacked. These guns were placed in a cabin close to the compass, and the mass of metal had attracted the needle from its bearing.

The claims of hunger began to assert themselves as they continued their voyage. Garibaldi had provided, for reasons of his own, that no means of landing should be on board, and the difficulty of getting ashore in quest of provisions placed them in a dilemma. Our hero's resources did not fail him in this extremity. He had given his boat away to the people who were on board the prize, and consequently a raft had to be constructed of the materials at hand—a table and some casks. On this he ventured with a single sailor, Maurice Garibaldi—not a relative. After vast labour, which consisted chiefly of swaying the raft with their feet, as a substitute for oars, they reached the beach, and Garibaldi went on his foray. After several failures he came to a farm occupied only by a young woman, the wife of the master, of whom he essayed to purchase a bullock. This could not be done in the husband's absence; besides, it occurred to him that there would be some difficulty in getting back to the shore the same night. He therefore awaited the husband's return, and engaged his hostess in conversation. He found to his amazement that she was a person of great culture, familiar with the masterpieces of Dante, Petrarch, and Tasso. She inquired whether her visitor knew the works of a Spanish poet, Quintana, and learning that he did not, gave him a copy, recommending him to learn Spanish. He suggested that perhaps she was a poetess. Without waiting to be asked, she recited several of her own compositions, full of feeling and harmony. The memory of Maurice and all else vanished in this intellectual surprise; but in course of time the husband returned. The negotiation for the bullock was successful, and at daybreak on the morrow the farmer drove the animal to the seaside.

The animal was slaughtered and cut up into strips, and then arose the question of its embarkation. Half-a-mile of furious sea, and a ricketty craft, did not promise an easy undertaking. The mast was lowered and used as a paddle, and the cargo was transferred to the deck; but it was too heavy. The water rose above its surface, knee-deep. The

American cheered, and the distant crew cheered; but how to steer the two Italians knew not, for the sea had become rougher, and the water too deep for the pole to touch the bottom; besides which the wind rose and carried them far out of their course. The crew saw that the only chance was to set sail and overtake them; which was done. This incident led to the purchase of a canoe a few days later from a passing vessel.

Next morning two barks appeared in the distance. Garibaldi, seeing cause for suspicion, ordered sail to be set and the muskets to be brought on deck. The barks came nearer, and the first appeared to have only three men on board. But one of these suddenly summoned them to surrender; and at the same moment the armed crew started up and commenced firing without another word. Garibaldi cried, "To arms!" and sprang to his gun with an order, "Brace the foresails!" Finding that the helm did not work, he looked round; and the steersman lay dead—shot in the first discharge. The fight was furious. The enemy had grappled them, and some of her men were already clambering up the side. Shot and sword cleared them off, and Garibaldi himself sprang to the helm, when at the instant a ball struck him, entering his neck, and he fell senseless. Without their leader, the Italians and Maltese fought bravely for an hour; the others hiding themselves down in the hold; when the enemy, having lost a dozen men, and becoming fatigued, cleared away. Presently the wind rose, and they floated up the river in safety.

The commander soon recovered his senses. There was no physician or helmsman on board; his own eyes were half-glazed still; he was speechless, and in fever. Making signs for a chart, he examined it, and with his finger pointed to Santa Fe. The sailors were terrified at his condition, and at the sight of their dead companion; none of them had ever navigated the Rio de la Plata, and they imagined an enemy everywhere. For several days no landing could be effected, and with much grief it was determined to commit the dead Fiorentino to the deep. Garibaldi's recovery, under the loving care of a certain Luiji Cariuglia, occupied nineteen days, by which time they had reached Gualeguay, having met on the way with another ship, whose commander had supplied them with food, which was much needed ; for, except coffee, all their own stores had been consumed. Not only did he shew this humanity, but he added letters of introduction to persons in Gualeguay, where Garibaldi found a physician to extract the ball.

CHAPTER III.

SOUTH AMERICAN WARS.

"—But foes are gathering—Liberty must raise
Red on the hills her beacon's far-seen blaze ;
Must bid the tocsin ring from tower to tower ! —
Nearer and nearer comes the trying hour !"
—WORDSWORTH.

STAY of six months in Gualeguay established friendships among the people there, but it became evident to Garibaldi that he was virtually a close prisoner.

The invalid had recovered from the effects of his wound, and had begun to take exercise on horseback within prescribed limits. Strength and energy had returned to him. Meanwhile his companions had been thrown into prison, and his ship confiscated; but a sufficient allowance, that of a crown a day, was punctually paid to him. The insatiable craving for liberty was upon him, and there presently came invitations to escape, which were made in good faith, and accompanied with an intimation that the governor would not trouble himself about the flight. Garibaldi had been scheming for such a chance, and the hint was irresistible. Hitherto the governor had been kind to him, and this confirmed him in the belief that success would attend a daring effort, seeing that no notice was taken of him or of his movements. Now at this time it happened that, for some reason or other, Garibaldi's friend was obliged to absent himself from Gualeguay ; and his temporary substitute was a man of very different disposition. It became necessary for our hero to conduct his plans with great caution and secrecy. One rough night he rode out a distance of three miles from the town, to visit a brave old man with whom he had made acquaintance, and, informing him of his intention, begged that a guide and horses might be provided, that he might fly to a farm kept by an Englishman on the left bank of the river Parana, where he hoped to find a vessel by which he might get away unobserved, either to Buenos Ayres or Monte Video. The old man acceded to his friend's request most cheerfully. By break of day the journey of forty miles was commenced, and the guide and Garibaldi travelled without any noteworthy incident, making the best use of their time until they had arrived within half-a-mile of the river, when the guide ordered a halt, that he might go on to reconnoitre. Left alone, Garibaldi dismounted, hooked the bridle of his horse to a tree, and lay down a few hours to wait. His guide not returning, as had been arranged, he became impatient, and thought he would try and reach his destination alone ; but just as he was arriving a gunshot was heard behind, and the ball whizzed through the grass. Turning sharply round, to his dismay a detachment of horse was seen in hot pursuit, with drawn sabres. They were already between him and his horse, which he had left where he dismounted. There was no chance of flight; resistance was folly, and he surrendered. Binding his hands behind him, they placed him on horseback, his legs fastened to the saddle-girths, and all went back to Gualeguay.

The next day he appeared before the governor, who forthwith demanded of him the name of the persons who had connived at his escape and provided the means. Garibaldi disclaimed co-operators, and took upon himself the sole responsibility. He was standing before Don Leonardo Milan—the governor who had taken the place of his friend—bound, and the cowardly fellow struck him with a whip, renewing his demand, which was promptly met by a repetition of the denial. A few directions were whispered to the officials, and Garibaldi was sent back to prison. Those orders were to his discomfort, for on reaching the cell, his hands still bound behind, a cord was passed round his wrists and over a joist, and drawn tight, until he was suspended in that torturing position some four or five feet from the ground. Presently the governor entered, and again repeated his interrogations. Garibaldi's blood was up. He would have wrestled with his enemy, but that was impossible. What he could do, he did, and that was to spit in his face.

"Ah," said the governor, "that is all very well;" and turning to the warders as he left the place, he added, " When the prisoner shall be willing to confess, send for me, and on hearing his confession I will let him be taken down."

Two hours of this misery ensued ; his wrists were bleeding, and his joints all but dislocated ; his body was in a burning heat, and he begged for water, which the more tender-hearted guards supplied. This gave but little relief ; and he realised the torture inflicted by the Holy Inquisition in the Middle Ages. More dead than alive he was let down ; with just the assurance of existence which the sensation of severe pain could afford. Mercilessly put into fetters, he was made the fellow of some imprisoned assassin ; and to add to his grief, he learned that the hospitable Spanish gentleman, who had for six months been his friend, had been cast into prison.

In this deplorable plight a sister of charity ministered to him, and her succour sustained his fainting life. She found ways of supplying all his necessities during the incarceration, which continued some days. The governor began to fear he had taken upon himself more than his position justified, and as all his endeavours to obtain information were of no avail, he deemed it prudent to shirk the responsibility of any more violence by ordering his prisoner's removal to Bajada, where a further detention of two months ensued ; after which Garibaldi was informed that he might leave the country. There was no trial, nor any notice taken of his repeated protestations. It is possible that the first governor had interfered and obtained for him his liberty.

At Bajada—better known as Parana—there lay an Italian brig, the captain of which undertook to convey Garibaldi down the small stream which flows into the River Parana, from which he embarked to Monte Video in a balandre—a small vessel constructed to travel safely in rapid and dangerous waters—where he was joined by troops of friends, and by them warmly welcomed. He had not been there long before his much-loved Rossetti appeared.

The successful resistance Garibaldi had made to the attack at sea rendered him obnoxious to the authorities, and concealment was necessary. A Mr. Pizante therefore entertained him at his own house for a month, and the visits of compatriots cheered his solitude. At the end of that time Rossetti and he departed for Rio Grande on horseback, a journey of about two hundred miles. The abundance of horses in that country enabled them to use the ordinary practice of long journeys—namely, to have a supply of fifteen or twenty unladen horses to follow the travellers, who dismount when the ridden horse appears to be fatigued, and shiftiug the saddle, take a fresh one, the other following with the herd. There were no hostelries, so that the bait had to be taken from the herbage where the changes were accomplished.

It was not advisable to approach the capital of the province of Rio Grande, Porto Allegro, for the enemy held it. They consequently made for Pirantinim, whither the seat of the Republican government had been removed. The journey and the scenery invigorated the party. Vast plains adorned with the banana tree, the sugar-cane, and the orange, and mountains clothed with verdure, filled their hearts with cheerfulness, and made the long ride a delightful recreation. Here and there they had come upon human habitations, all with open doors, into which any one might enter, and stay as long as was convenient to himself. Strange country!—a mixture of cruelty and simplicity, romantic adventure and arrogant authority.

The end of the ride recalled them to the consideration of politics. Pirantinim, the temporary seat of the government, had become the camp of the Republic, whose small forces scarcely justified the name of an army. Garibaldi was getting weary of protracted idleness. Not long before he had written to a friend :—" As for myself, I can only say that fortune does not smile upon our undertaking. And what grieves me chiefly is the conviction that I am doing nothing in aid of our cause. By heaven! I am wearied of dragging on a life useless to our country; but we are destined for better things, though here we are out of our element." He obtained permission to join a column, just marching for San Gonzalo, some twenty or thirty miles to the east, where was the President, a man who hnd raised the welcome cry of war, and was much esteemed for his disinterested devotion, skill, and personal bravery. Added to these virtues he possessed a commanding presence, and was "the idol of the citizens." They had not gone far when they found that the Imperialist leader had retired in a hurry on hearing of the Republican advance. He was not worth following, and the party wheeled round and took the road to Pirantinim, where the good news of a victory to their arms at Rio Pardo, some hundred miles to the north, gladdened their souls. Panting for action, Garibaldi gathered a band of thirty of all nations, and of various personal characteristics, some sailors and some filibusters

With these he set about arming two little vessels, mere
pinnaces—one of eighteen tons, the other twelve. These
vessels lay in the Camacuam, a little river which runs into
the Lago Des Patos, and had been constructed by an American there. The crew was increased by forty negroes, and
each vessel was provided with two small bronze pieces.
One little craft, named *Rio Pardo*, was commanded by
Garibaldi; the other, *The Republican*, by an American—
John Griggs. When all was ready, the saucy pair emerged
upon the lake, making in a few days prizes of no inconsiderable value. On the water were thirty Imperialist ships of
war and a steamer. These were compelled to keep in deep
water, and the little craft preferred the shallow. There was
only one channel of deep water, and that was on the eastward, the seaside of the lake; and this is the only excuse
that can be urged for the Republicans' temerity. The inner
edge of the lake consisted of sand-banks, and shoals running
at right angles from the shore, making bays for every two;
and when any interruption to landing occurred, it was
caused by the pinnace blundering on one of those sand-
banks. Garibaldi would then shout out, "Now my ducks,
to the water!" when overboard they tumbled, and lifted
the whole craft and cargo off into deeper water. But, for
all that, it was a profitable business. They made many
captures, and the spoil was fairly divided.

The Emperor of Brazil had a force on this lake large
enough to be active; but instead of acting, it looked on
these transactions with immense contempt. They were
pretty enough for its amusement, but that was all. By-
and-bye things looked serious. These contemptible tubs
were taking prize after prize unchallenged, and it was to
them a losing game. Boats were put on the lakes to protect commerce, and then Garibaldi retired to take something in hand on *terra firma;* and he was employed in
command of a fortified position at Camacuam. It was a

happy life. With him intrepidity was natural, variety was agreeable; and the strangeness of novelty gave to every incident a romantic charm. All his sailors were horsemen, and of horses there was no end in that land. Two hours, and his jack-tars were a mounted squadron—of all colours and nations, it is true, but one of which he was not ashamed. The country was very rich. The proximity of the war had caused a temporary desertion of the homesteads; and corn, cattle, potatoes, and all the riches of the land were left behind. These were utilised on behalf of the protecting army. There were residents who had not quitted their homes, and with some of them Garibaldi passed many happy hours. Of two homes especially, belonging to the President's sisters, he spoke of as " Paradise Regained." He was then but twenty-six, and of an impressible nature; this may have given a roseate hue to all he met. It happened, however, that whenever the day was stormy, or foraging drove them from the arsenal at Camacuam, the occasion of a general holiday was seized, and he repaired to the villa of his kind and engaging friends, who had, in addition to their own cheerful society, several visitors of intelligence and education.

Garibaldi, in the midst of this dramatic existence, emerged from isolation by reaching the conclusion that he ought to be married. " I then wanted," he says, "a wife; nothing else would cure; for she would be my refuge, my consoling one, the star in the tempest; she would hear the implorings of my heart always, but most in misfortune." He had come to know a few of the people at Languna, and among them Le Bana, who had a mansion within sight of the sea. One day, turning his eyes in that direction, he beheld several pretty young women busy in the household duties of the place. He went thither immediately, with a beating heart, but firmly bent on his purpose. When he reached the house, a man he had known asked him to come in;

which, he says, he should have done if he had not been asked. There he saw a girl whom he liked, and said to her, "Maiden, thou shalt be mine!" And so it came to pass. The Anita of whom the world has heard so much became his wife, his consolation, his refuge, his star in the tempest —for a little while, until she, too, passed away!

Marriage did not involve inactivity. Garibaldi was summoned to sea service. While his colleague, Canavario, was operating on land, he required assistance on the water. The Imperial vessels were cruising about in the north, on the coast of Brazil, and they were to be attacked. It was an unreasonable mission, because of the inadequate force of the Republicans. The three vessels they had taken comprised their whole fleet, and the entrance to the harbour was blocked by the Imperialist ships. However, orders are made to be obeyed, and under cover of the night the *Rio Pardo* (Garibaldi), the *Cassapara* (Griggs), both schooners, and the *Seivel* (commanded by Lorenzo, an Italian) put to sea unobserved. Anita would not stay behind. They had all been furnished with war material, and went on their way north as far as Santos—about three hundred miles, where a corvette chased them to no purpose. After making several prizes during eight days, they turned the vessels for return. A separation from Griggs's ship had taken place several days back in the darkness of the night, and there were but two vessels in company, when, directly in the course, and not to be avoided, they came upon a Brazilian war pinnace. Steering straight on, Garibaldi immediately attacked the enemy.

Most of the prizes escaped, or were retaken. One, in the command of a Spaniard, was steered safely to a port held by the Republicans, and that was followed by the *Seivel*, which had had its cannon dismounted, and was shipping water. Garibaldi could not hold out single-handed, and he also entered the harbour, driven by a north-east wind.

He would have much preferred sailing for Laguna, because he knew that the vessel he had parted with would touch St. Catherine's Island, and report its adventures, and that his fleeing to this port would expose him to attack, and that without delay. It was not his wont to indulge in a fool's paradise, but to be ready for the worst. Hoisting the dismounted cannon from the *Seivel* he placed it on a projection of the land which formed the bay, and there constructed a gabooned battery. The forecast proved correct. Scarcely had the morning dawned when the sight of approaching ships proclaimed the danger at hand. His wife was as enthusiastic and active as himself. She would not hear of being put on shore, and he was proud of her for refusing. The enemy cannonaded most effectually. The fight became closer; carbines were used; and there was much slaughter. The *Rio Pardo* had her rigging shot into rags and threads, and her sides riddled by bullets, but her crew refused to yield, preferring to sink rather than surrender. Garibaldi says, "No doubt we were animated to this devotedness by the presence of the Brazilian amazon on board;" for Anita took her turn in the fight. The land battery also helped by its constant "peppering away" as long as the engagement lasted. The enemy had set their minds on capturing Garibaldi: his name was known already and feared. The attack became furious. However, after five hours' sharp work, a bullet closed the Brazilian commander's life, and the enemy cleared away.

This was a most serious danger, out of which no escape at one time appeared to be possible. It had its little romance. The General says: "I experienced during this fight one of the most lively and cruel emotions of my life. Whilst Anita, on the deck, was cheering our men, sword in hand, there came a cannon-ball, which knocked her down, and two men who were close by. I sprang towards her, expecting to find her dead, but she rose safe; the men were killed.   I then begged she would go below.   'Yes, I will go,' she answered, 'but only to drive up the cowards who have gone down there to hide.'   And so she did, and they came up looking terribly ashamed at their discovery, and the more so that a woman was behind them."   It took them all day to repair the injured ship and to bury the dead.   This done, night offered a welcome rest, for the morrow had its prospective peril and toil.

The expectation of a repetition of attack from the enemy on the morrow proving illusory, the guns were re-embarked in the evening, and at night the homeward journey was resumed.   Without anything of importance having occurred they reached Laguna, and received the welcome of their friends, who did not fail to express surprise at their safe arrival.

But the gathering of Imperialist troops everywhere around filled Garibaldi with dismay.   The province was disaffected towards the Republicans, and almost inclined to expel their new friends, as they had the old possessors; and indeed one city had set an example.   The general in command bade Garibaldi take charge of a force to reduce that city to sub-mission, and this order he was obliged to execute.   He did it, but much to his regret.   Landing at a distance of three miles, he made an attack from the hill-side at an unexpected moment, surprised the garrison, who fled, and marching in, took possession of the place, which, according to the usages of war, was sacked—abandoned to pillage.   His feelings on the subject were very acute : although by dint of great exertion, and even blows, he was able to maintain the sanctity of person, and to keep violence within stricter limits than in any previous instance had been possible. The horrors of drunkenness and the waste and destruction of property harrowed his very soul.   He never drank any-thing but water himself, and the sight of officers and men given over to degrading excess wrung from him this ejaculation : " May God look on and pity me, but I never in my whole life had a day which left in my soul so bitter a memory as that." The "unchained wild beasts" were at last got on board, the spoil brought down to the ship and embarked, after which the expedition returned to the lake.

The tide of prosperity had been flowing, and now came its ebb. The causes of that change in the aspect of affairs— namely, the want of discipline amongst the new levies, and the high spirit of the Imperialists—sufficiently account for it. Canavario's advance guard, sent out to obstruct the enemy's approach, had returned unsuccessful, and brought intelligence that the march he could not hinder was a rapid one, and the force numerous. The general directed a transfer of the camp to the opposite shore of the lake, and when Garibaldi arrived the baggage was being sent across under great peril; for, although the number of the army could not embarrass the operation, the countless petty belongings did. Moreover, the current had become doubly dangerous; its natural narrowness being made more difficult by increased rapidity and violent winds. After eight hours' toil the enemy's vessels came in sight, and simultaneously his troops co-operated by land, evidently intending to join them at the entrance of the lake. The force despatched to hinder this union did not arrive in time, and the fleet entered. A battery had been mounted, but the unskilful artillerymen did not produce any perceptible effect, their only guns being very small. The three vessels, half-manned, were under the command of Garibaldi, and virtually the contest had to be undertaken by him alone.

Wind and tide in their favour, the enemy bore down in full sail. Our hero took up his post; his wife had already commenced the cannonade, pointing and lighting herself the piece she undertook to use, and doing her best to excite the men to enthusiasm. But it was of little avail. Out of six officers all presently lay dead but himself, whilst half of the men still remained on land.　The guns were dismounted, and they had indeed produced little effect upon the enemy.

Amid these thrilling scenes Anita stood close to her husband in the midst of danger, and nothing could induce her to change her purpose.　Garibaldi made an excuse to send her ashore, giving her a message to the general, asking for reinforcements, and promising that if they were sent he would follow the Imperialists.　He also declared that, if not otherwise able to prevent their landing, he would fire the fleet.　The general could not supply men, and Anita, who had promised to stay on shore and reply by a messenger, came back herself with orders for Garibaldi to burn the fleet, and to return with what fire-arms and ammunition he could save.　A hard undertaking ; for the enemy's fire did not relax.　At length the arms and ammunition, under the direction of Anita—the only "officer" remaining—were carried ashore, while her husband employed himself in depositing inflammable substances in all parts of the ships, clambering over the dead with an agonised heart.　His poor friend and brother soldier, Commander Griggs, lay cut in two, and the third commander, "with a hole in his body three inches in diameter," lay slaughtered among more than half his little crew.　In an instant a cloud of smoke enveloped them all, and the funeral pile was ignited !

Anita surpassed all in the heroism of that scene.　She went backwards and forwards with the boats which bore arms, standing upright while the enemy's fire whistled around, yet passing to-and-fro unhurt some twenty times. Her husband gratefully writes, "God, who extended His arm over me, at the same time covered her with the shadow of His hand."

The army of the Republicans had begun its retreat to-wards Rio Grande, and the discouragement of all contrasted bitterly with their former hopes.　Garibaldi collected his few survivors, and on horseback, with his wife at his side, rode along, " proud of the living, the dead, and almost of myself." His disinterestedness never left him. He knew that no money would ever come from the Republic, and that if it did he would not take it. Therefore, the changes of life pressed less heavily on him. He could accept events with composure ; and he had a wife after his own heart. And on the other hand, peril and danger, camp and war, things to almost every one else terrible and exhausting, had charms for her, in her husband's society, which no safety or ease could afford.

On they went until the frontier of Santa Caterina was passed ; and they reached As Torres without being harassed by a pursuit. Andrea and Acunha, the generals of divisions, joined the camp in the neighbourhood of the mountains of Rio Grande, before mentioned. The inhabitants were in jeopardy, being invested by the Imperial forces in strength greater than their own, and they sent down to them for help. Texeira, the commander of the advance division, went to their aid, and with him went Garibaldi. At Santa Vittoria they confronted the Imperialist force under Colonel Aranha and beat him ; losing, however, Acunha, one of the division generals ; and the greater part of the enemy were taken prisoners. Thus two sections of Santa Caterina were recovered, and the Republicans triumphantly took possession. But the successful movement which the Imperialists had made at Laguna had encouraged them ; and their persistence compelled great activity on the part of the Republicans. In Council, Texeira determined on a division of forces, in order to intercept and annihilate an important company of cavalry. This division produced disaster. The recent victories, small indeed in comparison with the issue, had generated a feeling of self-confidence ill befitting the circumstances. They began to despise an enemy so little able to obstruct their movements, and fancied half their party to be a sufficient host.

Garibaldi's division encamped, after a three days' march, and lay down to rest; he himself, as he says, "sleeping with one eye open." The sentinels on the river received an attack in the night of so sudden and overwhelming a character as to leave them only time to return fire and flee. He heard them coming, and, starting from his rest, exclaimed, "To arms!" and all the camp prepared for action. No sooner had the daylight come than the enemy appeared, crossed the river, and formed for battle. Texeira could have sent off for the other division, but fancied that the enemy would retire—so self-confident had he become—and that the opportunity for chastising him would be lost by delay. He therefore dashed on at once, without heeding the orderly disposition of, and the favourable ground occupied by, the Imperial forces. The enemy pretended to fly, and the Republicans rushed on, firing as they went; but, to their disaster, a party in ambush, unperceived in the excitement, took them in the flank, and the camp had to be regained with loss. Forming again, they returned to the fight vigorously, and the enemy retired precipitately, eagerly followed by the Republicans, who however, after a nine miles chase, could not overtake them.

News from the advance-guard that the enemy had continued their retreat, and that oxen and horses had already been conducted to the other side of the river, incited Texeira to follow instantly. He ordered Garibaldi and his infantry to join him as speedily as possible, little supposing that the flight was a feint, and that, although horses and oxen had been taken over, the soldiers remained concealed in the hills at the sides of the pass. These saw the Republican cavalry approach, unsupported by infantry, and emerging from their hiding places, took them again in flank, scattering the whole force with ease. Garibaldi had foreseen all this; for, being mounted, he rode on before his soldiers, and from an eminence observed the catastrophe.

All is not lost while heart remains. The poor fellows could not conceal their mortification, and something must be done, if only for the honour of the corps. Garibaldi took measures promptly; and calling a score of his trusty friends by name, received a hearty response. They came, and while the body of the force remained under the command of a deputy, went with him to the top of the hill, where grew some trees, and there awaited battle. The defence was obstinate, as may be imagined, but it soon changed to attack, in which the enemy suffered. The men saw this, and the little party became a rallying-point for such of the rest as had not lost courage. The muster raised them to over seventy determined self-elected men against a cavalry force of five hundred. The enemy knew not how to conquer the resolute infantry, although it was seven to one in their favour, and exhausted themselves in the fruitless attempt. And on the other hand, the infantry could not remain and permit the enemy to obtain reinforcements, which he would very soon have done. They therefore retreated steadily, although harassed at every step. About a mile distant there stood a belt of trees, and thither the retreating force betook themselves. The thicket was soon sufficiently cleared for a night's bivouac.

But staying there did not coincide with Garibaldi's idea of safety. He was learning here what in Italy did such useful work : how to dispose small forces in irregular ways, so as to confound the more regular dispositions of professional warfare. It was his genius so to act; and this genius gathered its practical force in these South American campaigns.

A little before midnight Texeira ordered a march northward, in hope of joining the other half of the army. The night march of a wearied troop along the side of the great forest did not allay the nervous irritation caused by the day's work. One of the myriads of wild horses started from his disturbed slumber, and in a moment, from mouth to mouth, the cry of danger was passed. Those who calmly took their odds of seven to one in open warfare became terrified by the mysterious noise, and fled like sheep. The voice of their leader did, after a time, recover the wanderers, who might, by their irrational conduct, have betrayed all to the enemy.

It was a tedious and difficult march. Fatigued almost beyond their strength, hungry and thirsty, many of them covered with wounds, their case was by no means an enviable one. Their road lay over the rough rank herbage; their only food consisted of such roots as they could get out of the ground. No wonder if the little force became thoroughly disheartened; and though desertion meant almost certain death in the jungle, they began to desert in very despair. "But there is a spirit in man, and the inspiration of the Almighty giveth it understanding." To that spirit Garibaldi appealed. Calling the men around him, he demanded that those who would go should go at once, and take their chance; but that those who remained should march in a body, helping the weak and defending one another. After that there was no more desertions; no more disloyalty to each other. The next day brought them to a track which led to a house, where they obtained food and rest.

Resuming their travel, a short time brought them to Lages, from whence their victorious march had been made. But they did not find the old welcome. Worshipping the winning side, as most people do, the inhabitants had hauled down the Republican flag on the departure of the Republicans, fearing, or hoping—one hardly knows which—that the next visitors might be Imperialists. The place was a trading place, and commerce cares little for political principles, although upon the selection of political principles depends the success of commerce. The reappearance of the

Republicans created a panic, and the people fled. The stocks of goods were left behind; and as their allies had proved faithless, there was no scruple about appropriating for present need all that could be of service. As the place had every variety of store, their necessities were abundantly supplied.

The strength of the company now became a main consideration. To take a town and keep a town with a small force often falls to the lot of irregular expeditions; but if the expelled employ every effort to regain their lost possessions the irregular force at once feels its weakness. It can accomplish by surprise what it cannot, as a rule, retain. Lages became the centre of new plans. General Texeira wrote off to the commander of the other division, directing him to return and rejoin the army, for he had heard that another Imperialist force had been sent on their track, and might speedily appear.

This news of the enemy's designs could only be utilised in one way. He might approach from any quarter; and therefore to cut him off, or offer him resistance in the open field, could not be contemplated. The town must be defended, and pending the arrival of succours, the enemy must be harassed and delayed as soon as he appeared. The Imperialists came upon the other side of the river Canoas, but they did not venture to cross it. After some days the Republicans received the much-desired reinforcements, and immediately offered battle. This offer the enemy declined, and retired some ten or fifteen miles into another province; hoping in his turn to receive reinforcements. Hesitation and delay test the morale of soldiery to the utmost, and Garibaldi's men flinched. So long as an enemy was in sight, and fighting was to be done, the *esprit de corps* could be maintained, but any interruption produced impatience, and that led every man to go his own way, even to the extent of desertion. They would not run away from an enemy, but when an enemy ran away, they did so too ; and thus the force, instead of growing in numbers, became liable to chronic incoherence. Desertions were frequent, until Lages could not be defended; and the party, which might have been victorious by union, was dissolved by negative success.

Of such a nature, in fact, is the history of most of the struggles in which Garibaldi was engaged in South America. That he, personally, had military genius and even generalship of a high order has been testified by competent European witnesses, who were from time to time enabled to judge of his strategy and to be present at his victories. But the leaders of the Republican armies were for the most part utterly unequal to their position. They could collect men, but could not drill them, nor equip them, nor clothe them, nor even lead or command them. Discipline was almost unknown amongst the Uruguayan forces, and even Garibaldi's Italians were occasionally disorganised by association with their lawless allies.

Garibaldi's band of seventy had dwindled to forty, and with these, and a small force of marines, he repaired to a little farm, which had been forsaken, and in the confusion and violence of the times partially destroyed. His object in resorting thither was to construct a number of canoes, which would be useful in navigating the shallow borders of the lakes, or conveying material or provisions down the many strands. These canoes were formed from a single tree, and are the principal means of water communication in the country. After waiting many months without obtaining suitable trees for the purpose, that project had to be abandoned, and some other employment discovered ; for idleness was insupportable. It happened that this neighbourhood possessed, what many parts of South America do possess, large numbers of wild horses ; and it occurred to Garibaldi that, as he was hindered from making boats and training his marines in their use, he might as well catch colts and convert his people into a troop of horse soldiers.

The place he had taken into his own hands had been an excellent homestead, inhabited by a Spanish count, an exile. Under the exigencies of the time, the abandoned house might not unfairly be made available in the cause of the young Republic, which was now contending for its independence. There were plenty of buildings about, and the cattle had contrived to increase and multiply without tending; indeed, the colts may be said to have belonged to the exile. All the establishment was utilised, the building made suitable for its new purpose, the cattle converted into provisions, and the colts put under training.

Garibaldi had begun to want a home. His wedding was unmarked with holiday, and from day to day his wife and he had shared the weariness of war, and peril by land and sea. He took possession, and not long after, in September 1840, his son Menotti was born. The child of storm and danger, such as must have killed most women, came into the world safely, to the indescribable relief of the loving father and the devoted mother. It was born with a scar upon its head—the result, it is supposed, of a wound sustained by its mother's fall from her horse.

Here, then, at home are mother and child, and father "must go a-hunting." Clothes for the infant must be obtained, and he must obtain them. Mounting his horse, he turned out to reach a distant little town where he had friends. Riding across country, then in a state of inundation, with water over his horse's knees, he reached the house of a military acquaintance, who gave him a hearty welcome. It was evening, and rain came down in torrents. He consented to stay over the night, but the morning proving no better his friend begged further delay. But rest under his circumstances was not to be thought of. Out into the open, now more like a lake than fields, he turned, and presently the sound of firing fell upon his ear.   It puzzled him, and caused uneasiness and apprehension ; but pressing on to Settimbrina as rapidly as he could, he bought his few requirements, and the return journey commenced.

Passing his previous halting-place, he stayed and inquired about the firing that had been heard on the previous day. There he found that the Imperialist general, Moringue, had taken a large number of horses from the Republicans by surprise, and had then re-embarked with his soldiers, sailing towards the north part of the province of Rio Grande, in which Simon's farm was situated.   Garibaldi saw at once the seriousness of the danger, and when he reached his homestead his fears were realised.

In that dreadful rain and wind Anita had taken horse, half-clad as she was, and, with her babe across the saddle, had sought refuge in the forest.   When our hero arrived the place was empty.   He found them soon on the borders of the forest, where they had halted, not knowing which way to go to avoid the enemy, and in a state of alarm as to what further evil might await them.   But Moringue, after his successful raid, quitted the neighbourhood, and Garibaldi returned to Simon's farm, and set himself with his usual energy to repair the disaster.

Home-life, thus interrupted, was again renewed, and father, mother, and child were blessed with some further days of peaceful love.   The repose of mankind in such a form is a phase in life's progress which governs the future as well as the present.   In the hurry of action, when beset by interruptions, the potency of love operates unseen and imperceptibly ; but in an enforced peace this angel of human life fills the throne, and showers blessings on all her subjects.   The " Amazon," the outcast, the babe, were all the world to one another, and there needed no words to assert the fact.   In that wild place rested obscurely the great spirit which was to change the map of Europe

After staying some time Garibaldi determined on quitting Simon's farm, and forming a camp on the other side of the river Capivari, where twelve months ago he had had such hard work in preparing his expedition to Santa Catherina; and here he busied himself in constructing canoes for the shallow waters, and in making several expeditions to the western shores of the lake, for the purpose of establishing communications with the more civilised and populated districts. He found the political situation daily becoming more embarrassing. The Republican cause had suffered grievous disasters, and the expedition was at its weakest. The enthusiasm of its early stage had given way to disappointment, and that generated indifference. Two lost battles had decimated its numbers, and no means or money could be obtained for its reconstruction. This, and the extreme privation which ensued, had produced a strong conviction on all hands that the game was played out—that the whole enterprise must soon come to an end. From being a contest for the supremacy of certain political principles, the war had become one of personal ambition among the leaders; and petty jealousies, tyrannies, and ill-faith abounded. It was determined to retreat from Rio Grande. The Imperialists had offered accommodating terms, and these should have been accepted. They were, however, refused by the Republicans, and the refusal augmented the disaffection, and nullified all schemes for continued united action.

The retreat from Simon's farm broke up the home; the little vision of bliss was dissolved, and toil in a more rude form than before followed. The summer and autumn had passed, and now came the " winter of their discontent," physical as well as mental. Winter in South America has many terrors. The mountains are washed by incessant rains of great copiousness, which swell the innumerable rivers, and these, overflowing, deluge the plains. Roads there were none, and the few tracks were obscured in the storm season. The march of an army under such conditions is most distressing. The only provisions that could be taken consisted of a herd of cows, to be killed as necessity required. The three months' march of this retreat were months of misery beyond expression : few of the women and children got through it at all ; they perished in the wilderness from hunger, fatigue, and cold. In this scene of distress Anita had to bear her part, and her very life and that of her child was in extreme jeopardy. The few inhabitants of the boundless forest shewed what kindness could be shewn, but nature could not be controlled. Garibaldi feared exceedingly that his wife and child would and must perish. The passage of rivers tested their power of endurance to the last strain. He would carry the babe suspended from his neck by a handkerchief, and by that means keep him warm while crossing the stream. Almost all the mules and horses for his own service had died, and to add to the desolation the guides had lost their track. The forest was dense, and how to obtain food became an awfully pressing question. He thought it best to send his wife on before with the two horses that were left, taking with her a servant and the child, hoping they might thereby get sufficient food for themselves. She obeyed, and at last emerged from the forest, where she met with a small party of soldiers resting themselves, having lighted a fire. These had saved from the breaking up of the camp some woollen garments, which were of the utmost value, for the infant was perishing from cold ; and when they saw the mother and child, they soon scattered themselves to obtain for them all the comforts the district could yield, so that when the weary father came up the next day on foot, he found that loving hands had for his sake been ministering to his dear ones.

The forest was at length passed, and the weather became fine. It would seem that the rains and storms are attracted by the tall trees, for on emerging there was an immediate change. And upon the plains oxen were to be obtained in the chase by means of the lasso; an idle instrument in the woods, but invaluable in the open country. Here also could be caught some wild colts, by which their loss of horses and mules were partially repaired. This horse-taming business often became very exciting, and its events amusing. The lancers had lost all their cattle, and the young strong black fellows would leap on the backs of the wild animals, who had never seen or felt bit, saddle, or spur, and hold to their manes as the frantic creatures dashed across the open fields for miles away, until they recognised their conquerors. It was often a long struggle, for the animals would exert every faculty they had to discover some way of ridding themselves of their tormentors. The negroes stuck upon their backs, fixed their knees in their sides, and every now and then a pair would roll down and rise again, never separating until, in a lather of foam, and with a dire trembling of the limbs, the creature patiently accepted the inevitable, and became the servant of man. After three days' discipline it usually took the bit.

The journey had now continued a long time. They had traversed more than two hundred and fifty miles, and were nearing San Gabriele, the headquarters of the Republican army, where barracks had been built, and where what was left of them were to be housed, rested, or disbanded. As their destination was neared, Garibaldi became increasingly desirous of changing his way of life. It was evident that mother and child could not exist in a course of privation like that through which they had been passing, and the repetition of such privation was inevitable in those wars. He became more and more home-sick. He had not, of course, heard from his parents, nor had any tidings reached him concerning what he called his " other mother "—Italy— of whose fate and fortune he longed to hear.

He resolved on settling down for a time at some place near the sea that had direct communications with the distant parts of the world, and applied to Gonzales, the President, for leave of absence, which was granted. He left the camp on a long journey to Monte Video, having first obtained permission to collect wild bullocks, which he could dispose of on the way to procure necessary supplies.

Here, then, was the hero of a hundred adventures, who had rendered good service to the Republic, allowed to depart on a journey three hundred miles without any other means than could be gained from a herd of bullocks, which bullocks were not his until he caught them. The Republican officials gave him some assistance, but it took twenty days of vast toil to get together the herd of nine hundred which he collected for his journey, all as wild as nature made them. But the toil of collecting was nothing to be compared with the toil of driving them. Things went tolerably until a big river had to be crossed. The Rio Negro could be forded by men ; but eight hundred wild bullocks were a sorry set of voyagers, besides which the conductors availed themselves of the difficulties of transit to such an extent as to drive some of the animals away purposely, and then start off in pursuit, forgetting to return or to bring their bullocks. Out of the nine hundred four hundred were lost, and Garibaldi found that he would have a good many rivers to cross and a good deal of weariness to endure, all ending in certain loss. He therefore directed the slaughter of what remained, and the sale of the skins. After completing the business and paying the charges, there remained for the family chest one hundred crowns, and that sufficed for the wants of his family and himself until his arrival at Monte Video, and for a little while after.

This capital of the Republic of Uruguay was and is the trading port of the whole State. The greater part of its trade was with England, but Italy, France, and Belgium had considerable dealings with it. Garibaldi's occupation as a man of war had come to a temporary end, and although his friends were glad of his society, and entertained him hospitably, he did not choose to be a burden to them any more than he was compelled. He therefore took a turn at trade, and became a vendor of goods as commercial agent, trudging about the city with samples of every kind and variety of merchandise—as he says, "from Italian paste to Rouen goods." This occupation filled up the day, and for the remainder of his hours he took the post of mathematical tutor in the family of a friend, one Semidei. By these means, although in a straitened case, he obtained sufficient for the wants of his family; and so the days passed away in the dull routine of commerce and profession.

Banda Oriental, which was the name of that part of the Republic of which Monte Video is the capital, had for its leaders men who knew Garibaldi well; and now that the Rio Grande business had terminated, and he was at liberty, overtures were made him (in 1843), with a view of enlisting his services in the cause of the new emancipated Republic. The terms were too good for refusal. He would, moreover, be placed in hostility to Rosas, the dictator of Buenos Ayres, and on the side of those whose principle was held by him as the most sacred of truths—the right of men to govern themselves. He accepted the command of a small ship, a brigantine, of eighteen guns and two pivoted guns; and in company with her was commissioned a smaller vessel as consort, with general directions to assist Corrientes in his operations against Rosas.

There had already been several fights between the opposing squadrons, but none had brought about any positive change in the general situation. The affairs of the Republic were grossly mismanaged. Individuals took upon themselves autocratic power, thus actually practising a despotism against which their very existence as Republicans was bound to be

a living protest.   We often see this tendency in new democratic institutions, and it caused to Garibaldi many a sorrow,
many a disappointment, and many a hindrance.   Here was
one Vidal, a minister, actually ordering the dispersion of the
squadron, which had been brought to its then condition at a
prodigious expense, and formed the nucleus of a force that
might soon have been able to control the whole traffic of
La Plata.   Garibaldi had cause to suspect more than once,
that in the selection of duty entrusted to him, there was a
covert desire of getting rid of him altogether.   He saw with
pain, and knew not why it should be so, that he had many
enemies, and that these were powerful.   He was known as
a born ruler of men: a man of fearless integrity, and
animated by pure Republican principles; and he might
have known, had he not been so dimly conscious of his own
powers and their natural operation, that such as he were
terribly obnoxious amongst the more self-seeking of mob-
leaders.

Monte Video, a trading port, had, as it happened, a great
number of commercial Italian residents who had been
attracted thither by the opportunity of commerce, or driven
by exile from their native land.   Garibaldi issued a proclamation to these Italians, urging them to requite the
hospitality they had enjoyed by taking up arms in defence
of the place and people.   No offer of pay could be made,
except as far as food may be deemed payment, but a stipula-
tion for lands at the close of the contest had been tacitly
accepted by all parties.   In answer to his appeal five
hundred men enrolled, and that number soon increased to
eight hundred, every European vessel bringing fresh victims
of home proscription to take refuge in South America.
From them he selected three divisional commanders, and
formed three battalions.

These arrangements could not be hidden from Orribe,
but his self-confidence bade him take little heed, and he

continued his march towards Monte Video. The place had continued in its chronic disorder, and he thought there were many of his partisans in the city who would get up a manifestation of some kind in his favour. He might have taken the place, but chose to stop short at Cerito, and there pitch his camp. His friends, if he had any, made no sign, and the delay enabled the inhabitants to put the town in a better state of defence, and to organise the forces.

There had assembled some thousands of negroes who had regained their liberty: these were willing to take arms. They made good soldiers almost instantly, and their efficiency enabled the town to get together a total of nine thousand men, to cope with the twelve or fourteen thousand of the enemy. Orribe grew tired of waiting, and saw no chance of his being invited to enter the town. He therefore strengthened his position, and commenced desultory action. Meanwhile the town had fortified itself.

When the Republican soldiers were first brought face to face with the enemy they ran away without firing a shot ; a proceeding that must be attributed to the incapacity of the leaders. One of these had to be dismissed, and the others, growing familiar with their work, Garibaldi thought he would test their mettle by offering himself to take charge of an expedition to attack the division of Orribe's troops which had now assembled near their little fortress of Cerro. A general, whose name was Pacheco, accompanied him. They came on the enemy at two in the afternoon, and put them to flight by five o'clock, losing only half-a-score of men, but inflicting a loss of one hundred and fifty, besides taking two hundred prisoners. The homeward march to Monte Video was triumphant. Speeches of congratulation and commendation became the order of the day, and they were merited. This first " baptism of fire " had been nobly borne, and the leaders were now honoured by the bestowal of distinctions and gifts. For the Legion itself another watch the success of the march which had been stolen upon him.

In the meantime Colonel Bacz had collected two hundred and fifty horse from the frontiers of Brazil, which he now brought up and placed at Garibaldi's disposal. Word also came from General Medina that he was on his way with five hundred more, and that, on a certain day, he would be upon a neighbouring height, where he would await instructions. Garibaldi resolved to meet Medina in person; and on the appointed morning he set out with about two hundred Italians and a portion of Bacz's men. Anzani remained in Salta, in charge of the sick and wounded, which numbered something like sixty. About half of Garibaldi's force consisted of the foot-soldiers of the Legion, and these he stationed in a large shed upon the route which he had taken, whilst he rode forward with the horse.

A body of the enemy under Servando Gomez had observed these movements, and when the Italian leader had advanced for about a couple of hours, and was approaching Medina's rendezvous, he perceived a large force galloping across the plain. It was afterwards ascertained that the enemy's cavalry numbered twelve hundred, whilst three hundred of the horses carried double, bringing up the number to fifteen hundred.

Instantly turning, Garibaldi hurled himself upon the foe, and drove back without difficulty such as had ventured too far from the direct line of their leader's attack, which proved to be centred upon the shed containing the infantry. But as for Bacz and his recruits, no sooner did they perceive that the enemy was in superior force, than they shewed their mettle by a precipitate retreat. An incident now occurred which Garibaldi shall relate in his own words:—

"Perceiving clearly that resistance was only to be expected from my brave soldiers of the Legion, and that wherever they were the heart of the struggle would be, I galloped towards them; but just as I gained their front ranks, through the midst of the enemy's fire, I found my horse sinking, and in falling he dragged me with him. My first idea was that, on seeing me fall, my men would suppose I was dead, and that the belief would throw them into confusion. I had the presence of mind to draw a pistol from my saddle, and fire into the air to shew them I was safe. The consequence was, that before I was really down, eager hands sustained me, and I stood on my feet in their midst."

Surrounded by his faithful followers, who had never failed him in the hour of need, Garibaldi was more than equal to the occasion. He addressed them cheerfully and confidently.

"The enemy are numerous," he said, "we are few: so much the better! The fewer we are, the more glorious must be the fight. Be calm! Don't fire until they are close, and then give them a bayonet charge!" Every word was as a spark to combustible matter. They saw the crisis: cowardice was fatal, courage their only hope. Retreat was impossible. On came the enemy, and at sixty yards fired. This only inflamed the courage of the Italians, who replied with tenfold vigour. The commander fell. Garibaldi sprang to the head of his company, and led them to the thickest of the fight. It was a daring charge, made with a gallantry almost incredible, for the cavalry of the enemy was not only in front, but upon both flanks. A terrible *melée* ensued, when those of the enemy's infantry who had not fallen began to save themselves by flight. Garibaldi gave word to fire upon the cavalry; and this was done with disastrous effect.

At this juncture a brave officer of Baez's troop appeared with a few of his men. He had been disgusted at the cowardice of his general, and persuaded some of the

fugitives to turn their horses and rejoin Garibaldi. On they came, dashed through the opposing ranks, and pulled up at the side of their friends, throwing the enemy into fresh confusion by their unexpected arrival and the suddenness of the exploit. But Gomez's men were brave, and the check gave them renewed spirit. They retreated a few yards, dismounted, and to the number of six hundred encircled the gallant band. The plain was strewed with dead, and the fight became wild and furious. A young Italian trumpeter, only fifteen years old, was pierced by a lance. Away flew his trumpet, out came his knife, and springing on the lancer, he plunged it in his side, and they fell together. After the fight the two bodies were found clasped in deadly embrace. The lad was covered with wounds, and the lancer had in his thigh the deep mark of his assailant's thrust.

The combat had nearly exhausted both sides, and, moreover, the light began to fail. The enemy remained numerically strongest, but they had suffered terribly by the effective firing of the Itálians. Garibaldi ordered a retreat; but it was a deliberate movement. "In retreating," he said, "we will not leave, I hope, a single wounded comrade on the field." The enthusiasm and confidence he inspired by every word he spoke were unbounded. Calmly and steadily, fighting as they receded, they began their retreat. There was scarcely one who had not been wounded, save Garibaldi himself, although he had been as fully exposed as any of his followers.

The enemy could not understand the extraordinary spectacle presented by this movement. Too exhausted for the moment to offer serious resistance, they stood watching the slow retreat of the Italian Legion, who, bearing with them such of their companions as were too gravely hurt to march, withdrew leisurely and in good form, singing as they went the patriotic songs and hymns of their native country.

Night was closing fast about them as they fell back upon the shelter of a little copse. Even here the enemy disputed possession with them, but they were compelled to give way.

The retreat was, however, only a feint; or, if Garibaldi's first intention had been to snatch a few hours' rest, his unwearying spirit soon roused him to fresh action. The enemy was between him and Salta; and he was informed by scouts that the men had dismounted, and had even removed their horses' saddles. In little more than an hour, when the bulk of Gomez's troops had fallen asleep, never imagining but that the Italians were more exhausted than themselves, Garibaldi formed his men into close column, stole down upon the enemy, and as the trumpets of the latter were sounding the alarm, swept through their encampment without the loss of a man.

It would have been too rash to attack them on the spot, but Garibaldi did better. He reached a patch of high grass on the other side, and ordered his men to lie down on the ground. The enemy, as soon as they had mounted, rode in pursuit, and when they were within a few yards of the ambush Garibaldi gave the order to fire. At least thirty horsemen fell to the ground, and the rest, routed at last, fled in disorder.

"Now, my children," cried Garibaldi, "I think the time is come for us to go and drink." Skirting the wood, they hastened to the river, and after quenching their thirst marched back to Salta. Anzani came forth to greet them, weeping for joy, and not knowing how to testify his congratulation and relief.

He had had his share in the glory of the day. In the absence of his companions he had been summoned to surrender by a second force from Urguisa's camp. "Italians," he replied, "do not surrender. Go, or though you are many, I will annihilate you. So long as I have a companion we will fight; and if I am alone, I will set fire to the powder and destroy both you and myself." Cowed by his determination, the enemy, probably ignorant of the garrison's weakness, departed.

Few deeds of greater gallantry are recorded in the history of war; and if it be thought that a needless risk was run in the attempt to join forces with Medina, it must be allowed that the brilliancy of the exploit amply condoned its rashness. Medina does not appear to have reached the rendezvous; or if he did, he was not in time to render assistance, or not aware of the danger of his ally.

Garibaldi wrote the following despatch to the Commission of the Italian Legion, at Monte Video :—

"Brothers,—The day before yesterday we fought, in the plains of San Antonio, within a league and a half of the city, the most terrible and the most glorious of our battles. The four companies of our Legion, and a score of horse, who took refuge under our protection, not only defended themselves against twelve hundred of the men of Servando Gomez, but entirely annihilated the enemy's infantry, which had assailed them, to the number of three hundred men. The firing commenced at mid-day, and ended at midnight. Neither the number of the enemy, their repeated charges, their mass of cavalry, nor the assault of their infantry could prevail, although we had no other shelter than a ruined shed, supported by four posts. The Legion steadfastly repulsed the assault of the furious enemy, and every officer fought like one of the soldiers on that memorable day. Anzani, who had been left at Salta, and whom the enemy summoned to surrender, replied, with match in hand, and his foot on the store powder of the battery, that he would there die with them; although they had assured him that we were all dead or prisoners.

"We had thirty killed and fifty-three wounded. All the officers are wounded except Saccarello the elder, and Travers.

"I would not give up my name as one of the Italian Legion for a world of gold.

"At midnight we returned towards Salta. There were about a hundred left safe and sound. Those wounded but slightly marched first, to drive back the enemy when they became too troublesome.

"This affair deserves to be commemorated by a medal.

"Adieu! I will write to you at greater length another time.   "Yours,

"GIUSEPPE GARIBALDI."

The return of Garibaldi to Monte Video took place about three months after the close of the Salta struggle, and the event awoke the popular enthusiasm to the highest pitch of excitement. The foreign service there joined in the jubilation: the French Admiral wrote our hero a congratulatory note from on board his frigate *L'Africane*, averring that the skill and intrepidity of that feat of arms would have added lustre to the renowned Grand Army of France, and bestowing a personal compliment on Garibaldi for the simplicity and modesty of his narrative, in which praise is meted out to others when it was mainly due to himself.

Not satisfied with having written to Garibaldi, the Admiral wished to pay his compliments in person. He came on shore at Monte Video, and proceeded to the street where Garibaldi resided. The poorest legionary could not have had a humbler abode. The door, without fastenings, stood open to all by night and by day, and as our hero humorously said, "particularly to the wind and the rain." The Admiral's visit was after dark; he pushed open the door, and stumbling against a chair, exclaimed:—

"Halloa! Is it necessary to risk one's life to see you, Garibaldi?"

"Ho! wife!" cried Garibaldi, on hearing the sound, and not recognising the Admiral's voice, "don't you hear some one in the passage? Bring a light?"

"And what am I to light?" answered Anita; "don't you know there are not two sous in the house to buy a candle with?"

"Very true!" was the philosophic answer. Turning towards the door, he called to the visitor to come in.

The Admiral entered, but it was too dark for mutual recognition, and he therefore announced his name.

"Admiral," said Garibaldi, "when I arranged with the Republic at Monte Video for rations, I omitted to include candles. So, as Anita has just said, inasmuch as we have not two sous, the house is dark. But I presume you wish to speak with, rather than to see, me."

On leaving, the old Admiral went off to the Minister of War, General Pacheco, and told what he had seen. It happened that the decree of the Government was at that moment lying before him. He at once despatched a messenger with a hundred patagous (£20) to Garibaldi's residence. The Italian accepted the gift: it would have been rude to act otherwise; but the next morning he was distributing it amongst the widows and children of the dead soldiers; keeping enough to buy a pound of candles with, "in case," as he said to his wife, "Admiral Lainé should pay us another visit."

He settled down at Monte Video for some time, steadfastly refusing all grants of land, or other gifts by which the necessaries of life so well deserved and so much needed might have been secured to him. No argument availed, no remonstrance moved him : and in consequence he was often in penury. He rented a little land and worked it ; but his heart continued hungering for news from home ; and whenever that news came, his heart beat fast with excitement. The atmosphere of Europe was charged with revolution, and more especially the land of his birth. Sicily, Tuscany, Naples, Lombardy, Piedmont, the Roman States, and Venetia were all in agitation. There needed no prophet to shew what lay in the future. Organic political change became daily and increasingly imminent. Every vessel from Europe brought tidings. Garibaldi's thoughts, his hopes, his love turned towards home ; and when news came of the death of Gregory XVI. and the accession of Pius IX., his sanguine heart bade him believe that for the land of his fathers the hour of deliverance had come. Thus ceaselessly hoping that the opportunity of returning might be vouchsafed to him, in answer to his earnest prayer, the exile chafed and waited. It was in 1847 that Jacopo Medici, afterwards a general in the Italian army, brought him a message from Mazzini that Italy needed his assistance.

CHAPTER IV.

RETURNS TO ITALY.

"Italy, what of the night?
  Ah, child, child, it is long!
  Moonbeam and starbeam and song
Leave it dumb now and dark;
Yet I perceive on the height,
  Eastward, not now very far,
A song too loud for the lark,
  A light too strong for a star."
                                    —SWINBURNE.

IT will be remembered that when Garibaldi fled from
Europe he belonged to the young Republican party of
Italy, the *Giovine Italia*. Their sect—for sect it was
—died down; the noble enthusiasm of its founders not
receiving the full sympathy and assistance of the maturer
minds of its day. Many of the enthusiasts insensibly fell
into the ranks of moderate Liberalism in Piedmont, and
the efforts of those who remained faithful became spasmodic
and powerless. An expedition from Savoy to reunite Italy,
for instance, could not be expected to command general
concurrence, seeing that Savoy was Italian only by treaty,
although its inhabitants might reasonably deem themselves
Italians. But as the doctrines of Young Italy lost the
power of combining the disaffected, their principles made
way in the Marches and lower Provinces, and the leavening
process went on. In the meantime petty disputes arose;
the old Radicals, as we may call them, and the new came
into conflict, some acknowledging an element of religious
motive, and others scorning it as only another form of

slavery. Hence arose a weakness in every attempt that was made to advance from opinion to action; but a feeling was generated in the national mind which promised to ripen into union whenever change of circumstance should provide a common basis.

It will be well here to give the reader a short sketch of the state of Italy at this time. The Congress of Vienna adopted a rough and ready way of repairing, so far as possible, the effects of Buonaparte's aggressive career. It aimed at restoring the map of Europe to the form which it presented at the date of the French Revolution, heedless of the fact that nearly a quarter of a century had elapsed in the meantime, and deliberately refusing the grand opportunity afforded to it of reaping a certain harvest of good from the results of the great European catastrophe.

Nowhere was this opportunity so fairly offered as in the case of Italy. The peninsula had been broken up into ten several States, most of them contemptible in power and influence, and several of them foully stained with the crimes of oppression and dynastic cruelty. Buonaparte had at least attempted to found a united kingdom of Italy on the basis of her old and glorious autonomy; the unification of the country in 1815 would surely have been a lighter offence against justice in the abstact, and a greater gain to the entire Italian population, than the bare renewal of the petty tyrannies which had virtually forfeited their title to exist. But diplomacy is not wont to play the part of an intervening deity, and it was hardly possible that Italy should have been dealt with on different principles from those which were applied to the rest of Europe. The old States were consequently restored; and it is as well, for the better understanding of the narrative which is to follow, that we should take a rapid survey of their actual and relative positions.

The States of Italy, as defined in the Treaty of Vienna,

were as follows :—The kingdom of Sardinia (to which Genoa was attached), the Lombardo-Venetian kingdom (to which was annexed the republic of San Marco), the kingdom of Naples and Sicily, the Papal States, the republic of San Marino, the principality of Monaco, the grand duchy of Tuscany, and the duchies of Palma, Modena, and Lucca; the latter of which was subsequently annexed to Tuscany.

The State of Sardinia, or more properly of Piedmont, was of French origin, the King of Burgundy having, in the year 1000, conferred the fief of Maurienne, in Savoy, upon one Beroldo, whose successor Oddone, by marriage with Adelaide of Susa, added thereto a large portion of Piedmont. Oddone was the fourth of the line who had held the title of Count of Savoy. His descendants long continued to deem themselves rather Frenchmen than Italians; and they reckoned amongst their possessions Geneva and Vaud, in what is now Switzerland, Bourg en Bresse, Bugez and Valromey, now constituting the French department of Ain. Circumstances, however, led them to cede these provinces one by one, and to extend their sway southwards; but it was not until within the last few years that Savoy itself reverted to France. No century passed without a substantial addition to the territories of this State; of which we need only mention a few instances. In 1386 Nice voluntarily accepted the sway of Amadeo the Seventh. In 1720 the acquisition of the island of Sardinia gave its name to the entire kingdom, as the conquest of England had given a new title to William of Normandy. In 1815—a notable violation of principle on the part of the Congress of Vienna —the Republic of Genoa was delivered over to the King of Sardinia.

Sardinia was perhaps the best governed of the large Italian States, but the influences set a-going by the French Revolution, and the unscrupulous severity of Austria's suzerainty operated very strongly upon her citizens. In

1820 the Liberal party demanded from the government a policy of reform. The King, Charles Felix, was absent, but his cousin, Charles Albert, temporised with the memorialists, and at least suffered them to conclude that he was favourably inclined to their demands. But the King's reply was stern and uncompromising. An Austrian force occupied Alessandria, the strongest town of Piedmont, and Austrian influence was supreme. The leading remonstrants were banished; amongst them Cesare Balbo, who in his exile wrote a book, entitled *Le Speranze d'Italia* ("The Hopes of Italy"), in which he designated the King of Sardinia as the future chief of an Italian Confederation.

Lombardy and Venice.—As a result of the wars ended by the treaty of Utrecht, in 1713, the Duchies of Milan and Mantua, then united under the name of Lombardy, passed under the rule of Austria. In 1796 Napoleon, who had previously induced the Republic of Venice to annex herself to France, ceded that country to the Emperor Francis II., as the price of the latter's non-interference with the French invasion of the peninsula. After the battle of Austerlitz Venice was restored to Italy, but the prestige of Austria in 1815 sufficed to confirm her in the possession of both provinces, in spite of the boasted restitution of the map of Europe.

The Lombardo-Venetian kingdom was ruled by Austria with a rod of iron; but, though the efforts of patriotism were more desperate and hopeless here than in any other part of Italy, the inhabitants did not submit quietly to the hated yoke. Always vigorously repressed, demands for reform and incipient insurrection manifested themselves again and again. Here also Mazzini's doctrines and exhortations penetrated and bore fruit; but it was not until during the War of Italian Independence, waged in 1848 by Charles Albert against the foreign oppressors, that events specially demanding our notice occurred in Lombardy and Venice.

Naples and Sicily.—The two Sicilies, comprising the island of Sicily, and the foot and ankle of the peninsula, as far north as the States of the Church, were united in one kingdom, in 1745, under Charles of Spain. In 1812 England interfered, to avert a revolution in Sicily against Ferdinand, and guaranteed the constitutional independence of the island. But Ferdinand soon forgot the oath which he had taken to respect the covenant imposed upon him, and England suffered her guarantee to become a dead letter. From being the most influential portion of the United Kingdom, Sicily had fallen to a subservient position, and thus internal disaster and disaffection were added to the national animosity against Austria, whose yoke was, if anything, more galling in the south than in the north. The rule of Ferdinand was corrupt and cruel in the extreme, and Sicily experienced the full bitterness of his oppression.

The Papal States.—The temporal power of the Popes may be dated from the conferment of the Duchy of Rome upon Stephen II. by Charlemagne. Subsequent bequests and conquests increased the dominions of the Church, until they extended from the Adriatic to the western Mediterranean, and from Naples to Tuscany.

The overwhelming influence of the Roman Church in Italy is, undoubtedly, the key-note of the country's disorganisation throughout the Middle and Modern Ages. The *imperium in imperio* was utterly incompatible with strong or united national institutions. As the power of Rome increased, the independence of civil government gradually diminished. It has ever been the policy of ecclesiastical Rome to "divide and rule;" and the quarrels of Italian States were fomented rather than appeased by the intervention of the Popes.

The ministers and administrators of the Pontifical dominions were naturally all cardinals and priests; a circumstance which tended directly to produce that incredible corruption of the Church which has been the most glaring scandal of Christendom. These are facts, to the truth of which even Roman Catholic historians, writing candidly and dispassionately, have not been able to demur. At no time was the administrative corruption of Rome more aggravated than during the pontificate of Gregory the Sixteenth, the predecessor of Pius the Ninth. The extortion, cruelty, and immorality of Gregory and his tools not only exceeded in themselves the crimes of Austrian and Neapolitan oppression, but they added, as it were, a sanction and encouragement to the almost universal tyranny under which Italy groaned.

The accession of Pius in 1846 to a certain extent broke through this dark reign of cruelty and impiety, feeding the minds of Italians with bright hopes of an amelioration of their hapless lot, and contributing largely to the formation of that moderate Liberal party which became hereafter necessary to add solidity to the less stable Radicals. But in the meantime the Papal States were, under Gregory, the most lamentably misgoverned in the whole peninsula.

"In the Roman States, every sentiment of patriotism, every desire for the public good, every glimmering of moral rectitude was extinct, if such had ever existed, in the sensual, grasping, cowardly priesthood who held the reins of administration. The well-known reply of Pope Gregory XVI. to any remark on the impoverished state of the treasury, and the enormous debt of twenty millions of dollars with which he had saddled the country: 'My successor will look to that,' might be taken as the device of all surrounding or depending on him. Railways, scientific congresses, and infant asylums were systematically opposed; the laws against the freedom of the press rendered still more stringent; heresy and political offences no less rigorously punished. Bands of robbers were known to purchase the connivance of the military authorities charged with their repression. It required but money to secure immunity from any violation of the criminal laws, or to obtain a favourable judgment in any of the civil tribunals. Places of responsibility and trust, and titles of nobility, to which capacity, integrity, and years of faithful service had been the original qualifications, were bought and sold with unblushing effrontery, or else became the wages of dishonesty and intrigue. The gross immorality of the clergy scarce sought concealment or feared detection. Commerce was hampered by the monopolies enjoyed by private individuals, or the imbecility of the ministers, many of whom, ignorant of geography and the first principles of trade, passed measures diametrically opposed to the development of the industrial resources of the country. The post-office had become a vehicle for ascertaining the sentiments of private persons; the boasted secrecy of the confessional was made subservient to the same end. Everywhere tyranny, fraud, corruption; vice rampant; morality sunk immeasurably low; truth a myth; religion bartered for grovelling superstition or else totally discarded—such is the summing up of this dreary catalogue of wretchedness and misrule."

Tuscany.—The Grand Duchy of Tuscany embraces the old republics of Florence, Pisa, and Siena. Lucca, assigned in 1815 to Charles Louis of Bourbon, in lieu of his rightful inheritance of Parma, which had been granted to Maria Louisa (the wife of Napoleon), reverted to Tuscany on the death of the ex-Empress in 1847, when Charles resumed the Duchy of Parma. Tuscany received an admirable constitution from Leopold, son of Maria Theresa, whose code of laws formed the basis of civil and religious liberties in the duchy down to its absorption, a few years ago, in the Italian kingdom. But the curse of Italian misrule did not escape this comparatively fortunate State. Leopold's grandson, Leopold II., who married the sister of Ferdinand of Naples, copied the example of his brother-in-law, and did

not scruple to set at naught the institutions of his grand-
father. Nevertheless, in the earlier portion of his reign
Tuscany was well governed, and formed the only powerful
bulwark in Italy against the encroachments of Rome; and
for a long period Florence, the capital, deserved to be called
the freest and most liberal city in Italy.

Parma.—The Duchy of Parma came into the possession
of the Bourbons in 1731, and continued to be held by
them, with the exception of the period during which it was
governed by the Empress Maria Louisa, until 1859. "The
fortunes of Parma," writes Mr. Gretton, "had varied (from
the year 1815) with the tastes and dispositions of the
favourites who successively swayed the facile mind of the
widow of Napoleon. In the history of her amours lies the
clue to the history of her reign. Splendid and munificent
under Neipperg; grasping and parsimonious when Werk-
lein held the ascendancy; oppressive and inquisitorial while
Mistrali occupied her affections—the acme of misgovernment was finally reached by the elevation of the Count de
Bombelles, an Austrian diplomatist, to the post so many
had previously enjoyed. First grand major-domo, then
inspector of military affairs, lastly Chief President of the
Privy Council — an office he had himself created — the
whole control of the State was vested in his hands. The
ministers, from fear of being displaced, were content to
transform themselves into mere instruments of his will;
every description of injustice, extortion, and political rigour
was permitted or enforced; and as a last refinement of
tyranny, the privilege of claiming an audience from the
Duchess was abolished, so that no channel remained whereby
her subjects could address their supplications and complaints
to their sovereign." Under such circumstances, it was
natural that Parma should be regarded as little else than
an Austrian province.

In Modena, also, the influence of Austria and Rome was

predominant ; and the apostles of liberty met with no mercy at the hands of Francesco and his son. The attempted revolt of 1831 commenced by movements in the Roman States and in Modena, which were suppressed by Austrian troops with ruthless severity.

The Republic of San Marino, on the northern frontier of the Papal States, and the Principality of Monaco, on the Sardinian coast between Nice and Genoa, are of no political importance. Numbering respectively about seven thousand and five thousand inhabitants, their insignificance has protected them from most of the convulsions which have distracted the remainder of Italy.

Such were the divisions into which Italy was cut up, and the disjoined miserable conditions the different States had fallen into. But the leaven of Freedom was working in the minds of many, and deliverance was nearer than any expected.

A basis for common action was found in the universal hatred of Austrian arrogance, and in the ever-increasing popular resentment against Austrian oppression. As has been shewn, the Treaty of Vienna had made Austria the sole arbiter in the internal discords of Italy ; but the trust fell into hands little fit to be invested with arbitrary power. With all the far-inherited duplicity of the Asiatic, and all the dogged obstinacy of the Teuton, no power was less qualified to determine controversies arising in a land of traditionary intellectual acuteness. The pride of the land of song and literary glory, the prejudice and jealousy of the Imperial City, which since its great decline had become the shrine of Christendom, could excite no other emotion in the guardian State than that of violent antagonism, whenever the least breath of excitement stirred the pulse of Italy.

No stranger could heal the breaches of Italy. She must be her own deliverer, and the process of such deliverance involves, in nations or individuals, a terrible prelude of suffering and convulsion. Shut out from the correcting

influence of free and frank intercourse with others by her
own sensitive pride, as much as by the selfish combination
of the Great Powers of Europe, she had to acquire the
hardihood necessary for her salvation by the bitterness of
internal dissension and disunion. By her own temporary
disunion only could the common basis of her new life be
reached.

The changes which occurred in France during the Revolution of 1830 included the virtual abrogation of the Treaty of
Vienna. The French again claimed a position among the
Great Powers; and eager to resume their traditionary
attitude toward Austria, occupied Ancona at the invitation
of the Pope, an important city on the Adriatic, of great
influence in the Marches. Austria at the same time held
the Legations. Both abandoned their position in 1838,
much to the relief of all Italian patriots. The faithful
champions of Young Italy had in the meantime been
indefatigable. They had laboured effectually in the
South and in Sicily, to the alarm of the King of Naples;
but the parental condition of Rome was not invoked, and of
course France and Austria did not interfere. The Pope,
lulled by the absence of complaint, determined to pay a
visit to the southern Provinces, and the usual rejoicings,
illuminations, and flattery took place. But the emissaries
of the *Giovine Italia* had likewise been travelling over the
same ground. These came back with assurances that
Naples and Sicily were ripe for revolt, and they urged the
inhabitants of the Romagna and the Marches to cast in
their lot with them. The news of these intrigues disturbed
the authorities at Rome, and a messenger was despatched
from Bologna to ascertain the condition of Naples, who
confirmed the evil tidings. Mazzini and his friends had succeeded in obtaining the adhesion of many sons of noble
families, and these were soon proscribed, and fled from place
to place until they finally took refuge in France or Switzer-

land.   Guerilla warfare sprang up throughout Southern
Italy.   An honourable and gallant youth, Muratori, collected
about him a number of those who had been or expected to
be proscribed ; they were attacked by a body of Papal
Carbineers, who captured their chief and shot him.

The agitation of the country produced what may be
described as a Liberal party of order.   These agreed with
the Young Italy party in ascribing the sufferings of the
people to the Austrian rule, but endeavoured to shew that
patriotism and religion did not demand violent measures.
But the more ardent spirits laughed at these counsels.
Their patience was utterly exhausted, and not unnaturally.
The rule of Pope Gregory was abominable.   That of the
King of Naples was but little better.   Austria held the
Lombardo-Venetian Provinces, oppressing her immediate
subjects, and lording it over the whole peninsula.   Tuscany
was fairly ruled, and Piedmont, under Charles Albert, was
progressing, but until all Italy could be united it seemed
vain to hope for freedom.   The patriots therefore continued
their plots, labouring incessantly to light the flame of a
general insurrection.

In 1844 their hopes seemed to be near fulfilment.   The
popular excitement spread throughout the two Sicilies and
the Roman States.   The whole of the Italian Governments
were on the watch, and each supplied the others with such
information as could be gained.   The principal European
States, everywhere in dread of civil commotion, bound themselves to render aid, even to the extent of intercepting
the correspondence entrusted to them as public carriers.
Austria, being in the greatest danger, and dreading lest
even a spark of insurrection should fall within her own
dominions, and create a conflagration a hundredfold more
dreadful than an Italian Revolution, set her police actively
to work.   France kept jealous guard over the refugees.
Even England opened their letters !   To talk of moral suasion

and the inherent force of non-resistance sounded like a mockery in the ears of the Italian patriots. The conspirators formed, in every town from Rome to Bologna, bodies of men ready to take arms and try the issue. Down in the Calabrias there existed men desperate enough for any attempt, and in Parma and Tuscany sufficient popular excitement was maintained to hinder their Governments from rendering much service to the oppressors. Outbreaks occurred here and there, and considerable slaughter ensued. The moderate party now grew more imperative, and issued at last a manifesto, which, after recapitulating past wrongs and present oppressions, concluded by demanding:—1. An amnesty to all political offenders, from 1821 until that date. 2. The concession of equitable civil and criminal codes, parliamentary government, trial by jury, the abolition of confiscation and death for political offences. 3. The reliuquishment by the Holy Office of the Inquisition of control over laymen. 4. That political trials should be referred to the ordinary tribunals. 5. That municipal bodies should be elected by the people. 6. That no clergy should have any civil, military, or judicial dignity or employment. 7. That public instruction, except on religion, should be in lay hands. 8. That foreign troops should be disbanded, and a Civic Guard established, and that the governments should enter upon a course of social reform in harmony with the age, and after the example of the freest European States. "We will replace our sword in the scabbard," declared the memorialists, "and become tranquil and obedient subjects of the Pope the moment he guarantees by the Great Powers these just concessions."

This political programme was of course rejected.

Then came fresh severities and sufferings. Military commissions were issued, men of wealth and character were sent to the galleys for no other crime than acquaintance

with the absent leaders ; the press was put under more rigid
censorship; but the issue turned in favour of the subject
and against the government in the minds of all candid and
reasonable men both in Italy and elsewhere.   The Italian
despots, and the intolerant Austrian government, could not
endure the free expression of opinion in any part of the
peninsula, and they took every opportunity of suppressing it.   Mazzini, Gioberti, Cesare Balbo, and many other
writers of independence and ability, had been banished soon
after the restoration.   But books continued to appear that
had increasing influence; books of moderate tone, but
reviewing the crisis most searchingly, explaining the pre-
scriptive rights of the Italian to Italy, and reciting the
perfidy and corruption of the Austrian Court.   This was a
novel method, and possible only in Piedmont.   The hopes of
independence gradually acquired a vigour that could not be
repressed by policemen and dungeons, even had such means
been tried.   They could not be tried in Piedmont, for King
Charles Albert was "every inch a king," and consciously an
equal among princes, as the writers of those books knew and
said.   Austrian journals replied by depreciatory reviews and
sneers at the saucy little house of Savoy.

Then the Emperor bethought him of another way.   He
resorted to fiscal vengeance, and enacted a prohibitory duty
on the wine produce of Sardinia.   Charles Edward met it
adroitly.   There had been a question on the salt duties, in
which reason and policy put Austria out of the field, and
in a State paper the King narrated the facts, and in reference to the wine tariff ended his criticism thus: "Upon
these grounds Austria has adopted the measure by way
of reprisal."

Reprisal ! That was the word.   The spirited resistance
had roused both Italy and Austria. Reprisal ! Are we
equal? Yes, said Piedmont, at least I am as good as you,
who are only the conservator of despotism and of the corrupt

government of Italian States. The leaven worked wondrously, as we shall see by-and-by. Rome, under Pope Gregory, persisted in believing that repression meant governing, and oppression preserving; but on the 1st of June 1846, after a short illness, God called that pontiff to the judgment-seat about which he had once bearded Nicholas of Russia, when the latter had dared to question his right to parcel out the earth and its people. And the land had a brief peace.

The death of a Pope is not like the death of a king. It is a break in historic continuity. A hundred things might happen before a new Vicegerent of God could be selected. The strifes and struggles of human ambition, veiled under ecclesiastical titles and ideas, must have their little day, and in this case it included some sixteen of earth's revolutions. Gizzi, the popular favourite, was set aside by the conclave. The man was too good. A weak, plausible, and obscure person, Mastai Ferretti, was preferred, and he took the designation of Pius IX. Men waited hopefully. Nothing could be worse than that which had been endured. Pio Nono's first act, the appointment of a provisional Commission of Consultation, and his giving of alms, his ordering of weekly audiences, and the end of political inquisition, indicated a *régime* of gentleness and justice. " As wretchedness makes the smallest gifts seem great, so the subjects of the Pope opened their eyes at these twinklings of light as to the dawn of brighter destinies. They cheered themselves by gazing on the tranquil and majestic countenance of the Pontiff; they commented with eager care on every amiable and noble word that was said to have issued from his mouth. They magnified every act of clemency, of charity, or of justice; and when some of his household or court reported (for the Pope's court is full of gossip) that Pius IX. thought of conceding a general amnesty for political offences, the hearts long saddened opened to joy." The popular mind,

content with small things, hoped to gain the Pope to itself;
and some politicians attached themselves to the idea that it
was practicable to bring about harmony between the Papacy
and freedom, priesthood and laity; forgetting that the Pope
had been a Cardinal, and that the Sacred College was too
powerful to be set aside with impunity.

On the 16th of July, however, one month after the Pope's
election, his amnesty was published; and when the intelligence had flown through Rome, and the conciliatory edict
had been perused, it seemed as though a ray from the love
of God had unexpectedly descended upon the Eternal City.
Hosannas multiplied; "Pius IX., the Deliverer," passed
from mouth to mouth, as each man embraced his brother;
the torches blazed in thousands; the people shouted for
him.   He appeared, they prostrated themselves, and received
his blessing in devout silence.   These solemnities of love and
gratitude spread to the utmost borders of the States; the
intelligence flew over Europe and across the seas.

Garibaldi in his exile heard the glad tidings which Mazzini lost no time in conveying to him. With all the
ingenuousness of his nature, and the spontaneity of his
country, he believed in the dawning of an era of liberty for
Italy.   He resolved to second the generous resolutions of
the Pope by offering him his sword, and also the services of
his companions in arms.   He had no insuperable antipathy
to the Pope, and he reverenced religion; and wherever the
tones of Liberty's call rang, the echo of his heart was "I
come!"   It was in this sense that American troubles had
enlisted his service; that ended, the claim of the mother—
Italy—was irresistible; and especially if the aspiration of
his heart could be indulged by serving under a Messiah of
his country.

Anzani, too, accepted the hopeful tidings. The two
friends believed that, after all, a Pope was to be the sublime
emancipator.   They wrote to the Nuncio, begging the

transmission of the desires of themselves and the Italian Legion in the cause they had at heart. For they had heard that that cause was in jeopardy from the hostility of the Pope's antagonists, and that His Holiness must have recourse to war.

Their letter ran thus :—

" Most Illustrious and Honoured Seigneur,—From the moment the news came of the accession of the Sovereign Pontiff Pius IX., who has granted the amnesty to poor outlaws, our attention and interest have followed the radiance which the Supreme Head of the Church has shed on the course of liberty and glory. The commendations echoed from beyond the sea, with which Italy rapturously welcomed the convocation of deputies and the sagacious concession to the press, the institution of the Civic Guard, the impulse imparted to popular education and to industry, and many other acts for improving the welfare of the poorer classes, in the forming of the new administration—the whole, in fact, convinced us that there had come out from our country the man who comprehended the necessities of the age, in accordance with the precepts of our sacred religion, ever new and ever immortal; who, without lessening their authority, could apply them to the exigencies of our times ; and although these benefits have no effect upon ourselves, we have yet followed with our plaudits and our wishes the general concert of Italy and Christendom. But again, we are apprised of the sacrilegious crime of a faction maintained and fomented by strangers—not yet tired, after so long a time, of rending our poor country—to reverse the selected order of existing arrangements. Our feeble tribute of enthusiastic admiration imposes a grand duty upon us.

" We, the undersigned, most illustrious and honoured Highness, are men animated with the same spirit which caused our exile, who took up arms at Monte Video for an apparently just cause, and have combined some hundreds of our compatriots, who came hither to escape troubles in their own country. During the five years of the siege all of us have given many proofs of courage and resignation, and, thanks to Providence and the ancient spirit which warms our Italian blood, our Legion has distinguished itself on several occasions, taking advantage of every opportunity— so that without vanity we, in the path of honour, have surpassed all rivals in any other corps.

"Therefore, if now these men of arms are accepted by His Holiness, it is useless to offer the assurance that they will be for ever consecrated to the service of their country and the Church.

"We shall deem ourselves fortunate in coming to aid the work of redemption of Pius IX.—we and our companions in whose name we speak, and who are willing to give their blood.

"If your illustrious and honoured Highness thinks that our offer would be acceptable to the Sovereign Pontiff, will you place it at the foot of his throne.

"It is not the childish pretension that our service is necessary which makes this offer. We very well know that the throne of St. Peter rests on foundations which need not human succour, nor will by men be shaken, and that also the new order counts on many defenders who will repel with vigour the unjust aggressions of its enemies. The work must be given, a part to the good and a part to the strong, and we ask the honour of being reckoned among the latter.

"Meanwhile, we acknowledge the hand of Providence in preserving His Holiness from the machinations of the Tristi, and offer our ardent prayers that he may have many years for the good of Christendom and Italy.

"We now end, asking your illustrious and honoured Holiness to pardon the trouble we cause, and to accept the proffer of the esteem and profound respect of the

devoted servants of your most illustrious and honoured
Holiness.   "G. GARIBALDI.

"LEO ANZANI."

To this communication neither the Nuncio nor the Pope
made any reply, direct or indirect. The intelligence which
followed revealed the disappointed hopes of the Italians,
and the friends came to the resolution of returning to Italy,
with as many of the Legion as were willing to accompany
them, so as to join in the struggle where arms had already
been taken up, or to stimulate it in such places as had
hitherto remained dormant. But amongst the whole company there was not a sou wherewith to defray the cost of
travelling.

The Government of Monte Video could not be expected
to lose with a good grace so useful an instrument as Garibaldi had proved. Remembrance of the past and hope for
the future prompted them to put every impediment they
reasonably could in his way. The merchants in the port
had come to learn the potency of his name and character,
and had depended on his help when commercial affronts
and damage raised quarrels between them and the native
traders, and they naturally sought to deter him from his
cherished projects. He became fretful, exclaiming, "We
shall arrive too late : there will be nothing left for us to
do," and complained of the obstacles and delay.

A subscription was set on foot among those who had
means, which went on very well until the jealousy or
treachery of some in the Legion vented itself in traducing
the character and motives of their leader, and urging his
followers to abstain from joining a venture so perilous and
impracticable that it must end in death at the executioner's
hands. This proceeding winnowed away the faint-hearted
to the number of eighty-five, and when the hour of departure
arrived they were still further decreased to nine-and-twenty
staunch and valiant fellows, almost all of whom had been

present on the plain of San Antonio. A few natives joined, and among them Garibaldi's negro Aguyar, whose untimely death in the siege of Rome subsequently grieved him so much. A Genoese merchant advanced the greater part of the funds, and the Government of Monte Video supplied two cannon and eight hundred muskets, which was really all it could afford.

The little band left Monte Video on the 27th March 1848, but now, even at the last moment, without great difficulty. The captain of the ship they had arranged to sail in adopted every method in his power to increase the expenses, and did so beyond the means so hardly collected. Rather than be foiled, the brave fellows sold their clothing, even to their shirts, to satisfy his rapacity, some of them having to lie in bed on the passage for want of clothing to cover them.

After crossing the equator and sailing in the open sea, through 400 miles of north latitude, whilst Garibaldi was passing the time in an amusement common to Atlantic voyagers, that of harpooning dolphins, suddenly a cry of fire startled the crew. One of the men engaged in getting out and distributing the rations had the imprudence to draw the brandy with a lighted candle in his hand, and the running stream of spirit was ignited. He lost his presence of mind, and rushed about crying, "Fire," leaving the lighted fluid flowing, until that part of the hold had become literally a lake of fire—separated from the powder-room only by a wooden partition not an inch thick. Anzani, too, had heard the cry, where he lay in his hammock, sick of a consumption. He, like Garibaldi, was collected enough to rush to the spot, and was fortunately able to assist the leader, who extinguished the flame.

The voyagers crossed the Atlantic in safety, and passed through the Straits of Gibraltar, taking what is known as the Marseilles route, though they were bound for Nice.

The Sardinian Consul at Palo, where the ship anchored at, had an interview with Garibaldi, and explained the course of events as they had happened during the last few months, not only in Europe generally, but particularly in Milan, Naples, and Sicily.

The Pope had disappointed all the expectations of the public. He had shewn himself the feeble vacillating tool of the ecclesiastical party, and in his weakness had offended Austria, as well as disgusted all Italy. Piedmont had granted a constitution which was likely to work, and her king was maintaining at least his defensive attitude towards his antagonist. The Lombardo-Venetian province, the capital of which is Milan, had risen. Sicily had been the scene of a terrible explosion. The Neapolitan king had violated the ancient constitution beyond the endurance of the Sicilians, and dreadful results had followed. France had sent Louis Philippe after Charles X., and proclaimed itself Republican.

But Garibaldi heard with most interest the intelligence from the North of Italy: how that Charles Albert had granted the constitution containing great financial reforms, extending the franchise so as to include municipal representation, establishing a Volunteer Civic Guard, with government arms and at government charge, providing an increase of ministers, suppressing the separate Sardinian Ministry, and establishing the identification of that island with the mainland, with other like measures. He also heard the full particulars of the "five days" of Milan, the faint-hearted, which at last had turned upon Austria, and he was rejoiced.

Moreover, the Consul told him that he had seen Italian vessels pass, flying the tri-colour flag. This circumstance determined ·Garibaldi's course. He saw that the most powerful popular sentiment was the thirst for national independence; that men of wealth and learning could shed

their blood in that cause, and that their names and martyrdom were already sung by the wild mountaineer and the
industrious peasant. He saw that while kings granted
reforms, they were accepted from the Alps to Sicily, not as
for Piedmont, or Sardinia, or Tuscany, or Parma, but as for
Italy. He saw that all reforms brought kings and peoples
nearer to each other, and made all seek for the complete
union of Italian princes and provinces. Then he foresaw,
also, an Italy so united, able to meet Austria in the field, in
the senate, in the diplomatic world, and to answer for herself everywhere. He went on board again. He hauled
down the Monte Videan flag, under which he had come so
far towards home, and out of a bed-sheet, a red scarf, and
some green facings of their worn-out uniforms, he made a
tricolour flag and hoisted it. His sanguine spirit rushed
on like a torrent to conclusions yet remote, but which his
clear vision saw distinctly to be near. With the truthfulness
of a child, as well as the heart of a hero, he heard and acted.

In three months from leaving Monte Video the vessel
came in sight of Nice. They were boarded by the harbour
people, and Garibaldi was recognised. There had been some
anxious discussions among the exiles on board as to the
prudence of landing at all, and especially of the landing of
their leader, who was under sentence of death. He did not
hesitate, and if he had it would have been useless. His
name was reported from one to the other, and in a few hours
half the inhabitants had flocked down to force upon the
exiles, first their joyful exclamations, and secondly a hearty
welcome. This welcome touched the hearts, the hospitality
comforted the bodies and spirits of the long-banished
Italians; and when it was known that the motive of their
return was a desire to render such service as the cause of
Italian independence could accept at their hands, volunteers
flocked in from all the districts for enrolment.

This ardour exceeded Garibaldi's wishes. He had a

natural and sincere faith in men, and a most delicate sense of honour. The King of Piedmont having conceded the demands of the moderate party, and shewn a disposition to bind in sympathy the Italian peoples, had a claim on him that he would recognise. Some might like revolution for revolution's sake; he submitted to it as an evil to be endured for freedom's sake. He would go and see the king, and offer him his services. He had believed in Pio Nono and been deceived, but why should he not trust some one else? Besides, he had determined on exciting an insurrection in Reggio, and on coming found that not only had it begun, but the king was the source of its inspiration.

Our hero might have spared himself the visit to Charles Albert, although the feeling which prompted it did him honour ; and it is due to him that this loyal offer of service to the King of Piedmont should be borne in mind. Charles Albert did not appreciate Garibaldi or his services, and the General came to have exactly the same sentiments towards the king. The Pope would not have him, and now the king would not have him.

It appears that the interview had deeply annoyed the visitor. The manner of the king was bad : his treatment worse. He had referred the matter to Ricci, the Minister of War, who, after a few days' delay, had sent for Garibaldi, and advised him to proceed to Venice, and obtain a few small vessels by which he might serve the Venetians as a privateer, adding, "I believe that is your proper place." It was an answer natural enough in the mouth of a Minister of War, but it was no answer from a patriot. Garibaldi determined to go to Milan, for the news had just arrived that the Piedmontese army opposed to Austria had met with reverses.

The events at Milan excited the sympathies of liberal men all over Europe. There had been a five days' fight. The sleepy city had vindicated its honour in the eyes of the world. But the fight had had its victims. These were honoured with a public funeral, one of the most sublime and splendid description. The magnificent interior of the Duomo, and the wealth of space before it, had been selected for the solemnity, and no grander place could be found in Europe. The whole interior of the cathedral was hung with black ; a funeral trophy in the centre, bearing commemorative inscriptions ; a profusion of wax-lights and innumerable banners ; the floor covered with green baize ; the throng of people ; the colossal organ rolling out its music ; the hundreds of choristers singing patriotic hymns, which the people outside repeated, making the very edifice vibrate with human sentiment ; the procession of ecclesiastics ; the mourning relatives, sobbing as they walked ; the presence of the new Provisional Government, the Foreign Consuls, and the ladies—made up a spectacle and incident never to be forgotten.

Outside, in the Piazza before the Duomo, it seemed as if all Milan were gathered. A pyramid had there also been raised, with inscriptions, and as the first act of their existence the National Guard just formed stood round dressed in black velvet and Tyrolese hats. Every person wore mourning : every window had a tricolour flag : every breast a tricolour riband. The whole scene was pervaded by a fervid religious emotion, tempered with a gravity like that of old Rome in its best days.

The cause of all this naturally and deeply moved Garibaldi. The Lombardo-Venetian territory had had to bear the brunt of Austria's aggressiveness. They were not Piedmontese, nor did they wish to be. Ever since the Treaty of Vienna they had been deprived of their status through Austria's protection thereby guaranteed ; but they would never be Austrian, nor even Lombardian, but Italians. This was their sole political demand. In the proclamation of grievances this appears as the central idea, and in asserting this inalienable right they insisted that, as they were not even by that treaty made Austrian, they should have their own National Guard. They recapitulated a score of methods of oppression and occasions of bad faith to their hurt, which had arisen from the unjust subjugation. No sooner had they constituted their National Guard and Provisional Government, or rather resolved to do so, than the cannon of Austria rent the air, and the sword of the tyrant their hearts. Piedmont was called on to aid. The ambition of the House of Savoy, and its comparative enlightenment, combined to produce a favourable response ; and Charles Albert took the field with 55,000 troops against the veteran Radetzky, while the Provisional Government of Milan directed the local aid.

On assuming its independence Milan addressed the Pope. It had succeeded in its first effort, and at a great expenditure of all that patriots and citizens most value. Pius IX. had ever since his accession been virtually urging the Italian people to assert their freedom, and nothing could be more natural than that to him should be their first communication, and nothing more just than the expectation of his sympathy and benediction.

On the 29th of April the famous Allocution, in reply, was issued, and from that date the historian may commence his narrative of the decline and fall of the "Temporal Power." To the utter astonishment of Italy, which had been literally egged on by the Pontiff, and after having given a constitution himself, he addressed the Consistory thus :—

"More than once, venerable brothers, we have in your presence expressed our abhorrence of the audacity of some who have not hesitated so far to calumniate us, and in us this Apostolic See, as to pretend that we have departed in several particulars from the holy institutes of our predecessors, and even, dreadful to say, from the very doctrine of the Church herself. Nor are there wanting at this moment men who speak of us as though we were the chief author of those public commotions which have recently taken place, not only in other parts of Europe but in Italy itself. Especially have we heard from the Austrian part of Germany that a report is there disseminated among the people, that the Roman Pontiff, both through various spies whom he has sent, and by other arts, has excited the people of Italy to introduce fresh changes of public affairs. We have also heard that some enemies of the Catholic religion are seizing this opportunity to inflame the minds of the Germans with a desire for revenge, and to alienate them from the unity of the Holy See."

His Holiness then recites the concessions to the laity extorted from Pius VII., and the interference of the European Powers in 1831, when Gregory XVI. promised what he never did nor ever meant to perform.

He then speaks of the excessive joy exhibited, and mentions how he had to repress it in order to maintain concord and charity.

He forgives his slanderers, and asserts that his own soldiers had no instructions to leave the Pontifical States, and complains that he is now called upon to wage war against the Germans (Austrians), and that he abhors it, because his vocation is peace. And, finally, notes that his own people's wishes are in common with those of other Italians.

"And here we cannot but repudiate openly, in the sight of all nations, the private designs set forth in public journals and pamphlets of certain persons, who would wish that the Roman Pontiff should preside over some new Republic to be made out of all the people of Italy. Moreover, we take this opportunity most earnestly to admonish and exhort the people of Italy themselves, out of our great love towards them, that they be most diligently on their guard against cunning schemes of this sort.

"Nor can we refrain from lamenting in this assembly that most calamitous habit of publishing all sorts of pernicious pamphlets, which either wage war against our holy religion or inflame civil tumults and discord ; which seek to lay hold of the property of the Church, and to attack its most sacred rites, or assail the most excellent men with false accusations."

This was on the 29th. On the previous day his people had sent a deputation, who waited on him that night, demanding that war be proclaimed by him against the Austrians. Their sympathies were altogether Italian ; the Pontifical troops and the National Guard had crossed the frontier in that cause; but before giving them an answer he called the Consistory, and sent out this Allocution in the *Gazette* on the Saturday night. His Ministry had already resigned ; the following day passed off quietly. But one accustomed to such things might perceive that beneath the surface was no ordinary excitement. National Guards were placed at all the gates, which were closed to all egress. This was to prevent the Allocution being published. The correspondent of the English *Daily News* could not obtain a copy.

On Monday the excitement grew. At an early hour another deputation waited on Pio Nono, to express the public discontent at his Allocution, and to warn him that the refusal to declare war against Austria would cause him to be stripped of his Temporal Power, and that a Provisional Government would be set up. The Pope would not so much as see them. The Post-Office was seized by the populace, and the Cardinals' letters read in the market-place, whilst the Cardinals were imprisoned in their own houses. Pio sent orders for them to come to the palace. The officers refused, and threatened the bayonet.

On the 2nd of May the Holy Father wrote a further address, repeating his determination not to declare war, and

7

repudiating the acts of his soldiers, appealing to the concessions he had made, and quoting Scripture; finally threatening
the exercise of the spiritual powers with which he was entrusted. The address was torn down as fast as it was
posted up, and his Holiness virtually became a prisoner. A
new Ministry was formed, but it proved to be as national in
its sympathies as the former. War was proclaimed against
Austria, and six thousand men under Pamphili were sent
off to co-operate with the Lombardian forces.

The determination of Garibaldi and his friends was amaz-
ingly strengthened by these proceedings. Pius had said to
a distinguished remonstrant, "You forget. I am an Italian,
I know; but I am also Pope!" The story flew through the
country, and people said, " As long as we remain in the
hands of the Pope we shall never be more than a nation of
buffoons, opera dancers, singers, fiddlers, priests, and slaves."
The fast and loose game that had been played shewed them
that the Pope desired the humiliation of France and Austria,
and the extinction of Piedmont, only to augment the Roman
Empire, or rather to rebuild under ecclesiastical conditions
that empire which had crumbled and wasted away. And
now we shall trace the working of this popular commotion—
not as an episode in the life of kings or priests, but as the
career of Garibaldi may exhibit its operations.

To the Milan Council, therefore, Garibaldi repaired, on
hearing of the reverses which they had sustained, and he
received a hearty welcome. The enthusiasm had permeated
every class. Men of the most wealthy families—men of
every degree—demanded enrolment, and prompt pursuit of
the enemy. The Provisional Government gave to Garibaldi
the rank of General, and he was appointed to organise these
volunteers. The entire country was up. A large company,
of similar material, had come from Vincenza, and had been
organised at Pavia; thus forming a nucleus for larger operations. The young men of Milan who, with four hundred guns,

had driven Radetzky and his twenty thousand away from the city, could not remain undisciplined. Medici undertook this service, and Garibaldi formed a battalion, named, after his friend, the Anzani Battalion, in which Mazzini accepted the post of standard-bearer.

But Provisional Governments usually have crude notions, and the members hug their prejudices. When the demand for arms came before the Council, difficulties arose, and petty sinister remarks were made. The volunteers therefore insisted on providing themselves. Then came the applications for clothing. What could they do? Some Hungarian and Austrian uniforms were at their service. A pleasant risk—to put on the enemy's clothes, and then be shot in the field by a comrade for a foe. But by one means or another an equipment was supplied, and the troop marched off towards Bergamo, where Mazzini joined the ranks, and a regiment of conscripts raised there for the Piedmontese army was added to the force.

It was not fated that Garibaldi should be able to effect much in this last struggle of Charles Albert, whose ruin was virtually complete before the General was enabled to take the field. What different results might have crowned the gallant struggle of the Piedmontese and Lombards if the king had frankly accepted our hero's assistance, or if the authorities at Milan had energetically seconded his efforts, it is impossible to say.

CHAPTER V.

ITALY IN ARMS.

"Thou too, O splendour of the sudden sword,
　　That drove the crews abhorred
From Naples and the siren-footed strand,
　　Flash from thy Master's hand!

　　　　*　　　*　　　*　　　*

In the fierce year of failure and of fame,
　　Art thou not yet the same
That wert as lightning swifter than all wings
　　In the blind face of Kings?
When priests took counsel to devise despair,
　　And princes to forswear,
She clasped thee, O, her sword and flag-bearer,
　　And staff and shield to her,
O Garibaldi!"

　　　　　　　　　　　　—Swinburne.

IN the summer of 1848, Garibaldi, at the head of five thousand compatriots, was marching northwards in the hope of carrying the war into Austrian territory, when an order reached him from the Provisional Government at Milan bidding him return at once. He obeyed the order, and on nearing Monza, he heard of the capitulation of Milan, and, at the same time, of his own pursuit by a body of Austrian cavalry. He therefore determined upon a strategical retreat in the direction of Como, where, under the altered circumstances of the war, he considered that he should be better able to choose his own time and place for a trial of strength with the enemy.

For, deeply distrusting both Charles Albert and his generals, he would not for a moment accept the defeat which they had sustained at Custozza, and the evacuation of Milan, as a signal for the cessation of his own efforts. He thought that the time had come for a more or less independent attitude on the part of Italian patriots. His military genius lay especially in sectional, if not in guerilla warfare; and he may be excused if he felt himself equal to succeeding, with his five thousand enthusiasts, where Charles Albert had failed with ten times the number. But the news of the great disasters of the regular army acted very differently upon the majority of the volunteers. Moreover, their forced marches, followed by the rapid retreat—tactics natural enough to the disciplined soldier—took the courage out of these raw hands. The result was that four-fifths of them deserted into Switzerland, leaving their general with a bare eight hundred men. Garibaldi was not disheartened. At La Camerlata several routes towards Como meet; there he took up his position, planted his battery, and despatched messengers to the revolutionary leaders, with the view of securing concerted action. It was of no avail: few responded to his appeal. He further retreated to San Fermo, called his soldiers together, and delivered an address in his own animated and inspiring manner. He explained the advantages of a war of detail, assuring them that it did the most service and was attended with the least danger; but that its issue depended on the confidence placed in leaders, and in the spirit of ready obedience amongst followers. Desertions, however, increased; three hundred more stole away in the night; and in the morning Garibaldi, convinced that this unfaithfulness would destroy all chance of success, for a moment thought of returning. The thought brought shame. Never to fire a shot, or draw the sword in a cause so dear, was insupportable. He sent off Medici to ransack the district, and recover the deserters; and by this means the army was put up to seven hundred and fifty.

It was at San Fermo that he learned the manner and

method of Charles Albert's evacuation of Milan, and heard
of the armistice which, by the interference of England and
France, had been arranged.   He liked neither the one nor
the other.   The King of Piedmont had been, as he felt,
foiled in a contest of ambition, which had merely assumed
the sacred sanction of liberty.   He believed Charles Albert
to be a virtual traitor to the people, only willing to serve
them so long as the service brought him power.   Although
he knew that such service had of late tended to the exten-
sion of liberty, he counted the motive thereof to be inadequate for the great end which he had set before himself.
He therefore determined to defy the Austrian and disregard the armistice.   On the 12th of August 1848, he issued
a proclamation announcing the resolution to which he had
come, and assigning his reasons for it.

The Piedmontese, in the meantime, were retiring from
Lombardy in every direction, and returning towards Turin
and Genoa.   The king had issued his address of explanation
to the exasperated Milanese, who were kept in a feverish
agitation, not only by a sense of wrongs endured, and of
hopes disappointed, but also by the machinations of Austrian
spies.   They carried their rage so far as to endanger the
personal safety of Charles Albert.   He also wrote to his
people at Turin, lauding their work and announcing his
return march.   But Garibaldi lost no time in carrying his
resolution into effect.   Skirting Lago Maggiore, where he
captured two Austrian steamers and a number of smaller
craft, and obtaining hostages at Arona, he continued his
march rapidly down the valley of the Ticino.   These proceedings scandalised the king, who issued an order pro-
hibiting him from entering Piedmont, alleging that he
would himself be deemed an accomplice in the violation of
the armistice arranged ·between himself and the Emperor
of Austria.   This did not alter Garibaldi's plan—that of a
war carried on by details.   His next exploit was against

four hundred of the enemy, in which encounter he was successful. This movement, and indeed his every step, was carefully watched and promptly reported. He had cause to expect an Austrian attack, and occupied a homestead and buildings in as good a position as could be selected; but his recent exertions had well-nigh exhausted his strength, and he claimed of his friends a few hours' rest. Scouts were sent out in every direction as a matter of caution and prudence. It was well thought of, for in half-an-hour they returned in terror, crying, "The Austrians!" Garibaldi instantly awoke and sprang from his couch, although he felt that an attack of fever had taken hold of him. After calling his men to arms, and giving Medici a number of directions, in ten minutes he appeared at his post. Dividing the troop into two columns, a favourite method of his, he placed one in position to meet the foe, whilst the other took position in flank, awaiting orders. On they came—twelve hundred men against little more than five. It was no new disadvantage to him; but here he was face to face with highly-disciplined men, a part of the finest European army. He combined all his strength at once, and returned the attack. His men were all on foot; he alone was mounted. It was a wild business—the one side doing the best they could, how they could; the other endeavouring to conduct operations in a more orderly manner. The fight soon became a general scramble; running under the walls, clambering over them, rushing up the house-stairs, firing out of windows, barricading passages and doorways. When the *mélée* had lasted some time, Garibaldi cried, "Charge!" Emerging from every lurking-place, the men obeyed, and amid a hail of bullets drove their adversaries into a panic, and off the field in great confusion.

Medici was ordered to pursue. A hundred killed and wounded, and eighty prisoners, testified to the punishment of the Austrians. All the way was strewn with ammunition, knapsacks, and guns. Meantime another column of Austrians, much more numerous and quite fresh, were reported as being near. Garibaldi took up his defence of the village whither he expected they would arrive, but from some cause the tug-of-war was not resumed. He therefore divided his band into three companies, and sent them out in search of the enemy without result. Marshalling all his forces, he went off on the road to Varese, hoping to effect there a junction with Colonels Aprici and Griffini, who were expected by way of the mountains of Como. He reached the neighbourhood of this place on the 18th of August, and made a triumphal entry into the town of Varese, but retired to a secure height, overlooking the place, as a safer retreat. An Austrian spy, who had ascertained their force and direction, and held a special commission from the Austrian divisional columns to report Garibaldi's whereabouts to either or all of them, was taken and shot. The movement evidently had the design of interrupting the retreat of the Italians. One column had orders to go to Larino, on the border of Switzerland, on the west; the other was sent to Como, at the southern end of the lake of that name, and the remaining one to Varese, which lay between the two, the Austrians hoping thus to hinder escape either into Piedmont or Switzerland, by hemming him in near the lake Lugano. The Italians' advance-guard was directed to move forward in the direction of Como, and there attack the Austrian column, the first division of which was led by D'Aspré, and comprised five hundred men.

The work was undertaken by Medici, with a hundred men. He occupied three small villages, commanding all the roads leading into Como, and sufficiently near to the frontier of Switzerland to offer a safe asylum in case of a reverse.

Medici himself held Laguna with forty men, and ran up

in haste such fortifications as he could. The other section
of his hundred was divided between the two remaining
points. In the night one of these succumbed to a surprise;
and the morning found the enemy facing the general.
Choosing his ground, he sent for the outposts, who had no
sooner arrived than rockets and balls proclaimed the vigilance and activity of the foe. The hill was ridged with
cavalry, and Medici, with bad guns and very few cartridges,
could not hope to effect much. The firing awoke the villagers, who came out to see a genuine battle as a curiosity,
and some of them, who had guns, joined and helped. The
last cartridge was gone, and Garibaldi not appearing, the
retreat was quickly begun, and the woods of Switzerland
were reached in safety. They had done well. Four thousand
on the one side and less than one hundred on the other
shewed what stuff the men were made of. The Austrians
announced a glorious victory.

Garibaldi occupied the westward corner of Lago Maggiore; but this event had disconcerted his plan by liberating the Austrian force, which instantly marched to intercept his progress. He had heard the tumult of the fight,
and longed to be in its midst, although under such a great
disadvantage. Encamping in a strong position, at some
distance from the point he had intended to have reached, he
very soon received the attack of five thousand Austrians,
against whom he had scarcely as many hundreds. For the
whole of one day he bore the attack, but he knew that a
long resistance under such conditions was impossible, and
certainly imprudent. Under the cover of the night he
roused his men, formed them in compact column, and with
bayonets fixed gallantly forced his way, though with some
loss, into the open country beyond. After traversing a few
miles a halt was called, and then the little band scattered
itself in every direction over a country quite favourable
to their cause, and therefore able and willing to afford

temporary succour. He did not disband his men, as the Austrians would have us believe, helpless and uncared for. They knew as well as himself, for he was thoroughly confidential in all his intercourse with them, that the work in the North was for the present done. The seed had been sown. The people had learned what could be achieved in spite of Pope, Emperor, and King, and had not disliked the lesson. Garibaldi took pains to ascertain what each man wanted to reach home with, and although clothing and food they had none, the municipal authorities at Arona made no difficulty in providing all the money that they required. That—let all other patriots know—was only two hundred and eighty pounds for five hundred people.

Garibaldi himself accepted the offices of a native guide, disguised himself as a peasant, and fled into Switzerland. The bodily fatigue he had undergone, and the hurts he had received, made him little fit for a march of nearly twenty miles, beset as he was by enemies who knew him well ; and when he reached the village of refuge he threw himself on a bed, severely stricken with the marsh fever of Lombardy. He intended to have been up the next day to look after Medici's wing, hoping to render him assistance, but a hand none can control had stopped him.

The armistice that so seriously affected the king's conscience, as to make it seem a crime for Garibaldi to enter Piedmont, had not been observed either by Austria or Sardinia, except in so far as was convenient to either.

As soon as Garibaldi was able, he left Switzerland and repaired to Nice, and from thence to Genoa, where he rested until the fall of the year. Charles Albert had learned another lesson which, like so many in his life, came all too late—namely, that in this disinterested man there was Italy's truest-hearted friend ; and he offered to Garibaldi a distinguished position in the Sardinian army. We, who know him by the light of his history, need not be surprised to find that the offer was declined, and that its non-acceptance was accompanied with an intimation that he thought Venice needed his services, it being then besieged by the Austrian army and gallantly defending itself. The Lombardo-Venetian provinces had been the subject of diplomatic barter. Piedmont was to have the first, and Austria the other. The drowsy old city of glory, lying like a pearl in the Adriatic, had dared to defy Austria, and claimed its right to rise from the dead and be free.

Garibaldi meant what he said when he spoke of placing himself at the service of Venice. He collected about two hundred and fifty men from Genoa and the neighbourhood, and setting sail with them, had arrived at a small seaport on the Adriatic when all his plans were at once changed by the news which reached him from Rome.

The constitution which Pio Nono had granted to his subjects was little better than a delusion. The Encyclical Letter of 29th April 1848, which protested complete neutrality in the struggles of Northern Italy, had convinced the Romans that Pio's sympathy was not with those who aimed at the reunification of Italy. Count Mamiani, who was at the head of the Ministry, used every endeavour to incline the Sovereign Pontiff to a more popular and enlightened course, but in vain. The latter did indeed assert that, if Charles Albert should triumph over Austria, he would with his own hands crown him King of Northern Italy ; but beyond this he would not go.

The Chambers met for the first time at the beginning of June, but Pio Nono declined to sanction the speech which Mamiani had prepared to be read on his behalf at the opening of the session. A struggle arose between the Pontiff and the Chambers, and it was at once forcibly impressed upon the minds of all that the pretentions of the Vatican were utterly irreconcilable with liberal institutions.

Mamiani soon found his position untenable, and he was

replaced in September by Count Rossi, an Italian whose apprenticeship in the art of diplomacy had been served under Guizot. He took office with the express purpose of championing the Vatican against what he held to be the encroachments of popular excess, and he had the entire confidence and favour of the Pope. He naturally became an object of intense hatred to the populace; nor was he fitted by nature or training to be a popular man. "Proud with the cardinals," it was said of him by a dispassionate writer, "haughty with the patricians, and insolent with the people: with all he passed, with the utmost ease and promptitude, from disdain to insult." On the fifteenth of November, barely two months after his assumption of power, he was assassinated by an unknown hand upon the steps of the capitol.

Mamiani was absent from Rome, and there was no one else of sufficient influence and skill to curb the passions of the mob. The city was thrown into the wildest disturbance; the populace rose and paraded the streets; whilst the Pope and the Sacred College shut themselves up in terror, expecting an instant outbreak of violence.

On the next day a crowd besieged the palace of the Quirinal, where the Pope then was, demanding the formation of a democratic cabinet, with the election of a National Convention. In reply to this demand the Pope, who had already ordered the troops to disperse all public assemblages, a command which could not be executed, bluntly refused his consent. The populace was in no mood to be denied. Cannons were placed against the palace gates; and a prelate who incautiously shewed himself at a window was killed by a musket-shot. It was said that the Swiss Guards had fired first; but, however this may have been, Pio Nono saw the uselessness of braving a resolute people. He ended by agreeing to select his cabinet from a list to be submitted to him, and to refer the question of a Constituent Assembly or National Convention to the Chambers.

"In the secret councils of the Quirinal, of which Count Spaur, the Bavarian ambassador and temporary representative of Austria, was the moving spring, it had been resolved that Pius should depart from Rome; and by skilfully appealing to his instincts as a churchman, all opposition was speedily overcome. To guide the sacred barque of St. Peter into the harbour of refuge proffered by the Catholic Powers was clearly his allotted task; this interval of apparent calm had been vouchsafed for its accomplishment. The greatest secrecy was maintained. The Pope himself was kept in the dark by Count Spaur and the Neapolitan ambassador as to his real destination; while the ministers of France and Spain were respectively led to believe the plans they had suggested would be adopted. The one anticipated receiving him on board a French man-of-war; the other was confident that Minorca had been selected as his place of refuge. But the count was too well aware of the value of the prize, of its bearing on the interest of Austria, to relinquish it to any other competitor. With consummate address, confiding his determination to none but his wife, he planned and carried out the Pope's flight, and had him many miles on the road to the Neapolitan frontier ere any one within the Quirinal, or the baffled diplomatists, who had each relied on the success of his own project, suspected his departure.

"Arrived at Gaeta, Spaur, leaving the disguised Pontiff with his countess and Cardinal Antonelli, hurried to Naples. No sooner had he received the welcome intelligence than Ferdinand repaired with the queen to the presence of the fugitive, where, falling at his feet, the royal pair entreated him to accept their hospitality and service."

The Pope, from Gaeta, called upon the Roman Catholic Powers to interpose by force of arms for his restoration to his temporal sovereignty, and was responded to by France, Spain, Austria, and Naples, who agreed to unite on his behalf. "Contrary, however, to the impatient desires of the Papal Court, the avenging sword was still delayed. The caution of the Austrian Cabinet, which foresaw that a fresh campaign against Piedmont was impending, and concentrated all its resources in Northern Italy—some lingering scruples on the part of the French diplomacy, which resulted in a feeble effort at an adjustment which the clericals would have been the last to desire—retarded the longed-for hour of retribution. It was not till the battle of Novara had laid low the armies of Charles Albert that the allies judged it expedient to fulfil their contract."

The Austrians in the Adriatic and the French in the Mediterranean simultaneously appeared to champion the cause of the Pope ; whilst a Neapolitan force of 20,000, led by King Ferdinand, prepared to cross the southern frontier. The French force, afterwards increased to 30,000, was commanded by General Oudinot, who landed at Civita Vecchia on the 24th of April. Both by himself and by M. de Lesseps, the French Representative in Rome, the young Republic was assured of the pacific intentions of France, and allowed itself for a time to believe that its visitors had no sinister design. But the disillusion was not slow in coming.

About the time that the French landed at Civita Vecchia the Austrians marched upon Bologna, and the Neapolitans crossed the southern frontier. These steps were doubtless hastened by the proclamation of the Roman Republic. Garibaldi had been elected by Macerata to represent her in the Constituent Assembly, and he came to Rome and took his seat in February. At the first meeting the Republic was proclaimed, amidst the wildest enthusiasm, by a vote of one hundred and thirty-nine members out of one hundred and fifty.

The Assembly issued its decree, in the form which has

already been quoted. The citizens hailed the new Government with unbounded delight, and men walked about the streets as though a great weight had been taken from their shoulders. Never had Rome been more orderly, more enthusiastic, more united. Hardly a single scene or act of disorder is recorded of this critical period, and the subsequent conduct of the Romans, both during the consolidation of the novel constitution and during the long and trying siege, proved at once their heroism and their moderation.

Garibaldi stayed but a short time in Rome. Mazzini could see to legislative business; but for himself he preferred action. "It was ever his highest ambition to serve Italy in the battle-field, and lay down his life in her defence." Returning to Rieti, he fortified the place, and set to work drilling and exercising his volunteers. Forty of his Monte Videan Legion remained behind; these wore the red blouse with green facings. Three hundred who had returned from Venice, 400 university students, 300 public servants, and 300 others, added to the force previously there, made up a total of 2500. Pisacini, a superior officer of the Roman Republic, describes him at this period in the following terms :—

"Garibaldi was stationed at Rieti with the rank of colonel. His refusal to conform to army regulations rendered him a stumbling-block to the partisans of the old system, who deemed him more injurious than useful. But being gifted with that peculiar genius found in so few men, of keeping straight in difficult circumstances, and knowing how to utilise every element, he was regarded as a unique and precious being, if employed in such a way as not to be removed from his sphere of action. The war committee were convinced of this truth, when, during the formation of the army, and upon dividing it into two camps, they declared Garibaldi's corps a partisan band independent of the army. Personally brave, and of most agreeable character, continually on the field of battle, making his arrangements with the utmost calmness, this chief was extremely dear to his soldiers. His handsome appearance, his peculiar way of dressing himself, all his habits, in a word, had surrounded him with an extraordinary prestige."

Garibaldi was scarcely recovered from his illness when he undertook the arduous duty of preparing his men for service. He allowed himself no rest, and them but little. The energetic general might be seen daily traversing the mountain paths in the dreary winter weather; and his men saw it, and emulated the example. No complaint of cold or weariness, no disaffection for the cause, ever escaped their lips. His life infused courage in other lives; and when for practice he would order forced marches, direct the troops into a distant plain for open camp, leave the commissariat uncared for, by design—or, in short, do anything to prove the worthiness of his men, or to strengthen worthiness where it was weak—they knew their leader, and gladly learned to follow him; until they came to love endurance for his sake.

Meanwhile (as already briefly recorded), the army of Charles Albert had been idle since the truce of Milan, and ill-disposed for fighting. The Government, knowing fresh strife to be inevitable, raised it to 135,000 men; but these were untrained, and without a taste for war. The officers were not loved by the men, the old ones were not esteemed, and the merits of the new ones were unrecognised. Only two-thirds of the force could be trusted for service. Victor Emanuel and his brother held commands, but the king no longer did so. The Austrian army had been industriously preparing during his truce; and when its term expired, Radetsky (now eighty years old), issued a lying proclamation, charging the war on the ambition of Piedmont and the evil passions of Italians. The Piedmontese marched in the direction of Milan, but waited on the Ticino to decide whether their work should be offensive or defensive. The

Austrian had no such scruple. He resolved on the offensive, concentrated his forces upon Pavia, and was kept well informed by spies of what was going on in the opposing army.

On the 24th of March the battle was fought at Novara, the Piedmontese army being vanquished and driven back— the Duke of Savoy's division to the foot of the Alps, and the General (Chrzanowsky) to Borgho. The result of the battle determined Charles Albert to abdicate; and he issued a proclamation announcing that he had resigned his crown in favour of his son, Victor Emanuel, Duke of Savoy. The unfortunate ex-king quitted his dominions and took refuge in Portugal, where, in about three months, he died broken-hearted.

An armistice was concluded in terms that deeply mortified the Sardinian people, and riots occurred at Genoa, so that Victor Emanuel had not only an imperious antagonist insisting on impossible conditions, but the greater evil of intestine revolution. The Genoese demanded resistance to the Austrians, and the new king had to attack the rebellion. The spirit of the people was up, and Genoa was declared to be in a state of siege. Other cities were reduced by the enemy; in particular Brescia, which resisted the Austrians for eight days behind barricades. At last General Haydau came and bombarded the place until it was half in ruins. Victor Emanuel and his Chamber quarrelled about the capitulation, and the king made a spirited remonstrance, asserting his motive to be pure and patriotic, and also his confidence in the loyalty and good sense of his subjects.

Tuscany had also undergone a violent commotion, for on the 7th of February the Grand Duke had abandoned his dominions, and on the following day a Provisional Government had been formed, consisting of Mazzini and two others. But after two months the sovereign was called back and the monarchy restored.

The courts of Naples, Rome, and Tuscany were rejoiced

by the tidings of the disaster at Novara; but not so the young Republic at Rome, which had to bear the further sorrow of hearing that the infamous Haynau had extorted large sums from various Italian towns, and had remitted them to the Pope at Gaeta. The busy operations for improving the city and constructing a Roman army had to be suspended, and on the 29th of March a meeting of the Assembly took place with closed doors. The debate was stormy, and the council divided, some desiring to declare war against Naples, and others to renew the fight in Lombardy. Finally, the Assembly decided on entering with all its resources into the war of Independence, by giving aid to Piedmont. The executive of the State passed on this occasion into the hands of Mazzini, Saffi, and Armellini. The chief conduct of affairs fell to the share of Mazzini, who represented from that moment the spirit, as Garibaldi did the active force, of Italian nationality.

The morning of the 29th of April brought intelligence to Rome of the arrival of the French at Civita Vecchia. The Assembly called a permanent sitting, and the question of who should hold Rome—the French or the Romans—had to be discussed. Oudinot's proclamations were utterly disingenuous, and the party of Mazzini, who had some experience of the immoralities of public men, saw through the craft. The first said that the authorities of Civita Vecchia had yielded to the wishes of the inhabitants, and opened the city gates at the first summons; and then it proceeded to make professions of respect and friendliness. Whereas, scarcely had he landed when he closed and nailed up the printing-offices, disarmed the national troops, occupied the fort, and then sought to hinder a band of five hundred Lombards, who were coming to serve Rome, from landing. It is true, that by virtue of their peaceful professions, the French had obtained hospitality at Civita Vecchia. They declared that they had not come to Italy to restore the Pope's temporal power, but to avert great misfortunes which might come upon an unprotected land. France said she did not arrogate the right to regulate the affairs of her neighbours, but to assist in establishing good government, interrupted by the anarchy which had followed the Pope's generosity. The flag she hoisted was that of "peace, order, conciliation, and true liberty," and Oudinot invited the Italians to "co-operate in the accomplishment of this patriotic and sacred work."

This absurd hypocrisy had no lasting effect on the policy at Rome. Mazzini, ever disposed to trust French Republicanism, was for a moment inclined to hesitate; but Garibaldi, at once and strenuously, advised the utmost resistance, and that measures should be promptly taken. He believed that similar tactics would be tried on them at Rome, and thought that the falsehood about this visit being in the interests of the Republic should be answered by blows. Preparations were therefore instantly commenced, to the surprise of Oudinot, who did not expect discernment in "enthusiasts," or vigour in "dreamers."

The Triumvirate, or permanent irresponsible Committee, addressed a protest to General Oudinot which had been voted by the Assembly, and issued two proclamations to the Roman people, in the following terms:—

"Citizens,—The Roman Assembly, moved by the menace of invasion of the territory of the Republic, and conscious that this invasion, not provoked by the conduct of the Republic toward foreign powers, not preceded by any communication on the part of the French Government, and calculated to excite anarchy in a country which reposes with calmness and order on the consciousness of its rights and the concord of the citizens—violates the law of nations, obligations contracted by France in her constitution, and bonds of fraternity that ought to unite the two Republics, protests in the name of God and the people against the unexpected invasion, asserts its firm purpose of resisting, and declares France responsible for the consequences."

And again :—

"Romans! A foreign intervention threatens the territory of the Republic. A body of French soldiers has appeared at Civita Vecchia. Whatever its intention, the salvation of the principle which has been freely consented to by the people, the law of nations, the honour of the Roman name, command the Republic to resist—and the Republic will resist. The people must prove to France, and to the world, that it is a people not of children but of men, and men who have dictated laws and given civilisation to Europe. No one shall say that the Romans desired freedom and knew not how to obtain it. The French people shall, from our resistance, our declarations, our attitude, learn our wish, our irrevocable decision, not to submit any more to the abhorred government which we have overthrown. The people shall prove this. Whoever opposes this determination dishonours the people and betrays the country. Let there be order, calm solemnity, concentrated energy. The government watches inexorably over whatever might attempt to throw the country into anarchy, or to rise against the Republic. Citizens, assemble, rally round us. God and the people, law and force, shall triumph."

Resistance having been determined on, Cernuschi, who had constructed the barricades of Milan, was directed to undertake a similar duty at Rome, and to mount cannon wherever it could be placed. But the great hope of the people was elsewhere.

Suddenly, amid the excitement of the city, the cry rang along the streets, "Garibaldi! *viva* Garibaldi!" They marched on before him, a huge gathering crowd, filling the air with their caps and flying handkerchiefs, shouting, "He is here! He is here!" The enthusiasm was indescribable. None of the heroes of old Rome elicited such acclamations or inspired like faith. Miraglio describes him in his *La Rivoluzione* di 1849–50 :—

"This mysterious conqueror, environed by a brilliant halo of glory, a stranger to the discussions of the Assembly, and not caring to know them, entered Rome on the eve of the very day on which the Republic was to be attacked. The spirit of the Roman people saw in him the only man capable of affording resistance.

"Therefore, on the very instant of his appearance, the multitude rallied to him as the one who personified the wants of the moment, and on whom all could rely with hope."

The French General did not believe that anything could resist French arms and French will. On the 28th of April the advanced guard reached Paolo, on the coast, and on the next day Capo Guido. Oudinot sent his brother with a small company to reconnoitre; and at the crossways, where the old and new roads divide, they encountered the Roman advanced posts : the officer in command demanded their business. The foreigner replied :—

"To go to Rome."

"That cannot be."

"But we have come from the Republic of France."

"And," was the prompt reply, "the Roman Republic orders you to return."

"But suppose we are not willing to return?"

"Then we must make you," said the Roman.

"How?"

"By force," quoth he.

With the spontaneity of his race the French officer turned and ordered his men to fire; setting an example. The response was prompt.

"Fire!" cried the Roman to his sentinels;—and the French ran away.

When they reached the camp, Oudinot was embarrassed

at learning the attitude of the Roman Republic ; but as he had come from Louis Napoleon, in whose service scruples would be thrown away, he ordered an instant march on Rome.

It cost the world a ten years' scandal ; it cost Europe a disgrace ; it cost liberty a foul stain. But what did the Buonaparte care for that? He could at his pleasure flatter and deceive the world ; he could on a certain New Year's day decree the desolation of Europe ; and he could so work upon men by vulgar expedients as to bind round his brow the laurels of a Cæsar. As for the Pope, did not the other Napoleon make the Pope his groom.

On the news of the French attack reaching Rome, the Assembly in permanence issued this decree: "In the name of God and the people. Confiding in the fidelity of the Romans, as we do in their valour, we are convinced that, while we, the Roman people, who are determined to defend to the utmost the independence of the country, do not make the French people responsible for the act of their Government ; for in the people, and the Republican principle they embody, we have unbounded trust ;—We decree :—That strangers, especially French, residing in Rome, are under national safeguard. All offenders will be deemed guilty of dishonour to Rome. The laws of hospitality shall be watchfully respected."

Garibaldi was called to the post of honour. Few believed that Oudinot would persist, but it was necessary to take the counsels of precaution.

The French had made their reconnoitre. They knew how far the city had military protection. But the Italians also had learnt somewhat. A French officer, who was killed in the skirmish at the outposts, had upon his person this General Order :—

"A double attack should be made upon Porta Angelica and Porta Cavallegieri, to make a diversion. The first is to occupy, or force the enemy at, Monte Mario. After that Porta Angelica is secure. Occupying these, press on to La Piazza San Pedro. The blood of the French people is to be specially spared."

On the day before the battle the correspondent of the *Daily News* wrote home thus :—"The enthusiasm of the citizens and troops, instead of flagging, is every hour rising with energy. The National Guard was passed in review before the Assembly and the Triumvirs this morning, and all swore to defend Rome to the last drop of their blood. The lower orders are in a state of perfect frenzy, and brandished pitchforks, knives, and every imaginable implement, crying out for the infamous French invaders to come in if they dare. The Princess Trivulzio di Belgioioso is at the head of a committee of noble ladies who are busy preparing bandages for the wounded, and wadding for the cannon. All the bridges of the city from Ponte Molle to Ponte Sisto and San Bartolomeo are undermined, ready to be blown up. The Tiber is now swollen. The artillery staff are erecting batteries, and the engineers redoubts, at which the people work with zeal and alacrity. All the paving-stones of the city are up in heaps, and are being carried to the tops of the houses. Oudinot is within twenty-five miles, and hesitates to advance. He is said to have asked for an armistice of nine days, no doubt to allow the second division of his men to come in from Toulon. This won't do now ; he is come too far to get back with honour, and a horrid butchery must ensue."

Later in the evening he writes : "General Oudinot and his crusade have fallen back on Paolo, a wretched village. It were sheer insanity to try his luck here against a whole population in arms, backed by 14,000 regular troops, 25 pieces of cannon, and having in prospect barricades, sharp-shooters, paving-stones, knives, and every imaginable man-trap in the shape of mines and covert batteries.

"Garibaldi's division had been ordered out to the heights of Monte Mario, which, with Janiculum, will command the approach on the sea-side. I saw the daring adventurer yesterday. His battalion was drawn up all round the colonnade that stretches out before St. Peter's Church, and the hero himself was seated in the centre, under the shadow of the great obelisk, squatted on the bare flags, eating his dinner—viz., a cold sausage, a lump of brown bread, and two raw onions. His negro servant, with a long pike, stood over him, as a sort of Mameluke to this Napoleon of Monte Video."

Oudinot would probably have preferred to delay his attack on any reasonable excuse; but his own acts in the first place, and his general instructions in the second, absolutely compelled him to go on. He was determined to go to Rome at any risk, to anticipate his friends and to gratify his chief. He gave out that he had 15,000 men, whilst he had not half that number; and Garibaldi knew this, though the world did not.

Garibaldi stationed his battalion on the heights of Monte Mario, and himself occupied a villa called Pamphili, or Pamfili; and the others were placed as will be found described in the official report presently produced. The French sent forward their Voltigeurs to the 20th Line in great force upon the right, and these found the country very rough, cut up by woods and difficult of access. Upon the heights on the left advanced the Chasseurs of Vincennes, at about two hundred yards from the walls.

An English correspondent, writing on the 30th of April, gives the following account of the battle :—" Yesterday evening a party of French cavalry, sent out as *éclaireurs*, was met by an equal squadron of Garibaldi's division, about a mile off, and after a sharp encounter fled, leaving four killed and their officer a prisoner. Night closed on this trifling affair, but all knew it to be the prelude of to-day's business, which promised to be decisive and serious. At daybreak all Rome was on the alert, and the various positions assigned to the National Guard and the regular troops were taken up in calm order and silence. The three gates of St. Pancrazio, Portese, and Cavallegieri were considered the most probable points of attack, and were consequently manned by the best and most resolute of the disposable force. At eleven o'clock the French *corps d'armée* made its appearance in good array, and commenced a simultaneous fire of cannon and musketry on the three points first mentioned. A bold and dashing sortie was made, headed by Garibaldi, from St. Pancrazio, which resulted in the capture of four of the French guns, with a French colonel, the dispersion of that wing of the Gallic army, and shortly after, in the rout and defeat of the whole line of attack by a general charge of the Roman troops. The French did not yield till they had six hundred killed on the spot; and they have left four hundred and fifty-two prisoners in the hands of the victorious Romans. Their wounded are probably a thousand or so, as the commandant has sent an urgent request, in his flight, for surgeons from Rome, a dozen of which operators have been sent after him and his broken brigades. The loss on the part of the Romans is only eighty killed and a hundred and seventy wounded.

"The French prisoners, in traversing the town, loudly declared that they had been tricked into this expedition by a promise of being led against Austrians. The officers captured are highly indignant at being sent on this wild-goose crusade against a sister Republic. All are treated with respectful care, and the wounded are particularly attended to by the Roman women, and in the various hospitals."

The French had gone; but the Romans bivouacked under arms, and the Civic Guard remained at their posts, fearing the enemy might rally his scattered forces, and make an attempt to gain one of the hills commanding the town, for the purpose of a bombardment. Monte Mario Garibaldi resolved on protecting, and ordered up strong reinforcements. There followed, however, a tranquil night. At daybreak the *génerale* was beaten in brisk style. The cry "to arms"—Garibaldi's watchword—resounded in every street. A sixty-eight-pounder from the battlements of St. Angelo was fired to invite the French to come up; but they had had quite enough, and preferred to encamp three or four miles off, in a spot called *Val d'Inferno*, where they were badly off for food, as they had contemplated dining and supping at the expense of the Romans, and brought no supplies with them from their ships. Major Callendrini shewed them good generalship from the top of Adrian's Mole, for, observing the Villa Pamphili (discarded by Garibaldi) to be a kind of rendezvous for the enemy's staff, he pointed a quantity of heavy ordnance at the Casino, and knocked the whole building to fragments, with all its inmates, from a distance of nearly a mile.

In the afternoon the French sent a white flag, and begged a truce. Three spies had been taken who were supposed to be in Holy Orders: these were shot. A priest tried to harangue the people in the Pope's interests, but his audience instantly set on him and killed him.

Congratulatory proclamations were issued, addressed to the citizens, urging vigilance and order, reminding them that their enemy had not finally departed, and it was most probable he would be reinforced, and return to renew his attack.

On the 2nd of May an English correspondent writes:—"It is now quite certain that the French troops are in full retreat for Civita Vecchia, which place their vanguard, at least, may reach this evening. General Oudinot's visit has been a most serious one, and such as in some degree compromises the military reputation of the French army. By his hasty advance to Rome, his hurried attack and his precipitous retreat, he cuts but a ridiculous figure in the eyes of Europe. It is now clear that he must have counted more upon the co-operation of the Pontifical party within Rome than upon his own force, and finding the resource fail him completely, he retires. Was there ever, on his part or on that of his government, a more flagrant blunder?"

On the 1st of May, at dawn, Garibaldi, who had obtained from the War Minister authority to attack the retreating French with his Legion of twelve hundred men, divided them into two columns. One, under Masa, set out by the Cavallegieri gate, the other, under himself, by the Sancto Pancrazio gate. His cavalry he strengthened with a squadron of dragoons. He wished to surprise the French in their own camp, but on arriving there he found they had quitted it in the night, and were retiring on Castel Guido. Masa, by taking the shortest roads, had fallen upon their rearguard, and was already hotly engaged. With all possible haste Garibaldi followed, and joined Masa near Malagratta, where the French were gathering together apparently for battle. Taking up an advantageous position on the height, on the flank of the French army, he prepared to charge, when a French officer advanced on the main road and desired a parley with Garibaldi. He represented that he was a messenger from the French General Oudinot, with orders to treat for an armistice, and to receive assurance that the Romans had resolved to accept the Republican Government, and were also determined to defend their rights ; at the same time offering a hostage in proof. While this was proceeding, Avanezza, the Roman Minister, sent an order recalling Garibaldi to Rome, whither he returned at four in the afternoon with the French officer ; and an armistice was granted.

From the improvised telegraph station on the top of St. Peter's the defenders of Rome watched the receding columns of the French as they hastened towards the place whence they came, and the sight cheered them. It was but a short time before the watchman signalled the oncoming of the Neapolitan army. The public animosity was intense. The French they had regarded as dupes of a designing and conspiring government, which perhaps was ignorant of the intensity of the Roman feeling; but these Neapolitans knew well who Garibaldi, Mazzini, Avanezza, Cernuschi, and all the other leading spirits of the Republic were, and seemed bent on a fight that would not respect mercy or kindness. The Assembly, sitting in permanence, resolved to send out Garibaldi to meet the Neapolitans and oppose their march.

Farini, the skilful historian of the Roman State between 1815–1850, thus describes the entry of the King of Naples into the Roman territory, and the movements of Garibaldi:—

"The Neapolitan army, consisting of 16,000 men, was posted between Albano and Frascati, and was commanded by the king, who had his headquarters at Albano, with two Swiss regiments, three regiments of cavalry, and a good quantity of artillery. His entry into the Roman States was not signalised by a battle, nor by any noble deeds, but by numerous arrests of Republican magistrates, of peaceful travellers, and of honest citizens, whom he threw into filthy prisons, where they were associated with thieves and vagabonds. The uncertain projects of France, who, disdaining his alliance, promised liberty to the people, disturbed him greatly, and Garibaldi, who was roaming all over the country, would not allow the courtiers and prelates that swarmed in the royal camp to enjoy a night's repose. Such accounts of the diabolical disposition of the leader and his followers had been spread about Gaeta, that the Neapolitan soldiers had got their heads filled with them, and perhaps trusted more in the virtue of their amulets than in the strength of their arms to fight the Garibaldians. These men had, in truth, strange and singular manners; their chief was dressed in scarlet, without any ornaments, and without any mark of rank; they wore hats of every fashion and of every colour; they rushed hither and thither; they dispersed; they threw themselves wherever the peril was greatest. During their moments of repose they left their horses at liberty, or mounted them without saddle or bridle, and scoured the country in quest of cattle; then they returned with their booty, and distributed it among the soldiers; they helped in dressing it, and afterwards shared in the frugal repast. Garibaldi, who, in his countenance and bearing gave one the idea of the head of an Indian tribe, when danger was distant, either reposed under his tent, or from the summit of a hill reconnoitred the ground, or went about, in disguise and quite alone, to explore it. When the trumpet sounded for battle he was everywhere, giving orders, encouraging his men, and fighting. His Legion was composed of young men, spurred on by enthusiasm; of old soldiers, trusting in their bold chief; and of rascals, who were in eager search of booty, not of glory. The officers, selected from the most courageous soldiers, were sometimes raised at once to the highest grades, and then thrown back again amongst the common file. There was neither discipline nor order; audacity and fortune governed all.

"Having come out against the Neapolitans, they were at Palestrina by the 7th of May, and from that place Garibaldi sent a few soldiers, the day after, to harass such of the enemy as were scattered about in the villages. Accordingly they went, put them to flight, and took some prisoners. On the 9th two regiments of infantry belonging to the Royal Guard, and one division of cavalry, having moved against Palestrina, Garibaldi sent out only four companies to meet them, drawing up the remainder of his people near the gates of the city. After a skirmish, which lasted three hours, the Neapolitans, having lost about a hundred men, took flight, and retreated to their encampment. The prisoners, on being brought before Garibaldi, thinking of nothing but how to appease the monster who they fancied was so terrible, cried out for mercy, cursing Pius IX. in their dialect. The Romans had only twelve killed and twenty wounded; so that they might, with undiminished force and courage, have continued to molest the enemy; but Garibaldi having been made aware of the movements of the French towards Rome, raised his camp, and passing within two miles of that of the Neapolitans, marched twenty-eight miles in one night, and on the morning of the 12th re-entered the capital."

The Assembly, while depending absolutely upon Garibaldi, choose to make Roselli his superior in the enterprise. The opportunity of crippling the King of Naples (who at Palestrina had had to scramble on his horse, and with his Old Guard take flight before Garibaldi's skirmishers) was a chance which in justice and policy should have been put into the General's hand alone. Garibaldi's friends were displeased at the slight; but he himself said: "I confess I have never been accessible to questions affecting self-love: whoever gives me the opportunity of drawing my sword against our common enemy, if only as a soldier, deserves my gratitude. I would have served as one of the National Guard, and therefore I thankfully accept the post of General of Division."

The army of the Republic, consisting of ten thousand men, including a thousand cavalry, with three batteries and twelve cannon, proceeded out of the gate of San Giovanni in Laterano, the high road to Naples; when the enemy, either from a doubt of the loyalty of their soldiers, or a dread of the French—who, really being bent on glory only, seemed quite as likely to fall on the Neapolitans as upon the Romans—retired precipitately from Albano, and went to Velletri.

Taking the Palestrina road they went as far as to Teverone, and from thence, turning to the right, left Tivoli and reached Zargarola at about eleven: a sixteen hours' march. The distance is not great, but the column was very long, and the road covered with dust, and so narrow that in many parts the march had to be done in single file. They had left Rome in such haste that the commissariat had been overlooked—a thing not unusual in the enthusiastic enterprises of the Legion—and the little place had not wherewith to supply ten thousand hungry men. Moreover, the Neapolitans had not been so improvident in arranging their flight. They had taken out of the place all that could be eaten, and almost all the drink. Garibaldi had, however, brought a few head of cattle, and his Legion, taking up their lassos, went out and caught others. He complained to the authorities of Zargarola of this lack of foresight, which might have caused so many to perish of hunger; and he did not feel the validity of the excuse that the omission was due to a desire to avoid letting the enemy suspect that an enterprise was on foot. On the 18th the marching order was given, but it could not be obeyed, or was not, until six in the evening.

At six o'clock Garibaldi, placing himself at the head of the brigade in the vanguard, s t forward toward Valmontone. The force marched in profound silence, as he had ordered. The utmost vigilance was enjoined; for he received information that the king was at Velletri with twenty thousand soldiers, and all the cannon saved at Palestrina, namely thirty-three. The King of Naples held Frascati and Albano, beside Velletri, with advanced posts, as far as Frate Vecchia, thus commanding the whole valley leading from Rome. Silence was therefore golden. Roselli favoured the idea of clearing the territory as the one object before them; Garibaldi the idea of destroying the baneful power of Naples, now that it was within grasp. Both concurred in the opinion that, whether the king fled or fought, Monte Fortino should be taken and held. It commanded the road to Naples, and formed a basis of advance towards Velletri.

Garibaldi shall here tell his own tale :—"In the dusk of the evening we reached an obstructed road, which led to Valmontone, which it took two hours to clear. Manara and his regiment, who came last of the van, were supported by dragoons and cannon. It was only fair. We reached Valmontone in the thick darkness at about ten, and found a place having no water w thin a mile, where we were obliged to encamp. The next day the march was vigorously pursued. Palestrina we had found empty, and Valmontone was likewise abandoned. We now found Monte Fortino, which it would have been so easy to have kept us out of, empty. The enemy had gone. In the morning I left Monte Fortino, having with me my Italian Legion, the 3rd battalion of a Roman infantry regiment, some cavalry, and my brave Marina, in all nineteen hundred men. My old friend, who had been made prisoner and had been ransomed, served me as officer of ordnance; but would often, very often—even when danger and death were nearest—run to me and say, 'General, nd me where there is danger, and not any one who may be of more service.'

"At sight of Velletri I sent on orders for a detachment to advance close under the city walls, that they might not only reconnoitre, for I wanted to know the weakness and strength, but that they might attract the notice of the enemy, and provoke him to attack. I did not suppose it possible for nineteen hundred men to beat the army of the King of Naples, but I hoped to begin a fight which, by drawing them on towards me, would in the engagement afford time for the rest of our army to come up and take their post.

"I placed the half of my Legion on the height which flanked the road leading to the town; in the centre two or three hundred men: the battalion took the right, and Marina's cavalry had the road to Velletri: the other half of my Legion were in reserve. The enemy observed our meagre numbers, and were not slow in attacking. A regiment of foot soldiers came out and spread in line, firing on our advanced posts. We let them. They had received no orders to retreat if such an occurrence happened. They pressed on, and then more of the enemy, in battalions, and cavalry followed in great numbers, and gave us a spirited attack. It did not last. We let them come to half-gunshot, and began a calm and well-directed fire, which stopped them short. After half-an-hour's firing their general sent on two squadrons of cavalry. I saw instantly that a desperate charge would decide the contest, and placing myself at the head of my fifty or sixty horsemen, we charged the five hundred. Down they crashed, and the very impetus brought them right over us. I was knocked down and carried some yards from my horse, but springing to my feet, I remained in the thick of the fight, striking right and left that I might not be struck. My horse did not lie down long, and I leaped on his back, calling to and cheering my men, who thought I was dead. They recognised me when putting my hat upon my sword I waved it. Besides, my distinctive white cape, lined with red, ensured me a speedy recognition, and loud huzzas testified their delight at the resurrection.

"The enemy had borne down with an impetuosity which carried them through as far as our reserve, and the infantry in close column followed. It was disastrous to them, for our men sprang up the hills on either side, and our reserve contested their progress. Their mass became a mere target for the pouring in of our shot. I despatched a messenger to Roselli for reinforcements, and stating my belief that the battle we sought had really commenced. His cool reply was that I could not have it, as the men had not eaten their porridge.　I then determined to do what I could with my own forces, but knew that my strength alone could not produce the decisive result I saw might be attained with assistance.　We were 1900 against 5000, and charged the whole line of the enemy.　In an instant we placed our two cannon in position and fired, and the sharp-shooters doubled their speed; my forty or fifty lancers dashed at the same time into their 3000 infantry.

"Manara had heard the noise of the battle at two miles' distance, and sent to Roselli asking permission to join me. After keeping him in suspense for an hour this was granted. The brave young Lombardians came to me in double-quick march, by the high road, under the fire of the enemy's guns. Our rearguard opened to let them pass, and amid the greatest enthusiasm, the trumpets sounding, the young, short, brown, and vigorous fellows, with the black feathers in their caps, came eagerly in, and whilst ours were exclaiming 'Vivent les bersaglieri,' they responded 'Viva Garibaldi,' and fell into line.　In a second the enemy was driven from point to point, and began to retreat, protected by the cannon of the place, of which the greater part was mounted upon a convent.　Two of these commanded the highway, the others fired upon the left flank of our column, where the riflemen were.　Fortunately the ground was uneven and afforded shelter, so that my men did not suffer much damage.

"The moment Manara reached the scene of action he looked about for me, whom he soon recognised by the white puncho, and came galloping up.　But he was stopped by a little circumstance which I must relate, for it shews the spirit of our men.　When his party came up our men made way, and played their lively music as the new comers passed through.　A score of his men could not resist the influence of the tune, and although cannon balls and shot were hailing down, they began to dance.　Manara looked on, and was heartily laughing when a cannon-ball swept away a dozen of the dancers. A slight pause ensued, when Manara cried out, 'Well, the music?' The music resumed, and the dance went on more gaily than ever.

"When I saw Manara and his party coming up, I asked Ugo Bassi to go and tell Manara I wished to speak to him. His first concern was to know whether I was wounded. Bassi said, 'I believe the General has been shot in his hand and his foot, but he does not complain. I dare say the wounds are not serious.' Now I had received two slight wounds, of which I took no heed until the evening, when I should want something to do.

"Manara then told me about the dancing incident, and ardently inquired whether with such men we could not carry Velletri by assault. I laughed at him. I could not help it. 'What!' said I, 'with two thousand men and two cannon carry that city, which is perched on the top of a height like an eyrie, and defended by twenty thousand soldiers and thirty pieces of cannon?' However, Manara, the brave-spirited fellow, would not believe in the impossibility, and I therefore sent to headquarters for more strength. Had I had nine thousand I would have attempted the affair, for my men were in a state of high enthusiasm, and the Neapolitans disheartened. I could without telescope perceive a kind of breach in the walls, closed up with fascines, which one or two cannon balls would have opened ; and I could send attacking columns under the covering of the trees and the rising ground to that breach unobserved, while the sappers or pioneers could clear away obstructions. Two pretended assaults would leave a principal one pretty certain of success.

"This project had to wait a reply from Roselli, and Manara's company amused themselves in picking off the men on the ramparts, while the convent artillery kept hurling into them its fearful showers. Roselli at last made up his mind to come to us with the whole army. He did so, but the opportunity was gone. I did not for a moment doubt that the Neapolitans would vacate the city in the night, for I had heard of the king having taken his departure with six thousand of his men, and proposed to send a strong detachment to the Naples gate of the city, and fall on the enemy's flank when they were retreating in disorder. I was overruled by the apprehension that we might be much weakened by such an enterprise.

"In the middle of the night I desired Marana to despatch an officer and forty men whom he could trust up to the walls of Velletri, and if they could get in, to enter the city itself, in order that I might know how we stood. A reconnaissance was accordingly made, when it was discovered that Velletri had been suddenly abandoned during the night.

"We could not be said to have obtained a victory in any event, for the Neapolitans would certainly have retreated had we attacked Velletri; but a panic had evidently got possession of the troops, and compelled this hasty evacuation, so little to their honour. With twenty thousand men, and masters of the place and the surrounding heights, surely they might have stayed as long as they choose, and after inflicting on us much injury, have effected an honourable retreat at their leisure. From what could be learned the whole army was demoralised; only a few companies of cavalry preserved sufficient courage and discipline to cover the retreat. In two days the invaders had passed the frontier."

Garibaldi followed at daybreak, but it was quite impossible to overtake them. Roselli, moreover, sent after him as he was on the high road to Terracini, the frontier town, ordering him to rejoin the column. One-half returned to Rome, and the other half was sent to clear the district round Frosinone from the volunteers of Zucchi, by whom it was infested. Dandalo's and Marana's rifles went with them, while Garibaldi's marched on to Rome, which was re-entered on the 24th of May. Could he have assaulted Velletri as he wished he would have gained a glorious victory ; but the miserable cowardice and pusillanimity of Bomba had caused the affair to be a mere success of having, at little loss and with indomitable pluck, driven twenty thousand men and the king out of the Roman territory, while the French army lay under the walls of Rome awaiting the result of negotiations.

On the 10th of May Oudinot returned, and came within four miles of the Tiber, investing the whole of the Travestere side of Rome. His reinforcements amounted to six thousand. The Neapolitan advanced-posts came up close to the walls of St. Paul and St. John Lantern, on the side of Albano and Frascati. The city was in consternation, expecting an attack within twenty-four hours ; they had had no suspicion of such tactics, for this seemed to be the beginning of a blockade, and a combined attack of thirty or forty thousand men with a force of heavy artillery. It occurred to some there that the news of the disastrous movement of General Oudinot on the 30th April had reached Paris, and that in consequence reinforcements had been hastily forwarded. That surmise contained the truth. Louis Napoleon trembled like a leaf at the tidings of Oudinot's reverse, and his opponents in the Assembly irritated him beyond measure. The French people at large sympathised with Rome, and disliked the French interference in Italian affairs, especially in so glorious a contest as that between Pope and people. He dreaded another revolution : the word had been named. He therefore had the audacity to send off to Oudinot the following letter, and the soldiers followed :—" My dear General,—The telegraphic news announcing the unforeseen resistance which you have met with under the wall of Rome has greatly grieved me. I had hoped, as you know, that the inhabitants of Rome, opening their eyes to evidence, would receive an army which had arrived there to accomplish a friendly and disinterested mission. This has not been the case. Our soldiers have been received as enemies. Our military honour has been engaged. I will not suffer it to be assailed. Reinforcements shall not be wanting to you. Tell your soldiers that I appreciate their bravery, and take part in what they endure, and that they may always rely upon my support and gratitude. Receive, my dear General, the true assurance of my sentiments of high esteem."

The tidings of the advance of the French did not produce dismay in the hearts of the Roman Assembly. Garibaldi was sent for, and begged to press homewards immediately. The Triumvirate issued a proclamation to the people, in the spirit of one who wrote a short time after these troublous days had passed.

> " Peace-lovers we—sweet Peace we all desire—
> Peace-lovers we—but who can trust a liar ?—
> > Peace-lovers, haters
> > Of shameless traitors:
> We hate not France, but this man's heart of stone ;
> > Italians, guard your own !
>
> We hate not France, but France has lost her voice,
> This man is France, the man they call her choice.
> > By tricks and spying,
> > And craft and lying,
> And murder, was her freedom overthrown,
> > Italians, guard your own !"

CHAPTER VI.

REVERSES.

"Still, graves, when Italy is talked upon,
  Still, still, the patriot's tomb, the stranger's hate.
    Still Niobe ! still fainting in the sun,
  By those most dazzling arrows violate,
    Her beauteous offspring perished !—has she won
  Nothing but garlands for the graves, from Fate ?
    Nothing but death songs ?—Yes, be it understood,
  Life throbs."

—E. BARRETT BROWNING.

EARLY in May 1849, M. Ferdinand Lesseps arrived in Rome, having been deputed by the French National Assembly to enter upon negotiations with Mazzini and the Constituent Assembly of the Roman Republic. In an interview with the Triumvirs, in which he informed them that he was commissioned to inquire into the truth with regard to the opinions and desires of the Romans, and that his instructions were to use all care to prevent a deplorable struggle between the two Republics, he begged that the rulers of Rome would study to bring about such a result, taking into consideration the dignity of France and the honour due to her army. The Triumvirs were partly deluded by his fair words ; Garibaldi was not. Mazzini, like so many Italian great men, was ever liable to fascination by France. Its pitiful struggles against its own tyrants, and its sprightliness of address, won upon his honesty and sincerity to the extent of diverting his judgment. French arms needed no vindication for a blunder. Their best vindication would have been a voluntary retirement. The Assembly at Paris meant well enough in sending Lesseps. They were themselves on the very verge of another revolution, thanks to the intriguing of the son of Hortense and the aspirations of the Buonaparte family, who were willing to make him their stalking-horse. Lesseps was in great straits under such imposing influences and in such inharmonious ideas. Oudinot was a man of war, and the President of the Republic's instrument.

"On the 31st of May Lesseps signed with the Triumvirs a treaty to be submitted to the ratification of the French Government. The treaty was sent the same day to General Oudinot, who refused his sanction on the ground that it was in opposition to his instructions. This refusal he notified to the Triumvirs, who in turn communicated it to M. Lesseps. On one occasion a rather violent scene took place between the minister and the general, the cause of which was as follows :—While M. Lesseps was following up his negotiation, the Triumvirs rejected the first proposition, and a delay of twenty-four hours was accorded. Before this period expired the Triumvirs presented a counter-proposition, which General Oudinot refused to take any notice of, and mentioned that he should attack Rome immediately. M. Lesseps protested against this act. This protest was apparently attended to, but preparations were made for an attack the same night. M. Lesseps being informed of what was going on again interfered, but his interference was too late to prevent the army from occupying Monte Mario, where no resistance was encountered, owing to the fact of M. Lesseps assuring the authorities in Rome that it was merely come to prevent the position from being occupied by the other armies who were marching on Rome. It was at this moment that the despatch arrived recalling M. Lesseps to Paris. In the meantime the government instructed the directors of the telegraph not to transmit, and even not to receive the despatches of M. Lesseps; the result of which was that the despatch ordering the bombardment of Rome crossed on the way that of M. Lesseps, announcing the conclusion of the treaty submitted for the ratification of the French Assembly.

"In obedience to the orders last received, Genera Oudinot prepared his troops for the attack, and at three o'clock on the morning of the 3rd instant, active hostilities recommenced, and the Villa Pamphili, the Church of St. Pa crazio, and Villas Corsini and Valentini were successively taken. The Villa Pamphili was defended by numerous barricades and 2000 men. More than 200 prisoners, includir ten officers, were taken by the French before five the same morning. Three standards and 200,000 cartridges were also captured. The Church of San Pancrazio was taken at seven o'clock A.M., and the Villa Corsini at ten o'clock, and at the same hour the Villa Valentini. The Romans set fire to these positions with their mortars, and the French had to abandon them, but they were immediately retaken. Garibaldi tried to turn the left of the French position, but failed. On the night of the third the Romans had attempted a sortie, but were driven back. In the taking of these important positions the French had 165 men wounded, of whom seven were officers. The amount of killed is not stated. The despatch states that the French troops behaved admirably."

"The following proclamation was published at Rome on the 3rd June by the Triumvirs :—'Romans! To the crime of attacking a friendly Republic with troops led on under a Republican banner, General Oudinot adds the infamy of treachery. He violates the written promise we have in our hands not to attack us before Monday. Arise, Romans, to the walls, to the gates, to the barricades! Let us prove to the enemy that Rome cannot be conquered even by treachery. Let the Eternal City rise to a man with the energy of one common thought! Let every man fight! Let every man have faith in victory! Let every man remember our ancestors, and be great! Let right triumph, and let eternal shame attend the ally of Austria! Viva la Republica!'"

Garibaldi has himself furnished notes on these memorable events, which are well worthy of a place here.

"On the 24th of May I re-entered Rome, attended by a vast multitude, who hailed me with the most joyful welcome.

"The Austrians were threatening Ancona, and the first corps of four thousand men had left Rome for the purpose of defending the Legations and the Marches, and the sending a second was in contemplation. Before orders to that effect were given, General Roselli thought it most conducive to the safety of Rome to write to General Oudinot, thus :—

"'CITIZEN-GENERAL,—It is my perfect conviction that the army of the Roman Republic will fight side-by-side with the French Republican Army one day, for the purpose of maintaining the sacred rights of the people. I am impelled, therefore, to make you proposals that I hope you will accept.

"'I am aware that a treaty has been signed between the Government and the Minister Extraordinary of France, which has not received your approval; but as I am not involved in political diplomacy, I address you as the General-in-Chief of the French Army at Rome. The Austrians are on the march; they intend to concentrate their forces at Foligno, and thence advance, inclining their right wing toward the territory of Tuscany, pass the valley of the Tiber, and, by the Abruzzi, join the Neapolitans. I cannot think you will see with indifference the realisation of such a scheme.

"'I deem it my duty to inform you of my suppositions as to the movements of the Austrians, because at this moment your attitude of indecision paralyses our force, and may give assurance of success to the enemy. These reasons appear to me to be sufficient for me to request of you an unlimited armistice, subject only to a fifteen days' notice before hostilities are resumed.

" 'General, this armistice is, I believe, necessary for the safety of my country, and I ask it, therefore, in the name of the honour of the army and the Republic of France.

" 'In the event of the Austrians bringing the head of their column to Civita Castellana, it is upon the army of France that History will cast the responsibility of dividing our forces just at the very time when their union is so necessary; and upon it will be charged the success of the enemies of France.

" 'General, I have the honour to ask you to send prompt reply, and to receive my fraternal salutation.

" 'ROSELLI.'

" Had Roselli been less confiding, or had Louis Napoleon, the President, through his willing agent, been less wicked, this appeal would never have been written, or when written, would have been irresistible.

" The Algerine replied :—

" 'The orders of my Government positively order me to enter Rome as soon as possible. I have repudiated the verbal armistice which I consented to grant, at the request of M. Lesseps, to the Roman authorities, and have written orders to my advanced posts that the two armies were at liberty to commence hostilities.

" 'Notwithstanding, to give the opportunity to those of your people who desire to quit Rome, and at the request of the Chancellor of the French Ambassador, of doing so without discomfort, I defer the attack on the place until at least the morning of Monday *("je déffère l'attaque de la place jusqu'au lundi matin au moins")*.

" 'General, receive the assurance of my high consideration.

" 'The General-in-Chief of the Army Corps of the Mediterranean.   " 'OUDINOT, DUC DE REGGIO.'

"In accordance with this assurance the attack would not commence until the 4th June.

"It is true that a French author, Folard, has, in his commentaries on Polybe, said—'A general who goes to sleep on the faith of a treaty awakes a dupe.'

"On 3rd of June, about three in the morning, I was awakened by the sound of cannon, and was lodging in Via Crozze with two friends, Orrigonni and Daverio, of whom I have spoken—of the last as captain of a company of youths at Velletri. This sound, so unexpected, caused us all to leap from the bed. Daverio was suffering from an abscess. I ordered him to remain in the house and rest; but I had no reason to hinder his accompanying me. I therefore took to horse, leaving him the liberty of following me when he could, and where also, and galloped away to the gate of San Pancrazio.

"Everything was on fire. I will tell you what happened. Our advanced posts of the Villa Pamphili consisted of two companies of Bolognese Volunteers and two hundred men of the Sixth Regiment. The midnight bell was striking, and we were entering on the morning of the 3rd of June, when a French column was stealing through the obscurity towards the Villa Pamphili.

"The sentinel, hearing the sound of footsteps, exclaimed, 'Qui Vive?'

"A voice replied, 'Viva l'Italia!'

"The sentinel thought he had to do only with compatriots, and he permitted them to approach. He was disarmed, and the column rushed into the Villa Pamphili, wounding or making prisoners all whom they met. Some of them leaped from the windows into the garden, and when they were there clambered over the wall. Those who in haste had rushed behind the convent of San Pancrazio, cried 'To Arms!' the others hurried away in the direction of the Villas Corsini and Valentini. These, like the Villa of Pamphili, were taken by surprise, but not without offering the best possible resistance.

"The cry of those who had taken refuge behind San Pancrazio, the thunder of the guns fired by those who defended Villa Corsini and Villa Pamphili, had awakened the gunners, who, as soon as they heard of the French occupation of those country mansions, directed their fire upon them. The noise of the cannon awoke the drums and the bells.

"On my arrival at the gate of San Pancrazio, the Villas Pamphili, Corsini, and Valentini were all taken; Vascello was the only one left in our hands. Corsini was a great loss to us. So long as we dominated that, the French could not draw their parallels. Therefore, for Rome, its recovery was a matter of life and death. The cannon on the ramparts were increasing their fire, the men at the Vascello were increased in numbers, and the French in the Villas Corsini and Valentini were augmented. But fusilade or cannonade could not effect a victory. Nothing but an assault, terrible and victorious, could restore Corsini to our hands.

"With a sudden leap I jumped into the road, not heeding whether my white puncho and hat of plumes might make me the target of French riflemen, and by call and energetic emotion called the scattered ones about me. It seemed as if officers and soldiers rose from the earth: in an instant Nino Bixio, my officer of *ordonnance*, was beside me; Daverio, who I had every reason to believe was at Via Crozze; Masina, my commander of the lancers, besides Sacchi and Marochetti, my old companions of the Monte Videan wars. These rallied round me the remnant of the Bolognese company, placed themselves at the head of the Italian Legion, and dashed on first, and others were immediately drawn after them. Their sudden rush defied all arrest: the Villa Corsini was regained; but before they reached it so many men had been left on the only road to get there that it was not possible to resist the assailing columns. They were compelled to retire. But during this charge others had come on, and others had joined; the chiefs, who were furious at their having been checked, would insist upon their marching on again. Masina, who had received a ball in his arm, raised it high in the air, and cried, 'Forward.' To second these brave soldiers I drew all the men I could from Vascello, the charge was sounded, and the Villa Corsini was retaken.

"In one quarter of an hour it was lost again at the cost of most precious blood! Masina, I have before said, was wounded in the arm; Nino Bixio had received a ball in his side; Daverio was slain! Just as I was imploring Masina to go and have his wound dressed, and ordering Bixio to be carried away, Manara was at my side, having disobeyed the orders to the contrary which I had given him. I said, 'Bring out your men; this paltry place, you see, must be regained.'

"His first company, commanded by Captain Ferrari, a former *aide-de-camp* to General Durando, were then deployed as skirmishers outside the gate San Pancrazio. Ferrari was a brave man, who had made the double campaign of Palestrina and Velletri with us, and had been wounded in the charge at Palestrina in the leg, but now was recovered.

"Manara ordered the recall to be sounded by the trumpet. Ferrari rallied his men and came to receive his colonel's orders. 'Fix bayonets, charge, spring forward.' From the instant of his arrival at the gate, that is to say, three hundred metres from the Casino, a shower of balls began to pour upon him and his men; he however did not stay his rushing haste on the Villa, which like a volcano belched forth flames; when his lieutenant, Mangiagalli, took the sleeve of his dress and exclaimed: 'Captain! Captain, why, do you not see there are only us two?' Ferrari, for the first time, looked behind him. Twenty-eight of his eighty men were lying dead or wounded, and the others had retreated. Mangiagalli and he also retreated.

"Manara became enraged as he saw his men abandon the company of their officers before his eyes. He called up the second company, commanded by Captain Henri Dandolo, a wealthy Milanese noble of Venetian origin, as his ducal name indicates, and gave him the like orders, crying, 'Lombards, forward! The business is to retake that Villa or lay down your lives. The eye of Garibaldi is upon you!'

"Ferrari signified his wish to speak, and Manara said, 'Speak, then!' Ferrari said to me, 'General, what I wish to say is not with a view of lessening the danger, but of ensuring success. I know the place I have just come out, and you may have observed me hesitating more at that than in going in.' I nodded assent. 'Well, I propose, therefore, that instead of following the path by the garden and attacking the front we shall silently take the myrtle hedge, Dandolo's company on the left and the first company on the right. When I throw a stone to the Dandolo company they will know that my men are ready, and they will throw a stone to shew that it is understood. Then the eight trumpets shall sound instantly, and we shall from the very foot of the terrace rush to the assault.'

"'Do as you like, I said,' 'only regain that beggarly place.'

"Ferrari parted with me at the head of his company; Dandolo did the same. I then ordered Captain Hoffstetter and fifty students to follow, and charged them to occupy the house on the left which I have named, and which was afterwards known as *la maison brûlée* (the burnt house).

"In about six minutes the sound of the trumpets was heard, almost at the same time as the fusilade. This was what was passing:—

"The two companies, protected by the hedges and the vines, had reached to within forty yards of the terrace, as Ferrari hoped : then, the signals having been exchanged, the trumpets sounded, and my brave company rushed to the assault. But from the terrace of the grand saloon on the first storey, and from the round staircase leading thereto, as well as from the windows, a frightful fire was poured down upon them. Dandolo fell backwards, his body pierced by a ball. Lieutenant Sylva was wounded, close to Ferrari. Lieutenant Mancini received almost at the same time two balls, one in his thigh, the other in his arm.

"And yet Ferrari, who assumed the captain's place when Dandolo was dead, led on the company, and by great effort kept pushing forward ; they scaled the terrace and drove back the French as far as the round staircase. But there was an end. The French were in front and at their sides : the guns they used almost touched them, and every shot killed a man. I witnessed their disastrous fall, and saw that every one of them would perish, and no result ensue ; I therefore sounded a retreat. I had two thousand, and the French twenty thousand men. I had taken the Corsini Villa with a company ; they had retaken it with a regiment. The French knew as well as I the importance of the position. My men came back to me—almost all of them were wounded —leaving forty comrades dead in the gardens, and I saw I must wait for more soldiers. I despatched Orrigoni and Ugo Bassi, and charged them to send in all they could meet ; I wished, for the satisfaction of my own mind, to make one last and supreme effort.

"I moved my men to a place of shelter behind the Vascello ; and in an hour's time there arrived, pell-mell, the companies of the line, students, the civic officers, and fragments of other corps, among whom was Masina, who had brought with him twelve lancers. He had had his wounds dressed, and came to take his part in the action.

"Then I left the Vascello with a small group of dragoons; at the sight of me, 'Viva l'Italia! Viva la Republica Romana!' was shouted: the cannon thundered from the walls, and the bullets passing over our heads announced a new French attack; and altogether, without order, pell-mell, Masina at the head of his lancers, Manara at the head of his riflemen, and I at the head of all, now rushed against, I do not say the impregnable, but the untenable villa. Arrived at the gate, we found it impossible for all to enter in: the torrent flowed off to the right and to the left: and these spread themselves about, taking position as sharpshooters on the two sides of the Casino; others scaled the walls of the villa garden, leaping down: lastly, others went off to the Villa Valentini, took it, and made some prisoners.

"There I beheld a deed that would be thought incredible. Masina, followed by his lancers, took the lead of his column and advanced; the intrepid horseman devoured the ground, cleared the terrace, arrived at the foot of the staircase, and clapping spurs to his horse, galloped him up the stairs so well that in an instant he appeared on the saloon landing-place like an equestrian statue.

"The apotheosis did not continue one minute. A fusilade of guns close to him brought down the cavalier; his horse fell upon him, having received nine balls.

"Manara followed, leading a bayonet charge which nothing could resist. For an instant the Villa Corsini was ours. That instant was short, but sublime.

"The French now were joined by their reserve, and altogether, before the disorder inseparable from victory could be repaired, and the fight recommenced, more desperate, more bloody, and more mortal, I saw pass before me, repulsed by two irresistible weapons of war, fire, and steel, those who but an instant before had passed on. One among these wounded was the brave Captain Rozat. 'I

10

have run out my account,' was his saying as he passed me, and pointed to his bleeding breast.

"I have seen very terrible combats. I saw that of Rio Grande, that of the Boyada, that of San Antonio, but I never saw anything parallel to the butchery of the Villa Corsini. I came out last; my puncho riddled with balls, but I without a single wound. After ten minutes we re-entered the Vascello, in the line of houses held by us, and from the windows recommenced firing upon the Villa Corsini. There seemed nothing more to be done.

"Nevertheless, in the evening a hundred men, at the head of whom was Emile Dandolo, brother of the dead one, and Goffredo Mameli, a young Genoese poet of great promise, came to ask me to allow them to make another attempt. 'Do so, my poor boys: perhaps it is God who inspires you,' was my reply. They went and came back, leaving half their number behind—Emile Dandolo pierced by a ball in the thigh, Mameli wounded in the leg.

"We had suffered terrible losses. The Italian Legion had, in dead or wounded, 500 men *hors de combat.* The Rifle Battalion of 600 had lost 150, and the others in the same proportion. The traits of courage and devotion on this remarkable day were wonderful. In the last charge Ferrari and Mangiagalli, who could not go in with us, threw themselves upon the Villa Valentini with a few men who followed them, fighting from chamber to chamber—not with guns, for they were useless, but with the sword. Mangiagalli's blade was broken in two, but he continued to strike with the stump so well—Ferrari also being equally brave—that they remained masters of the villa. The quarter-sergeant Monfrini, eighteen years of age, had his right hand broken by a bayonet, but ran, got it dressed, and in a few seconds was in his rank again. Manara saw him, and said: 'What do you come here for? You are wounded and good for nothing. Away.' 'I ask your pardon, colonel,' replied the lad, 'I shall serve to make up the number.' The brave youth was killed. Lieutenant Bronzelli's orderly, for whom he had a great affection, was killed in the Villa Corsini ; he took four determined men, and went at night, entered the place, and bore off the body, which he had buried secretly. A Milanese soldier, Della Longa, saw the fall of Corporal Fiorani, whose wound was mortal, just as we were being repulsed. He could not endure to leave the body in the enemy's hands, so he carried it upon his shoulders ; after pacing twenty steps a ball struck him in the chest, and he died under his dying burden."

Garibaldi's military skill has undergone much criticism, but of his personal valour there can be no dispute. Both friend and foe agree in the recognition of his heroic courage during the terrible scenes of war. At one moment leading a battalion to the bayonet charge—at another rushing to cheer his men if he observed them to be discouraged, and by exposing himself continually where the fight was thickest ; it seemed as if he had a charmed life. The bullets hailed about him, piercing his clothes, but leaving him untouched. Dandolo complains of his defective judgment in estimating his own and the enemy's strength, but we must remember that a thousand times his enthusiasm had made him strong enough to face the most terrible odds, and to come off victorious.

He certainly changed his tactics on the 4th of June, for the loss of the choicest of his officers, irreparable as it was, compelled a modification while there yet remained to him so many kindred spirits as had survived the first day. He feared that a fresh assault would be made on the 4th, and committed to Giacomo Medici the defence of the advanced line, which then commenced at the Villa Vascello, whereto the little remnant of a brave party had retired on the previous evening, whom Garibaldi had sent with orders to spare their shot and resort to the bayonet. The night was spent in organising means of defence. He had come to the conclusion that an army of 40,000, having six-and-thiry cannon, resolutely sitting down before the city and selecting at their discretion the best approaches for siege operations, must in the end succeed. It was only a question of time. The object he and all else had was therefore limited to the hope that, since the city must fall, it should not fall ingloriously.

Taking for his headquarters some high ground commanding the Pancrazio gate, and affording a view of all that was going on at Vascello, Corsini, Pamphili, above the ramparts, but in very dangerous proximity to the French sharpshooters, being only at half-shot distance—Garibaldi awaited the day.

The French in their turn had used the time to some purpose. The places that had been taken they retained, at least those of greatest importance. These they had strengthened; and they had also planted on the inaccessible heights two siege batteries. These operations of the French were thoroughly scientific. Their earthworks exist still, to challenge observation and admiration.

During the night Garibaldi had sent for his old friend Manara, and had entreated him to resign his colonelcy of the Lombard Rifles, and become chief of his staff. The sacrifice was great, but the extraordinary bravery, self-possession, and penetrating tact of Manara, which had made his regiment the most perfect in the army, impelled the General to press his request with much urgency. Manara was in addition a scholar: he knew four European languages, and possessed the natural dignity of a commanding presence. He gave way to Garibaldi, and at once began his duties by reorganising the staff,

The Villa Savarelli—the headquarters—commanding the whole country, was a favourite resort for all the officers on that account, as well as because it was the General's headquarters, and everybody wished to be near him. The French knew to what use this house had been put, and bullets, cannon-balls, and other projectiles fell thickly about it, as Garibaldi said, "meant for him." At the top of the villa was a little observatory, whereto he frequently repaired for a still better view of general operations. Hither he was pursued by a tempest of balls; "and I can safely say," he writes, "that I never heard a tempest make such a hissing noise in my life. The balls made the house shake as if there were an earthquake." Frequently he had his meals there, and "was favoured with music, which enabled him to dispense with the services of his regimental band."

Avezzana, the Roman Minister of War, went up to see Garibaldi in a few days after the siege operations were commenced, and as he entered the great room he had transformed into headquarters, asked whether he could not obtain a greater elevation to observe the general works. Garibaldi took him up to the turret which commanded the prospect, and they had no sooner reached it than the usual music commenced in full chorus. Avezzana surveyed the country, saw the enemy's outposts in silence, and came away. The next day Garibaldi found the entrances stopped with bags of earth, and on inquiry learned that the Minister of War had so ordered it. And none too soon had he done so. He had been there before, when Vecchj, the accurate collector of so much concerning the revolution, and a dear friend of the General's, had called at the dinner hour. Avezzana and Rita had come, and a dinner had been sent for from Rome. It was brought in a tin case, and Vecchj was invited to stay. They sat down on the ground in the garden, for they could not use the room because of the violence of the firing upon the house, which made the place more like a ship's cabin in a storm than a dwelling. In the midst of dinner a bomb fell within a yard of them, and caused some of them to flee. Vecchj seemed inclined to do likewise, but Garibaldi seized his wrist, and exclaimed to him, as a member of the Constituent Assembly, "Conscript Father, don't leave the chair," laughing heartily. He knew which way the thing would burst, and it did, as he anticipated, on the opposite side of the room, doing no more damage than to cover them with dust.

War has its horrors : it has also its more entertaining escapades. Let Garibaldi here tell the tale of an incident in the siege.

" Vecchj was one of the advanced guard at the vineyards of Castabili, which is the name of one of those near the Corsini Villa, and had his report to make. He found me at dinner, and on a table, for the attention of the French artillery had been so kind as to give me a little intermission, there was before me a dish with a savour that stimulated appetite, and I made room for him at my side, and asked him to join me. He was just about to sit when Manara interrupted—

" 'Do nothing of the sort, Vecchj ! Three consecutive days have officers who have joined the General at dinner been killed before they have had time to enjoy it.'

"It was true : David, Prosser, and Panizzi had been so killed. Vecchj replied—

" 'Well, that has a marvellous correspondence with a prophecy made about me.'

" Manara was curious to know it, and Vecchj said—

" ' A Bohemian gipsy drew my horoscope when I was an infant, and predicted that I should die in Rome at the age of thirty-six, and very rich. I was on a journey in 1838 on foot from Naples to Salerno, and near Sarno I saw a gipsy in a field by the road-side, whose beautiful eyes tempted me to kiss her. She kept me off with her knife, and I could only offer a bright new crown. She took the money and gave this prophecy. Now I am thirty-six : I am not rich : but I have no wish to die, although well off.

I am a fatalist, like a Mahommedan, and what is written is written.'

"Manara grew more serious, and said it was all very well, but he would like to see the day over; and, turning to me, said—

"'For heaven's sake, General, send him nowhere to-day.'

"Vecchj did not object to that idea. He had been up two nights, and after dinner was over he asked leave to retire for a brief sleep. Manara offered him his bed, and enjoined his seclusion for the day. It was accepted. About an hour after I saw the French officers placing gabions in the trenches opposite to our battery, and I looked for an officer to order a dozen riflemen to fire into them, for I was alone. I thought of poor Vecchj, who was sound asleep, and it went against me to wake him, but the balls were making fearful havoc. I aroused him by pulling his leg, calling out—

"'Come, arouse; you have had twenty-four hours' sleep. Manara's fatalism is no longer to be feared. Take a dozen of your best shots and silence those fellows.'

'Vecchj did not need another word; he took a dozen riflemen, the best he could find, stationed them behind a barricade, and commenced a murderous raking fire which caused them to resort to cannon-ball in reply. In half-an-hour one of the men came up to me, and said—

"'General, have you heard that poor Vecchj is killed?'

"It cut me to the heart: thinking that I had been the cause of his death, and I reproached myself exceedingly. In a half-hour I saw him approaching me, and exclaimed, 'In God's name let me embrace you: I thought you were dead?' He replied that he had only been buried. I inquired what he meant, when he related how a ball had cut open a sack of earth, the contents of which came over him, and that beside that sack there were a dozen more, which fell, when struck, and had literally buried him."

Three thousand men had now fallen on both sides, by far the greater part being French. But this only incited to the utmost energy the spirit of those who survived, and on the evening of the 6th a sharp encounter took place between Oudinot's riflemen and Garibaldi's Legion. These latter fought with the more ferocity from the fact that two hundred of the Roman soldiers had been drawn into an ambuscade on the previous day, and made prisoners by the French, through the contemptible deception of a cry of " Fraternité." The attack of the Italians became so fierce that their treacherous enemy had to retire. The fame of Garibaldi, to whose efforts the repulse of the French on the 3rd was mainly due, spread through the city after this day's work with still more rapidity ; and indeed throughout Italy and Piedmont the populace indulged in cries of " Long live Rome ! Long live Garibaldi !"

On the 10th of June General Roselli sent orders to Garibaldi to assume command of a great sortie, which should consist of half the Roman army, and be made through the Cavallegieri gate. There had been a small one on the previous day, for the purpose of interrupting the French works ; but this was intended to effect the recovery of the Villa Pamphili, or of Vallentina. To carry out the project Garibaldi was relieved by Avezzana, the Minister of War, of the command of the San Pancrazio line. He took his Italian Legion and the Lombard Rifleman, and repaired to the Palace of the Vatican, where he was to be joined by two other regiments and the Polish Legion. He there reviewed his troops on horseback and distributed his orders, explaining the object of the enterprise, and the method for its accomplishment which he contemplated. Ammunition was dealt round, and the army awaited in impatience the hour when the attack should be commenced.

The inexperience of the men in this mode of warfare defeated the design, and the French aptitude and vigilance converted it into failure. Garibaldi describes in his journal the incidents.

"In order to avoid the common misfortunes of night attacks, whereby enemies are often accounted friends, and friends foes, and mistaken firing ensues to great loss, I ordered the soldiers to put their shirts over their uniforms, and the operation created much laughter, on account of the condition of some of the under garments now made outer ones. At ten o'clock the gate was opened, and Hoffstetter's Polish Legion marched out as vanguard, followed by the Italian Legion under Manara : the Lombard Rifles and the other two regiments bringing up the rear. I was scarcely out of the city when the blunder of dress was palpable. My men were as conspicuous as in broad daylight. I saw that before they had gone a hundred yards the French would deem themselves attacked by an army of ghosts. The shirts were at once taken off, and I think I may assert that not a single soldier took the trouble to replace them where they had been taken from.

"I was riding on the flank of the Italian Legion when some soldiers who were passing one of the villas and carrying a ladder, wishing to know whether the place was really as abandoned as it appeared to be, raised it to the first storey. The regiment halted to watch the event, and the vanguard marched on. Five or six men mounted the ladder, and all at once the step on which the top man mounted broke off short, and all of them came tumbling down one upon the other with a frightful crash; and to add to the confusion two of the muskets went off. Hoffstetter's Legion in advance heard the report, and fancied they were surprised by the enemy whom they had intended to surprise. They were instantly panic-stricken, and broke away from their commanders, who were left with about a score of men, and came hurrying back to us in despair, overturning everything in their fright and disorder. Manara did his best to stop them, but to no purpose. I flung myself in the midst of them, swearing and striking right and left with my whip, but it was no use: and I verily believe that all would have run back to Rome had not the Lombard riflemen, at the head of whom was Captain Ferrari and two officers, formed across the road with fixed bayonets. The noise of this disturbance could not but be heard by the French, and the enterprise had to be abandoned. As for me, I was fatigued from striking the cowardly fellows, and returned to the city with Manara, regretting to him that he had not placed his brave company at the head instead of the Poles, for they were fine soldiers. Manara would say to them, when he had received orders, 'Now, men, I want forty of you for an expedition in which one quarter of you will be killed, and another quarter wounded.' They were never alarmed at such a programme, for the whole regiment would present themselves, and lots had to be cast to avoid jealousy."

The brave Anita, whose calm spirit never flinched from the fatigues of war, and whose presence was so strengthening and consoling to her husband, had, for the sake of her child not yet born, been persuaded to remain at Rieti much against her will. She now rejoined him, attended by two or three friends who could not prevail on her to abide where she was in safety, whilst her husband was exposed to the imminent risk of life and limb.

Repeated efforts to drive back the enemy were daily made, and sometimes also in the night. The activity was unceasing, and could not have been maintained had there not been an indomitable spirit inspiring the defenders, and also the existence of a moral support arising from the indefeasible justice of the position they were driven to assume. People are never anxious to take the reins of government into their own hands for the sake of possessing and exercising power; they are willing and desirous of leaving that province to those who devote themselves to the administration of political affairs. It is only when, as in Rome, the government itself ceases to govern by any righteous laws that the long-suffering community ultimately take the helm. No living man dare justify the unleavened mass of hypocrisy and iniquity which sat in the seat of judgment at Rome ; nor can we wonder at the angry rising of an infuriated people, who were determined to regenerate Rome. They had done so: and now, in resisting an alien interference, were supported by the consciousness of a righteous cause.

The bombardment of the city became daily more and more violent. The Foreign Consuls had tried their best personally at interposition, seeing the fearful havoc which, day after day, was made in the homes of the innocent people. But the French General turned a deaf ear to all such representations: his savage thirst for blood—partly due to his Algerine training—rendered him callous to the claims of humanity, of reason, of justice, and of truth. The French pressed on their works: every day new batteries opened their fire on the bastions 6 and 7, so that at last a breach was made there to the left of the San Pancrazio gate—the part of the city committed by Garibaldi to the protection of his own Legion and their comrades. These were well aware that, a breach once made and a battery planted, their undisciplined valour would be of no avail in a contest with scientific strategy, skilled soldiers, and an army possessing infinite power of reinforcement. The Casino Savorelli, where Garibaldi had latterly taken up his residence, became untenable. Every hour caused increased apprehension lest it should sink to the earth as a ruin, and bury its tenants alive. He therefore repaired to the Villa Corsini, which was at an inconvenient distance from the walls, and had only the single advantage of being tolerably quiet and safe. Medici had, consequently, much to do in repulsing the minor attacks upon the points Vascelli and Corsini. Now, as in the earlier

time in Piedmont, he served his General with fidelity and
indefatigable zeal.

The 20th of June, however, more clearly revealed to the
besieged their oncoming fate.   Another day's fire could make
breaches in two or three places; and though to a soldier the
prospect of assault—when, hand to hand, the dagger decides
everything—excites rather an appetite for the struggle than
a dread or revulsion, the truth dawned upon them all that
the end of the siege could not be long deferred.

The French now commanded the one-quarter of the city,
and of course, as soon as their cannons were mounted on the
breach, the disaster of Rome would culminate.   Losing no
time, they immediately commenced the fortification of the
acquired position; but within the city the event was a prelude to discord, or, at least, to difference of opinion.
Roselli, the General, urged the necessity of assuming the
offensive by attempting to regain the lost position by a
bayonet charge; but Garibaldi, who knew the effect of such
a grave loss on the minds of men, the discouragement that
is sure to follow even among the best, and fearing also the
vulgar suspiciousness so ready to attribute treachery, and
therefore to abandon hope, warmly opposed Roselli's proposal.   Ferrari attributes to the General a spirit of jealousy
and conceit—a disposition to set up a rivalry—but we have
seen abundantly that those tendencies did not, and never
could, find entrance into the nature of Garibaldi.   His
judgment was right.   A siege under the conditions of that
of Rome—an innumerable host on the outside, and poor and
limited resources within—even where the cause of the assailant is the most unjustifiable, and that of the defenders holy
and good, must have for conclusion a catastrophe.   The tocsin was sounded: the Assembly met; time was spent in idle
words; and when the evening drew on, the French had
crowned the breach with their cannon, and the plan of
Roselli was rendered impracticable.

On the sounding of the tocsin the streets of Rome were crowded by the populace, wildly demanding arms, that they might be led forward to drive the French from the walls. Garibaldi protested against the useless sacrifice, but the Triumvirs and Roselli were obstinate. He urged the disorders which the infusion of a mere mob would produce in the ranks, and he dreaded another panic, like that of twelve days before, which was the more likely to follow with men who had never had any familiarity with fire-arms. After having given his judgment, and failed to persuade his friends, he insisted on waiting till morning, because then they would see what enemy they had to meet, and whether there had been treachery.

In the early morning the division was called out, and strengthened by some reinforcement from the other regiments which Roselli had placed at Garibaldi's disposal. Medici and his Lombards went first, and the cannon of their batteries were turned upon the lost bastions: a bayonet charge was ordered, and the sappers and miners and the Grande Garde were held in readiness. Garibaldi saw the force he had to face. It was clear enough to him that another 3rd of June would soon rob him of half the men he loved more than himself. There was not the least hope of effecting the dislodgment of the foe, but a certainty that a step further would cause useless butchery. He ordered a retreat, and named five in the evening for renewing the attempt; doing that, however, merely to keep his men in good temper, not meaning to be responsible for so futile a proceeding. By the sacrifice of a thousand of his best soldiers, he knew that the French could be driven from the two villas; but he knew also, that whilst he lost a thousand men whom years could not replace, the enemy would hurl upon him, in true Buonaparte style, any number of human beings, when by so doing they could effect their purpose. There was also now less reason for holding out, as we have seen. The French Constituent Assembly had been cleverly manipulated, and the generous enthusiasm of the Roman Republic could not meet in open field an army of such skill, training, and prestige as traditionally distinguished the French. The Corsini Villa in Garibaldi's hands might have hindered the French approaches ; but now that the walls had been broken through, nothing could save the city.

The spirit of Garibaldi was unsubdued amidst all these contentions and calamities. He had ordered a retreat, but it was only for two hundred yards. Oudinot had indeed extended the scope of his operations, for from the 21st, notwithstanding his professions of regret for the monuments of Rome, and its innocent people, he had ordered bombs to be discharged all over Rome—an act of indiscriminate and outrageous Vandalism which has left the marks of France for all time on the Eternal City.

The report of Garibaldi is interesting here, because it gives some idea of his strategic skill and insight, and also of his popularity.

"The behaviour of the people of Rome in these trying days would have given glory to ancient days. While during the night they were pursued by showers of projectiles crushing in the roofs of houses, mothers could be seen flitting from one place to another with their children pressed to their bosoms; and the streets resounded with cries and lamentations ; but no word could be heard about surrendering. Often a scorning voice was heard when some missile injured a house,—*Benediction du Pape!* A benediction from the Pope! The night was busier than the day. Many bombs fell upon the Transtiberian quarter ; many upon the Capitol, the Quirinal, the Place d'Espagne ; one on the small temples that contains the Hercules of Canova, another into the Spada Palace, damaging a fresco.

"The marvellous fire of our cannon during the 25th, 26th, 27th June silenced the batteries raised by the French upon the curtain and bastions they held. But two French batteries opened their fire against our batteries of San Sabine and San Alexio. Two others, one on the curtain and the other bastion No. 6, opened against our battery St. Peter in Montorio. A fifth battery on the breach, placed at the foot of bastion No. 7, and sheltered from our fire opened also. A sixth, at the side of bastion 8, in front of the Church San Pancrazio, opened on our battery No. 8, and my late headquarters at Savorelli. A seventh, before Corsini Villa, threw its force against Porta di St. Pancrazio, my old quarters, Savorelli, and against us at the Aurelian. I never saw such a tempest of flame, such a torrent of shot. We were, I may say, stifled by it. And after all, there was Medici and his gallant Legion holding the Vascelli and the Corsini as if nothing were capable of disturbing them ! "

"During the evening of the 28th the French batteries seemed to rest for a little while, as if to take breath. But on the beginning of the 29th the fire was resumed with new violence.

"Rome was in a condition of immense agitation. The 27th had been terrible for our troops, and the number of killed almost equalled that of the 3rd of June. The streets were choked with mutilated human bodies. The pioneers had no sooner taken in hand the spade and pickaxe than they were cut in two by cannon-balls, or dismembered by howitzers. Our artillery, too, you will observe, had all been killed at their guns, and the work was now being done by soldiers of the line. The national guard was all under arms, and—a thing unheard of—the only reserve was the wounded, and these, still with unclosed wounds, came and did their relief guard or duty. And all this time, in admirable contrast, calm and unmoved, the Assembly in permanence at the Capitol deliberated under bullets and balls.

" As long as one of our cannon rested upon its carriage

we responded to the fire.   But on the evening of the 29th, our last was dismounted—our fire had ceased.   The breach at bastion No. 8 was practicable.   The wall of La Porta San Pancrazio and the bastion No. 9 were crumbling.   On the night of the 29th there came over Rome the winding-sheet : we could no longer see to repair the breaches, but the French artillery thundered right on through the night, and such a night !"

The attack was expected that night.   Rome was illuminated even to the cupola of the Vatican.   Men who saw that night's work describe it as a scene never to be forgotten. Amidst the noise of thunder, the wind, the cannon, the flying bombs, the city in all its glorious historic grandeur became the theatre of struggle of two armies—the whole brilliantly lighted up as though for the representation of a ghastly drama.   Perhaps to many a spectator, as well as actor, it brought to mind the Armageddon of John the Divine—being as it was a sublime conflict for the spiritual rulership of men and the domination of the world—a struggle whether Christ or Antichrist should possess the souls of men.

The storm ceased about midnight, and stealthily the French crept up to the last breach at bastion No. 8, favoured by the night, and perhaps by the inadequacy of the guard.   The other breaches were also forced.   A fearful uproar ensued at two o'clock.   Three reports of cannon, ominously fired at equal intervals, proclaimed the assault. The cry of alarm was given, and the drum beat to arms ; the night had become pitch dark, and the sky was stormy, whilst the discharge of musketry, mingled with the shouts of the approaching enemy, the crashing of roofs and sheds, and the tumbling of houses, increased the general confusion and dismay.

Garibaldi came to the head of the Lombard riflemen, springing forward with his drawn sword in his hand, and shouting the popular hymn of Italy, having, as he averred.

in his discouragement concerning the future, only one wish
—to throw himself on the French and be killed. He had
no recollection of what took place in that hour, whilst he
was lashing about him unceasingly, covered with blood, and
still unhurt. He had rushed in to strike a last blow, not
for the safety but for the honour of Rome, and brought
with him companions like-minded. They all rushed to the
breach, striking with lance, sword, and bayonet; for powder
and ball were spent. The French met the shock and re-
coiled; but others came up. "At the same time," says
Vecchj, Garibaldi's friend, "the artillery pointed against
them began to carry away whole files at once. The
Aurelian Amphitheatre was taken and retaken several
times; there was not a foot of ground uncovered by the
wounded and the dead. Garibaldi was greater that night
than anybody had ever seen him. His sword was like
lightning. Every man he struck fell dead. The blood of a
new adversary washed off the blood of him who had just
fallen. . . . I trembled in the expectation of seeing him
fall from one moment to another. But no, he remained
apparently saved by supreme protection."

In the middle' of this night's work a message reached
Garibaldi, requiring his presence in the Capitol to meet the
Assembly, and as he was descending towards the Longara
with Vecchj, who was a member of the Assembly, he heard
of the death of his poor negro, Aguyar, which had just
occurred. He was holding an exchange horse for his
master when a ball passed through his head. This was to
him not merely the loss of a servant—he ever spoke of
Aguyar as a friend.

On arriving at the Capitol he found that Mazzini had
already announced to the Assembly his view of the position
of affairs, and had set forth a choice of three courses: first,
to come to terms with the French; second, to defend the
city from barricade to barricade; and third, to leave the

Assembly, Triumvirate, and Army, carrying away with them the palladium of Roman liberty.

Garibaldi shall describe this last scene :—

"When I appeared at the door of the Chamber all the deputies rose and applauded. I looked about me, and upon myself to see what it was that awakened their enthusiasm. I was covered with blood; my clothes were pierced with balls and bayonet thrusts; my sabre, from the force of my strokes, was not more than half in the sheath. They cried to me, 'To the tribune! to the tribune!' I went. Then they asked me questions from all sides. I replied :—

"'The defence is from this time impossible, unless we are resolved to make of Rome another Saragossa. On the 9th of February I proposed a military dictatorship : that alone could have placed on foot a hundred thousand men in arms. The elements were existent, they had to be sought, but would have been found in one courageous man. At that time such daring was repulsed, and small measures prevailed. I could not urge the argument further, and yielded : modesty restrained me, although I am free to confess that I might have been that man. In this I was wanting to the sacred principle which is the idol of my heart. Had I been listened to with attention, the Roman eagle would again have made its eyrie on the towers of the Capitol : and with my brave men—and my brave men, it is pretty well known, know how to die—I might have changed the face of Italy. But for the past there is now no remedy : let us regard with heads unabased the ruin of which we are no longer the masters. Let us take with us from Rome all of the volunteer army who are willing to follow us. Where we shall be, there is Rome. I pledge myself to nothing ; but all that man can do I will do.'

"This proposition, already made by Mazzini, was rejected Henri Cernuschi himself—the brave Cernuschi—one of the heroes of the five days at Milan, President of the Commission of Barricades, rejected it. He ascended the tribune after me, and, with tears and a voice trembling with emotion, said :—

" ' You all know whether I am an ardent defender of my country and its people. Well then, it is I who tell you we have not a single obstacle which we can oppose to the French : and Rome and her good people resign'—and tears choked his speech—' must resign themselves to the occupation.' "

After a short deliberation, the Assembly issued the following decree :—" The Roman Republic. In the name of God and the People. The Roman Constituent Assembly ceases from a defence which has become impossible. It will remain at its post. The Triumvirate are charged with the execution of this decree."

We return to the last episode in the siege, as it is described by Dandolo. " After the breaches had been taken the fighting became general. All the bastions were occupied by the French, and also the roads and barricades. They had taken almost all the cannon, but these were spiked by our gunners : many of these men were seen still clasping their pieces in the death struggle, scarcely a gun being taken till the last of its defenders had fallen.

" The day dawned, and with it the spirit of our men revived ; mustering their forces, they attempted with their usual courage to drive back the enemy, who were pressing in on all sides. All order was at an end, and every moment increased the French ranks. Our riflemen collected at Villa Savorelli, and Garibaldi's troops stationed themselves among the vineyards and along the road. The word of command was given at last, and all rushed forward with a last impetus of courage, whilst the French were driven back at all points by this desperate effort of opponents already vanquished. Meanwhile the enemy's cannon roared without intermission: our ruined batteries, without artillerymen (for they were

lying dead in heaps round their pieces), could not return
the fire ; and the ground was strewed with our soldiers, for
the most part mortally wounded. Villa Spada was surrounded : we shut ourselves into the house, barricading the
doors, and defending ourselves from the windows. The
cannon-balls fell thickly, spreading devastation and death ;
the balls of the Vincennes chasseurs hissed with unerring
aim through the shattered windows. It is maddening to
fight when confined in a house where a cannon-ball·can
rebound from every wall, and where if you are not struck,
you are likely to be crushed in the *debris* : where the air,
impregnated with smoke and powder, brings the groans of
the wounded more distinctly on the ear, and the feet slip
along the pavement covered with blood, and the whole
fabric is reeling and tottering under the repeated strokes of
artillery. The defence had already continued two hours.
The fighting continued all this time most fiercely. Garibaldi came back from the Assembly to his men to finish his
work. The riflemen charged for the last time with the
bayonet, and he led them. The French were driven back
behind the second line. There soon came a report that the
Assembly had sent offers of capitulation, and the firing
gradually died away, while the gloom of night silently came
over all. The posts had, as we have described, been abandoned, and the loss in dead and wounded was very great.
The courage of those who survived did not forsake them,
but it was easy to see that that day marked the fall of
Rome.

The determination of the Assembly did not disturb Garibaldi.   He never did accept the *dictum* of mobs or monarchs,
and did not feel disposed to acquiesce. It leads our story
into further sadness, and still further glory, to state the
events which resulted from such a determination ; but this
much is clear, that an unseen hand not only led him on through
those fearful sorrows, but gave him strength to bear them.

Whether or no we be of Italian blood, every reader must, in the words of Ferrari, "bless those who in dying defended the honour of Italy, fighting against the foreigner. Here there is neither party spirit nor question of party—it is Italian soil on which the foreigner tramples: those who have fallen are the defenders of their country. Peace and honour to their memory!"

But the amazement of the Italians at the conduct of France added grief to their defeat. They would not, and do not believe that the French people meant to hurt them. In this we may find an explantion of more than one apparent mistake. Garibaldi, writing to Hugo some time after this, penned these lines :—

> "Can it be France—who once so proud and free,
> Gluts everywhere her hate of Liberty?
> Is yon her Master? *that* Man? that false Thing
> Fuddled with blood?—that nephew of a King?
> Is he the Lord to whom, Hugo, thy land
> Yields up the place she held? is *His* the hand
> Which, using France for smithy, forges chains
> And plots to bind whatever free remains?
> That one your Master? whose paid varlets swear
> To order. That one, the Pope's Grenadier?
> Oh France! that thou shouldst be to this fate sunk!
> The Queen of Kings, to mount guard for a monk!"

On the 2nd of July Garibaldi assembled his troops in the Piazzza San Pietro, and proposed to them to quit Rome, that they might avoid the abhorred sight of the victorious army. He exhorted them to march into the provinces, to attack the Austrians, who were inflicting a dreadful scourge on the minor cities of Italy, and raise a general revolution, not only against them, but against Naples, which also had returned and invaded Italian ground.

"I offer you," he said, "new battles and fresh glory. Whoso is willing to follow me shall be received among my own people, but it will be at the price of great exertions and great perils. I require nothing of you but hearts filled with the love of country. I can give no pay, no rest, and food will have to be eaten where it is found. Whoever is not satisfied with this fate had better stay behind. The gates of Rome once passed can never be re-entered while the French are here. Having dyed our fingers in the blood of the French, let us go and plunge our hands into that of the Austrians."

The acclamation which greeted him on this was immense. The enthusiasm knew no bounds. Five thousand men rallied to his standard, one thousand of whom were horse-soldiers. His name was lauded to the skies, and they swore to follow him. These composed two-thirds of the surviving army.

His wife Anita dressed herself in man's clothing. Father Ugo Bassi, his old companion and faithful friend, the man of many subsequent as of many previous sorrows, and many other leading men accompanied him, when in the evening, their hearts wrung with sadness, though fired with indomitable energy, they marched out by the Tivoli gate.

The departure of Garibaldi and the entry of the French aroused the energy of Austria, Naples, and Spain. They were mortified at the French success; and they trembled at the name of Italy's champion. The French General despatched a flying column in pursuit of Garibaldi. The Neapolitan army, strengthened, or rather increased, by some three hundred Spanish, and the Austrian army, were put in motion for the purpose of surrounding and destroying him.

Garibaldi, his wife, his friends, and his army marched away in silence, followed by ammunition and baggage-waggons, along the Tivoli road, through all that night, and at day-dawn they bivouacked at Tivoli. Volunteers came flocking in, and he found it necessary to divide the army into two legions, placing these recruits entirely with one-half, in order to keep an experienced force together, which would not be likely to be the victims of panic and disorder. After one day's rest he gave orders to march again, and the camp was struck. The journey was one of weariness and hardship, which continued for five days, and had caused great prostration and exhaustion by the time they reached Terni on the 9th of July.

The supply of such a force in a thinly peopled country caused excessive trouble, not at all lightened by the toil of mountain climbing which had to be undergone. Garibaldi made it a habit to avoid trespassing on the goodwill of the villagers and householders in small towns; but considering that the Church had so much of the soil, and had brought under its dominion so much of the productive industry of the country, he thought it only right that it should now contribute to the necessities of his forces. He therefore, while obtaining from the open country provisions for man and beast, bivouacked in monastery gardens, in which the district abounded.

There was always plenty of buildings capable of affording rough shelter. If it happened otherwise, the soldiers and their General slept under the open sky. There was indeed little of hardship in all this. Anita and the officers shared the same fate. In shelter, in food, in exposure, all were equal: the most perfect trust and sympathy being thereby maintained.

By some strange mistake Oudinot had sent off his flying column in the wrong direction. He imagined that Garibaldi, with his five thousand men, was bent on guerilla warfare, and had betaken himself to the mountains south of Rome, or south-east, near the towns of Albano and Frascati; and upon those towns the vultures descended. The next day half of them went back to Rome; but the other half stationed itself there, being quartered upon the inhabitants. Another arm of the French force under General Morris went northward to subjugate the towns of Civita, Catalana,

Todi, Viterbo, and Orvieto; for these, like many other towns, had awoke to a new life by virtue of unwonted liberty.

On the Abruzzi, General Statella had mustered a force, but Garibaldi was not there. He imagined, from the natural position of Abruzzi, and Garibaldi's knowledge thereof, that it would be the *dernier ressort* of the warrior, but he was mistaken; for on the night of the 11th July Garibaldi quitted the town of Terni and entered the Neapolitan territory.

Garibaldi wished to reach San Germano with his eight thousand men, and there to rest after the great fatigues and hardships already endured. He knew that, if he fought, he was fighting single-handed the four European Powers—a battle, they, in all their greatness, could not afford to disdain. He felt the righteousness of his cause, and the consciousness sustained him. The odds against him were fearful: and it cannot be a matter of surprise that human nature should shrink from so great a strain. His army had travelled six days, and were exhausted and fatigued; they began to question the purpose of their enterprise, and to think it impracticable. Want had looked them in the face, and they felt that it would do so again. Dangers had beset them; and more peril loomed in front: the risks were daily increasing. Rome had fallen, and how were they to deliver her? Faith failed them, and they lost hope.

The raw recruits that had rushed into the ranks at Terni fell away in this time of trial. The boys, who with the wild enthusiasm of eighteen had espoused the popular cause, now began to desert. They began to fear, fear lead to suspicion, and that to disloyalty. Many in the weary march passed by their own homes, through their own villages: they stealthily dropped out of the ranks, and did not return. The horse-soldiers began to sell their horses, and the infantry connived at the transaction, sharing the spoil; and again Garibaldi had to fret at the spectacle of Democracy calumniating itself and exhibiting the worst vices of human nature ; for one wrong led to another. These men ran away, and then made illegal requisitions ; committed theft and indulged passion, making their cause odious in the eyes of their countrymen, and compromising their leader, whom they were bound to honour.

Garibaldi, in traversing this Valley of Humiliation, underwent intense mental sorrow. The simplicity of his nature had been gratified by the alliance of the youth of Italy : and his sensibilities were hurt at their desertion. Brunetti, Anita, and the others continually exhorted to patience and loyalty the remaining corps. They personally distributed the reserved supply of spirits, and with it gave the most generous and helpful words of hope and encouragement. But the General had a weight of grief and apprehension that could not be cast off.

What a journey he had from the time he left Rome ! First to Frascati, then to Tivoli, and leaving the Abruzzi on his left, onwards to Terni. Then following the Tuscan frontier to Montepulciano, and on to Arezzo, he had re-entered the Roman States at Citta de Castello Mercatello. He had then crossed the Apennines and taken refuge in San Marino, and had been driven even from that sacred soil, hunted for the greater part of a hot summer month. His difficulties on the march were overwhelming. Armies all around, and seeking to encircle him, did not daunt his heart, but his followers from many causes dwindled and dwindled, till on reaching San Marino the eight thousand had become one thousand five hundred !

At San Marino, where the right of asylum was inviolate, he expected to have been out of the reach of the Austrians, but they had no scruples about the sanctity of the soil attached to the Republic. They surrounded the town and hemmed them in on all sides. The difficulty now was to get clear of the circle that surrounded them without

attracting attention : if that were effected, he would leave
to his own skill and the aid of his guides the work of
deceiving the reserved troops stationed at Rimini and
Cesanatico. He made his resolution, and rose suddenly :
called up his officers, and issued orders for immediate departure, exclaiming : "Let who will follow me. Again I
offer fresh combats, more privations and exile, but I will
never make covenant with a foreigner." He mounted his
horse as he said these words, and started off, preceded by
his guides. Those who had been sleeping in the streets
were up instantly, and followed; but many had gone to
private houses; these did not know of their chief's departure. Others put faith in the Austrian treaty, and determined on accepting the offered discharge. The result was
that only about two hundred persons went with the General.
They got away two hours before the enemy had any knowledge of their departure, and the news was sent off by
express to Rimini. This small force was further reduced
by the capture of one hundred and fifty of his men as they
were sailing for Venice in fishing boats.

The morning of 3rd August found Garibaldi with his
beloved wife, Padre Bassi, Cicero Vacchio, and a few others
of his truest friends on the shore at Chioggia. Then and
there the question arose, What was to be done? And it was
resolved by them all that in their diminished numbers and
increased dangers there was no possibility of effective united
action. The best, and indeed the only chance of escaping a
general calamity, lay in their scattering, in the hope of re-
union at some future time. To abide together was certain
death, for a dozen armed men could dispose of them.
Scattered, there remained the chance of escape. Garibaldi
asked no one to compromise himself: he would have one
friend, in case he might fall, to take care of his wife, but the
others must do as best they could. He would bear his own
burden alone.

Repairing to one of the country people's cottages, the three changed their dress, and then set out toward Ravenna. Exhausted as they must have been by the incessant excitement described in the last few pages, they were little fitted for the perils and dangers of the wild country which intervened; besides which, poor Anita, in her unhappy circumstances, was exposed to tenfold greater danger; and her strength was already failing. Through these wild forests— which the long story we have to tell will not suffer us to describe beyond saying that they are trackless and mapless —they struggled for two whole days; aided humanely, but stealthily, by the peasants, and not interfered with by what we should call the county police. Sometimes, indeed, the latter rendered aid.

The wolves of Austria were again upon the track: they had missed their real prey, whatever else they might have gained. The men captured in the boats were nothing to them, except for liberty of insult, which is the proudest gratification of innate brutality; all they wanted was the General and his wife—the proclaimed ones. For them they strained all their powers.

Anita was sinking. Love to her husband she had shewn far beyond the point usually found in our frail nature. When she took the oath of affection she was a true and perfect woman; and being a true woman then, she could not be false at any other time or in any other circumstances. She did not marry for home, support, honour, rest, troops of friends, wealth, and all the externals of comfort. She married from love and sympathy, and had indeed passed through a career which some man will one day relate to her renown, but which it is beyond our power now to dwell upon. She was still devoted to the cause which her husband served—the liberty of the old centre of religion and art, Italy; she remained thoroughly faithful to the husband who had chosen her; and her mother's heart clung to the

unborn child and those in the old house at home.   Then
again, the uncertainty concerning Padre Bassi and the other
brave Monte Videans, and those new friends gained in
Europe; whether they were dead or alive, whether imprisoned or maltreated, and beyond that, the sad look-out
into a future which must for a time dim the glory and hide
the worth of her dear husband, the diminution, if not the
deprivation, of those supplies without which life is impossible
—all these troubles weighed upon her.   She could not be
reproachful : when the world reviled, she would not revile :
she certainly would not utter a word, to even the dearest
friend, of any suspicion concerning the imprudence of one
man engaging the four European Powers in single combat.
Not she.   If by faith she could not, or he could not be
saved, she would rather die.

She was sinking at last.   When the third day of their
flight arrived, Anita made sign that she could go no
further.

Poor Garibaldi and his friend sprang to her assistance, and
carried her to a homestead not very far off, to assert the
claims of humanity in distress by asking for food and
help.

They had not got far on their errand before they learnt
from some fishermen that the enemy was in the neighbourhood in earnest search.   They were compelled to flee at
once in an opposite direction; but a private gentleman in
the neighbourhood provided a small travelling carriage, and
that aided them to flee several hours beyond the reach of
the bloodhounds on their track.

But it was evident to them all that premature confinement
was her lot.   While making their way beside a small stream,
which runs not far from Chioggia, Anita was suddenly
seized with the pains of childbirth, and fainted.   Garibaldi
rushed to her aid, taking her in his arms.   He carried her to
a cottage, where dwelt some touch of mercy and goodness,

and laid her on a bed.   The neighbours sent off to the town
for a physician, but the devoted woman, after faintly asking
of her husband something to allay her thirst, expired before
the doctor could arrive.   Mother and child were at rest.

> " Dead for Italia, not in vain has died,
>   Though many vainly, ere life's struggle ceased,
>   To mad dissimilar ends have swerved aside ;
>   Each grave her nationality has pierced
> By its majestic breadth, and fortified
>   And pinned it deeper to the soil.   Forlorn
> Of thanks, be, therefore, no one of these graves !
>   Not hers—who at her husband's side, in scorn,
> Outfaced the whistling shot and hissing waves,
>   Until she felt her little babe unborn
> Recoil within her, from the violent slaves
>   And bloodhounds of the world—at which, her life
> Dropp'd inward from her eyes and followed it
>   Beyond the hunters.   Garibaldi's wife
> And child died so.   And now the sea-weeds fit
>   Her body like a proper shroud and coif,
> And murmurously the ebbing waters grit
>   The little pebbles, where she lies interred
> In the sea-sand.   Perhaps ere dying thus,
>   She looked up in his face (which never stirred
> From its clenched anguish) as to make excuse
>   For leaving him for his: if so she erred
> He well remembers that she could not choose."

Garibaldi's heart was stricken.   All his grand life since
that time has the evidence of that day stamped thereon.   His
precious true-hearted wife was dead, just when he hoped
for a new life to be given in token of coming good.   The
fountain of tears was sealed : he had passed that consolation.
Deep called unto deep : all the waves and billows rolled over
and back upon his heart.   Those who saw him years after,
when he passed triumphantly through London, could have
no difficulty in tracing the lines of that sorrowful day.   The
farmer on whose hospitality he had entrenched very kindly
permitted the use of his field for a burial-place, and with his

friend's aid he there deposited, " in sure and certain hope," his best earthly treasure. Garibaldi begged that this resting-place might not be made known. He hoped that no harm would come to his host from rendering him assistance, and he also hoped for better times, when he might redeem the body of his beloved out of the hand of the spoiler, and place it near his future home.

It is the most touching part of Garibaldi's eventful and sorrowful life ; an episode, too, which history will preserve as an ineffaceable blot upon the honour of Austria. We used no metaphor in saying that our hero and his wife had had to flee from the pursuit of bloodhounds; for it was thus that the ruthless Gorzgowski followed the track of the fugitive Italian and the pregnant woman. The hounds soon discovered the resting-place of Anita ; and, maddened at the loss of their victims, the brutal Austrians wreaked their vengeance on the hospitable peasant who had harboured the dying woman. *He was hung, drawn, and quartered* on his own homestead !

To stay at his wife's grave was impossible for our hero unless he wanted to die : and indeed many men under less distressing trials have destroyed themselves. But his energy was unabated. He determined on starting again, and finishing his work in the world. To that end he struck off into the woods, aiming to reach Sardinia. During thirty-five days he wandered in various disguises among the woods, mountains, and caves of the Apennines, sometimes receiving hospitable shelter in the farmhouses of the country through which he passed ; for there were some who were not afraid to " obey God rather than man," by giving shelter to a solitary and sorrowing man, whose only idea in life was disinterested devotion to his maltreated country. Sometimes he had no place to lay his head. Sometimes, like David in Engedi, pursued by Saul, he found it necessary to hide in caves in the day and journey by night.

IIis name was always a power. Italians could not betray *him.* The country was swarming with Austrians, and money was ready for the man who would bring him in, but the country-folk scouted the idea. They shewed him where the path was safe, and where it was dangerous; and aided in any way they could, changing clothes with him, feeding him, harbouring him, anything to render service to their friend and benefactor. The great privation of thirty-five days under such conditions can be felt—if a man does not die of exhaustion in the process—but they can never be described. There was often no food to be had: he was too self-denying to ask more than shelter. The wild fruits of the woods, and herbs fit for human food, were his supply. Many of the poor people could not have fed him. With them in so many places he left a memorandum of their kindness to him under such privations, and these are preserved with affectionate care.

After all these hardships he contrived to reach Porto Venere, a small harbour in Piedmont, having only his one faithful friend with him, on the 5th September, and his arrival caused the greatest excitement. IIis long march, his many adventures and escapes, the terrible sufferings which he had endured, had centred upon him the interest of all men.

From Porto Venere he proceeded to Spezzia, and thence to Chiavari, where he arrived in the evening. Notwithstanding the late hour, he was recognised, and a crowd assembled around him. The intendant immediately proceeded to the spot and begged him to avoid causing disturbance, and to stay there until communications with the Piedmontese Government could be made, for which he would instantly apply. The orders of the Ministry came very speedily, and a captain of the Gendarmerie was instantly despatched to Chiavari to invite Garibaldi to let himself be conducted to Genoa, where he might remain in safety until means were found for his departure to some foreign country.　With characteristic deference to the will of the government he cheerfully complied.　The news having spread that he was about to leave, and at whose request, many came about him to satisfy their curiosity, perhaps, or to shew their sympathy: these he requested to leave as a matter of prudence, and to maintain order, observing that popular demonstrations under existing circumstances could only do him harm.　Piedmont could not then have him avowedly resident in the Sardinian States; but she determined on treating him with every consideration, and to render all the necessary aid to his departure for any foreign country he might prefer.　But meanwhile he was, of course, under arrest, but it was the arrest of protection

VIEW OF NICE

CHAPTER VII.

IN EXILE.

" O well for him whose will is strong !
  He suffers, but he will not suffer long ;
  He suffers, but he cannot suffer wrong :
  For him nor moves the loud world's random mock,
  Nor all Calamity's hugest waves confound,
  Who seems a promontory of rock,
  Compassed round with turbulent sound,
  Tempest-buffeted, citadel crowned."
—TENNYSON.

IT soon transpired at Genoa that Garibaldi would leave there for Nice on board the *San Giorgio* steamer. Crowds assembled at the port, and many took to small boats for the purpose of seeing and cheering him. These boats waited an hour round about the steamer, when she suddenly put on steam and moved towards the outlet of the port. The people asked the sailors whether he was on board, and they declared he was not. However, before leaving the port she stopped, and a boat left the *San Michaele* frigate, and approached. The people saw it, and set up the cry, "There's Garibaldi ! pull away ! Viva Garibaldi !" Before they could get close she was under way; but they were in time to know that he was on board.

His visit to Nice was to see his mother. Heaven only can know how ardently his heart yearned for that joy, after so many and such personal sorrows as he had undergone. It was arranged that he should return in twenty-four hours. His language, according to the semi-official papers of the date, was constantly that of one who thoroughly understood

12

the necessities of the political situation of Piedmont and Rome, and who, above all things, sought to avoid anything like discord. Not only did he desire to see his aged mother, but at Nice were his children. He was on his parole. He went about freely through the town, and on the 13th returned tc Genoa. Immediately after landing he returned on board the *San Giorgio*.

From thence he wrote thus to one of his friends :—

"MY DEAR FRIEND,—I am to sail to-morrow for Tunis on board the *Tripoli*. I have seen what you have done for me, and what your generous colleagues have done. Convey to them my expressions of gratitude. I have no cause of complaint against any one. Our times, I believe, require resignation, for they are times of bitterness. Remember me to all who bravely defend the Italian cause, and love your   "GIUSEPPE GARIBALDI."

He was informed by the Royal Commissioners that he would leave for Sardinia and go thence to Tunis, but that in two or three months the temporary exile would end, if the public tranquillity remained undisturbed.

But on reaching Tunis he was not permitted to land. The French had intervened by an envoy, and influenced the authorities. The Bey of Tunis kindly offered a steamer which should proceed to Malta; but Garibaldi declined, for he remembered that some Italian refugees had not been received there on a previous occasion. The Sardinian vessel had turned back as far as to Cagliari, where he arrived on the 22nd. After being quarantined for two days he landed at the small island Maddalena, and there had his freedom upon parole under Colonel Focchi.

When Sardinia exiled her best friend, whom she had not enough courage to acknowledge, he accepted the order without out a murmur, and refusing the many offers of money which came to him, determined, with an empty pocket, to fall back upon himself. He sought employment. He took up his commission and agency life at the various seaports, just as when he had returned to Monte Video from the revolution in Uruguay. But trade happened to be bad, and he did not get enough to live upon. What was to be done? Rome had gone from the grasp of its best friend, the combination of self-interested reigning families had overwhelmed the man who dared them; his companion and consolation had left him for the "land of the leal," and he remained alone, a mere "bagman," asking by work to earn bread! The bagman's work did not produce enough. He made up his mind to emigrate to America, and took up his residence for a time in New York.

Spini writes of this incident: "In one of the obscure streets of New York there was, in 1850, a small candle-factory, by the side of which was a tobacconist's shop, kept by General Avezzana, formerly Minister of War, who now sold cigars to support himself in exile. One of Garibaldi's friends, an officer in the Genoese navy, happened to come to New York, and his first care was to see him. He came up to the candle-factory and found him with his shirt-sleeves turned up, busied in one corner of the shop in dipping wicks attached to short rods into a pan of boiling tallow.

" 'Ah,' said he, 'I am glad to see you.'

" 'And I should be glad to shake hands if you don't mind the tallow. You have come at a critical time. I have just settled a difficulty in navigation which has worried me ever so long.'

"Then he forthwith narrated the formula of the problem and stated his solution, saying cheerfully:

" 'How singularly humorous it is that all this came out of a cauldron of tallow! But never mind. I am weary of this occupation, and have a strong desire to go to sea, where, I am sure, we shall meet again.'

"In this wretched capacity of candle-making he was not exempt from the insulting remarks of New York City; nor would he have been alone had those remarks or observations been tenfold more violent.   A distinguished member of the late German Parliament was then constrained to accept the work of a barber to save his wife and two children from starvation.   A popular representative of the French Assembly was selling cabbages in the streets ; another, Miot, had by their insults been driven to Boston because he was starving, and there he died from want.   They were with glee anticipating the pleasurable arrival of Ledru Rollin as a shore-porter, Louis Blanc as a dancing-master, Felix Pyat as a scene-shifter, and Lamartine as a mendicant ; and they urged that these presumptive appointments were honourable and appropriate to the European peoples.   It will, therefore, excite no surprise that under a homicide like Sickles, who has since acquired a memorable notoriety in the annals of murder, but was then only noted as supported by the most profligate woman in their city ; a select body of them assembled to mock Garibaldi at his 'melting tub,' while a body of venal wretches belonging to their press, comprising a Scotch vagabond named Bennett, a noseless knave who bore the designation of Raymond, and a strange compound of idiocy and rascality named Greeley, who had duped the expatriated Irish out of 30,000 dollars on the pretext of once more raising insurrection in their native land, daily insulted him with their jibes.

"This Sickles, enjoying in a special degree the protection of the American bench, under the auspices of a pettifogger, who subsequently saved him from the gibbet, was, moreover, amply provided with funds by the despotic governments of Europe, for the purpose of hunting down those who, after passing their lives in vain resistance to tyranny at home, had been constrained to seek shelter in exile when they could resist no longer.   Garibaldi felt in vain to apply to the law for protection ; and he, accordingly, quitted the city in disgust, when he at last found it irksome to move about armed with a 'bowie-knife' by day, and to sleep with his revolver in his hand. Sacrificing the remainder of his property, to the infinite satisfaction of the rapacious natives, he set sail for South America."

Here lived many of his countrymen. They had become more numerous and influential since the time when he dwelt among them, and held the merchant trade and shipping pretty much in their own hands. Many of the smaller traders of his country were in the city of Lima, and what attracted Garibaldi thither most of all was the circumstance that many emigrants who had been among his volunteers had gone thither. When the news of his probable visit was bruited about, a meeting of Italians and the men of Genoa and Naples was called, and it was determined to send a deputation to Callao, the port of landing, and give him a triumphal entry into Lima. This was accordingly done. There was their brave chief, looking as of yore, with his long beard and long hair, wearing a broad-brimmed felt hat, and a short puce-coloured loose tunic belted at the waist. So he passed up the main street amid the tumultuous cheers of the population, bearing his honour with the same meekness as he had borne his sorrows, but grateful for the sympathetic gladness of his friends.

He settled there for a couple of years engaged in merchant traffic, a friend having offered him the command of a vessel trading from thence to China, a work that better suited his disposition and capacity than the occupation he had had in New York ; and when that voyage ended he visited Genoa in 1854, in an American trading vessel, and carefully watched the phases of politics as they then appeared, and learned the particulars of what had transpired in his absence. For the supply of his wants he followed a sea-faring life, running a steamer from Nice to Marseilles, and spending his time continually on the water in the vigorous fulfilment of the duties and responsibilities of his position, busy on the wharfs and quays, and too much intent on work to excite any observation or to engage public attention.

By diligence and tact he realised a respectable sum, and with it purchased his little farm at Caprera.   There, throwing aside the sword, he took up the plough, and laboured with his own hands in the intervals of his continual merchant trading between Nice and Genoa and elsewhere.   But he did not forsake politics.   He began to see the possibility of Piedmont yet being in a position to redeem Italy ; and without separating himself from his somewhat extreme but beloved friends, he determined to do all he could for the national cause in connection with the growing influence of the King of Sardinia.

It was in the year 1854 that he returned to Europe, and responding to a warm invitation from the men of Newcastle-on-Tyne, he visited them on his way.   Having kindly but firmly declined any public demonstration, it was resolved to present him with an address of welcome and sympathy, accompanied by a sword and telescope, to be purchased by a penny subscription.   The proposal, when made public, was received with great enthusiasm, demands for subscription lists coming in from all parts, and the expressions of approval and sympathy being warm and numerous.

The presentation took place on board his ship, at Shields, on Tuesday, 11th April, the day before he sailed.

The sword was a handsome weapon, with a gold hilt, on which this inscription was engraved :—"Presented to General Garibaldi by the people of Tyneside, friends of European Freedom, Newcastle-on-Tyne, April 1854."   The telescope bore the same inscription.

In replying to the address presented, and thanking them for their gifts, Garibaldi said :—

"One of the people—a workman like yourselves—I value very highly these expressions of your esteem ; the more so because you testify thereby your sympathy for my poor oppressed and down-trodden country. Speaking in a strange tongue, I feel most painfully my inability to thank you in terms sufficiently warm.

"The future will alone shew how soon it will be before I am called on to unsheath the noble gift I have just received, and again battle in behalf of that which lies nearest my heart—the freedom of my native land. But be sure of this: Italy will one day be a nation, and its free citizens will know how to acknowledge all the kindness shewn her exiled sons in the days of their darkest troubles.

"Gentlemen, I would say more, but my bad English prevents me. You can appreciate my feelings, and understand my hesitation. Again I thank you from my heart of hearts ; and be confident of this, that whatever vicissitudes of fortune I may hereafter pass through, this handsome sword shall never be drawn by me except in the cause of liberty."

CHAPTER VIII.

WAR WITH AUSTRIA.

" Ev'n now we hear with inward strife
    A motion toiling in the gloom—
    The spirit of the years to come
Yearning to mix himself with life.

A slow-developed strength awaits
    Completion in a painful school ;
    Phantoms of other forms of rule,
New Majesties of mighty States.

The warders of the growing hour,
    But vague in vapour, hard to mark ;
    And round them sea and air are dark
With great contrivances of power."

                                   —TENNYSON.

IT has been the good fortune of Italy, and the reward of
all the services which she had rendered to civilisation,
that even in the most sombre period of her history,
and when her children were separated by governments interested in maintaining mutual distrust and animosity, all
who were not engrossed, like the ox in the furrow, by the
memory or the actuality of grief, saw on the horizon a
purified image of an united Italy ; and the breath of evening
brought home to every rising generation the dreams and
ambitions of the poets, of the writers who called their
country into existence, crying to her with the voice of filial
piety : "Mother, come forth from thy tomb !" Before
diplomacy and success in the field had liberated Italy, poets
and authors had aroused the desire and passion for independence, the aspiration to be free and united.   From the

Florentine who sets in the circles of his *Paradiso* those who delivered Italy from the stranger, to the impassioned verses of Giusti, one and the same cry has ever issued from the hearts of the oppressed: "Fuori Barbari!" Out with the foreigners! ("Non vogliam Tedeschi?") We will have no Germans! It was amidst these circumstances and with these thoughts that Cavour awoke to manhood. With him Italian patriotism enters upon a new phase; it leaves behind the shadow of conspiracy, wherein so much devotion and heroism have been expended at an absolute loss; it renounces revolutionary agencies, in order to shew that the independence of Italy is a question of European order, and enlists public opinion in its interest.

Cavour was not one of those reckless men who would set Europe on fire to get themselves out of a difficulty. He had the patience of a firm, resolute man who relies upon the justice of his cause, and has no reason to call into existence accidents and chances in order to bring his long-ripening plans to issue. If fortune does not seek us out in our sleep, she ever avoids the imprudent capricious people who would take her by storm, unable to wait until the force of circumstances causes the object of their ambition to fall into their hands. Austria made a point of soothing his impatience, and hastening the issue which he desired. Boasting in her veteran armies, renowned for their discipline, accustomed to dictate her will throughout Italy, whose princes were her vassals and dependents, she could no longer endure the spectacle of this petty State becoming day after day the arsenal of liberty, the refuge of all who had sworn the oath of Hannibal against her tyranny in Italy. As sometimes happens with tyrants whose power begins to totter, she did not resist the temptation to assert her will, never striving to keep up the appearance of legality and the sympathies of the European courts. Suddenly throwing over existing treaties, she no longer concealed that she was organising a crusade in favour of absolutism against liberal Europe, and summoned Piedmont to disarm.

Later on, when circumstances brought their contrasted natures into opposition and strife, Cavour shewed his intellectual superiority by forbidding the passion and resentment which murmured round about him to despise the pure character and real greatness of the leader of the Thousand.

"Garibaldi," he said, "is a man by himself; his ways are peculiarly his own; others would not do what he does, and he could not do what others do. Garibaldi is more than a general; he is a banner. We have misunderstood each other for the moment; and I am sure that, if there were no one between us, we should understand one another again."

Such, then, was the statesman who had brought about the second great struggle between Piedmont and Austria; who had spent a decade in preparing for it, and who had strained every nerve in deserving the success which he attained. We rob Garibaldi of none of his glory by giving Cavour his due; and the following pages will amply prove how indispensable the soldier-patriot was to the triumph of the diplomatist.

The time had come when Cavour's patient labours were to bear their fruit, and when, moreover, by a fortunate coincidence, the ambition and policy of Louis Napoleon ensured the co-operation of France and Sardinia against their common enemy Austria. It was not without a view to this contingency that Cavour had forced his country into alliance with England and France during the Crimean war, whereof one result had been to wipe out on the field of battle the rankling memories of 1849, and to familiarise French and Italian soldiers with the idea of fighting side by side. The Sardinian Government left no opportunity of letting all Italy understand how necessary to them, and how useful would be the co-operation of France, " without which

Sardinia's position would be a forlorn one, England's friendly attitude having given place to decided indifference." On one occasion Cavour stated, in the Chamber of Deputies, that as early as 1849 Napoleon had desired to aid Sardinia in a war against Austria. Than which, indeed, there were many things more improbable. ∟

In the year 1858 the relations between Sardinia and Naples were much disturbed from causes into which we need not enter. Whatever these were, there can be small doubt that Cavour rather kept the sore open than attempted to close it; and one advantage of this somewhat Machiavellian conduct was that a colourable pretext was afforded for the continued armament of Sardinia, which had already excited grave jealousy and alarm on the part of Austria. Moreover, Cavour was by this time perfectly ready for the outbreak of hostilities, and it was in exact accordance with his provisions that the Government of Vienna now gave him to understand that an attack upon Naples by Sardinia would be considered by Austria as a " cause of war."

After these events, and these unmistakable forewarnings, no time was lost by either country in making itself ready for immediate action. Austria was sorely crippled in her resources, and an attempt to raise six millions sterling in London was successful only to the extent of about one-fifth of the amount. Sardinia contracted a loan of two millions, granted an amnesty to her political and military prisoners, and made no secret of the news that before the end of March she would be able to place 120,000 men in the field. Cavour sent for Garibaldi, as we have already stated, and gave him the rank of general of division, relying upon the noble free-lance to raise his own troops, which was effected without the slightest difficulty. No sooner was it known that our hero would work in hearty concert with the king than volunteers flocked in to his standard from all parts of the country, and especially from the Lombardo-Venetian provinces, where men were eager for the opportunity of fighting against Austria.   At Coni, Garibaldi raised and trained three battalions of troops, the nucleus of a force which was to do effective service in the coming war, under the title of the Alpine Chasseurs (Cacciatori degl' Alpi).   France also busily prepared her contingent, mobilising five *corps d'armée* —one consisting of Imperial Guards—and three regiments of artillery.   Austria, with no less alacrity, managed by immense sacrifices and labour to mass six divisions in Lombardy and Venice, so as to be prepared for any violation of the peace which might be attempted by Sardinia.

On the 27th, after a solemn service in the capital, attended by the king and his ministers, Victor Emmanuel's staff received marching orders for Alessandria, and the king's proclamation to the army appeared.

The die was cast, and the war began.   We cannot attempt in these pages to follow it in detail, or to do much more than indicate the part which Garibaldi took in it.   His Alpine Chasseurs numbered originally 4500 men, consisting of representatives of every State in Italy, and of more than one foreign country—the Poles amongst them.   A small contingent of Romans had arrived, bringing 200 horses and 30,000 scudi; but the bulk of the "Cacciatori" were Lombards and Venetians, who fought not merely for the ultimate unification of Italy, but for the immediate liberation of their own home from a hated yoke.   Our hero was left almost complete liberty in the disposition and handling of his force; for the king and his advisers knew that his genius lay in irregular action, in rapid surprises, in unfettered enthusiasm, rather than in the subordination of scientific warfare.

Garibaldi's movements were entirely characteristic of him.   The Austrians had massed their force upon their left, anticipating an attack from the French on the road from Alessandria.   Seizing the opportunity, our hero pushed in haste towards the north, crossing the Ticino, and advancing some fifteen miles in the direction of Como. It would have been easy for Gyulai to divide him from the Piedmontese army, and thus ensure his destruction, so that the movement of the volunteer General cannot be said to have been either sound or safe. His object was not—it need hardly be said—to turn the flank of the Austrians, but principally to excite the Lombards of the west to take up arms; and in this he was to a great extent successful. At Varese he issued the following proclamation :—

"LOMBARDS ! You are called to a new life, and you will respond to the appeal, as your fathers did of yore at Ponsida and Legnago. The enemy is the same as ever, pitiless, a black assassin and a robber. Your brethren in every province have sworn to conquer or to die with you. It is our task to avenge the insults, the outrages, and the servitude of twenty generations : it is for us to leave to our children a patrimony freed from the pollution of a foreign domination. Victor Emmanuel, chosen by the national will for our supreme chief, sends me to organise you for this patriotic fight. I deeply feel the sanctity of this mission, and I am proud to command you. To arms ! Then bondage must cease. He who can seize a weapon, and does not, is a traitor. Italy, with her children united, and freed from foreign domination, will now know how to recover by conquest the rank which Providence has assigned her among the nations."

Garibaldi left Turin with three thousand seven hundred men ; and the day after his departure he quitted Biella and proceeded to Borgomanero, where he passed the night and part of the next day. He then prepared his plans, and put them in harmony with the instructions he had received from headquarters. The principal object was to cross the Ticino, and effect the passage and invasion without danger to himself or his men. He knew that all these men risked their lives, inasmuch as, before becoming soldiers, they were

refugees, and by bearing arms they incurred, according to
the Austrian Code, the penalty of death. He accordingly
spread the report that he intended to stop at Arona, and he
even wrote himself to have stores and lodgings prepared
there, and the churches fitted up for the reception of horses.
No sooner had he sent off these orders by special messengers
to Arona, which is on the Lago Maggiore, than he gave
orders to his men, each of whom carried two muskets, to
leave for Castelletto, where they crossed the Ticino in a
ferry-boat on the 24th May, to Sesto Calende, and by a
forced march proceeded to Varese. The Austrians, on
learning how they had been tricked, assembled at Calarata,
and intercepted the line of the Ticino at Varese, believing
that they would thereby cut off the retreat of the force and
surprise it. Garibaldi troubled himself little about that proceeding, and induced the towns and villages to revolt. His
success in this was so great that he had to write to the king
for eight thousand muskets and eight thousand great-coats.
Foreseeing, however, an attack on Varese, he barricaded the
town—which does not mean that he barricaded himself in
the town. That done, he left two hundred of his men, and
they, with the assistance of the population, heroically resisted
the Austrians, who soon attacked the place. In the meantime he marched with the main body of his army from the
town towards the hills; and some time afterwards, surprising the enemy in flank, defeated and routed them. The
Austrians retired in great disorder, and only re-formed at
Camerlata, a very important position, from which Como can
be defended without great loss. But Garibaldi scarcely left
them time to count themselves, as he attacked them again,
and after a sharp combat, in which many of their officers
were killed, dislodged them.

Accounts differ with respect to the conduct of both sides
in this brief episode of the war; but the following well-
authenticated anecdote may be construed by the discerning

reader as explaining such a natural and only too familiar discrepancy. Garibaldi, on being told that the Austrians, having laid their hands on one of his followers, broken down by fatigue near Varese, had hung him on the nearest tree, exclaimed: "The cowards! I will sift this story to the bottom, and if I find it true, I will shoot every Austrian officer that I have made prisoner." Money, so much wanted at other times, poured into Garibaldi's military treasury, together with gold necklaces and other valuable trinkets from fair Lombard ladies. In two days the sum collected reached 2,000,000 francs.

Faithful to his promises, Garibaldi had no sooner returned to Como, after having beaten the Austrians, than he marched southwards to aid the allied armies of France and Italy.

The main body of the Austrians, after recrossing the Ticino and the Naviglio 'Grande, a ship canal running parallel with the river, halted at Magenta, half-way between Novara and Milan, where it was considerably reinforced by the arrival of Clam-Gallas with the first *corps d'armée;* Gyulai's plan being, it is alleged, to turn and attack the allies on the 5th of June. But the latter did not wait for him to offer battle.

The van of the French army reached Novara from the south-west on the 1st of June. Hence the forces were separated into two divisions; the road through Trecate to the bridge of San Martino being followed by the divisions of Generals Wimpffen, Clerc, Martimprey, d'Angely, Niel, Vinoy, Canrobert, and Trochu, in the order named; whilst Generals MacMahon and Espinasse marched to a higher point of the Ticino, where they were to construct a bridge and cross over to Turbigo, so as to join General Cialdini, and move down upon Magenta from the North. Napoleon himself was with the Guards, under Martimprey and d'Angely; and upon them devolved the first and most critical part of this sanguinary battle. On the morning of the 4th of June the Emperor himself gave the order to cross the bridge over the Ticino, and from thence to push forward to the Ponte di Magenta over the Naviglio Grande. It was between these two lines of water that the Imperial Guard had to bear the brunt of a powerful and murderous attack from the enemy, whilst there was as yet no sign of MacMahon's approach from the north, and whilst the divisions of Canrobert and Trochu were still far in the rear. As it happened, perhaps this bold, and, as some think, premature commencement of hostilities by the Guards won the battle of Magenta ; but if they had been driven back across the Ticino it is not improbable that the Austrians might have gained a decisive victory.

The second French corps had had some trouble at Turbigo and Cuggione, and south of the latter place it was threatened by Clam-Gallas, who, with a little more activity, might have cut of the lagging division of Espinasse from the more advanced forces of MacMahon and Cialdini, and so have taken the latter in the rear. But the Austrian missed this opportunity, and the sound of French guns at Buffalora soon gladdened the hearts of Napoleon and his generals. Meanwhile, Canrobert, Trochu, and Vinoy had crossed the Ticino, and turned the fate of the struggle at Ponte di Magenta. The weakness of the Austrian generalship on this eventful day was almost incredible. It was not until two o'clock in the afternoon that Gyulai, who had been informed at an early hour of the French movements, thought fit to mount his horse and leave his headquarters at Abbiate Grasso for Magenta ; of course too late to do any good.

All the afternoon the battle raged fiercely on the banks of the canal. Seven times was the bridge lost and won; but at length the Austrians retired upon Magenta. During this retrograde movement they were taken in flank by a murderous fire from Espinasse's artillery ; and in Magenta itself a terrible *mêlée* ensued. The slaughter was vast on both sides, and it was not until eight P.M. that the village was fairly in the hands of the French. It was then that the Austrians felt themselves, for the moment at least, beaten, and they retired along the Milan road.

Next morning Gyulai ordered a fresh attack, but nothing came of it. Clam-Gallas and Leichtenstein had seen more clearly than their leader the real significance of the battle of Magenta, and when, on the 5th of June, Gyulai ordered Hartung and the Hessian troops to advance, he was in actual ignorance of the position of Clam-Gallas, who steadily pursued his march towards Milan ! The Austrians were therefore soon recalled, and the retreat soon became general.

The fact is not to be denied, as a contemporary writer points out, that through this affair on the Ticino "Lombardy was lost to the Austrian crown." The only hope now lay in the line of the Mincio, in the neighbourhood of the famous quadrilateral formed by the fortresses of Verona, Peschiera, Mantua, and Legnago.

"The day after, the Emperor Louis Napoleon and the King of Sardinia made their triumphal entry into Milan, amid cries of exultation and welcome, and a state of excitement difficult to describe ; a sort of delirium seemed to have seized the people.

"Victor Emmanuel expressed himself with unmistakable clearness :—'Inhabitants of Lombardy ! The right of nations re-established, let your voices be heard in favour of a union with my kingdom.' He spoke of the sacrifices which Sardinia had already made for the common cause, and urged the Lombards at once to recognise the fact and the consequences of their deliverance from the Austrian yoke."

In the meantime Garibaldi, with his Chesseurs of the

Alps, was always in advance of the left flank of the Allies, rousing and organising the country on the southern slopes of the Alps, recruiting and following on the heels of the enemy. Before the Allies entered Milan he was in Lecco, on the eastern branch of Lake Como; before they had crossed the river he appeared at Bergamo; and while they were crossing the river Adda he appeared at Brescia.

The Austria's now withdrew, in three large columns, behind the Alps. In the centre was General Benedek, who was retreating in the direction of Lodi. On the right wing was Urban, who operated the passage of the Adda at Canonica and Cassano, not, however, without being somewhat annoyed by the French. On the left wing marched the main body of the Austrians, along the left bank of the Po, crossing the Adda below Pizzighettone. The head-quarters were established at Casatigozzi, on the road from Cremona. The line of retreat on to the left bank of the Mincio was in no way threatened. The communications, however, lying more northward than the direction the Austrian army was following—*e.g.*, that going off towards Goito, or even that leading to Peschiera—seemed imperilled; for Garibaldi had pushed forward as far as Bergamo, and was making preparations, amid the acclamations of the insurgent population, for marching *via* Brescia towards the Lake of Garda—an undertaking that, in spite of the five thousand men and four guns at the disposal of the guerilla chieftain, must be designated as a very bold one, as it exposed the little band on its march to the danger of being attacked in the flank from troops descending from the Tyrol.

The more immediate danger for Garibaldi lay, however, in the approach of Urban's flying corps. In spite of his numerical inferiority, Garibaldi determined, on the 15th of June, to attack the troops under Urban, and at Castelnedolo the advanced corps of the two parties came to blows. The numbers engaged were not inconsiderable: Garibaldi had drawn to his aid Piedmontese troops of the brigade Voghera, which rendered his corps more of a match for the Austrians.

The Garibaldini had strongly occupied all farmhouses in the neighbourhood of Castelnedolo that admitted of a hasty barricading, &c., and pushed forward a corps of sharp-shooters, shewing a determination to attempt to cut off the Austrians from their line of retreat on Montechiaro. The conflict became very sanguinary. By an attack on the enemy's front the Austrians could obtain no advantage whatever; on the contrary, this turned out much to their prejudice. Major von Bourguignon therefore attempted, at the head of the 3rd battalion of the Archduke Rainer infantry, a squadron of Haller hussars, and a detachment of artillery, to turn the enemy's position and disperse the Piedmontese reserves.

In the meantime Major von Welsersheimb, with a battalion of the regiment Rainer, and Major Schmidt, with the 1st battalion of the regiment Zobel, had got into a very critical position. These battalions were completely surrounded by the Garibaldini, and were being decimated by ball and bayonet. They kept well together, however, till Bourguignon's artillery was heard in the direction of Civilerghe, and the jäger of the 19th battalion, together with the infantry regiment Keller, came up and broke the destructive cordon of the foe round Welsersheimb's and Schmidt's troops, whereupon the Garibaldini retired once more to the farm-houses. The conflict lasted some four hours, till at length Garibaldi, feeling his numerical inferiority, withdrew his men out of the battle, and made a retreat on Brescia. Several small detachments in the farm-houses were not quick enough in their movements, and fell into the hands of the Austrians. These latter, however, did not push forward beyond Civilerghe and Treponti, but on the advance of Cialdini with a part of his division to the aid of Garibaldi, retired slowly, and soon after evacuated

Castelnedolo, attempting to destroy the bridge over the Chiesa, at Bertoletto, which was, however, soon rendered passable again by the Piedmontese and Garibaldini.

The famous leader who with his daring movements had astonished Europe had already been rewarded by the "Gallant King." An order of the day, dated Milan, the 8th June, conferred upon him the gold medal of military valour. A life pension of five hnndred francs is always granted to those who are deemed worthy of that distinction.

The award of these honours gave great satisfaction to the people of Lombardy, because it shewed Victor Emmanuel's recognition of all the great services which had been rendered by Garibaldi's force to the main army.

Steadily and cautiously the allied armies continued to roll on after the retreating masses of the Austrians, who abandoned successively the lines of the Adda, the Oglio, the Chiese ; the French marching on the right, the Piedmontese on the left, and Garibaldi acting with them on the north, till on the 22nd of June, Lonato and Castaglione were occupied by the allied troops, and the Austrian army crossed the Mincio to the eastern side.

The Emperor of Austria had now resumed the command-in-chief of the army, and his headquarters were at Villafranca, which lies within the famous quadrilateral, and not far from the famous town of Oustozza. The battle of Solferino was fought on the 24th June. The Austrian army numbered about 170,000 men, and the allied forces were not less than 150,000, two of the largest armies that had ever come into conflict in modern times. The Emperor of Austria in person was opposed to the Emperor of the French and the King of Sardinia.

The battle commenced about five o'clock in the morning, when the Emperor Napoleon, who was at Montechiaro, proceeded in haste to Castaglione, where the Imperial

Guard were to assemble. The main collision of these two vast armies took place about ten in the forenoon. The village and heights of Solferino, an exceedingly strong and commanding position, became the grand object of contention. Marshal Baraguay d'Hilliers directed the assaults, which were resisted with the greatest obstinacy, and sometimes repulsed, but the heights were at length won. The Piedmontese, advancing by Pozzolongo, were assailed by a strong Austrian force, which they successfully resisted, and at length won the heights of San Martino. Marshal MacMahon and General Niel were hotly engaged to the right of Marshal Baraguay d'Hilliers. Marshal Canrobert was chiefly occupied in keeping watch for an expected attack from Mantua. The Emperor Napoleon was seen everywhere, directing the operations.

The Emperor of Austria, who had occupied a house at Cavriana, quitted the field about four o'clock in the afternoon. The Austrian army then commenced its retreat, which was skilfully conducted, favoured for a time by a terrific storm of thunder, hail, and wind, which raged for nearly an hour. The fighting continued until about eight o'clock in the evening. The allies took 30 pieces of cannon and 7000 prisoners. The loss of the French in killed and wounded was 12,000 rank and file, and 720 officers. The loss of the Austrians was doubtless considerably more, but it was never made known. General Niel was created a Marshal of France.

Two great battles had been fought, but Austria had not been driven from Italy. There remained still the almost impregnable fortresses of the Quadrilateral. Besides, other European Powers began to look on the struggle with dismay. The intentions of Napoleon were more than doubtful, and English newspapers did not hesitate to say so. The German Confederation, fearing that the nephew was about to carry out the designs of his uncle, threatened an invasion of

France. Russia took a similar view of the situation. Prussia began to mobilise her army, but, as usual, declined to say for what purpose.   Lord John Russell, who was then English Secretary for Foreign Affairs, wrote a stirring despatch to Berlin, in which he said:—" Her Majesty's Government observes, with great concern, a disposition to take part in the war which has broken out between France and Sardinia on the one side, and Austria on the other.   The Emperor Napoleon has declared that he has no intention of attacking Germany.   It is hoped and believed that the Prince Regent (the present emperor) will not become a party to an attack upon France."   The Emperor Napoleon had become alarmed.   He had won two great battles.   But what might he not lose ?   He was uncertain of the action of Prussia, which might seize the opportunity to invade France.   He was uncertain as to his shattered armies taking the four great Austrian fortresses.   He was uncertain whether he had not already created a kingdom which might prove dangerous to France.   And he was uncertain whether that kingdom might not, in the end, extend itself from Sardinia to Rome.

To the great astonishment of Europe, Napoleon, who had already carried all before him, entered into negotiations with the Emperor Frances Joseph.   A truce was concluded at Villafranca on the 8th of July, by Marshal Vaillant and General Hess, by which the suspension of hostilities was to last for five weeks.

A council was at once called, and the Treaty of Villafranca was drawn up between the two emperors.   It is not necessary to give the whole of the facts.   The two sovereigns agreed to favour the creation of an Italian Confederation ; that the confederation should be under the honorary presidency of the Pope ; that certain boundary lines should be drawn (Austria ceding to France Lombardy, with the exception of the fortresses of Mantua and Peschiera) ; that the

French Emperor should hand over the ceded territory to the King of Sardinia; that Venetia should form part of the Italian Confederation, though remaining under the crown of Austria; that the Grand Duke of Tuscany and the Duke of Modena should return to their States, granting a general amnesty; that the two emperors should ask the Holy Father to introduce indispensable reforms into his States; and that a full and complete amnesty should be granted on both sides to persons compromised in the late events in the territories of the belligerent parties.

This preliminary contract was afterwards verified by a treaty of peace signed at Zurich, in the presence of the ambassadors of the several States. The treaty was condemned in the House of Lords by Lord Lyndhurst, who disputed the sincerity of Louis Napoleon. "If I am asked," said he, "if I can place reliance on the Emperor Napoleon, I reply with confidence that I cannot, because he is in a position in which he cannot place reliance on himself."

The design of the French Emperor was seen through by Lord John Russell, who wrote to Lord Cowley at Paris:—"Her Majesty has learned with concern that the question of annexing Savoy to France has been in agitation. If Savoy should be annexed to France, it will generally be supposed that the left bank of the Rhine and the natural limits will be the next object; and thus the emperor will become an object of suspicion in Europe, and kindle the hostility of which his uncle was the victim." On the 8th, Earl Cowley replied that, in the course of an interview he had had with Count Walewski (another creature of the imperial court), he assured the English ambassador that the emperor had abandoned all idea of annexing Savoy to France. Yet, on the 24th of March 1860, the treaty of annexation was signed. Comment on such perfidy would be superfluous.

The *Daily News* aptly summarised the designs of Napoleon:—"If a man is to receive praises in this world and

remission in the next, in consideration of all the offences he
has not committed ; if great criminals are to be pardoned
on account of all the harm they have left undone, why then
the author of the peace of Villafranca deserves the credit
done to peacemakers. Test the Emperor of the French by the
designs imputed to him last Easter, by the secret conspiracy
with Russia for the dismemberment of Europe—by the
projected invasion of England—by the descent upon Egypt
—the partition of Turkey—the capture of Malta, Gibraltar,
and Corfu—and a few other trifling enterprises, east and
west—and we cheerfully admit that Louis Napoleon has
well deserved of mankind for the clever feat of swerving
from the stone walls between the Mincio and the Adige.
He has, with impartial perfidy, disappointed his calumnia-
tors, and deceived his friends. . . . We see noble principles
prostituted, and substantial interests disturbed—for what?
To prove that an emperor can be a general without ever
having been a soldier, and that the art of war is more
easily learned than the arts of honesty and justice.
England is not without reproach in Italy, but we are thankful that, in the darkness of Villafranca, her hands at least
are clean."

CHAPTER IX.

GARIBALDI TO THE RESCUE.

'Alone in Garibaldi place thy trust ;
There shalt thou find a champion brave and Just."
—WALTER SAVAGE LANDOR.

THE first step of the authorities after the peace terms were published was a notification to the volunteers that they might depart to their homes: but in the perplexing uncertainty of affairs that order was temporarily countermanded. Garibaldi could not be brought to see its propriety, for his opinion went in the opposite direction. He, however, issued a proclamation to the army he conducted by an order of the day, dated 19th July 1859.

"Whatever direction political events may take, Italians ought not, under existing circumstances, either to lay down their arms or to feel any discouragement. On the contrary, they ought to enlarge their ranks, and shew to Europe that, led by the valiant Victor Emmanuel, they are ready to encounter anew the vicissitudes of war, whatever complexion they may assume."

As might be expected, after the hopes which had been raised in Sardinia and Lombardy, the rest of the peninsula was in a state of extreme agitation. Revolutions broke out in the States of Tuscany, Modena, and Parma—States in which despotism of the most painful type had been hereditary, and against which Mazzini strove with might and main. His proclamations were ceaseless. His fervent appeals were responded to by the youth of Italy, which, along with the whole of liberal Europe, turned round and called upon

Garibaldi as the liberator.   But Garibaldi was not satisfied
with the tortuous diplomatic arrangements which still left
Italy in slavery.   He therefore resigned his command.

"Finding," he said, "that by cunning device and vain
pretexts, my freedom of action is, by my rank in the army
of Central Italy, continually hampered—a freedom which I
have ever used for the object which every good Italian must
wish to attain—I leave the military service.   On the day
when Victor Emmanuel shall again call upon his soldiers to
fight for the deliverance of our country, I shall find an arm
of some kind or other, and a post by the side of my brave
companions in arms.   The miserable and tortuous policy
which for the moment troubles the majestic march of our
affairs, should engage us more than ever to rally round the
brave and loyal soldier of our independence, who is incapable
of repudiating the sublime and generous design which he has
conceived.   More than ever must we lay up stores of gold
and steel to prepare a good reception for whoever may
attempt to throw us back into our former miserable state."

Much dissatisfaction arose at the General's resignation.
The people were offended with the authorities, who, they
felt, had been treating their hero unworthily.

The fact was that Fanti, a strict military man, could not
endure the enthusiasm that filled the atmosphere of Garibaldi's presence.   He considered it evanescent, and preferred
to prescribe a perpetual drill as the best preparation for the
battle-field.   Garibaldi could make more dashing soldiers in
two months than the schools could in a year, and he could
infuse into them the moral element which mere military
men despise or disparage.   To that moral force Garibaldi
attributed the fine edge of his steel and the efficiency of his
guns.   Fanti preferred the mechanism of scientific military
education.

The king sent him, as a token of his personal appreciation
and regard, a handsome fowling-piece, which he himself had

used: for it happened that his leisure of only a few years before was relieved by shooting excursions among the little islands off the coasts of Sicily and Sardinia, one of which, Caprera, belonged to Garibaldi.

Bixio, his intimate friend, and several of the officers of the patriotic legions, resigned their commissions, and when our hero heard of it at Genoa, he issued the following:—

"To my companions in arms of Central Italy.

"Let not my temporary absence cool your ardour for the sacred cause you are determined to defend.

"My severance from you, whom I love as the representatives of Italian freedom, causes sadness, but I am consoled by the certainty that I shall soon be among you again, aiding in the completion of the work we have begun so gloriously. The truce must be short, for antique diplomacy is unable and indisposed to see things as they are. It regards you as a mere handful of malcontents which it has always despised. We desire to invade no foreign soil: let us remain unmolested on our own! Whoever attempts to gainsay this our determination will find that we will never be slaves, unless they succeed in crushing by force an entire people ready to die for liberty.

"But even should we all fall, we shall bequeath to future generations a legacy of hatred and vengeance against foreign domination. The inheritance of each of our sons will be a rifle, and the consciousness of his rights; and by the blessing of God the oppressor will never sleep soundly.

"Italians, I say again do not lay down your arms; rally more closely than ever to your chiefs, and maintain the strictest discipline. Fellow-citizens, let not a man in Italy omit to contribute his mite to the national subscription, let not one fail to clean his gun so as to be ready—perhaps to-morrow—to obtain by force that which to-day they hesitate to grant to our just rights.   "GARIBALDI."

The vexation he was suffering had its ordinary result in

his case—an attack of gout—which confined him to his bed for several days. As soon as a recovery commenced, his mental activity resumed its wonted supremacy, and he resolved to depart for Central Italy, taking with him those portions of the troops which adhered to him—the Chasseurs of the Alps and of the Apennines. He determined on moving from Lombardy exactly at the time it suited him, but gave permission for any of his faithful men to go and see their relatives and friends; but on no account would he extend the leave beyond two days.

The interval was occupied in communicating with the Tuscan and Modenese revolutionists as to the collecting of an army in those States, which would be ready to act there or in the Romagna. Every hour increased his intense restlessness.

The arrival of Garibaldi in the centre of Italy brought matters to a crisis. A defensive league of the States of Central Italy was formed as by magic, and the Legations joined it. The Florentines in their National Assembly voted unanimously the annexation of Tuscany to the Kingdom of Sardinia, and the following day the National Assembly of Modena resolved "to confirm at any sacrifice the union of their provinces to the House of Savoy under Victor Emmanuel," not a single deputy being absent or dissenting.

A letter from Bologna on the 9th September reveals that he was busy in every direction; and his singular tact in selecting the exact place where his presence would benefit the national cause, is good evidence of his insight into the nature of men and circumstances. Bologna had been in a terrible state of commotion for a long time. It had suffered more than many places at the hand of the Austrian, and their vote of annexation was marked by a paroxysm of delight and enthusiasm. The illuminations on the occasion resembled those at the opening of the Assembly of the

Roman States; but the programme of the *fête* was more complete. Twelve bands of music were placed in the public square or at the town gates. They were surrounded by the population, bearing torches, and they played till midnight, after which they marched to the Grand Square and gave a monster concert. On the next day hundreds of people were seen rushing into the courtyard of the Government Palace, and there saw driving away a post-carriage, amidst cheers and cries of "*Viva Garibaldi !*" It was indeed himself. He was on his way to inspect the troops at Ferrara.

Meanwhile, Mazzini, who was at Florence, foresaw the impending struggle. The Neapolitan frontier was lined with soldiers and mounted cannon. He determind to write the king a letter, and it thoroughly embodied the sentiments of Garibaldi. :-The following are extracts :—

To Victor Emmanuel, King of Sardinia, &c.,—"Say to Louis Napoleon, 'I mistrusted Italy, therefore I accepted your peace, not mine.' But Italy did not mistrust me, and I feel the obligations which that trust imposes. I withdraw my acceptance. I will do, freed from every bond, that which God and my country inspire me to attempt. I ask of you only one thing—to abstain from all interference in our affairs, and to leave Italy, as you promised, free to fulfil, by her own exertions, the work which you initiated with me. On this condition you will find me ever grateful, and Italy always the friend of France.'

"Say to the European Powers, 'You have destroyed the old treaties of 1815 in Poland, in Belgium, in France, in the East, and everywhere. In the name of Italian right I ask you to leave us alone and free. Against Austria, we ask aid only from our own swords : but let no one aid her : be the keepers of the field, and render a tardy justice to the people from whom sprang in a great measure that civilisation which adores your own dominions.'

"Say to the Italians, 'You have hailed me as the first soldier of your independence; and I will not betray the mission you have entrusted to me.   There is no independence for slaves, nor possible strength for those divided amongst themselves.   Be then a free and united people.   Free yourselves from your oppressors; and whenever you shall see under the tricolour banner the shining blade of the sword I now unsheathe, there rally around me   With God's help and yours, I will never replace it in its sheath until in Rome your representatives shall dictate the compact of love for the twenty-six millions who people our Italy.   But mark! I require from you, besides those I now count around me, two hundred thousand armed men.   I require the means necessary to maintain them in action.   I require unlimited trust; I require that you, in order to conquer, are ready, as I am, to die slaves or free men; for us there is no middle way.'

"I call you, in the name of Italy, to a great undertaking, to one of those undertakings in which the strong man numbers his friends, not his enemies.   Be great as is the object which God has put before you, sublime as duty, daring as faith.   Will and declare it; you will have all, and us amongst the first, with you.   Go, without looking to the right or the left, in the name of eternal justice, eternal right, to the Holy Crusade of Italy, and you will conquer with her; and then, sire, when in the midst of the applause of Europe, and the delirious joy of the Italian people, and joyful in the joy of millions, and blessed in the consciousness of having fulfilled a God-like work, you will ask the nation what post she assigns to him who has hazarded his life and throne in order that she should be free and one; be it that you may wish to pass to eternal fame with posterity as the Life President of the Italian Republic, or be it that the royal dynastic idea may possess your mind: God and the nation will bless and accept you, and I, a Republican, and ready to return and die in exile, to preserve pure and intact to the grave the faith of my youth, shall exclaim, with my brother Italians, 'President or King, may God bless you, and the nation for whom you have dared and conquered."   " MAZZINI."

In assuming the command of the Tuscan army Garibaldi was obliged, by military etiquette, to retain the greater part of the staff, so that he had not about him exclusively his South American coadjutors as he had at Varese and at Stelvio—he merely retained two orderly officers and his secretary. But the magical influence of his presence soon inspired in his new friends the confidence and affection that prevailed among the others. The same grave and gentle countenance, the same musical tenderness of voice when all was right, and the same ringing tone and black looks if he were made angry, yet, withal, such plainness and simplicity —these formed an outward individuality ever attractive to all with whom he was at any time brought into contact.

Garibaldi arrived at Turin on the 28th, having been summoned thither by the king. He had been enthusiastically received everywhere along the road, especially at Voghera, where, in addressing the multitude, he exclaimed : " With a king like Victor Emmanuel, with an army like ours, and with a people like you, Italy should not stop until she has freed the last inch of her soil from the heel of the foreigner."

It was soon known for certain that Napoleon's letter was the cause of the king's summons to Garibaldi. He and Fanti had an interview with Victor Emmanuel at Turin, and the discussion turned upon the affairs of Central Italy ; as, in fact, the North being secured, it could turn on nothing else. Parma, Modena, Tuscany, and the Roman States were in Garibaldi's hands, and could not be wrested from them, except by such measures as were adopted by the gentleman who devoured Poland, and that iniquity all Europe would prevent. The king and his generals denounced the letter of the emperor as utterly impracticable and ridiculous. Garibaldi declared that the hour for action was at hand, and the king also felt the time was come for a determined policy.

The king had replied to Napoleon that he could not accept the suggested policy. The Pope received a copy of the note, addressed by Napoleon, and replied, styling it " an absurdity." Thereupon the emperor intimated to Antonelli that if his counsel was to be treated in such a manner he must withdraw his troops from Rome, and they must look to themselves. Thus it came to pass that the tortuous policy of the monarchs defeated itself, as all such policy must, either public or private. The emperor did not learn reason—the king did. The chamois hunter, with all his rough and animal ways, proved himself a king.

For a few months our hero endured what he held to be a disgraceful peace with a certain amount of patience ; but the penalty of enforced idleness was, in his case, pain and illness, and the only remedy, work.

It was Macchiavelli who said that the unity of Italy would never be effected under ordinary conditions. Manin, Mazzini, Charles Albert, and a dozen more could see the remedy, but none could apply it. Broken into fragments for centuries, and misruled by contradictory governments which could only produce misery, the loyalty of the people was gone. They were utterly wild ; wishing to come together, fretting because they could not ; dreaming of a future, sick of the present, they were as " sheep having no shepherd." Garibaldi was the only man who had penetrated to the depth of the disorder. This fact the governments began to see, and some of them to face. It was therefore quite in accord with the principles and with the dignity of the Sardinian King, that the disposition of these dissolved States to cluster about his throne should not be discouraged ; and seeing that Garibaldi could not be hindered in any proceeding that he chose to initiate, his only policy lay in accepting the inevitable, and receiving, as he could bring them in, the crowns of the scattered kingdoms and duchies.

Victor Emmanuel had had from his childhood good practice in the art of government, and he had an adroit far-seeing mind. It has been stated that when the deputations from Parma, Modena, and the Romagna came to present him with the votes of their several Assemblies, asking for his provisional government through a representative, he urged upon them the necessity of developing the armaments of Italy. "It is not impossible," said he, "that the present situation, still critical, may compel us to draw the sword once more: and in that case you will understand that I rely upon the arms of those who proclaim themselves my subjects." And the king discerned that a military visitation by Garibaldi, however distasteful it might be to the prejudices or the jealousy of his regular forces, would do far more to strengthen their allegiance to his crown and interests, and to develop in them the national instinct of self-preservation, than all the glittering parade of military display, or even the pomp and ceremony of a royal journey.

In his anxiety to put into some tangible and serviceable form the many professions of zeal and sympathy from those who could not tender personal service, and also in order to exhibit to the world visible proof that Italians could and would work out their deliverance with some external help, Garibaldi wrote a letter to the Mayor of Cremona, requesting him to announce officially that he had caused a subscription to be opened for the purchase of a million muskets, and that he himself would head the list with 5000 francs, to which Trecchi, his adjutant, added a similar amount. This idea took hold on the population, and at Turin was especially well received and imitated.

Avezzana appealed to Italians, resident in England, to carry out the national subscription for the purchase of a million muskets, and Messrs. L. Serena & Co., 147 Leaden hall Street, were appointed by Garibaldi to receive subscriptions.

The Associazione Unitaria Italiana at Mil an took up this movement, and in connection with it increased their branch associations in all the towns of Lombardy, as well as Piedmont. These were crowded with business as soon as opened.

The *Times* newspaper threw cold water on the movement, and lavished its platitudes on the Italian effort for independence, informing the English public that Garibaldi was begging aid from England for a foreign purpose with which we had no concern; but the subscriptions flowed in steadily and regularly. Avezzana wrote an independent letter, avowing what everybody well knew, and the *Times* also, that the circular note of Garibaldi was addressed to all the world, in the sure faith that when it was known that he could have a million muskets, he could soon find, if necessary, a million men to use them.

Mazzini wrote, enclosing his contribution: "I send 200 francs as my contribution to General Garibaldi's fund, to which I feel sure that all who share my political faith will subscribe. The name of Garibaldi is a guarantee that those arms will not be employed merely in defence of Cattolica and the Mincio. The sacred unity of the whole of Italy, from the heights of the Tyrol to the Sicilian Sea, is an article of faith for him as well as for us. These arms, then, are to be used for us. It is essential that, rapidly fraternising in this subscription, Italians should display a manly resolution, and separate themselves finally from that unseemly collection of optimist cowards who look for liberty and nationality from hypothetical conferences between foreign sovereigns."

"There are Poles, Hungarians, Neapolitans, Romans, Piedmontese, Lombards, Venetians—all ready to die rather than yield; many of them young lads, but of the same uncompromising spirit. It is only necessary to see the Garibaldi men to convince oneself what there can be done with mere children, if they are led by a man of genius and have a noble cause to uphold. The name of Garibaldi is a tower of strength. You meet his officers everywhere ; many I have met just come back from California and other parts of America, on hearing of the war of Independence in Italy. They are weather-beaten, but soldiers of the stoutest fibre."

For the same object Garibaldi addressed the following proclamation to the "Ladies of Italy":—

"When the ladies of Milan, Venice, and other Italian cities asked at evening parties their children, friends, or lovers if they were not going to the holy war, and in this way increased the ranks of the liberating army with the young, the brave, and the industrious, then I say they gave to the character of this epoch the brilliant stamp of female patriotism, which, according to history, bears witness to us of the value of the Roman, Spartan, and Carthaginian women.

"Well, these ladies, these women, worthy of the times of ancient Italy, who sent to us their beloved ones, their brothers by blood, will they now refuse to throw their superfluities into the balance for the redemption of Italy ! The ladies Cairoli of Pavia, Martinez, Deorchi, Sinora, Biancardi of Como, Pallavicino, Speri, Pepoli, Salvi, have they no comrades in heart in the hundred cities of Italy ? Are there not thousands of women like the Verri, Casani, Montegezza, Araldi, Adamolo, Lomellini, who will throw in the face of those who wish to oppress us their superfluous ornaments, their jewels, their hair, their children even, as a holocaust of foreign princes, but desire to be placed on the same footing, and to take its position on an equality with the other European nations, who are our sisters, and of whom we feel ourselves worthy ?

"One lady, then, one woman of every Italian city, town,

or village, must invite the fair sex, for, by so doing, a religious and vital service is performed, the consciousness of which must invigorate and bless; and she should urge on them to offer of their superfluous ornaments some for the cause of Italy; and this can be done in a day. Do it generously and quickly; then shall the powerful ones of the earth bow before the million of men armed with a million muskets, for which you can contribute so much. Then shall our children no longer be exposed to death in the field, and God will bless our holy work.   "G. GARIBALDI."

Garibaldi proceeded to Milan, and there made a speech to the National Guard, in which were these remarkable words :—

"The peace of Villafranca left open a vast field for Italian bravery. France, who gave us her help to deliver Italy in part, has determined to leave to us the honour of emancipating such of our brethren as remain oppressed, and of liberating all Italy by the force of Italian arms."

The city of Milan heard of his arrival late at night, and though it was dark and snowing fast, a great crowd procured torches and assembled to greet him. Some visitors might wonder at the prestige of his name, but the secret lay in that early consecration of himself to the people, independent of any political creed or doctrine, and his descent into their sorrowful condition, by which he came to know them, and they him. Thousands of incidents attest his integrity and disinterestedness ; and those are moral attributes in man which a people cannot fail both to recognise and to honour.

Garibaldi, at the persuasion of some of his friends, resigned his position as President of the National Society, and accepted the presidency of another body called "La Nazione Armata," and issued a proclamation to the Italian Liberals.

But he did not hold this position many days, for at the request of the ministry, and by the advice of the king, he consented to dissolve the society. The fact was, that his impulsive, generous nature had been drawn into the scheme when idleness exposed him to temptation. The next day he issued this proclamation :—

"To the Italians.

"Summoned by some of my friends to try the part of conciliator between all the factions of the Italian Liberal party, I was invited to accept the presidency of a society, to be called the 'Armed Nation.'

"But as the Armed Italian Nation is a fact that terrifies everything disloyal, corrupting, and tyrannical, whether in Italy or out of it, the crowd of modern Jesuits has become alarmed, and cries out 'Anathema.'

"The government of the gallant king has been importuned by the alarmists, and in order not to compromise it I have decided on abandoning the noble object proposed to us.

"With the unanimous assent of all the members, I declare the Society of the Armed Nation dissolved, and I invite every Italian who loves his country to assist by his subscription the acquisition of a million muskets. If with these Italy, in presence of a foreigner, should be incapable of arming a million soldiers, we should despair of humanity. Let Italy arm, and she will be free.

"G. Garibaldi."

Central Italy was by this time virtually added to the kingdom of Victor Emmanuel, and one effect of the great moral demonstration by which this virtual annexation took place was to bring back to the front of Sardinian diplomacy the man by whom it was once more necessary that the fortunes of the kingdom should be guided. On the 10th of January 1860, Cavour had returned to office after six months retirement. Three of the Italian States, Tuscany, Modena, and Parma, had in the meantime got rid of their rulers, and a portion of the Pope's own subjects had thrown off their allegiance. Here was an opening for Cavour. Central Italy declared for annexation to Sardinia. Napoleon would not hear of it, and so Garibaldi had a roving commission given him to go through Nice and Savoy, and stir up the people against annexation to France. It is an old and savoury proverb that what is sause for the goose is sauce for the gander. Napoleon meant to go through the formality of a *plebiscite* before he took possession of Mont Blanc. But in Central Italy the *plebiscite* was a general fact, undeniable, unanswerable. Then Cavour for the first time found the value of England's moral support. The annexation of Central Italy was desired by the Italians; that was sufficient reason why it should be upholden by England. It was opposed by France, and that made the sanction of England enthusiastic. Cavour won this game. Napoleon, it is true, had taken the old kingdom of Savoy, but it was for the most part only a mountainous and barren possession, and the sparse inhabitants were already French in language, and to some degree in interests. But Cavour had won the fairest provinces of Italy, the centres of refinement and intellectual cultivation. Napoleon had won the biggest mountain in Europe; Cavour a score of cities, and a nobility of birth and intellect. All Europe declared that the victor was Cavour.

Within two months of his regaining the Premiership the arrangements above-mentioned were formally ratified, and he and his antagonist began a new game. Towards the middle of April 1860 Garibaldi left Turin for Nice, to arouse the people of his native place against the annexation to France. To go to Nice one must pass through Genoa. Garibaldi got to Genoa, but went no farther west. A fortnight later he and his thousand volunteers had set sail for the south. They landed at Marsala, in Sicily, on 11th May. The news was telegraphed to every part of the Continent. Europe looked on with various emotions. England rejoiced. Napoleon was furious. He wrote to Cavour urgent and insolent letters. Cavour shrugged his shoulders. "*Que voulezvous?*" he said. "My master is not King of Sicily. Garibaldi is there, and what can we do? We really are not now prepared to enter into an offensive and defensive alliance with King Francis against his subjects or against Garibaldi."

There is no reason to suppose that Garibaldi had been long and astutely plotting this expedition to Sicily, which was in point of fact the hinge and crisis of the national struggle for unity. His was the ready hand, not the calculating brain. He had resolved on action in some shape or other, and had been steadily and laboriously preparing a nation in arms, content to wait until the opportunity of launching it upon the foe might be presented to him. That opportunity came from the outbreak of an insurrectionary movement in the Two Sicilies—or rather from the sudden and general conflagration of a country in which the constant oppressions of a corrupt government had been gradually raising the wrath of the people to fever heat.

To this day, the strange fact of the landing being effected without the interference of the Neapolitan fleet remains unexplained. It has often been stated that the English squadron lay between the Garibaldians and the Bourbon men-of-war; but such was not in reality its position. It seems to us, however, certain that the vicinity of the English ironclads did deter the Bourbon commanders from attacking the *Piemonte* and the *Lombardino*, though how we do not pretend to understand. Possibly the Bourbons feared that a stray projectile might fall upon one of the houses along the coast hoisting the British flag, and that this might lead to English intervention.

On arriving at Marsala he telegraphed to Messina, and then cut the telegraph wires. He enlisted 750 volunteers, who offered themselves at Marsala, hastily armed them, and on the 12th set out in the direction of Palermo, followed by 2000 hostile troops in his rear, 1000 of whom were sent by sea. But on his route the extreme enthusiasm of the people foreshadowed success. His courage and decision, and the cause in hand, excited the utmost confidence that the island would soon be free of the Neapolitan power. When he landed at Marsala he issued a proclamation, commencing with the magic words, " Victor Emmanuel *Regnante*." The town had but a few custom-house officers and soldiers, and they gave up their arms. The courageous band having put their artillery in order, a reconnoitring party took the road to Salerni. A slight resistance was made on the way, but so brief as to be unworthy of note, for the soldiers took to their heels and retired to Alcamo.

King Bomba heard of the occurrences on the island, and threw himself into a great rage, accusing the commander of the steamers of conniving by treachery with Garibaldi to effect his landing. He summoned a Council of Ministers, and appointed General Filangieri and Prince Ischikla to the civil and military command of the island, which offer they both declined, for they knew right well that the Bourbon days were numbered. He also sent to England, complaining that we had connived with Garibaldi; and Lord John Russell telegraphed to the Admiral, requesting his report of the transaction, which, as a matter of history, should be reproduced here, bearing as it does on so many delicate points of international courtesy and general independence.

When Garibaldi landed in Sicily there were said to be about fifty thousand royal troops on the island, of which the majority were in the towns of Messina and Palermo. It was in these two ports that the popular agitation was known to be most dangerous; and on the other hand, it was here that the army was most likely to be of service in overawing any attempt at insurrection. They began by holding the audacious invader, who they outnumbered by something like sixty to one, exceedingly cheap. If the Garibaldians had been more numerous it would have been a serious question whether the royal forces, as a matter of strategy, ought not to have been concentrated in the strongest of the two fortified towns—Messina; for, as it was, their weakness arose from the necessity of repelling all demonstrations made against them in these strongholds, and at the same time of keeping open the communication between them, which lay along the north coast of the island, and was therefore menaced at every point, both by Garibaldi and his sympathisers—in other words, by the bulk of the population of Sicily.

According to this view of the matter, Garibaldi's expedition had some chances of success, always supposing that it was vigorously supported, as well by the inhabitants themselves as by its numerous and influential friends at home. It was particularly necessary that a sufficient sum of money should be forthcoming, to feed, clothe, and pay the Sicilians who took an active part in furthering the efforts of the Garibaldini in their behalf; for some had left their usual occupations—their daily bread—to shoulder the musket or handle the sabre in the national cause. The sums collected in England were therefore not without their great importance. The British Attorney-General had declared that collections in favour of Garibaldi and his plans were not contrary to the laws of the United Kingdom. Altogether the attitude assumed by England contributed greatly to the liberation of Lower Italy. Lord John Russell had, it is true, according to his own words in Parliament, requested the Sardinian Government to prevent the expedition; but Garibaldi once landed, the British Ministry refused to accede to a request made by France for a common guarding of the Neapolitan coasts, in order to prevent Garibaldi's landing on the continent and carrying on the war into the heart of the Two Sicilies; and France would not undertake such a measure alone. The Neapolitan Government was obliged to provide for the maintenance of tranquillity in the continental provinces of the kingdom, and was therefore unable to spare any overwhelming or irresistible force for the suppression of the revolt in Sicily.

There is no doubt that the king's forces in Sicily were surprised by the rapid preparation and carrying out of this heroic expedition. The place of landing had as much as possible been kept secret; but on the night after the disembarkation the principal insurrectionary leaders within the island met Garibaldi at Marsala, for the purpose of concerting measures with him for the approaching campaign.

Immediately upon landing, our hero issued one of his heart-stirring addresses to the people of Sicily, calling them to arms.

Another proclamation was issued to the royal army; and it was not without its effect. Fifty men escaped from Palermo and joined the invaders. Disturbances took place within the city, and the 6th regiment refused the orders of its general to fire upon the citizens.

On the road from Marsala to Trapani lies the small town of Calatafimi, possessing certain natural advantages of position. It was necessary that Garibaldi should push on at once to Trapani, which formed the centre of the insurgents' movements, and which was abandoned by the nine hundred Neapolitans as soon as they heard of the landing of the expedition in their immediate neighbourhood. The insurgents had established a fortified camp at Vita, and from thence they were making a simultaneous movement with Garibaldi's upon Calatafimi. No sooner did the Neapolitans at Messina learn these designs of their enemies than a force of eight thousand men was despatched to give them battle, and it was in the immediate neighbourhood of Calatafimi, on the 15th of May, that the first important action took place.

The *Cacciatori degli Alpi*, an ambuscade under Orsini, distinguished themselves by their great daring and dash, whilst at the same time a battery of mountain artillery, brought by Garibaldi from Genoa, kept up a well-directed fire upon the advancing forces. The Neapolitans seemed to fight without heart, but their numbers were overwhelming; so much so that at one time it seemed as if the gallant band of patriots would have to give way. The trained forces of the king were at least four to one in number against their half-disciplined opponents; for Garibaldi had only the thousand—actually no more than eight hundred effective men—who had landed with him, and the few *Picciotti*, as the Sicilian insurgents were called, who had been able to join him. Brave fellows they proved themselves on many future occasions, but they were at present totally unorganised, and not unsusceptible to panic. The plan was to carry each position at the point of the bayonet. At a certain juncture the struggle appeared hopeless; the best had fallen, the ammunition was gone, the glaring Sicilian sun was wearing out the hardiest. The commander of the first company, who had exposed himself all the day through with reckless gallantry, approached Garibaldi, and whispered in his ear, "General, I fear we must retreat."

The chief started as if he had been stung by a scorpion, but on seeing who it was addressed him, he answered gently, "Never say that, Bixio . . . . Here we *die.*"

"Sooner than hear these words, I had wished myself a hundred feet under the clod," Bixio used to say when he told the story. He made up his mind to hold his peace on the subject of retreating in future.

"My sons," said Garibaldi to the volunteers, "I require of you one last desperate charge. Five minutes' rest, and then—forwards!" The time past, he cried, "To the bayonet !" and the whole little host, repeating "Alla baieo-netta! Viva l'Italia! Viva Garibaldi!" dashed up the mountain side. In a quarter of an hour Calatafimi was won! ⸎

In the proclamation issued by Garibaldi the day after the victory, the chief made allusion to the effect upon the enemy produced by the bayonets of his soldiers.

"Surrounded by companions in arms like you one might dare anything: this conviction I displayed yesterday in calling upon you to undertake a labour of difficulty and danger, and leading you against a numerous enemy, I relied upon the fatal effects of your bayonets, and I see that I had reason to do so. Although it is much to be regretted that we must engage in a struggle with Italian soldiers, we must yet acknowledge that we encountered a resistance worthy of a better cause; and we have thereby acquired a knowledge of what we shall one day be able to accomplish, when the whole Italian family shall be united under one banner—that of our liberation."

This latter passage was calculated, and evidently intended, to enlist the sympathies of the royal troops in the national cause; and in reality a not inconsiderable number of desertions from the ranks of his Neapolitan Majesty's forces took place immediately after the publication of the above proclamation. Even officers, covered with the cloaks of privates, came into the patriot camp; and whole regiments became to a certain degree disaffected, or openly mutinied. Accordingly, all disposable troops, whose fidelity was con-sidered by the court of Naples as revolution-proof, were despatched in hot haste to the Island of Sicily.

Garibaldi at once advanced upon the town of Palermo. It is situated on the north coast of Sicily, on the mountainous coast of a bay of the same name, at the mouth of the little river Oseto. The old town is surrounded by a line of ramparts, once very strong, but which have been suffered to fall into decay.

The new town is without these fortifications, and extends along the coast almost as far as Monreale; the line of defences being broken between the city and suburbs. The fine port of Palermo is, however, defended by fortifications as strong for their size as any in the world—Castello Lucio and Castellamare, the latter completely commanding the town from the sea.

When Garibaldi had arrived about six miles from Palermo he was attacked by the royalists, but retired, in order to entice the enemy towards Corleone, and keep him occupied there with guerilla bands. This manœuvre was completely successful; he himself in the meanwhile approached the capital by another road. The gates were walled up half-way, in order to cut off all communication between the population and the insurgents; for the excitement of the Palermitans became something fearful when the fires of the camp on the surrounding hills became visible. Lanza, however, probably believed that his forts secured him the possession of the town; for, instead of sending patrols through the town to prevent all assembling or mutual communication of malcontents, as his predecessor had done, he determined to spare his troops this fatiguing duty, and concentrated the same in three parts of the city; between the different corps he arranged and kept open a constant communication. But the Palermitans took advantage of this favourable change to agree upon a common course of action for all conceivable cases. On Whit Sunday (27th May), the day after the arrival of Garibaldi on the neighbouring heights, an early meeting was held of all the chiefs of the movement in the old chapel of King Roger (dating from the year 1129), which was always much frequented at this feast by the people of the town.

The insurgents, who had been encamped on Monte Gibilrosso, with Garibaldi's *Cacciatori* in their van, attacked Porta Scala, Porta San Antonio, and Porta dei Termini; at four o'clock the same morning; and, within a couple of hours, our hero had established himself in the town-hall. He had drawn out about five thousand of the garrison to attack him in the mountains; and there were at this moment not more than fourteen thousand out of the original thirty-two thousand royalist troops in Palermo. No sooner was Garibaldi known to be within the city than the inhabitants, as he had confidently expected, rose *en masse;* even women and lads turning round upon the panic-stricken soldiery. About six in the morning the forts, ramparts, and batteries opened fire upon the streets, and the bombardment was incessant and murderous. The Neapolitan vessels in the port added their fire to that of the garrison. Garibaldi, however, was not daunted. He had stood his ground before a similar storm of shot and shell twelve long years before; and though the bombardment of Palermo was, perhaps, even more severe than that of Rome, it did not check the ardour of the gallant patriots. By ten o'clock the royalists had withdrawn to the strongest points within the city.

"The posts stationed to defend the prisons of Theamia were also obliged to give way, and were received on board three Neapolitan vessels set apart for such services. Those imprisoned here thus also obtained their liberty. Of the six thousand persons set free from the prisons there were about sixteen hundred to eighteen hundred political offenders, and twelve hundred galley slaves; the remainder had been arrested for petty offences. We mention here that Garibaldi caused all the prison warders belonging to the police that had been taken to be exposed a day in the market-place, and then had them hanged in presence of a concourse of the people.

"In the afternoon the struggle was renewed; the insurgents attacked the battery at the Porta Macqueda. Up till eleven o'clock two bombs per minute had fallen upon the

unfortunate city ; then the firing became weaker, only, however, to break forth with redoubled force in the afternoon.
From six o'clock in the evening till four the next morning
the firing slackened again, one bomb falling in about five
minutes.   Terrible fires raged in consequence ; but in spite
of the heat, the noise, the falling timbers and burning
embers flying about in all directions, the patriots advanced
undaunted to the attack.   The royalists now formed a line
extending from the Francesco-di-Paolo church to the barracks
of the Qauttro Venti.   But ere night set in Garibaldi's
troops had forced this line, and obliged Lanza to retire into
the royal palace in the south of the town ; and thus the
communication with the 'mole' was threatenad by the
whole hostile town. . . .

"The same evening important reinforcements, especially
in artillery, had arrived to second the efforts of the insur-
rectionists in Palermo, and the struggle was carried on all
night at the royal palace and at the barracks. . . .   Towards
evening the insurgents opened a well-sustained rifle fire on
the royal palace ; and being in possession of the archbishop's
palace, they were enabled to send such a destructive leaden
hail upon their opponents in the finance office that these
latter were obliged to evacuate this also.

"The royalists were now in possession of only the palace
and the citadel, while Garibaldi was taking measures, in the
town-hall, for driving them out of these positions.   For the
maintenance of order he published, in conjunction with the
town committee, an ordinance, threatening immediate death
to all convicted of murder or theft.   Another decree forbade
the indiscriminate bearing of weapons in the streets—every
one armed was obliged to join some recognised patriot
leader."

In the meanwhile the foreign consuls succeeded in bringing about a six days' truce, from the 20th May till the 3rd
of June. . . .   On the morning of the 29th, he received

scarcely less than a dozen requests from General Lanza for a cessation of hostilities, but he could not accept the terms. At first neither Garibaldi nor the people would listen to anything of the sort, but at last the former concluded that it would be the more humane course to adopt.

Knowing how little reliance could be placed on the future, our hero, having taken possession of the printing-presses, sent out in every direction copies of the following spirited appeal :—

"SICILIANS,—The tempest is almost sure to follow the calm, and therefore we must prepare ; for our object is not as yet entirely gained.

"The national effort in this cause opened brightly ; and the conquest was sure when the faithful people repudiated the proffered humiliations, and declared they would conquer or die.

"Ay ! it is true ! Our situation does improve day by day ; but we must do our duty the more faithfully to ensure, as we mean, the triumph of our sacred right.

"To arms ! then, to arms ! Sharpen your weapons, and devise every form of defence or of attack. We shall have leisure for the *vivas* when the enemy is forced off the soil of our country.

"'To arms !' I repeat, and 'To arms !' Whosoever does not, within three days, find something to arm himself is a traitor and a coward ; and those who fight amid the ruins of their fire-consumed houses, and for the lives of their wives and children in the nation's cause, cannot be cowards and traitors.

"G. GARIBALDI."

When, however, the three days and a little more were ended (for the armistice had to be extended to complete the negotiations), Lanza capitulated, not without having had very great difficulties at Naples. Ferdinand began to feel very suspicious about whether his turn would not come next. However, there was no choice. He could not re-take Sicily, for Garibaldi would have had 150,000 men in arms in a very short time.

The measures taken by Garibaldi to ensure order and restore confidence in the city were at once strict and judicious, and they soon had the desired effect. Robbery and murder were to be summarily punished with death, and this ordinance was not allowed to become a dead letter. Nine persons for instance, convicted of plundering, were all shot. But in other things also Garibaldi displayed great talent as a creative and organising spirit. A decree, published at Salerni, ordered the formation of a Sicilian militia, in which all persons from seventeen years of age to fifty were to be enrolled. The young men from seventeen to thirty were to serve actively throughout the land, those from thirty to forty in their provinces, those from forty to fifty in their parish.

Garibaldi needed more naval service to carry on his great work. Palermo is about one hundred and fifty miles from Naples, across the Mediterranean, and as his intention and policy bade him strike a blow at the royal city as the shortest method of determining the mighty issue before him, he wrote to England that the great services being rendered there might just at that time take that form in preference to any other. First, of Mr. Thomas Parke, shipbuilder, of Liverpool, he orders two large steamers carrying guns, to be delivered at Palermo for cash, and adds that he feels the want of "such gunboats as you have in England, or something in that way (not iron), and fully armed." After thanking him for good wishes, he adds : "Let England remember that she has no really sincere ally, except among free peoples, and that there are but few of these on the continent. An Italy free and united would supply the want, and be one of the greatest obstacles to the schemes of the Emperor of the French. Send us quick, arms, ships, guns, and material, and I vouch for the speedy realisation of this great object."

On the appointment of Prince Pandolfini to represent the Provisional Government of Sicily at the English Court, Garibaldi addressed Her Britannic Majesty thus :—

"YOUR MAJESTY,—I have been called by duty to my fatherland to defend its cause in Sicily, and have accepted the dictatorship of a noble people who have maintained a long-continued struggle to participate in national life and freedom, which they now desire to enjoy under the rule of the magnanimous prince whom Italy trusts.

"In presenting himself to your Majesty, the envoy of the Provisional Government in its name does not pretend to be the ambassador of a special and separate State, but only the interpreter of the thoughts and sentiments of two-and-a-half millions of Italians.

"I beg your Majesty to condescend to receive him under this title, and to bestow a gracious audience to what he may earnestly offer to your Majesty on the part of this most beautiful and very glorious part of Italy.

"G. GARIBALDI."

The warm interest felt by Englishmen and Englishwomen in the Italian cause found a new opportunity of manifestation in the sorrows incident to war. Under the patronage of Lady Shaftesbury and many other influential ladies, an association for the relief of the sick and wounded, and the widows and orphans of Garibaldi's followers, and the sufferers at Palermo and elsewhere, was formed, and one of its conditions ran thus :—

"None of the money will be applied to warlike purposes, but solely to those of charity and benevolence, and it is therefore hoped that many will join in this labour of love."

Many did join. The association represented every shade of English politics, and was carried on with zeal and personal devotion akin to the spirit of Florence Nightingale, who herself assisted in forming and promoting and guiding the work. Much sympathy was shewn in Sweden. A fund collected at Gottenberg reached 1046 thalers on 26th June, including the profits of a soireé, 365 thalers. The *Gotha Gazette* opened subscriptions for Garibaldi, saying that it was time that Germany, who had so many of her sons fighting against liberty, should do something in its favour.

The absolute power of the Dictator kindled a flame of jealousy at Turin which found its expression in the despatching of La Farina from the court of Victor Emmanuel to Sicily as his representative, with instructions inspired by Cavour. It is important to state the political operations of the time, not only because they bear witness to the artless skill of Garibaldi, but also because they shew the stupendous force of a single aim amid diplomatic confusion. All men, all kings, all nations had to succumb to one disinterested man who saw through the maze of politics. As we read the chronicles published day by day in the newspapers we cannot avoid this conviction. The *Times, the Daily News, the Débats* did not—could not—see what Garibaldi saw. Thouvenel, Russell, and the rest of the leading European statesmen, pottered about with "precedent on precedent," all hoping to maintain the Spanish Bourbon on the throne of Naples, but this was the very thing Garibaldi saw could not—ought not to be. Lord John Russell, in the celebrated debate evoked by Sir Robert Peel, and stimulated by the caustic dogmatism of Mr. Kinglake, spoke very sensibly: "The people of Italy should be free to select whatever government or ruler they might happen to prefer." The Pope fulminated message after message, calling the liberators of an enslaved nation "pirates and robbers;" the King of Naples sent out amnesty after amnesty, constitution after constitution, promise after promise, changed his ministers over and over again, and became a prodigal of virtue ; while the Emperor of the French looked innocently on, as Sicily slipped from the Neapolitan sceptre, watching for an opportunity to repeat his *coup* of Savoy and Nice on the island of Sardinia, and so to extend his sway in the Mediterranean; Austria, puzzled and perplexed, the lacquey of Rome, eager to give its magnificent army something to do, desired one more chance, whilst Garibaldi all the while was labouring on, laughing at the imbecility of the diplomatists.

A Neapolitan war-steamer, the *Veloce*, deserted the king's service, and came into Palermo on the 10th of July. She had belonged to the party of insurrection in 1848, and on the capitulation of Sicily escaped to Marseilles, where she was sequestrated by Naples. Now she was steaming off Messina, seeking an opportunity to desert, and she succeeded. Garibaldi received her commander on board the *Trentalore*, an American vessel, and proceeded to inspect the ship, whose crew loudly cheered them.

About this time an English gentleman met five Neapolitan officers in the King's Life Guards, who had thrown up their commissions, and were on their way to Garibaldi to tender their services. Their brilliant positions had been cheerfully sacrificed, and they reported that the great majority of their brother officers shared their sentiments. They had a firm opinion that the moment Garibaldi touched the soil of Naples the royal army would melt like snow in an April sun. The king dare not employ it against the ruler of Sicily, nor could he transport his troops safely to the Abruzzi, for it was felt that they would instantly desert to Palermo.

Besides these, four war-steamers came from England, and another, purchased by Lord Dudley for £8000, steamed out of Newhaven on the 28th. She had served previously in the Crimean war, but she was now rechristened *Garibaldi*, and augmented the forces of our hero.

How highly Garibaldi appreciated worthy and talented deserters from the royal army, and how well he received

them, may be gathered from the following characteristic confession which he made in the company of several Neapolitan officers in Palermo, and of which soon after copies went from hand to hand in the royal army:—
"Gentlemen ! We have to raise an army of two hundred thousand men. I know how to prize volunteers, and have a particular affection to them ; but when I want a colonel, I prefer a loyal captain who understands his business to a lawyer, and nominate a sergeant captain rather than a doctor. If you are royalists, so am I ; only, king against king, I prefer Victor Emmanuel (who will before very long again bring us face to face with the Austrian) to the Bourbon Francesco, who hounds Italians on to fight against Italians. Gentlemen ! you have to choose ; we shall conquer without you, but I should be proud to conquer with you."

The topography of the basin of Palermo should be known that we may realise the work in hand. Long before you arrive by sea there is before you a bold limestone mountain standing apart, resembling the rock of Gibraltar, but not so high. This rock forms the northern limit of the Bay of Palermo, and of the Concha d'Or (golden shell), the fertile plain in which the town lies. The plain stretches out in a north-westerly and south-westerly direction, and is bounded in a circular sweep by a mountain chain. The plain may be twelve miles long and about four miles broad. Between the isolated Monte Pellegrino and the rest of the chain the plain runs on to La Favorita, over which a carriage-road goes to Carini ; on the opposite side of the plain, skirting the shore, runs the high-road to Messina, passing through Bavaria and close to the ruins of Solento. These are the easiest outlets. The chain of mountains seems to forbid all other egress.

The army of Naples held this plain and the seaboard, as also the heights commanding it, from which there were, as we have seen, no roads into the plain, and therefore the position was apparently impregnable. There was only the plateau of Monreale open, a fine position, that had to be separately guarded.

As soon as the armistice drew towards its close Garibaldi hastened thither, hoping to reach it before the royal troops could do so, but he found that it could only be taken with great loss. He surrounded it with men, that none might escape, and kept beacon-fires burning for several nights, during which arrangements with the Committee of Palermo were agreed upon, and the prospect of success was rendered more certain ; but the town would not move until he was before the gates.

Seeing he had come too late for Monreale, he left a part of his followers, and with the main body effected a masterly march along the mountain chain, the guns being carried by the men, and appeared suddenly at Parco, on the road to Piani, with slight opposition, on the 23rd of July. The Neapolitans saw their blunder, and sent off all the forces that could be spared. On the 24th they made a second attack, for the skirmishing on the 23rd was indecisive, and Garibaldi changed his front. He was apparently on the defensive, but in reality was drawing the forces away from Palermo. Garibaldi withdrew and the enemy advanced, burning and pillaging the hapless villages.

When the Neapolitan troops left Palermo, a portion of them were despatched to Castellamare, and thence to Gaeta, evidently to be in readiness for an expected attack on Naples. Those remaining in the island concentrated themselves at Syracuse in the south, Messina in the east, Agosta and Milazzo in the north, and Lacata in the south-west. The General determined to push on his operations without delay, and General Türr undertook the advance towards Milazzo and Messina.

On the 14th July Garibaldi, at the head of three thousand men, effected a junction with Medici ; and on the next day Bosco, with four thousand men, quitted Messina for Barcelona, subsequently falling back upon Milazzo. On the 20th of the same month he advanced to the attack, and found the royalists under Bosco awaiting him in force at all events quite equal to his own. The fire began on the left wing, between Meri and Milazzo. A quarter of an hour afterwards the centre came upon the Neapolitan line, which was forced back out of the position it had taken up; while the right wing drove the enemy out of the houses he had occupied. In consequence of the difficult ground to be got over, part of the forces were retarded in their march, and thus Bosco was enabled to oppose near upon six thousand men to five or six hundred assailants, and those latter were finally repulsed, as may well be imagined. At this moment, however, Garibaldi sent the retiring columns reinforcements, and thus put them in a position to advance again to the attack of the enemy, who was sheltered behind rushes and Indian fig-trees. Garibaldi now placed himself, with some of his guides, at the head of the Genoese carabinieri, fell upon the flank of the Neapolitan army, and cut off a part of the same, but got thereby in the way of a cannon that was dealing out grape like hail at the short distance of twenty paces. Nissori and Captain Ratella hastened up with fifty men to Garibaldi's succour. The effect of the grape was terrible; and Garibaldi himself had the sole of his boot and the stirrup carried away by one of the bullets: his horse was wounded and became unmanageable, so that he was obliged to dismount, and unfortunately left his revolver in the holster. Major Breda was killed on the spot, and Nissori thrown by his horse, that had just received a mortal wound; while Captain Ratella remained unhurt in this scene of destruction. The critical moment of the conflict had now come for Garibaldi, but all his men behaved with a bravery and skill that promised well for the ultimate result. Becoming at length convinced that it was next to impossible to take the cannon by a front attack, Garibaldi gave Colonel Dunne orders to throw out some skirmishing parties, and advance through the rushes; while Nissori and Ratella, when they had penetrated through the same, were to spring on the wall that rose beyond, and fall upon the cannon which stood there. When these two officers, executing the orders thus given them by their chief, had reached the road, at the head of some fifty men, the first person they met was Garibaldi in person, on foot, sword in hand.

At this moment the cannon launched forth a volley that laid low some of the little troop here assembled: but the others precipitated themselves upon the gun, and bore it off in triumph, to be used against its former masters. All on a sudden the Neapolitan infantry opened to allow cavalry to pass through for the purpose of retaking the lost cannon. Colonel Dunne's men, who had been very little under fire, divided, and stepped back against the two sides of the road, instead of receiving the enemy with fixed bayonets. The Indian fig-trees here and a wall there prevented their further retreat; and soon recovering from their surprise, they poured in a volley upon the cavalry who were dashing through this living lane. The Neapolitan officer in command now seemed desirous of turning about and retiring, but he suddenly found himself surrounded by Garibaldi, Nissori, Stratella, and five or six others. Garibaldi immediately seized the bridle, and bade the officer surrender; but this latter made a cut at his detainer, which Garibaldi parried, and then in his turn dealt the Neapolitan a blow in the neck that brought him down. In the meantime, however, others had come up, and more than one sabre was flourished over Garibaldi's head. Swift as lightning this latter ran one of the assailants through, while Nissori wounded with his revolver two others and the horse of a third. One of the Neapolitans sprang from his horse and attacked Nissori, but received the fourth bullet of the revolver right through his head. While Nissori was thus engaged, Garibaldi had got the men together again, and led them on to the attack. The result was that of the fifty Neapolitan horsemen not one escaped; they were all either killed or wounded, or taken prisoners.

The whole of the royal army—Neapolitans, Bavarians, and Swiss—now turned and fled before the enemy's centre, which pressed forward to the attack, and this decided the fate of the day. The retreating royalists stopped not in their hurried flight till they reached the town of Milazzo, whither they were closely followed, even as far as the first houses, by the victorious Garibaldini.

The General then summoned the garrison in the citadel of Milazzo to withdraw, and leave guns, horses, and all war *matériel:* the demand was refused. Preparations were immediately made to attack and reduce the fortress.

On the next day the *City of Aberdeen* brought in a cargo under the enemy's fire, several native battalions and some guns; but meanwhile Bosco telegraphed to Messina that he could not hold out, and application was made to Naples for instructions as to capitulation.

Four Neapolitan frigates hove in sight two days afterwards, bearing Colonel Anzano, with full powers to treat. He assumed a high tone at first, hoping to obtain the terms granted to Palermo, but soon found that mode did not avail. Garibaldi simply informed him that he had already announced his terms, and that the whole fleet of Naples could not produce in him any change. He would not withdraw the terms he had conceded before the arrival of the naval squadron, but he would grant none more favourable. The colonel gave in and accepted the Dictator's offer.

The evacuation commenced accordingly on the next day. General Bosco, escorted by several officers, claimed to be the first to embark, but had the misery of being hissed by his people on the way. He had made a boast of taking Medici's horse, and had ordered guns to be spiked and some powder scattered about.   Garibaldi ordered him back, took away his charger, and let him walk off.

The wounded were sent down to the beach and embarked ; and the opportunity this gave many to desert was duly seized, especially among the artillery—some even took arms and baggage.   However, fifty guns, 100,000 rounds of ammunition, and 139 horses remained as the material fruits of victory over the man of highest repute in the Neapolitan army.

Immediately after the capitulation of Milazzo, Garibaldi ordered the advance upon Messina, which he desired to reach before the enemy had had time to concentrate his forces more completely than was already the case, and while his own troops were flushed with triumph.   He was alive to the danger of delay ; he knew also the force at Messina, and the number who had retired thither from Milazzo. Medici reached Spadafora the same night, with the intent of taking the heights commanding the last city on the morrow.

The Neapolitans harassed, but did not dispute our hero's progress ; and, in fact, the crowning difficulties which he had expected at Messina vanished before his steady progress. He not only found the heights abandoned, but the town likewise.   The troops had retired to the forts, having, before doing so, consigned the public treasure to the municipal authorities.

The evacuation on the one side and the entry on the other intoxicated the people of Messina.   The suppressed force broke out with true southern violence.   While all Sicily had been rejoicing, hoping, moving, talking, breathing freely, this town had groaned under the pressure of a garrison of five or six thousand, and under the shadow of hundreds of guns, deserted by all who could get away, dead to commerce and social life, and trembling for very existence.

The heart of the entire population poured itself out before the man of the people—one who felt and lived with the masses. They seemed to feel instinctively the presence of one who comprehended them thoroughly, who loved them in spite of their weaknesses and faults, and who had consecrated his life to their redemption.

Instantly began negotiations for a complete evacuation of the island and most of the forts. Beside other conditions the embarkation of the army of Naples stationed at Syracuse and Agosta was agreed to, so that no part of the island, except the royal citadel and its own forts, remained under the dominion of Naples, and these only pending future negotiations.

When the Municipal Council of Palermo and all the Communes of Sicily urged Garibaldi to effect the annexation of Sicily to the Italian kingdom, he answered that such an annexation was indeed his main intent and desire; that he was full of admiration for Victor Emmanuel; that with him and by him Italy could best become a nation; but that he did not for the present deem the annexation of Sicily alone an expedient measure; that the Italians should first become sufficiently strong. Were he to resolve on immediate annexation, he would have to receive orders from other persons when he might be under a necessity to withdraw.

Garibaldi's programme was clear and consistent. He would have no terms with any enemy of Italy. He had conquered Sicily, as before he had taken Tuscany; and he was now bent on taking Naples, as he had taken Palermo, by storm. After that he would settle matters with the Pope, listening to no compromise from Naples or Rome. He would shew the world that his only motive is Italy; he would never rest till his companion in arms, "*Il Rè Gal-antumo,*" was enthroned in the Capitol, and then, for his own part, he would retire to his rock-bound island of Cap-rera, and be seen no more in the ranks of war. Such was his programme; such were his aims. We shall see how he compassed them.

General Clary had retired with a garrison of two thousand men to the citadel, and measures were taken by Garibaldi to ensure the safety and order of Messina.   On the 28th of July the first body of nationalist troops, under the command of Medici and Fabrizzi, entered the city.

The appearance of Fabrizzi produced a wondrous emotion ; but still greater was the effect of Medici's entry.   Both these generals were tall, fine men, with a pleasing expression of countenance that contrasted strongly with the cold and lowering mien of the Neapolitan generals.   All of a sudden Garibaldi himself appeared at the gates of the town, although he had announced his arrival for the morrow. Not fond of pompous reception, &c., he had resolved to avoid anything of this sort at Messina by this little manœuvre.   But, on his being recognised, the people could not be restrained from taking the horses out the carriage and drawing the Dictator in triumph through the town to the Palazzo dell' Intendenza, where Fabrizzi and Medici had taken up their quarters.

The news of the great patriot's arrival spread through Messina like wildfire, and multitudes struggled through the streets towards the Strada Ferdinanda to get a sight of their deliverer,   ' *Viva Garibaldi !*' was in every mouth, and hats and handkerchiefs without number were frantically flourished in the air when the hero appeared at the balcony, and in a most friendly manner thanked the assembled thousands.   His dress was simple, and nothing distinguished him from his soldiers, were it not his eye, his forehead, and his noble bearing.   His late deeds of personal valour at Milazzo filled the Messinese with admiration ; as did also his antique simplicity.

The evening after the sanguinary and fatiguing conflict at Milazzo, Alexandre Dumas went about looking for the Dictator, the commander-in-chief of the Sicilian army, and at length found him stretched out asleep under the portico of a church, surrounded by his staff, his head resting on his saddle. Before him stood his supper—a piece of bread and a jug of water. He had allowed himself ten francs a day for his personal expenses, not a very extravagant sum for a generalissimo.

The Dictator's intention of landing on the mainland portion of the kingdom of Naples thus becoming every day more and more evident, the King of Sardinia, true to his promise to the Emperor Napoleon, made a last effort to dissuade Garibaldi from putting the said plans into execution. He wrote him the following autograph letter :—

"DEAR GENERAL,—You know that when you started for Sicily you did not have my approbation. To-day, in considering the grave circumstances of the moment, I must give you a warning; for I know the sincerity of your sentiments toward me.

"In order to terminate the war between Italians and Italians, I counsel you to renounce the idea of passing to the Neapolitan continent with your victorious and brave troops, if the King of Naples consents to evacuate the island, and leave the Sicilians to decide by free deliberation on their future government.

"I would reserve to myself full liberty of action as regards Sicily, in the event of the King of Naples declining to accept this condition.

"General, following advice, you will see that it is useful to Italy, whose grand development you would facilitate, that Europe should see that while she knows how to conquer, she also knows how to use her victories.

"VICTOR EMMANUEL."

Garibaldi replied in these terms :—

"SIRE,—Your Majesty knows the high esteem and devotion I have and feel for your Majesty. Much as I should like to obey your Majesty's injunctions, the present state of affairs in Italy precludes my so doing. I am called for, I

am urged on by, the people of Naples.   I have tried all my
influence to restrain them, for I felt that a more fortunate
moment would be desirable; but it has been in vain.   If I
should now hesitate, I should endanger the cause of Italy,
and fail in my duty as an Italian.   May your Majesty therefore permit me at this time to disobey.   When I have completed the task imposed by the wishes of a people groaning
under the tyranny of the Bourbon of Naples, I shall lay
down my sword at the feet of your Majesty, and obey your
Majesty for the remainder of my life.   "GARIBALDI."

Garibaldi did not lose a single day.   Before the end of
the month he had collected, at Capo di Faro, about four
thousand men and two hundred boats, with the intention of
crossing to Calabria forthwith.   It was at this time that
Garibaldi addressed the following proclamation to the
inhabitants of Naples :—

"To the people of the Neapolitan Continent,—The opposition of the foreigner, who is interested in our degradation,
and the work of internal factions, have combined to prevent
the unity of the Italian people.   Providence has now intervened, as it appears, to put an end to our misfortunes.   The
unanimity of the provinces has been exemplary, victory
smiling everywhere on the children of liberty; this proves
that the sufferings of the land of genius are drawing to a
close.

"One more step remains, and that I do not fear.   The
slender means that have enabled a handful of brave men to
reach these Straits are now developed into enormous force,
and the new enterprise is not a difficult one.   I desire to
avoid bloodshed among Italians, and therefore address
myself to you who are the people of the Neapolitan soil.

"I know that you are brave, for I have proved it; but I
do not want any further proof.   We will shed our blood
together upon the enemies of Italy, and therefore I call a
truce against further civil strife.

"Generous men, accept the right hand of a man who has never served a tyrant, and is experienced in the service of the people. Constitute a United Italy, I ask you, without the slaughter of her sons, and with me serve her, and, if need be, die for her. "G. GARIBALDI."

We have mentioned Garibaldi's preparations for crossing the Straits of Messina. The time of departure had not been divulged, though all things indicated the 8th of August. It took place in the evening. The army of twenty thousand, in four divisions, awaited orders;—one at Faro Point and the neighbourhood; two at Messina, under Medici and Cosenz, and Bixio's. Four batteries of heavy guns were constructed on the shore. Charybdis, at least the point known to readers of old story by that name, had the most powerful—six 32-pounders and two 65-pounders—to bear upon the opposite fort of Scylla. The intervening distance —only six thousand and seventeen English yards—needed this covering to prevent the Neapolitan men-of-war and the different floating batteries from interfering with their proceedings.

In the afternoon, Garibaldi, on board the *City of Aberdeen*, marched up and down the deck, following with his field-glass the movements of the enemy. He had devised an ingenious method of doing so before. The great fishery of the Straits is that of the sword-fish, and is carried on in a singular manner. The fisherman ascends a long pole in the centre of his boat, and when he sees the sword-fish in the current, he directs the rowers thither, and the man at the stern, with a long sharp spike, secures his prize. Garibaldi disappeared one day for two hours, disguised himself as a fisherman, and went so near the opposite shore as to reconnoitre all the fortified points on the coast. His fishing-boats, previously named, lay anchored in two lakes behind Faro lighthouse, and of course were concealed. These two lakes in ancient days communicated with the sea, but had of late years become choked. The channels he opened up by two canals, enabling him at pleasure to sail out unseen by a way his enemy knew nothing of. Previously to this Missori had been over incognito, and well examined the whole coast.

As the sun sank a south-west wind drove dense clouds towards the coast of Calabria. The rays of the rising moon could not disperse the vapours; and the whole gulf coast was concealed in a fog. Eight o'clock came, and Garibaldi gave his last orders to Major Missori, the officer in command. Ten men from each of the encamped brigade companies, fifty musketeers of Genoa, twenty guides and twenty engineers, were invited to join the select party; and the total amounted to three hundred and fifty men. These took the fishing-boats by half-past eight amid the ill-restrained mortification and entreaties of comrades who could not be permitted to go. At half-past nine the tower bell pealed from the church of Faro, and in the dim light off they went. The enterprise has scarcely a parallel, regarding the paucity of its means, the grandeur of its object, and the consummate skill of its preparation. A most dangerous, unknown coast before them, always well guarded with hundreds of guns, men-of-war floating up and down the Straits in swarms. In mid-stream they learned that the General's plan was to surprise or storm Fort Cavallo, just opposite Faro, standing on a rocky eminence close on the coast, from which the signal agreed on should be made. There were ten thousand on the Sicilian shore watching the fate of one hour's toil; and at last a faint light from the opposite shore indicated that, after eleven long years of sorrow and despair, the national flag once more floated on the misty tops of the Calabrian mountains.

Half-an-hour passed, and the rattle of musketry came over the ocean, and silence and mystery ensued. But in an hour Missori sent over a messenger announcing the landing, and explaining the ominous noise. Just as the boats touched the opposite shore, one of them, containing the French and English who had joined, drifted or chose to sail away from the company towards Villa San Giovanni; and not knowing either the coast or the General's orders, approached a Neapolitan battery. They were fired on and two were wounded, and this compelled them to retrace their way. Missori had gone on his way with his band, but the noise of musketry made him doubt the possibility of surprising the Fort Cavallo, and he took to the mountains.

But the most extraordinary phase of the transaction is the perfunctory way in which the Neapolitans guarded the straits. We use no wild word in saying they "swarmed" upon the waters; but they were mere lookers-on. Now and then, it is true, the sky was illuminated by signal-rockets; but it would almost seem as if the object of their being fired was only to advise their comrades to keep out of the way; for after the first party had landed Garibaldi despatched others in a continuous stream, purposing himself to follow, and no harm or hindrance ensued. The Calabrians from their village conclaves poured in their votes of adherence, and promised that upon his landing they would all rise to the cry of "Long live the Dictator! Long live Victor Emmanuel! and down with the Bourbons!" He, however, kept his own counsel. No one knew where he himself would land. No one knew, as each flotilla went off, where it was going; nor did they know if the General did not intend to fire the whole place by means of small parties on every side.

And indeed that turned out to be the case. But meanwhile the people set the place in a blaze. The men of the Abruzzi began. General Fleury, the commander, wrote on the 19th:—

"The day before yesterday Villa Foggia rose in insurrection. The dragoons in garrison joined the seditious cries, 'Viva Garibaldi! Viva Vittore Emmanuele!' I sent two companies of the 13th regiment, and they have joined the insurgents.   I went myself to get them away, and they began to obey, but just before leaving they turned and fraternised with the people, and I had to go back with nobody but my staff."

This northern example had its prompt followers.   The province Basilicata in the very heart of the kingdom cast off allegiance, and proclaimed, under Colonel Boldoni and others, " l'Italia e Vittore Emmanuele," and invited all the communes to send up their armed contingents to the central city Potenza.   There, to avoid civil war, the Revolutionary Committee asked the prefect and chief of police whether he would oppose or leave the people alone.   He asked for time, and then said he would fight it out ; proceedings began, but before an overt act he sent to the National Guard that he would join them, and took his four hundred *gens d'armes* to a hill outside the town. . . .   Potenza soon made up a revolutionary self-supporting army of ten thousand men, augmenting faster than could be utilised.   A Provisional Government, in the name of Victor Emmanuel, of course followed.

Garibaldi's landing had been known to Gallotti, the commander of Reggio ; but the latter did not anticipate so speedy an assault as he received, and the population refused to communicate intelligence that might be of use to him. He imagined that the attack would come from the sea, and to his astonishment it came from behind him.   He had eight companies, one hundred and fifty strong, under his orders, a battery of seven field-pieces, and two forts well furnished with guns, arms, provisions for a month, and ammunition.   He therefore went to bed on the evening of the 20th, but at half-past two in the afternoon the invading column had arrived at the northern gates from the hills, and within the town the National Committee had prepared eight hundred armed men ready to aid by an insurrection.

On the 21st Chiasso led the advanced guard, in which Garibaldi's son, Menotti, commanded a battalion and two companies of Sacchi's brigade. The recognised bravery and skill of Chiasso rendered his selection acceptable to the whole army, for they felt that all that arrangements could do would assuredly be done by him to ensure success. He determined to occupy the Piazza del Mercato before his presence could be known. Menotti Garibaldi took up his position at the north end of one of those wide streets parallel with the shore, ready to assail the enemy as soon as their arrival provoked resistance. Presently a patrol party came up from the shore road, and fell in with Chiasso's men, whom they engaged. This awoke the place, and an indescribable confusion ensued ; for the moon had set, and darkness hung over the streets. The Neapolitans, surprised, were running wildly about, not regarding their leaders, but pressing towards the castle. Boldrini had by this time come up with his men, and entered by one of the streets which led him to the rear of the little fort. Its four 32-pounders pointed to the sea, and could not be employed against assaults on the land side. These brave fellows rushed against the fort's walls with a loud cry of " Viva Garibaldi !" so as to paralyse the defenders by fright. They climbed the walls like cats, and speedily took possession. In a great panic the Neapolitans threw down their arms, imploring mercy, just as they had always done when opposed at close quarters.

This fort being secured, the two companies of Chiasso, which had helped Boldrini in his bold and successful operation, came up into the town, and by means of a movable barricade approached the steep lane which led to the castle, under great peril, for grape-shot and shells were sweeping the streets and bursting in many parts of the upper town. A strong barricade, put up by Chiasso and Boldrini, an artillery officer, prevented any effective sortie from the castle, and enabled Bixio to carry out his part of the proceedings. He had come from the heights into the piazza, where the business of fighting centralised itself. By a daring movement he advanced up a street on the right, and commenced a warm musketry fire against the castle gunners; but a slight wound in the left arm somewhat checked his advance. Egbert's brigade had in the meantime reached the heights in the rear of the castle, and two of its companies found an opportunity of firing into the town, where confusion waxed greater and greater.

Gallotti, the Neapolitan general, telegraphed to San Giovanni, a small fort seven or eight miles from Reggio, for General Briganti, with more than twelve hundred men, to come and help him. He did so, but on getting within four miles of his destination Garibaldi came out to meet him, and Briganti discreetly retired on Gallucco, leaving his colleague to help himself as he could. Garibaldi hastened back to Reggio, and, seeing a chance, ordered a storming party to prepare an attack, and get possession of the castle. It was then a quarter to twelve. One of the defenders' colonels had fallen, and Gallotti could not see his way to go on. The hoisting of a flag of truce was the signal for negotiation, and negotiation resulted in capitulation, which Garibaldi granted on certain terms—viz., That the royalists should retire by sea, leaving all the forts, stores, war *matériel*, mules, and horses in the victor's hands.

So fell the old Neapolitan rule in Reggio. Smart, well-dressed, well-armed soldiers threw down their arms at the presence of a ragged, ill-fed, dismal-looking army, which however atoned for all its roughness by an inextinguishable faith in its leader, and an all-absorbing attachment to liberty. The National Guard rendered much service in the conflict, and contributed to keep the energy of the invaders in full exercise, undaunted by the loss of one of their best officers, Camerini, and eight of their comrades. Garibaldi nominated Plotino to be the governor of the Reggio provinces *pro tem.*

The next day Garibaldi had an interview with Briganti and Accerello, but it came to nothing. He gave the order to march at twelve o'clock, and away the gallant band of patriots went over the ridge which faces the sea to a plateau, which they reached by dusk. Cosenz had arrived at Aspromonte, intending to combine with Garibaldi. He had effected his landing between Scilla and Bagnana, and encountered Neapolitan soldiers at Selano, who tried to oppose his march. With him were the English and French companies under the command of Colonel Flotte, the well-known defender of the barricades in the Paris revolution of 1848. The collision brought on a contest of two hours. The village had been carried at the point of the bayonet when Flotte rushed off towards a lane, sword in hand, summoning a small party there to surrender. He had scarcely reached the corner when a Neapolitan soldier, hidden there, shot him dead on the spot. The loss could not but be very much grieved over, and Garibaldi issued a touching order of the day recording the military capacity and social virtues of the lamented officer. Goodall took up the command, and the march had no further molestation.

At dawn the next day the bivouac broke up, and the march from the plateau was resumed, the object being to overtake the Neapolitans at Campo. In order to perform this march, and to reach one of the torrent beds which intersect those mountains, the little army had to pass within the range of Melandez's brigade, massed before the village of Piale, and outflank it. Well provided with artillery, it contested the ground. Half-a-dozen were killed, and a dozen wounded, when a charge was made, and that determined the question, and gave Garibaldi a position which governed most of the main roads of the district to the sea, and cut off Briganti from Melandez.

As soon as Garibaldi thought he had accomplished his object, and secured the result of his strategy, he sent Count Trecchi and Major Vecchy to General Melandez, summoning him to surrender (24th August). A flag of truce was hoisted, and the officers started to the enemy's camp, which they found thoroughly demoralised, many of the soldiers shouting "Viva Garibaldi!" Melandez denied at first that his condition was hopeless, and declined to give an answer without first consulting the military commander of the province of Calabria, which would require four hours. Two of the Neapolitan staff returned with them to discuss the terms of capitulation, and these had the impudence to ask Garibaldi whether, if they joined him, he would advance them a grado! He told them promptly that he could not do such a thing, for it would be scandalously unjust to reward men who had slain their brethren at Palermo, and now served a government that bombarded a harmless city of two hundred thousand people.

These were dismissed without any result, and at the expiration of four hours the General determined again to raise the flag of truce. No sooner had he done so than the soldier on duty received a shot in his head. Garibaldi, enraged at such infamous conduct, ordered an attack, but Melandez sent new messengers, and they had an interview not easily forgotten. He told them they commanded a band of brigands; that to shoot the bearer of a flag of truce was the most infamous act a soldier could be guilty of; he bade them begone, and tell Melandez that if he did not surrender by three o'clock he would attack him at once, and throw his brigade into the sea. Melandez complied, and two thousand five hundred more were disarmed by the "filibuster." Melandez's surrender necessitated that of Briganti before night, and twelve hundred more were disbanded. The fort was also evacuated, so that the victors captured on this day about two thousand muskets, four pieces of field artillery, and ten guns of heavy calibre. The moral effects of the capitulation were incomparably greater: two thousand soldiers, who adored Garibaldi, returned to their homes recounting his praise; and besides this, the position on the straits gained thereby was one of considerable importance for the southern army.

Between the 25th and 28th of August a march of eighty long mountain miles proved our hero's energy and determination to carry out his work to the utmost of his strength, and struck terror into the armed bands swarming about the country.

Seven thousand Neapolitan soldiers occupied Monteleone, and on Sunday the 27th our hero left his army, and went to Nicotera to receive a deputation, with a view of accepting a transfer of their allegiance; but he refused their terms and ordered his troops to press on thither. Cosenz took the advanced guard, and the Neapolitans bolted up the hills and wherever they could fly.

Once in motion, Garibaldi had great reluctance to halt; he left Cosenza at night on the 31st August, and reached Tarsi, some twenty miles farther to the north, by dawn, and there found General Pace and his company of Calabrians. They joined, and went forward together as far as Spezzana Albanese a few miles on the same road. The Albanese originally consisted of emigrants, and maintained still their Greek religion, their costume and habits, as when they came hither in the fifteenth century. These had always in Italian troubles fraternised with the Calabrians in the cause of liberty, and in return the Calabrian youth were sent there to be educated. The political tendencies of the people are determined by the entire sympathy maintained between the gentry and peasantry, who all in common are trained to arms amongst themselves, and are fired with the independence common to mountain tribes.

The oppressive heat hindered not the enthusiastic march

of thirty-five miles a day.　Bertani's six thousand from Milan were made the leading column, under Türr.　Cosenz's column, now placed under General Sacchi, Cosenz being fully engaged with the General as his confidential adviser, followed ; and Medici, with his division, had orders to go elsewhere.　Bixio and Ebert, with the rear of the army, made up a force, with the forty thousand Calabrians behind it, which was absolutely formidable.

Colonel Boldoni, formerly in the Sardinian service, had been conducting the Basilicata insurrection, and he arrived at Lagonegro, a large village near the western coast of the mainland, a hundred and fifty miles from the south point, with the news that his forces now reached fourteen thousand, including the insurrectionary bands under Mignano, and backed by the whole population ; and Garibaldi determined on leaving his. army behind, and pressing on thirty or forty miles in advance until he reached Naples.

On the Court at Naples the tidings of what was taking place in the south had a painful effect.　When the king heard the disastrous accounts of his army, and the popularity of the insurrection, he sorrowfully said, " My soldiers, nevertheless, had promised to defend me."　A true Bourbon-like answer.　The army, and all the brute force implied therein, has ever been the fatal rock on which they, and all rulers who dare not trust the spirit of loyalty in the community, have fallen to pieces.　A general standing by replied to the king : " Sire, when your soldiers are in your presence they cry, ' Long live the king ! ' but the moment they turn their backs, and have to be led against the enemy, they cry, ' Viva Garibaldi ! '　That sorcerer of a man has bewitched them, and none of them can be trusted."

The king had clung as long as possible to his royal city, the place of his birth, and the palace of his forefathers. Two years had not run their course since his accession, but the sins of his fathers and his own brought upon him a righteous banishment. The defection of his soldiers, before noticed, had much distressed him, and the generals and commanders of his land and sea forces daily corroborated the apprehension that all the instruments at his command were paralysed and powerless. Finally, he turned to the National Guard as a last resource, but for him or his like no National Guard in any country ever entertained a good-will. He thanked them for their conduct, and in taking leave informed them that a line of troops would be formed, and that it would respect the citadel, but diplomatic arrangements compelled his absence.

His ministers desired him to form a regency; he would not. The Council of State could take charge of affairs, and no minister should leave, but he demanded 260,000 ducats and eight thousand men for a six month's garrison at Gaeta.

He had accused his generals of treachery because they reported the corrupt state of the army, and the demoralising leaven at work. He soon learned the truth by experience. The navy refused to accompany him farther than within two miles of Gaeta, and the army melted away under the influence of the Revolutionary Committee, who guaranteed them a welcome in the Garibaldian army.

The announcement of Garibaldi's approach to Naples came as a surprise to its population. Men accustomed to watch events calmly questioned its possibility. When the flags began to be hoisted, and the Municipal Guard appeared, the public expectation quickened very rapidly, and crowds of people gathered everywhere. Then the sentinels took possession of the passages at Government House. Presently came on the portion of the army lately transferred to the new *régime*, and these fitly heralded the beginning of a new rule. At mid-day a cry was heard, followed by a popular shouting which swelled louder and louder, as the hundreds and thousands received the contagion. The trains had arrived at the station, and the red jackets filled every compartment. The object of popular enthusiasm could not at first be found, but many who bore some resemblance to him had to submit to the Italian huggings and kissings intended for their chief. As at Salerno, Garibaldi avoided the multitude, in order to avoid its violent ebullitions of welcome, and with his staff took carriages from another entrance, and through bye-streets reached the public building, with a following of three lines of carriages, crowded with persons bearing the Italian flag, who cheered, wept, and embraced in true Italian fashion. From every window the flag floated, and the ladies smiled their joy. As they passed Cannone Forte the soldiers gave their military salute, and received a gracious recognition. Amidst shouts and *vivas* to himself and to Italy, the thousands in procession passed to the palace of reception for State occasions, where the Duke of Tuscany had been the last visitor, and Garibaldi dismounted and entered. The pledge he had given to be there before the popular feast he had redeemed. No special preparation had been made, and in fact the committee of the people would have delayed his entry to make it more demonstrative, but the welcome was the more precious because of its spontaneity.

Shout after shout from the people outside brought Garibaldi to the balcony in his red jacket and wideawake. Leaning on the railings he looked on the masses of upturned faces and waved his hand, as if to silence the tremendous noise. The crowd would keep cheering, and he kept waving his hand, and saying, " Zitti, zitti !" (Peace, peace !) until he produced a perfect silence.

"People of Naples," said he, "this is a sublime, sacred, and memorable day. From being mere subjects under a tyrannical yoke, you become this day a free people. In the name of united Italy I thank you. The work you have done for Italy is a great work also for humanity, for you have vindicated its rights. Hurrah for liberty ! Liberty, more specially dear to Italy, for she has suffered more than any other nation.   Viva l' Italia !"

The response of the crowd rang out, as these words, so melodiously uttered, ended, and the Dictator retired to meet a deputation just come from Venetia, imploring his aid in their liberation, to whom he could only give his assurance that no one could be more anxious than he was for their freedom from Austrian rule.   He took a few hours' rest, for his weariness oppressed him, and then entered his carriage and drove up the Toledo to the Duomo and back to the palace, and there received the plaudits of the higher class Neapolitans.   At night Naples was glorious with universal illuminations and torchlight processions, and countless carriages moved to and fro in the streets and on the chief parade until very late.

At the close of the day the sounds of martial music reverberated through the city, indicating the king's departure, and the people collected as spectators on both sides of the street in perfect silence; no insult or any other offence occurred.   In the evening the flag of Piedmont was displayed in the chief cafés, and there were partial illuminations.   The royal arms were removed from public places, and armed bands were formed in accordance with a circular from Garibaldi, and by forced marches they drew nigh to the capital.   Every village complied, and the insurrection became universal.   The frontiers of the Papal States were not respected.   Blasis entered Benevento with several companies mounted on horseback, and dressed in red, with a band of music, in triumph.   Some of the gendarmes and soldiers fled, but most joined the new comers.   Victor Emmanuel was proclaimed King and Garibaldi Dictator, and the Papal arms were torn down wherever they had been placed.

The proclamation of the General to the people, published in the districts round Salerno, as well as in Naples, had much effect in feeding the flame.   These are its words :—

"To the beloved population of Naples, offspring of the people,—It is with true respect and love that I present myself to this noble and imposing centre of the Italian population, which many centuries of despotism have not been able to humiliate or to induce to bow their knees at the sight of tyranny. The first necessity of Italy was harmony, in order to unite the great Italian family; to-day Providence has created harmony through the sublime unanimity of all our provinces for the reconstitution of the nation, and for the same unity Providence has given us Victor Emmanuel, whom we may from this moment call the true father of the Italian land. Victor Emmanuel, the model of all sovereigns, will impress upon his descendants the duty that they owe to the prosperity of a people which has elected him for their chief with enthusiastic devotion.

"The Italian priests who are conscious of their true mission have, as a guarantee of the respect with which they will be treated, the ardour, the patriotism, and the truly Christian conduct of their numerous fellow ecclesiastics, who, from the highly to be praised monks of Lagrancia to the noble-hearted monks of the Neapolitan continent, one and all, in the sight and at the head of our soldiers, defied the gravest dangers of battle. I repeat it, concord is the first want of Italy ; so we will welcome as brothers those who once disagreed with us, but who now sincerely wish to bring their stone to raise up the monument of our country. Finally, respecting other people's houses, we are resolved to be masters in our own house, whether the powerful of the earth like it or not.   "GIUSEPPE GARIBALDI."

The National Guard and the General's soldiers took possession of the castles belonging to the city, those scenes of indescribable misery which first aroused Europe to an unchangeable hatred of the royal line. It was a grave question whether they should not be demolished, but after a while that idea faded out. The cannon were removed,

and they were thrown open to the public. Hitherto, silence
through repression had reigned ; now, like an heir entering
upon his patrimony, the people ran about here, there, and
everywhere, investigating, commenting, determining. A
hundred of the town-guard took their stations at each castle,
and thirty of the Sardinian artillery guarded them without.
Especially was the castle of Sant' Elmo hateful to the
populace, and that for sufficient reasons. It had been the
horror of many households, and the abode of indescribable
misery. About it the best tongues in Europe had remonstrated in powerless indignation. None dared to go
near it, for the sentinel's orders to fire had no alternative.
Here the guns had been ironically turned inward. The
people rushed in, tore down the Bourbon arms from every
gateway, and stamped them under their feet. Fearfully
strong they found the place ; all the winding passages
bomb-proof ; and such was the enormous thickness of the
walls that chambers were constructed in them of wonderful
strength, which could not be discovered on a hasty survey.
Stone platforms were the beds of the prisoners, and a slit in
the door and outer wall let in all the air and light allowed ;
each window, such as it was, had its lock and bolts.
Imagine such a man as Poerio being confined in such a
place for several years ! Other parts could hold greater
numbers, and had openings to admit grenades in case of
riot, and thus solve all difficulties by destroying the inmates.
The dungeons were not entered, because when the governor
went away he took the keys. They extend under the city,
and have witnessed grievous cruelties. But on reaching
the roof the intention of Bomba the younger to imitate his
infamous predecessor was revealed. New beds of wood for
mortars were there, and of recent construction, for the chips
had not been cleared away. The mason-work had also been
recently adjusted, for the mortar had not dried, and the
refuse lay about in heaps. Moreover the old gun-carriages

were reinforced by new ones, but the guns had not had time to come. Naples had transferred its Government just in time to avoid a horrible catastrophe, for no less than forty-two guns commanding the city stood in position.

In entering upon new responsibilities Garibaldi ever regarded, in the first place, the control of public order and peace; and these at Naples he directed in the same way.

The *Monitore Neapolitano*, now the *Giornale Ufficiale*, contained decrees headed "Victor Emmanuel and Italy—the Dictator of the two Sicilies," and signed "Garibaldi." These announced the new official appointments, in which the Neapolitan element preponderated; but some Republicans were included. Bertani had the general secretaryship to the Chief, and then followed the envoys to the Sardinian, French, and English courts. The Minister of the Interior, the commandant of the city, Romano, still kept his place, having so courageously done his duty in the transition, and being by his experience able to preserve the new administration from the influences of novices or selfish people. The Minister of Foreign Affairs, Martino, declined new honours from a delicacy caused by his intimate knowledge of past details and arrangements, and correspondence with other sovereigns and courts. The seals of State bore a new legend, "Victor Emmanuel, King of Italy." Passports inward were abolished; those outward were to have the *visa* of the Police Commissioner.

That first morn of Neapolitan freedom was ushered in by a hurricane of human joy. The garrison soldiers at Castel Nuovo no sooner got out than they set to running, jumping, galloping about the place like newly-emancipated slaves. Some had muskets, others bread, and that they flung about like mad people. The populace met them, armed with spikes, swords, and daggers, which they flourished about, and all were shouting the usual *vivas*. The excitement drew everybody out, for there was no danger, and then a curious scene occurred.   A garrison in the Pizzofalcone was peering over the walls as if to see whether the road were clear, and when the people saw them, all the gestures of invitation that can be imagined were made.   The place had iron doors and sentinels on guard.   Nevertheless, down came the soldiery like a torrent, making the doors bend and the bars yield, until they gained the street, when they set off to join their comrades, leaving empty walls and harmless cannon behind.

Garibaldi went to Pic di Grotta, like the Emperor Charles III., on the first morning of his entry into Naples, amid much enthusiasm, and to the theatre at night, where was much struggling for places from whence he could be seen.

King Francis had gone to Gaeta, and there he formed a ministry.   Garibaldi felt that he must prepare for a speedy renewal of hostilities.   He had not been in Naples many hours before he found proof that the king had not lost the cruel instincts of his race.   On leaving Naples Bomba had ordered Castel dell' Ovo to be blown up, and the forts should fire upon the city.   Garibaldi obtained possession of this order.   When the king, with his booty—for booty it was— reached Gaeta, he anxiously inquired of the first persons who arrived from the royal city for news, and finding that the forts had not bombarded, nor the wicked work of Palermo been done over again, nor the castle sent to the sky, he involuntarily exclaimed, "I *am* betrayed!" and remained for a few minutes in silent astonishment.

With such a spirit as that Garibaldi felt that any means of vengeance, however cruel or infamous, were to be appre- hended if time were wasted.   The experience he had acquired convinced him that, if possible, Naples, the Pope, and Austria would make an alliance again to reduce the millions to subjection, and that they would have no scruples whatever in effecting their purpose.

He therefore gave orders to the Neapolitan and Sardinian

fleets, and also to the army, to be ready for departure. Meanwhile the enthusiasm in the city did not abate. The people did not remain in their dwellings; they preferred the street. In the evening the unpassable thoroughfares resounded with loud shoutings of "Garibaldi!" "Victor Emmanuel!" and "Italia Una." Whenever the former appeared a vast sea of heads surrounded his horse or his carriage, and the people fell on their knees to kiss his stirrups or his clothes. Old men with tears running down their cheeks, and unable to speak, stretched out their hands towards him whom they accepted as the saviour of Italy; while flowers fell from the balconies upon his head. The fact of his entry occurring, as he said it would, on the day before the great *fête* of the Pic di Grotta, which was established a hundred and twenty-seven years ago by Carlo III. to commemorate the expulsion of the Austrians from his dominion, wrought a marvellous effect on popular enthusiasm; and Garibaldi attended it and kept holiday.

The whole of the National Guard, under arms, lined the streets from the Palazzo d'Angri to the end of the Riviera de Chiaja. The General with his staff drove down in carriages, amid the delight of the people, notwithstanding the heavy rain then falling.

The general sentiment of French and Italian politicians was urgently drawn to Garibaldi's northward course, and his professed intention to proceed to Rome, and there proclaim Victor Emmanuel from the Quirinal. Cavour trembled. France began to lose temper. Both remonstrated. To inquirers about his intentions the Dictator said, "What has France to do with us? Pio Nono may be Pope if he likes, but he shall not be an Italian prince." The diplomatic action of Cavour annoyed him, but he was neither surprised nor disconcerted in his patriotic policy. Having given the Neapolitan soldiers permission to return to their homes if so minded, there to await events which might make their recall necessary, particularly if Austria interfered, when he would not only recall them, but levy all under the age of twenty-five, he resolved to increase his present forces by organising more volunteers, which, in the unsettled condition of the country, was attended with no difficulty ; for men might as well be in the army as doing nothing—and, moreover, the spirit of the aroused people could be relied on for the pro-visioning of any temporary force. This he would attach to the army which was being despatched by Victor Emmanuel, and jointly they would march through a friendly country, in spite of mercenary armies or traitorous generals. Garibaldi declared to his friends, "I am the advanced guard of Victor Emmanuel, and he will follow me and take possession."

Garibaldi's determination to follow up his advantage evoked all the latent energies of his enemies, who believed that, by gaining time, the dead cause might be resuscitated, and the new birth killed. So, when the excitement had well-nigh spent itself, counteraction and petty disturbances arose. They were soon quelled, but they harassed the Dictator into a fever—a phase in his physical constitution which we have seen exemplified before. But he would not give up or lie down beyond his usual habit. The prospect of war kept him on the alert, and as Bonami, with a section of King Francis's army, took up position about twenty miles away, at Avellano, with an additional force in reserve at Ariano, he sent Türr after them, and a serious contest ensued, ending in Türr bringing a hundred prisoners after four day's absence. He had broken up Bonami's army ; they laid down their arms, and he bade them go whither they would, and many marched off to Naples, accepting service in Garibaldi's army.

Meanwhile Cavour had been working and waiting in the hope that a favourable opportunity would arise for interven-tion in Southern Italy. At this juncture he addressed an important note to the European Powers, the substance of which is contained in the following summary.

He had long realised the critical position of affairs, in Venetia especially, and was fully alive to the danger that Italians generally would sooner or later react against it. Yet he could not but yield to the general desire for peace, and seek to allay the fears of those who were apprehensive of another war with Austria. He had, therefore, suffered the Venetian question to remain in abeyance.

The fall of Ancona occurred at a most fortunate moment for the King of Sardinia. The Sardinian Chambers, not very united, received summonses calling them to Turin. Cavour read them a ministerial document, which set forth in detail the happy issues of the last few months, and announced: — "Henceforth Italy, with the exception of Venetia, is free. As regards the latter province, we cannot make war upon Austria against the almost unanimous wish of the European Powers. Such an enterprise would create a formidable coalition against Italy. But by creating a strong Italy we are serving the cause of Venetia. The same reasons also impose on us the duty of respecting Rome. That question cannot be solved by the sword; it is surrounded by moral obstacles which can only be overcome by moral force. . . . Parliament is convoked to determine the question of ministerial confidence. This is rendered imperative by the fact that a voice, justly dear to the people, has expressed a distrust of us in the discharge of our duties to the crown and the country." The Parliament gave the Ministry its vote, but begged that there might be no more divisions between Cavour and Garibaldi.

The king left Turin on the 30th September for Bologna, *en route* for Ancona, after learning the surrender of the city and the capture of the garrison, Cavour meeting him at the station. They both received the greetings of the people, but there existed nevertheless some popular uneasiness.

Garibaldi's judgment had so often been a truer guide than the wisest politicians, that the conviction could not be avoided that he had very good reasons for what he did and said.

On reaching Ancona Victor Emmanuel addressed the people of Southern Italy in a long proclamation, bearing his signature and that of Farini. It may be fairly characterised as an adroit production of the Minister to prove that the king had been the redeemer of Italy; whereas he had only been the honest and noble instrument, having accepted the confidence of Garibaldi, and received from him, step by step, the vast power which, but for Garibaldi, would never have come into his hands.

All this time our hero was preparing for his new campaign in the States of the Church. He had very sensibly allowed the armies of Victor Emmanuel to precede him there, but he was busily enrolling and preparing troops in order to co-operate with Cialdini. The Neapolitans enlisted in great numbers; ten thousand Calabrians were ready for the field before the middle of September, and a large force of foreign volunteers, amongst them being many Englishmen, were at Garibaldi's service.

General Türr, who had somewhat recovered his health, was entrusted with the command of a volunteer force from the south, which, without waiting for Garibaldi, proceeded to lay siege to Capua, about twenty-two miles from Naples. The town lies in a strong natural position, being surrounded on three sides by a bend of the river Volturno. On the arrival of Garibaldi at headquarters he announced his determination to take Capua by storm. He displayed on this occasion a military foresight and capacity which even his friends scarcely anticipated of him; and a few days were spent in completing his arrangements. The forces in Capua made sally after sally against his camp, but were as constantly repulsed, whilst a warm fire was kept up from the outposts on both sides.

"The fate of the campaign," which had planted the tri-colour flag in the kingdom of Naples, 22nd August 1860, was definitely decided forty days later by the battle of the Volturno. Till then Garibaldi had indeed led his legions along the way to victory, but this way lay across an abyss bridged over as it were by last night's ice. On the eve of the 1st of October the issue of the undertaking hung yet in the balance. The Neapolitans had collected in the fortress of Capua a well-armed, well-equipped force of about forty-five thousand men : they had brought Francis II. from Gaeta to witness what they thought to make their grand perform-ance ; they had chosen his birthday for its execution. Their troops were prepared to fight to the uttermost, and in fact did so. The 'general idea' of their plan was to break through the Garibaldian lines and march on to Naples. These lines Garibaldi had sketched out a month before—they stretched from San Angelo to Maddaloni, a distance of fourteen kilometres. In confiding to Bixio the positions he was to defend, the chief gave him one piece of advice—to look out that he kept them. Bixio answered, 'While we live they are safe.'

"The Volturno has been called Garibaldi's greatest battle; it certainly was Bixio's. The defence of Maddaloni was prac-tically a separate action from the fighting carried on at San Angelo and Santa Maria, and it was conducted by Bixio alone and unaided. The earliest assault of the *Regi* was made in the direction of Maddaloni, at about four A.M., they having come down from Capua under cover of the dense white mist which hung over the river. Some twelve hours later Bixio saw the last of them flying before his bayonets, and at almost the same moment Garibaldi telegraphed to Naples—'Victory all along the line!' The liberation of the Two Sicilies was an accomplished fact."

In spite of constant and urgent advice to the contrary, Garibaldi steadily refused to bombard Capua, and the town held out, to the no small annoyance of many of the volunteers. "It shall not be said of me," exclaimed our hero, "as of '*il rè Bombino,*' that I caused a town to be bombarded. Capua is so shut in that I shall certainly take it ere long without resorting to such means." It might be easy to prove that a short and sharp bombardment, which would probably have resulted in the speedy surrender of the place, would have been a less sanguinary measure than the prolongation of the campaign; but the cause of Garibaldi's hesitation does him infinite credit. He would not sacrifice the peaceable inhabitants ; and the approach of Cialdini was another good reason for his abstention. In fact, not many days passed before the advance of the Piedmontese army compelled the Neapolitans to abandon the town.

Cialdini was not inconsiderate to the Dictator. He wrote to him to ask if he should continue his march upon the Volturno, and Garibaldi, with the straightforward dignity of an honourable man, telegraphed his reply, "Come at once." It was on the 4th October that the first corps of the Piedmontese army quitted Ancona, whither Victor Emmanuel now came in person, with orders to join the Dictator. Others followed immediately by various routes. A few regiments were sent to Naples to recruit the force which Garibaldi had left there.

Meantime certain of Garibaldi's coadjutors had taken great umbrage against him on account of his steady loyalty to Victor Emmanuel. Mazzini persistently urged the proclamation of a Republic of Southern Italy, and his views were shared both by certain of the Dictator's ministers in Sicily and Naples, and by a large section of the volunteers. It was found necessary once more to disband the Calabrians on this account. Bertani was relieved of his office in the temporary government : and our hero, the better to impress his determination upon all, issued an order of the day in which he referred to " the brave soldiers of Piedmont who set foot on Neapolitan soil." In Naples itself the civil representative of the Dictator was Pallavicini, a staunch royalist, between whom and Crispi a warm dispute arose. Pallavicini tendered his resignation, but Garibaldi took his part, and declined to accept it. Mazzini had hastened to the capital as soon as it fell into the hands of the Garibaldini, and his machinations produced such a disquieting effect on the public mind that the pro-dictator was compelled to order him to depart.

Petitions now began to pour in to Turin from all parts of the rescued country asking for immediate annexation. The Turin Parliament met on the 2nd of October, and a bill was introduced for the purpose of declaring the unification of Italy. Cavour had to contend not only with the more irreconcilable of Garibaldi's partisans, who endeavoured to magnify the discord between the two distinguished patriots, but also with the friends of Mazzini, who argued against annexation. It is true that Garibaldi had suffered himself to protest bluntly against Cavour's compromising policy on more than one recent occasion, and that he had declared his intention of advancing upon Rome at all hazards ; but the Minister's speech disarmed much of the opposition at first displayed, without giving any ground of discontent to the Dictator's champions. "Europe," he said, "is averse to a war with Austria ; it esteems us alone too weak to free Venetia : let us make it manifest that we are of one accord : the weathercock of public opinion will veer : the Venetians will not quietly bear the galling yoke of the Austrian, in spite of all the latter's smooth-tongued flattery. France and England will become more liberal in their opinions of us, and enlightened Germany will wish us success."

The bill for annexation was carried by a majority of two hundred and ninety to six. At the same time a vote was unanimously passed to the effect that Garibaldi had deserved well of his country.

On Garibaldi's arrival at Naples he found the citizens busy in preparations for the arrival of Victor Emmanuel. A ball and illuminations, triumphal processions, and all outward displays common to royal visitations, occupied the attention of those not absorbed in politics.

On the 12th October Garibaldi issued the following proclamation :—

"To the Citizens of Naples.

"To-morrow Victor Emmanuel, King of Italy, the elect of the nation, will break down the frontier which has divided us for so many centuries from the rest of our country, and, listening to the unanimous voice of this brave people, will appear among us.

"Let us receive in a worthy manner him who is sent by Providence, and scatter in his path the flowers of concord, the evidence of our redemption and our affection, for that would be grateful to him as it is necessary for us. Let us have no more political colours, no more parties, no more discords ! The people of this metropolis have wisely accepted the principle—a United Italy and King Galantuomo. These are the imperishable proofs of our regeneration, and are the symbols of our national grandeur and prosperity. "G. Garibaldi."

On the 13th, in response to a public demonstration in his favour, Garibaldi addressed the people from the balcony of the Forestiera, in this characteristic speech :—

"Yesterday I said the king would enter ; to-day I have his letter. On the 10th the Piedmontese troops crossed the frontier of these provinces, and in a few days Victor Emmanuel will place himself at the head of his valiant army. In a few days, then, we shall see our king. Let this time of transition pass in calmness, with prudence and moderation, so that the Neapolitans may shew themselves to be the brave people they are. In a few days this provisional state will cease, and in spite of her enemies and those who do not desire it, Italy will be one!" Here, raising a finger, he was followed by a unanimous shout from all assembled.

From Naples Garibaldi now retired to Caserta. By this time he had come to the conclusion that he would no longer oppose the annexation, for he could plainly perceive that the difficulties in the way of immediately marching on to Rome were great enough to cause a dangerous delay, which might embolden the reactionary priesthood and court party.

The official journal of the 17th contained this important decree, dated San Angelo, 15th October :—

"The Two Sicilies, which owe their redemption to the blood of the Italians, and have elected me their Dictator, form an integral and indivisible part of Italy, with its constitutional king, Victor Emmanuel. I shall place in the hands of the king on his arrival the dictatorship conferred on me by the nation.   "G. GARIBALDI."

At three o'clock on the 24th an officer of Cialdini's staff arrived in disguise at Caserta, bringing news to Garibaldi of the arrival of the Piedmontese army in the vicinity of Venafro, and of the king's arrival at Iternia; and as Cialdini expected to find the Neapolitan forces somewhere near Teano, he wished Garibaldi to make some movement in that direction, that they might co-operate.

In the meantime Garibaldi having concentrated his forces at Calvi, sent Colonel Missori to compliment the king at Teano, and to state his near proximity. It was agreed that His Majesty should meet Garibaldi next day at the foot of Santa Maria della Croce, about midway between Calvi and Teano, and review the divisions of Ebert and Bixio when they came up. At eight o'clock on Friday morning Garibaldi drew up his force in order, and although ragged, they made a very good appearance. It was a sight for the artist to have seen the drawing together of these two men. Leaving his forces, and attended by his staff, Garibaldi advanced to meet the king, who was marching at the head of his army upon the line of the Volturno. They met between Teano and Sperangan on the 26th of October.

Seeing the red shirts, the king took a glass, and having recognised Garibaldi, gave his horse a touch of the spur and advanced to meet him. At ten paces distant the officers of the king and those of Garibaldi shouted "Viva Victor Emmanuel!" Garibaldi made another step in advance, raised his cap, and added in a tone which trembled with emotion, "King of Italy." Victor Emmanuel raised his hand to his cap, and then stretched out his hand to Garibaldi, and with equal emotion replied, "Thank you;" and such an answer well suited the facts of the case, the bluff honest nature of the king and the stern simplicity of the great Liberator, whose highest aim had been met in being enabled to hail his sovereign as King of Italy, and whose greatest reward lay in the fulfilment of his desire: and we shall shortly see how he left his work, declining honours or reward other than the grateful thanks of a freed people.

On reaching Capua, Garibaldi sent a flag of truce to demand, in the name of the king, the surrender of the place. The only answer was a brisk fire of shells and canister. In the night, however, two Neapolitan officers came to Santa Maria to confer with General della Rocca. He granted an interview, but it was only to receive the same answer as that given to Cialdini—that the commander at Capua had resolved to defend the place to the last extremity, and bury himself with the garrison under its ruins. Rocca reminded them that all communication with Gaeta being cut off, the position was indefensible, and adjured them to consider the character of the war; that both sides were Italians, and the fratricidal conflict, under impossible conditions, must be regarded as unjustifiable, for every man shot by their artillery might justly be considered as murdered by his brethren. It was of no avail. A tremendous fire was opened, and as that kind of reply convinced the camp that the urgent appeal of their general had made no favourable impression, a bombardment must be the other alternative, and for that the artillery made instant preparation. One of the mortar batteries that had been finished during the day threw three shells into the town, one bursting on the spire of the Duomo. The Neapolitans then opened a heavy fire, which silenced one of the batteries, and put a hundred and twenty men *hors-de-combat*, among whom were two captains and Colonel Fabrizzi, who had his right arm smashed by the bursting of a shell.

But the intrigues of those who surrounded the king had very nearly brought about a catastrophe which would have greatly damaged the Italian cause. The siege of Capua had, of course, to be effected by both the Piedmont and the Garibaldian armies, to cut off any attempt at retreat or relief and supplies. Rocca had been in charge of that department under Garibaldi, and his position remained the same now that Victor Emmanuel had come; but at the royal camp there had been some crafty influence at work, and a note from headquarters reached the General committing the artillery works to the sole care of Rocca, making him independent of Garibaldi. The warrior's spirit instantly quivered under the wound, which he thought inflicted by his friend from whom he had so recently parted, and with whom many confidential explanations and opinions had passed. He thought himself wronged, and forthwith wrote out his resignation, despatching Colonel Nullo to Sessa.

The king instantly refused it, and wrote a most kind letter to his friend, in which he explained the misunderstanding, and begged him to remain at the head of the army to which the operations of the siege of Capua were assigned. Garibaldi accepted the communication, and consented to remain until the end of the war. Had he not done so, his thirty thousand men would assuredly have gone away with him, for they had a very excusable spirit of jealousy. He broke up his staff, nevertheless, dividing between Cosenz and Sirtori twenty of them, but retaining Frecchi, Caldesi, Missori, and Nullo.

The besiegers pursued their preparations, erecting six batteries of mortars and rifled cannon ; one on the road that leads from San Angelo to the little town. There were only eight thousand inhabitants, and it seemed unlikely that the garrison would be so cruel as to sacrifice them. Their houses being close to the river Volturno, the people could not shelter themselves in the basements, because there was none, and nothing remained for them but to abide in their houses in hope of escaping the bursting shells.

Victor Emmanuel came across to San Angelo soon after mid-day on the 1st November, to give the signal for the bombardment in person, and Rocca went to meet him. At four o'clock His Majesty mounted the hill that slopes down to the village, and a red flag—the signal to open fire—fluttered in the wind. In five minutes a dense cloud of smoke covered the whole country from Carditello to San Angelo. The bastions of Capua opened their fire with heavy guns, and a dreadful cannonade ensued. Garibaldi was there, full of sorrow and melancholy, looking at the horrid tragedy of death preparing by terrible necessity for his countrymen at Capua. He became so dejected and heartbroken that none could speak to him. A band struck up under his window, but he turned away and begged to be left quiet. As the daylight gradually disappeared and darkness came on, the aspect grew more imposing and terrible. Nothing could be seen but the flashing of the guns and the terrible noise of falling houses. Even the screams of the women and children could be distinguished as the north wind brought the dreadful din into the camp. The projectiles from Capua doubled in number those sent thither, but the assailants lost but four men killed and wounded. The king, at San Angelo, grieved as did his friend, and the expression of his face concealed not his emotion. To his generals he said, "This is a sad scene, gentlemen; it breaks my heart to think that we are sending death and destruction into an Italian town. Oh, I fondly hope that the cries of those helpless inhabitants will induce Cerni to surrender."

The fire continued all the night, till in the morning a white flag waved over the Porta Napoli bastion. Liguori came to make proposals, but Garibaldi sent him to Rocca, who gave him answer that he would have given up to him the persons of those who insulted and threatened the soldiers of Garibaldi on the 1st of October, and bade him take that message as his final answer to Cerni, and bring his reply in an hour. His selection for such a work being a mere tool of the King of Naples's worst advisers, did not recommend to either of the opposing generals, and within an hour Cerni accepted the conditions, and engaged to effect the transfer at seven o'clock on the next day, being the 3rd November.

The *Nazoine* of Florence states that 10,500 men and six generals were taken prisoners, while 290 brass guns, 160 gun carriages, 20,000 muskets, 10,000 swords, 80 waggons, pontoons for 240 feet, 500 horses and mules, besides stores, ammunition, and several thousand articles of clothing, made the prize in material.

While at Naples on the 29th, Garibaldi wrote to Mordini, the Pro-Dictator in Sicily, a letter transferring him to the king's authority :—

"SIGNOR PRO-DICTATOR,—I have addressed to our *chargés d' affaires* at Paris and London the following despatch :—

"The decrees of the 8th and 15th of the past month, inviting the people of Southern Italy to recognise Victor Emmanuel as their king, must have informed you that we are appropriating the end we proposed to ourselves by the national war.

"That verdict of the people is now pronounced. I am going—as I have engaged to do, by several acts—I am going to place my powers in the hands of the fortunate king whom Providence has destined to unite in a single family the several provinces of our country. In consequence, my government gives place to that of the king, and your mission at his Majesty's court ceases *ipso facto;* the representatives of the King of Italy at foreign courts will have to undertake the duty of sustaining the acts of the national policy with the governments to which they are accredited.

" In discharging you from the employment which I have entrusted to you in the interests of the country, I feel that I ought to declare to you that in the difficult circumstances in which you have exercised it, you have deserved my entire satisfaction. Accept my best thanks and assurance that I shall ever remember your disinterested services.

" G. GARIBALDI."

The "two kings" rode into Naples together, and on leaving the railway took the route for the Cathedral in an open carriage, sitting side by side; Garibaldi on the king's left, and opposite to them sat the two pro-dictators of Sicily and Naples, followed by the suite. All along the road the public made one continuous ovation. The streets were gaily festooned with flowers and evergreens from window to window; pictures, tapestry, banners, and all the usual items in royal processions abounded; but the rain poured down without cessation, and the thunder-claps almost drowned the cheering of the vast crowd. On arriving at the Cathedral, the piazza of which had been beautifully decorated, His Majesty was received by the authorities and conducted to the high altar, amidst such a storm of shouts and applause as could only be compared with the outside storm. " Viva Victor Emmanuel! Viva Garibaldi! Viva Italia Unita!"

were the cries which rose from the many thousands who waved hats and handkerchiefs as the royal party advanced to the high altar. This was the Cathedral of St. Januarius, the special protector of the Bourbons, whose intercession had been evoked by Baron Brenier as an honour for M. Thouvenal. Some effort to produce silence only made the shouting louder and louder, as if an irrepressible and irresistible necessity impelled their joy.

The king did not take his seat on the throne, but stood a little below it, wiping his perspiring head and face vigorously, and then looking round with his natural bold and undaunted aspect. Shortly after this the ceremony began. His Majesty knelt at the *prix-dieu*, whilst Garibaldi and the others stood behind him. The *Te Deum* rang through the building in magnificent style, and, as soon as it ended, the royal party descended from the altar amidst the same long-continued and increasing shouts, and went to visit the treasury and the chapel of St. Januarius, where the blood of the saint is kept. Of course the observance could not be omitted, but who can imagine either of these men bowing reverently before this chemical deception.

As soon as the ceremony was over they came down the aisle, and, says an eye-witness, "I had an admirable view of the king and the liberator face to face, and as a gleam of sun shone out on the monarch, every line was visible. 'Humanity' came first, and 'Divinity' after. The difference in the two expressions could not fail to strike the most insensible. I looked at Victor Emmanuel's unvarying face and bold glance, and saw there the *rè galantuomo*, true to his word, and ready to maintain it with his sword; but I looked on Garibaldi and felt the moral grandeur of his character—not a statesman, but something higher. His face expresses his character; an amiability which wins all hearts, and an energy which overcomes all difficulties. The crowd around each of them was immense, although the soldiers did what they could to keep an open path. That was impossible; one of the poorest of the poor laid hold on the king's hand and walked with him, and the people clung to Garibaldi and kissed him and embraced him like a father. He was the greater idol in the temple of idols. So the royal party walked down the church and entered their carriage in the midst of long-continued bursts of applause. The king wore the uniform of a General of Division. Later on, Garibaldi issued the following address:

"To my Companions in Arms:

"We must now consider the period now terminating as the last stage but one in our national resurrection, and prepare ourselves for the worthy completion of the grand desires and hopes of twenty generations which Providence has reserved for our fortunate age.

"Yes, young men! Italy owes to you the glorious work which deserves the applause of the whole world. You have conquered, and you will conquer: because now you have acquired a knowledge of the tactics which decides the issue of battles. You are fit to rank with the men who entered with the close ranks of that Macedonian phalanx which successfully contended with the proud conquerers of Asia. To this wonderful page in our country's history another more glorious will be added, for the slave shall shew his free brethren a sharpened sword that has been forged from the very links of his chains.

"To arms, then, all of you! all of you! and the oppressors and the mighty will fly before you like dust.

"Women! you will spurn all cowards from your arms, for they will only give you cowards as children; and you, who are the daughters of the land of beauty, ought to have children that are noble and brave.

"Let timid *doctrinaires* depart from among us, to carry elsewhere their servility and their miserable fears. The people is its own master. I wish to establish fraternal relations with all other peoples ; but upon the insolent it desires to look proudly, and not to grovel before them to implore its own freedom. It will no longer be dragged along by men whose hearts are base. No ! no ! no ! Providence has given to Italy Victor Emmanuel, and every Italian must rally round him. By his side every quarrel should be forgotten, and all angry feelings disappear.

"Once more I repeat my battle cry. To arms ! All of you ! If March 1861 does not find a million of Italians in arms, alas for liberty ; alas for the life of Italy. Ah, no ! Far from me be the thought I loathe like poison. The March 1861, or if necessary the February, will find us all at our posts.

"Italians of Calatafimi, Palermo, Volturno, Ancona, Castel-Fidardo, and Isernia, every man of this land who is not a coward or a slave is on our side. All of us ! all of us ! I say, will be standing close around the glorious hero of Palestro, ready to strike the last blow at the crumbling edifice of tyranny.

" Receive, then, my gallant young volunteers at this time when we have honourably finished ten battles, one farewell word from me. I utter it with the deepest affection, and from my very heart. To-day I must retire, but only for a short time. The hour of battle will find me with you again ; with you, the champions of Italian liberty."

Basso, his private secretary, had the disagreeable tidings to report that, with every economy, they had only thirty pounds from the campaign. He replied, "Do not be anxious, Basso ; we have abundance of wood and corn at Caprera, and we will send them to Maddalena for sale." He had spent all his money, and now returned with less than when he left his home. Before leaving, however, he asked Colonel Missori to go to Admiral Munday and inform him that he hoped to pay him a farewell visit on the following day. After leaving the palace, Garibaldi retired to the Hotel d'Angleterre, and at dawn he embarked, as we have described, amid the grief of his friends. Before six o'clock the guns of the *Hannibal* announced his approach, and Lieutenant Welmont informed the Admiral that the General waited in his cabin. He had not put on his sword, but otherwise he retained his ordinary attire. Pointing to the *Washington,* he said, "There, Admiral, is the vessel that is to carry me to my island home; but I could not leave without expressing my sense of faith in the honour of the British flag."

Nothing in the life of Garibaldi is more touching than the noble simplicity with which he now retired from the proudest position which it is possible for a subject to occupy. The conqueror of Naples thus shewing himself determined to retire for a time, Victor Emmanuel, the heir of his conquests, desired to prove his gratitude by loading the hero with riches and honours. He proposed to reward Garibaldi with the title of Prince of Calatafimi, the rank of marshal of the Italian army, the grand cross of the *Annunciata,* and an income of 500,000 francs. But Garibaldi declined all these brilliant offers, and begged to be allowed to retire into private life. He assured his Majesty, however, that in the hour of danger he would again appear at the head of his veterans. He did not go away discontented, as many assert: this is proved by the fact that he accepted his nomination as general of the Piedmontese army—nothing more and nothing less than what he had been before he set out on his adventurous expedition to Sicily.

This was the hero's crowning glory, and had he been wrecked on the voyage, or landed with an unshaken determination never to revisit the mainland, his achievements would have gone down to posterity as a myth, hardly second to the deeds of the ancient demigods; and he would have been free from the alloy of the earthly passions which in almost all cases degraded their divine nature.

CHAPTER X.

ASPROMONTE.

'All—all—save one !   Rome still in fetters lay
  Writhing beneath the hierarch's heavy heel ;
  The eldest-born of all that bright array,
  From franchised kith cut off by warding steel.
  For fitful Gaul, whose trumpets first did bray
  Salvation o'er the hill tops, feebly leal
  To its own dream, from all high quests had ceased,
  Playing scorned gaoler to a trembling priest !"
                              —ALFRED AUSTIN.

WHEN the General arrived at Caprera, he was astonished to find his island quite changed. He had left it a stony desert, except around his dwelling ; but new cultivated fields and plantations, with groves and avenues, met his gaze. His cottage, too, had given place to a commodious villa and farm buildings ; no doubt he had known that a friend intended him a surprise. The full explanation faced him in the hall, for there hung the portrait of Victor Emmanuel, who had turned his absence to account in a practical manner.

After he had renewed acquaintance with his household gods, he paid a visit to his three horses. His first act after the usual caress was to remove their halters and let them have a run. He ordered a corn mill to be sent from Europe, one that should grind by hand, as Caprera has no water-course, and thus began again his rural life in all its simplicity.

On the 18th of April 1860, in the afternoon, Garibaldi went to the Chamber of Deputies amid the acclamations of a large concourse of spectators, and wearing his red shirt and grey cloak. After the usual formalities, on taking his seat for the first time, Ricasoli opened the debate with some direct questions to the Minister of War concerning the treatment of the Southern Army and the ideas for the future. Garibaldi followed, and accused the Ministry of despising the volunteers, and driving the country toward civil war. Cavour rose and said: "I earnestly protest against this accusation." The storm rose: the Ministers and Deputies stood, and the President took up his hat. On reassembling, apologies ensued as to warmth of language, and Bixio made a touching appeal in the interest of concord, begging Garibaldi and Cavour to forget the circumstance, on the ground that they both had served their country faithfully, and that the common love of country should produce agreement. Cavour followed, and shewed that although unseen he had really been among those who early prompted the General, and had quietly rendered all the help in his power to enlist the volunteers. Garibaldi thanked him for what he had done in 1859, but could not withdraw his reproaches, although he would tender them courteously. His soldiers should not have been treated in the manner they had been. He said: "When my country is at stake, I shall always yield; but ought I to shake hands with him who has made me a foreigner in my native land. The Minister of War says he has saved central Italy from anarchy. I appeal to those who then governed the country. I say there was never any danger of anarchy. It is not my wish to encourage personalities, but I am bound to defend mine own honour."

Victor Emmanuel had a castle outside of Turin, about six or seven miles, called Moncalieri, and there he invited Garibaldi to meet Cavour. The meeting took place; and the king entered into minute details on the affairs of the kingdom and its domestic and foreign relations. Cavour spoke afterwards with much frankness, and in the result Garibaldi gave him his hand. The king's heart was gladdened at this reconciliation. In the evening the king, knowing that Garibaldi intended a visit to the Marquis Pallavicini Trivulzio, arranged an interview between Cialdini and the General. Cosenz went with him, and Cialdini entered into explanations, alleging his jealousy of the Republican disturbers of the peace, who had no practical aim, and were therefore dangerous. Garibaldi, whilst defending his friends from suspicions quite undeserved, spoke in his natural frank manner, embraced his fellow-soldier, saying: "If Italy has need of us, we shall be united in her defence. I have no other ambition or desire but to render her service with those who love her as I do." The interview over, he repaired to the villa of Pallavicini Trivulzio.

The first anniversary of Garibaldi's departure for Sicily on the 5th May 1860, having come round, the people of Genoa got up a celebration of the events of the year in his honour. The *rendezvous* at the Villa Spinola was decorated for the occasion, and in spite of the cold and rainy weather a concourse of fifteen thousand assembled and went down to the spot on the sea-shore, more than three miles from the city, where a monument had been erected to mark the hero's last footsteps as he embarked for that nobly adventurous crusade. The stone was strewn with flowers, and orations were delivered by Brofferio, Ferrari, Guerazzi, and Mauro Macchi. The last-named speaker made a great hit in reference to the "gallant thousand" who left there last spring. "They were but a thousand when they left this lovely spot on the Riviera, but thirty thousand when they arrived at Naples and the Volturno; they went like men going to a certain death, but they returned with ten millions of Italians restored to our nation for their trophy. Here, then, we may see the power of an earnest will; here we may take courage for the combat to come." The other Italian cities also held celebration of this event.

In one month from that time Cavour departed this life, after an illness of seven days. When all hope was given up, the king called to take leave. Cavour was still sensible. He spoke of the "poor Neapolitans"—so full of talent, and yet so many of them corrupt. Their vice he ascribed to "that rogue Ferdinand." Then he went on to say how he would educate the people out of their corruption, and added, "We will have no state of siege; any one can govern with a state of siege." He said that he fully shared Garibaldi's desire to get Venice, but that Tyrol and Istria must wait for another generation. Then he referred to the American war, and said how passionate an admirer he had been of the United States; "but now," he added, "I am cured of my illusions." Lastly, he pointed to Ricasoli and Farini as his successors. The hand of death was upon him. Extreme unction was administered amid the sobs of the bystanders. Pressing the priest's hand, he said, " Frate, frate; libera chiesa in libero stato "—" Brother, brother, a free church in a free state." These were his last words, and a few minutes later all was over.

In spite of Papal excommunication, his body was buried in peace; in spite of Papal condemnation, his name will live evermore.

Cavour was succeeded as Prime Minister by Baron Ricasoli. This statesman had distinguished himself by his fidelity to the Italian cause, and by his making secondary all attempts to control affairs through diplomatic agents. The cause of Italian unity therefore lost little by the change. Garibaldi had left the Chamber sitting, and returned home after his daughter's wedding to recruit his broken health, and recover his mental elasticity in his favourite pursuit of agriculture. He rose early, took his cigar and breakfast, and then, until evening, occupied himself on the farm ; returning to his dinner, conversation, and correspondence. Some of his letters are didactic in tone ; as for instance, in invoking the Marchioness Pallavicini's acceptance of the presidency of a Ladies' Philanthropic Society for improving the condition of the poor, and educating their children, he alleged that much of the illness of women in the superior ranks arose from want of regular employment, and asserted that such labour, when done for the benefit of others, had a health-giving effect on the body. "Let once the power of mind over body be successfully established, vigour in body and mind must follow. Hearty industrious work is obedience to God's great law. Those who endeavour to evade that law and consult their own gratification suffer in health and comfort, whilst the sense of duty well done augments twofold all the delights of domestic life."

An attack of fever ensued in August, caused by worry. The Government of Naples, with its tiresome red-tapeism about the honouring and rewarding of his army, vexed him till he lost patience. The administration at Naples had become, like other regular governments, a little stiff and cold, and the priests and the old court faction took every advantage, and represented the facts to Europe in a sense hostile to the new *régime*. Of course, Garibaldi listened to the exaggerations, and thought matters worse than they were. But the people of Naples had not lost their regard for him ; in truth there was a danger of their becoming idolaters. The *Nazionale* published a letter which they addressed to him at Caprera :—"The people of Naples to their Garibaldi.—Every day, every hour, every moment, we bless the dear Joseph our father. You reign in our hearts ; our children have learned thy name, and mingle it in their prayers. You are the Father of our people. Quite alone, undaunted by difficulty or fatigue, and without caring for yourself, thou hast given us thy life and the lives of so many. Our hope in thee is undying, and so is our gratitude. We shall hand it down from father to son through all generations. May the winds of heaven bear to Caprera the echo of our voices: ' Viva Garibaldi !' "

Work at Caprera went on. Garibaldi brought more land under cultivation, and with the aid of new machinery and implements sent him from America, England, Scotland, and other countries, his management of the farm produced great results. His quiet was often interrupted by visitors, to whom he spoke with great freedom and kindness, and especially did he put aside any harsh language concerning the King of Naples, throwing all the blame on his bad advisers. Presents flowed in, and some were too rich for his use or taste ; and once he declined their acceptance and his visitors were hurt. He saw it, and said : "You might do me a great pleasure if you would ; there is much distress in a part of the Austrian dominions just at present. I have sent them a hundred francs ; that is all I can afford. If you would but sell those things, and give the money to those poor people, who want it so much, I should be very grateful to you." The gentleman remembering the flight of the General when he lost his wife Anita, listened in astonishment, and at last said, "But they are Austrians !" "And is that the way you read Christ's gospel ?" was the answer ; "did He not die for all, and has He not said that all mankind are brethren. If they have a bad government, the people need more of our pity than blame."

The craving for Rome pervaded all the towns of Italy, and Victor Emmanuel had the hardest work to keep matters in check, especially with so vigorous a Prime Minister as Ricasoli. The people of Florence deputed their best men to wait on him while staying in that city, and urge the matter on his prompt attention. He replied in these words : "Let there be no impatience, gentlemen ; be calm. I confess that the affair of Rome has become a very difficult one ; but the knot must not be cut, it must be untied, and it will be so in due time."

The people of Tricchina wrote to Garibaldi in a similar vein, and on Christmas eve, after thanking them for their kind words, he added : " Be good enough to listen to me ; you who were the first to throw down the glove have borne the brunt of misfortunes. We all, however, retain an approving conscience, and an inflexible resolve to do the like again very soon. The priests of Rome, and those who tolerate and protect them, are the cause of all your troubles. They must feed on the dead whom they have killed, or they could not live. . . . I hope soon to be with you. Meanwhile. . . . Arm, and bid the provinces around follow your example, and the priestly brigands will soon disappear. Adhere strictly to our programme, that which has made us strong—Italy and Victor Emmanuel. The audacious who may have forgotten will soon be reminded that this is the land of Massaniello and the Vespers.

On receiving the usual New Year's congratulations, the king said : " Italy must be prepared to make new sacrifices, in order to complete her independence ; " and at Florence the impression prevailed that Garibaldi was meditating some new action, and that the king had come to feel the necessity of acting in unison with him. When the Prince Royal went to inaugurate a local society, he said, " Italy has need to be assured that when the day of struggle shall come she will find in every citizen a soldier."

Garibaldi met Ratazzi by appointment at Turin, and the promises and engagements there made warranted him in endeavouring to secure for the new Ministry the support of his friends. All foreign influence was to be repudiated, and every act directed to the realisation of the national desire for Rome as the capital of Italy. On our hero's return journey to Caprera all that enthusiasm could express was lavished upon him by the Genoese.

COUNT CAVOUR

Garibaldi again left Caprera in the latter part of June, to accompany the heir-apparent and his brothers to Palermo. The municipality of that place issued a proclamation, reviewing his services to them and their deep obligations to him. And on his arrival at the Trinacrio Hotel the crowd assembled outside shouting for his appearance. He came out on the balcony and said: "I salute you, people of Palermo. We knew each other in the time of danger, and if there be a people for whom I have a special affection, it is you in Palermo, whose initiative work merits the gratitude of the whole peninsula and the admiration of the world. Yes! I am touched. This people moves me. I salute you. I am with you, and shall not immediately leave."

The next day the General, with the Royal Princes, his old friend Pallavicini, and the Mayor of Palermo, were present at the rifle contest and at a magnificent *fête*. The population, 200,000, poured out in large groups, and he frequently addressed them, exhorting to concord, and saying, "There are two who will never deceive you, and to them you should listen—Victor Emmanuel and myself. Rome and Venice will ere long be ours, but for their attainment sacrifices will be necessary. Italy must be *uno! uno! uno!*"

Garibaldi left Palermo for Trapani, and thence went to Marsala, the whole population turning out as at a gala to behold the man whom they designated "the hero of Marsala." The Mayor and Council, with the National Guard, went in procession some five or six miles to meet and congratulate him. Flags from all the windows, and thousands of voices welcomed their arrival at the cathedral, where the clergy awaited them. A hymn was sung and the *benedictus* pronounced, when a monk ascended the pulpit, addressing the people and the general in such language that, when he concluded, Garibaldi embraced him and designated him "a true minister of the Gospel of Christ." The people then carried the General to the residence assigned to him, amidst an enthusiasm not to be described. He appeared on the balcony, and profound silence ensued, while in calm and solemn tones he again enunciated the Italian idea of which he was the embodiment:—"The time is come when we can no longer permit the stranger upon the Italian soil. . . . Brethren, Napoleon did not make war in 1859 for Italy. We have given him Nice and Savoy, and that did not satiate him. He wanted more. Ay, I know it! His aim and labour is the aggrandisement of his family. He intended one prince for Rome, another for Naples, and would have renewed all the allotments. I know it. I know it. To petition him is not our duty or necessity, and I am sure that the people of France are with us. If Napoleon withdraws from Rome, the capital is ours. I have much joy in meeting you, and shall ever be your friend. Adieu!"

Ratazzi wanted, at the request of the French Emperor, to send Garibaldi back from Sicily to Caprera as a prisoner on parole, but Victor Emmanuel put a private check on this high-handed dealing, by sending a note to Garibaldi asking him not to make any more speeches like those at Palermo, for if he did, pressure might be put upon him to compel his return to Caprera. The king was shrewd, and his honesty controlled the double-dealing of the French Emperor and the reactionary leanings of the Turin Minister, who had forced from him the proclamation on which he proposed to act towards Garibaldi.

But the time was come when the French bubble must burst, and Garibaldi be the victim. The sacrifice forms one of the sublimest phases of European history. Austria looked on and learned in time, or she would have lost Hungary.

Ratazzi obtained the king's signature to a document, directing General Cugia, who had taken possession of the

Prefecture at Palmero, to request the Mayor and a delegate to see Garibaldi. They were to require him to break up his volunteer camp within twenty-four hours, and to send the volunteers to Palermo, where the Government would take charge of them and undertake to conduct them to their homes. Garibaldi declined a private interview, and met the deputation surrounded by his staff, that they might witness the whole affair. The king's proclamation being handed to him, he shrugged his shoulders, and said it wâs a document made up for diplomatic purposes; he knew all about Victor Emmanuel's intentions. His Majesty, he added, has been made to sign the edict by his Ministers out of consideration for foreign powers, just as he wrote two years before, desiring him not to cross the Straits of Messina, because negotiations were going on with the King of Naples for an alliance. The situation was exactly similar to this, and as he had disregarded that note he should now disregard the proclamation. But when he read the Minister of War's address he fell into a violent passion, avowing that while he recognised the King he did not care a fig for his Ministers. He bade the bearers return Medici's letter unopened.

At Rocca Palomba, he said to the people, "I am com· forted by your enthusiasm; what is well begun will surely end well." The people shouted "Romo o Morte!" "Yes, Rome or death," he replied; "we will keep our word." A group of women repeated the cry; he turned to them and said, "Yes, to Rome; you too, ladies, have a share in this new vindication of national independence. Instead of weeping, and keeping back your sons and lovers from aiding in this work of liberation, you must, like the women of Sparta, send them to the camp, and compel them if they hesitate. If not, they will be slaves, and death is better than slavery. The want of men left the Bourbons at Messina in 1849, from whence they returned to re-enslave you.　In 1860 we tracked the wild beast to his lair, though Napoleon tried to prevent it. . . .　And now he seeks to hinder me from going to Rome, which is the most ardent desire of the nation.　But, we go ; we shall punish him."

From Patrina, Garibaldi and his host marched into Catania, where the people had made great preparations to receive him, and just as these manifestations concluded a deputation of friends arrived with the request of the Ratazzi Ministry, that he would abandon his policy and retire, for Messina and Catania had been made impregnable. Garibaldi being already in Catania, the proposal was too late.　Every town being ablaze with affection, any strong measures were too likely to end in again creating Garibaldi dictator.　After General Cugia had declared the news of Catania being taken to be false, and within an hour finding it true, he actually declared Sicily in a state of siege. Garibaldi issued a proclamation, dated Catania, 24th August 1862, which concludes as follows :—

"If I have done anything for my country I desire you to believe my words.　I am resolved to enter Rome as a conqueror, or perish under its walls.　If I die, I know you will righteously avenge my death, and will also complete my work.

"Long live Italy !　Welcome Victor Emmanuel to the Capital !　　　　　　　　　　　"G. GARIBALDI."

No reporters could follow the General in his unknown track, but there is the faithful account rendered by General Guastela, one of the staff, and revised by General Cook, confirmed as it is by the official despatches :—

"General Garibaldi had been compelled to thin the ranks of his column, because of the difficulties of the voyage ; and the harassing marches caused more to drop out, exhausted by fatigue, privation, and the terrible heat. On the evening of the 28th August, the column encamped on the high table-land of Aspromonte, in the north-west of the province of Reggio, in Calabria, reduced to fifteen hundred men. The General had his headquarters in a very small room in one of the only two cottages on that spot; the night was cold and rainy, and the wind violent, which is not unusual in that high region during the summer season. The volunteers had great difficulty in keeping the bivouac fires burning while they rested and ate the scanty supply of food collected from the neighbouring villages. The royal troops following closely in their rear compelled them to avoid the mountain goat-tracks, and to ford the torrents; the country not being able to furnish supplies for fifteen hundred, Garibaldi divided his column into two, ordering their march by different routes to the same point. The royal troops arrived at Aztic (?) on the same day, and a part of the volunteers were at Pedargoni and Santo Stefano, scarcely a day's march from each other. Indeed, more than once the royalists entered as Garibaldi left the village, and some became prisoners. The volunteers had express orders not to attack, and, if attacked, not to defend themselves, but to march on as rapidly as possible. A little before noon on the 29th, the General broke up his camp at the forest of Aspromonte, for the royal troops had reached San Stefano, and could overtake them in two hours. He gave orders to ford a small river and move northward to the hill. We stopped half-way up the hill, at the edge of a pine forest, and turned about, facing the troops marching upon us, which had now reached the heights opposite. We had no outposts in the rear, nor did we retain occupation of the cottages. With our backs to the forest we stood watching the event, not intending to do battle, but to avoid encounter.

"Garibaldi stood in the centre of his men, sending off his staff officers to the front to repeat the order not to fire on any account, and watching the movement of the royal troops who were advancing—the rifles in front and the regulars behind, evidently intending to surround the volunteer force. The sharpshooters posted themselves within range, and waited in solemn silence. Some of our men, the best, knowing there would be no fighting, retired into the wood. Not a shout or a musket disturbed the silence. Garibaldi stood in front, wrapped in his grey American cloak lined with red, now and then turning to his soldiers and repeating his order, 'Do not fire,' and they repeating all down the line. But the commander of the royal troops had different orders—to attack. The rifles opened fire, and advanced. No summons to surrender, no flag of truce. The musketry became thicker and thicker, and we heard the well-known whistle of the bullets as they passed us and struck the trees. Unfortunately a few of our raw recruits disregarded the General's orders and fired a few shots, but the mass remained unmoved, some sitting, some standing. All our trumpets repeated the signal to cease firing, and the officers shouted the same order. The royal troops did not delay their advance.

"Garibaldi stood at his post, shouting, 'Do not fire! do not fire!' At that moment two bullets struck him, one wounding him slightly in the left thigh, and the other seriously on the right ankle. He did not fall, but elevating himself, took off his hat and cried out, 'Long live Italy! Do not fire.' Some of his officers surrounding him, lifted him up and seated him under a tree. Then, as calm as usual, he gave some orders, always repeating, 'Let the royal troops advance; do not fire.' Meanwhile the fire had entirely ceased all along our front; but in a few minutes Menotti was laid beside his father with a bad wound in his leg.

"Pallavicini was introduced to Garibaldi, to whom he removed his hat, and they entered into conversation and arrangements. These were the disarming of the volunteers, and after twenty-four hours, permission to return to their homes; the removal of Garibaldi and his staff to Scilla, retaining their swords; during the journey to stop where he pleased; to embark at Scilla on board an English vessel, and to be escorted to the shore by a company of riflemen at a given distance. Pallavicini told the General he must communicate with Turin as to the English vessel."

In the evening the disarming being completed, a rude litter was constructed for the General's removal, the burden devolving, at their desire, upon his own officers and men. They arrived at Scilla by two in the afternoon, where Pallavicini had taken a house near the sea-shore for the General's accommodation, and in the evening came to spend a little time with him. He was denied an English vessel. The Government ordered his disembarkation on the *Duke of Genoa*, with ten officers of his staff and some orderlies. A house had been prepared for him, but he declined to rest there, preferring to be taken on board where the royal steamer lay at the end of the jetty. When the vessel began to move, the familiar shout rang around, "Long live Garibaldi! To Rome! To Rome!" He stood up in his pain and raised his hands, bidding them adieu.

Europe was aroused by the news of Garibaldi's arrest and wounded condition. England sent Dr. Partridge at once, and a subscription of nearly £1000; and all classes called meetings of sympathy, and sent resolutions of condolence. Ratazzi became alarmed, and sought, through General Türr, to know what terms of amnesty would be acceptable to the chief; but the old bird could not be caught. He carefully and steadfastly resisted every attempt to elicit a word from him on the subject, thereby leaving the Minister in a dilemma. Pallavicini had not much cause for self-congratulation when he received from the Emperor of the French a decoration for his conduct at Aspromonte, and Cialdini's complacency was abated by the king's demanding his appearance at Turin. The people soon expressed their sentiments. For instance, his friends at Naples addressed him thus:—

" General ! to-day two years are completed since Naples witnessed the destruction of the Bourbon tyranny, and you, the soul and leader of a gigantic enterprise, entered our city alone, the first to unfold the banner of United Italy ; and you were enthusiastically received by the entire population. We should be wanting in gratitude—that holiest of human sentiments—if we were silent on the occasion of your misfortune, or disregarded or left unmarked this day. Illustrious prisoner ! Naples sends you, this day, her affectionate salutation. Whatever may be the vicissitudes of fortune, nothing can deprive you of the glory of having made us Italians, and nothing can deface the memory thereof in our hearts."

Meetings were held in London, Birmingham, Glasgow, Manchester, and all our great towns.

His landing at Varignano was a most affecting scene; the people sobbing, and he himself deeply moved, ejaculating : " Be patient, my dear children, and hope for better times ; you see that Garibaldi is not dead yet." At this he fainted, and was carried in that state to the appointed room in the convict prison at Spezzia, with no medical appliances for dressing his wounds. An Italian gentleman in the dockyard lent him a bedstead, and a Manchester lady arrived and purchased for him every needful comfort.

The French, Turinese, and some of the English desired to connect Mazzini's name with his, notwithstanding that Mazzini had written, a fortnight before, his disapproval of the step Garibaldi had taken. A friend wrote to Garibaldi expressing strong opinions on the intriguing disposition of the Mazzinian party, and accusing them of betraying them of betraying an old friend. He read it carefully, and said, " Our friend is deceived ; he must have got these ideas from the people at Turin." Then he added, " It is folly. I was induced by no one. I moved because it was my duty. After a hundred lucky marches, I have had one unlucky, and am disabled.   Had it not been for that I should have entered Rome as I entered Naples."

All that the surgical skill of Italy, France, and England could effect or suggest did not relieve his pain and misery for a long time, but from October his improvement increased, and the physicians strongly advised his removal to better ventilated and more cheerful apartments, with the best results to his appetite, his spirits, and the relief of his pain ; and as soon as the reaction set in he begged to be transferred to Pisa, which was carried into effect on the 8th of November.

On the assembling of the Italian Parliament, Antonio Morini rose in his place as member for Palermo, and delivered a speech such as had never before been heard in the Legislature.   He ended thus :—"Gentlemen, the Cabinet is universally disapproved.   The Ministry is destitute of authority, and the country is out of heart.   Anarchy is spreading, because the nation is losing hope.   We must speak of things as they are, and I appeal to my colleagues if my experience is not theirs.   Perhaps too hastily I say the nation has no hope.   It has hope—in Parliament—and from it the country waits the sentence of life or death."   It vindicated Garibaldi, and Ratazzi was hurled from power.

Garibaldi returned to Caprera, and became a delegate to the Italian Parliament in 1863 ; but he busied himself most in his sympathy with the oppressed, and sending kind words to his correspondents.   All activity for the time being was at an end.

CHAPTER XI.

GARIBALDI'S VISIT TO ENGLAND.

" Welcome, because the glory of thy wreath
  Had never shade nor stain,
Because thy sword sprang never from its sheath
  Except to cleave a chain ;
Because thy hands, outstretched to all who live,
  Armed not for thine own sake,
So strong to save, open'd so wide to give,
  Do not know how to take.
Because thy foes can reckon to thy charge
  Only the noble crime
Of faith too liberal, and love too large
  For this unworthy time."

GARIBALDI had arranged to make his long-deferred visit to England in the spring of 1864.   His health had not yet been restored, and the quiescence of political affairs gave him an opportunity which might not occur again of at once recruiting his strength and yielding to the pressing invitations of so many whom he highly esteemed.

Southampton went into a fever when his arrival in the *Ripon* was announced ; deputations from Bristol, London, Newcastle-on-Tyne, and other parts of England, and gentlemen deputed to represent the Poles, Hungarians, and Italians swelled the tide of welcome.

He landed at four o'clock on the Sunday afternoon, with his son Menotti and his secretaries, Bosco and Lugeso, Colonel Chambers, and his Italian surgeon.   On his arrival at the docks the quays were literally covered with the crowds of people. He went upon the paddle-box, and was hailed with tremendous cheering, which continued without cessation till the ship came alongside, he meantime repeatedly waving his cap in response.

Before leaving the *Ripon* he asked to make public this memorandum : "Dear Friends,—I do not desire any political demonstration, and above all, not to excite any agitation."

On Monday the 4th April, the town of Southampton did itself and its visitor honour by his reception at the Town Hall. The following is his reply to the address presented him :—

" It is not the first time that I have received proof of the sympathy of the English nation, and I have had these proofs not only in words but in deeds. I have seen that sympathy shewn to me in many circumstances of my life, and very particularly in 1860, when without the help of the English nation it would have been impossible to complete the deeds we did in Southern Italy. The English people provided for us in men and arms and in money—they help all the needs and wants of the human family in their work for freedom. What they did and what they say of us is worthy the eternal gratitude of all Italian people. To answer some of the words, noble and generous, of the Mayor, I will say to you that I did not sacrifice any part of my life ; but I think I did something, and a very small part it was, of my duty, and of the duty of every man. I finish by giving my thanks to you for your generous sympathy and your very kind and good welcome to me here to-day."

He had not been in the Isle of Wight more than two days before it was evident that nothing less than a *quasi*-royal progress throughout England and Scotland would satisfy the wishes of the people, the corporations and clubs, all over the land to do him honour. A powerful representation from Manchester by a committee of four hundred names, asking a visit, followed similar ones from Bristol and

London ; and after these came deputations of working men and official representatives of municipalities, such as those of Nottingham, Birmingham, Liverpool, York, Dundee, Greenock, Edinburgh, Glasgow, and Rochdale.

Before leaving Newport, the General planted an oak on the west side of the carriage drive, and Mr. Tennyson another opposite. Garibaldi then called on Mr. Tennyson, staying an hour-and-a-half with him. While there he planted a *Wellingtonia Gigantea* in the poet's grounds.

Garibaldi's reception in London baffles all description. No one had ever seen such a crowd assembled in the streets as on this day to welcome the single-handed, humble, unselfish man, who had fought and won the battle of freedom. The whole length of road from Nine Elms to Westminster is five miles, and every yard was crowded with human beings, obscuring the enormous trade procession, with its hundred banners, which headed the *cortege* of the General, and which of itself numbered fifty thousand men.

At about one o'clock the carriage of the Duke of Sutherland, drawn by four bays with outriders, drove up to the gate, and the people cheered again and again at the union of aristocracy and democracy in this glorification of a common sentiment. The large station-yard exhibited an exciting spectacle when the gates were thrown open. A sea of heads filled the whole space, and the windows all round were occupied by ladies saluting with their handkerchiefs, while from within and without rose a cheer, gradually increasing like the swell of a great organ, which burst out in full volume as General Garibaldi and his friends appeared at the doorway. He stood up, looked gravely round, and in an instant his smile made every one near him rush forward to seize his hand, and it was necessary for his protection that the police should make a way for him to enter his carriage. His grey military cloak carelessly thrown over one shoulder relieved the bright scarlet, and as he stood up in the carriage to enjoy and return the greetings of the people, one could scarcely imagine a more striking picture. At last his carriage left the yard, and the gates closed and shut in the others until the trades had defiled before him, after which they were re-opened, and the other carriages followed bringing up the rear. The remainder of the route need not be described.

Some idea may be formed of the vast multitude when it is known that it took more than four hours to reach Westminster Bridge Road. The scene at the bridge can readily be understood by those who know the locality. The centre had to be cleared by the troops, and then the high towers of the House of Parliament stood in full view against the blue sky and in the glow of the evening sun. Thence into Parliament Street up to Trafalgar Square, where the large area was filled by a solid mass of human beings ; but as Pall Mall was reached darkness came on, and the pageant, probably the most extraordinary and imposing that had ever been seen in London, either in royal progresses or visits of foreign sovereigns, came to an end by the General's carriage turning in at the park entrance of one of the most princely of English nobles. Garibaldi entered Stafford House leaning on the arm of the Duke of Sutherland, and was received by the Duchess and many of the nobility.

On Tuesday he visited the Right Hon. Mr. Stansfeld and Lord Palmerston, and in the afternoon Chiswick House, then occupied by the Dowager Duchess of Sutherland, where an elegant *dèjeuner* had been prepared.

On Wednesday he paid a visit to Earl and Countess Russell, and afterwards went to Woolwich to inspect the arsenal, accompanied by the Duke of Sutherland and General Ebert, returning in the evening to a magnificent banquet in his honour at Stafford House. Later in the evening he joined a brilliant circle, but retired soon after eleven, thoroughly exhausted.

On Saturday, at the Crystal Palace, after making a
speech to an assemblage of Italians, a concert followed, at
which the special musical event was the performance of "La
Garibaldina" by Arditi—a genuine Italian war song. Arditi
led off with a fire and effect quite electrical. The stirring
words—

> " O Garibaldi—nostro salvator,
>   Te seguiremo al campo dell'onor !
>   Risorgia Italia—il sol di Liberta !
>   All'armi ! all'armi ! Andiam "—

raised by thousands of voices, thundered along the roof and
reverberated throughout the vast interior.

Then followed a presentation of swords to Garibaldi and
his son Menotti, by Signora Serena, for the Italian committee, and an address. After a while he went on to the
terraces, had some rest, and returned amid cheers as hearty
as those which had greeted him on his arrival. He dined at
Cambridge House in the evening with Lord and Lady
Palmerston and a select circle.

On Sunday he received a deputation of "all the nations"
of the members of the Freemasons' Lodge, "Philadelphos,"
to which he belonged, he being the Grand Master of the
Sicilian Lodges. The "Grand Master of the Rite of
Memphis " headed the deputation. He conversed with him
in their respective languages, English, South American,
French, Italian, &c. Finding nearly all speaking a different
tongue, he exclaimed with emotion and delight, "What! is
the whole world represented here?" and large tears rolled
down his cheeks. The interview lasted an hour, and at parting his feelings overcame him, and he could only say, in
Italian, "I am with you, body and soul."

During the week his list of accepted invitations numbered
almost fifty, and there was no prospect of its closing. The
case began to involve the sacrifice of his health rather than
the promotion of his recovery ; but on Monday morning he

paid a second visit to the Crystal Palace to receive sundry addresses from thirty-seven deputations. On Wednesday that distinguished honour in the gift of the City of London—its freedom—was conferred on Garibaldi. The scene on Ludgate Hill and in St. Paul's Churchyard was one of extraordinary brilliancy. Flags streamed from the houses: the windows were all occupied by closely-packed groups, and the many city bells rang out their joyous peals. As Garibaldi passed in the carriage, he bowed from time to time in acknowledgment of the acclamations of the people.

On being asked whether he would accept the presentation in the Council Chamber or the Chamberlain's office, he characteristically replied, " Wherever Kossuth received his freedom." The record was given to him in a massive gold box, of oblong shape, in the style of Queen Anne, having in the centre of the lid the arms of the City of London, richly chased and ornamented with flowers. On the back is a star of burnished gold, with the letter " G " set in brilliants.

Wearing his ordinary grey cloak, and looking remarkably well, Garibaldi passed through the open space amid an ovation not loud but deep, expressing the esteem and admiration felt for him, accompanied by his son Menotti, Mr. Negretti, Dr. Basile, and his secretary. The court having been formally opened, and the resolution read, the Lord Mayor took his seat, whereupon the City Chamberlain delivered an address on behalf of the Corporation, many of its sentiments eliciting loud expressions of approbation. The following is the Address and Garibaldi's Reply :—

" Illustrious Sir, — The City of London invites you to-day to accept the highest honour and award at her disposal, placing your distinguished name upon the list of worthies inscribed upon the roll of honorary citizenship. It becomes my duty, accordingly, to address to you in her name a few words, however inadequate, of thanks, congratulation, and hearty welcome. We are well aware that no one shrinks more sensitively than yourself from the voice of eulogy ; and yet, living as you do to please not yourself alone, you will feel that there are occasions—and this would appear to be one of them—when, for the sake of others, truth, though flattering, should be listened to.   Bear with me, then, while 1 attempt to give feeble expression to the feelings of unbounded admiration and affection entertained towards you by the citizens of London.   I am not called to dilate upon the marvellous incidents of your eventful career, rivalling in interest the wildest romance, because the resolution of this honourable Court, devised so as to secure a perfect unanimity of welcome, directs my remarks rather to your character than to the political events of your life. History, it has been said, usually reproduces herself at intervals more or less frequent, but we turn her pages in vain to meet with the prototype of Giuseppe Garibaldi : 'none but himself can be his parallel.'   We find, sir, no counterpart to your career, even among the fabled legends of the early periods of that city with which your name is henceforth imperishably associated ; when Romans, in the interest of their country,

> 'Spared neither lands nor gold,
> Nor son, nor wife, nor limb, nor life,
> In those brave times of old.'

In your person that primitive spirit of self-sacrifice is reproduced in combination with characteristics and qualifications hitherto deemed incompatible.   The glories of an accomplished general, associated with the instinct and daring of the old sea-kings ; valour which liberated kingdoms and placed them at your feet, combined with the stern incorruptibility of a Dentatus and the severe simplicity of a Cincinnatus ; a heart in which the boldness of a Leonidas, dwells compatibly with the tenderness of a woman and the truthfulness of a child ; the whole strangely tempered and elevated by an earnest craving for the reign of peace, brotherhood, and freedom—manifesting faith in the world's future, in humanity, and in God. Twice, ere mature manhood, you had risked your own life to rescue a fellow-creature from drowning. Then, like our own Florence Nightingale, you devoted yourself to the suffering and the dying at a cholera hospital at Marseilles. Proceeding to South America, you are subject to the infliction of torture to the utmost point of human endurance, to compel (hopeless task) the betrayal of a friend; and, with generosity almost superhuman, you release with his life, liberty, and property intact, the monster who had so tortured you, when he falls into your hands. What shall I say of the magnanimity which distributed the spoils of war and of prize-money on the ocean to the most needy of your companions, and stripped from your own back even the last remaining shirt to shelter a comrade? Restored to Italy and to the work to which your life is devoted, victory places at your disposal the revenues of two kingdoms and spoils which might have graced an oriental triumph; but you reserve not to yourself sufficient to convey you to your sea-girt rock of Caprera; and, grandest of all, when stricken down in the name of your country, 'wounded in the house of your friends,' suffering and helpless during thirty weary days and sleepless nights, no taunt or reproach escaped your lips. . . . We have no selfish interest to promote in relation to this your visit. The era of revolutions is, to us, closed. . . . You will go back to that beautiful but long misgoverned country, to tell of a sight you have witnessed—unique of its kind in Europe—of a million of men contributing to a triumph to the uncrowned champion of liberty, without the presence of a single soldier; and you can acquaint those who rule that the securest throne rests solely upon the affections of a free people, and that the power to 'terminate the era of revolutions' is in the keeping of rulers, and at their own disposal. And now, sir, permit me the privilege of offering you the right hand of fellowship as a citizen of London, requesting your acceptance, in the name of the Corporation, of this souvenir of your visit to their city. We regret exceedingly, in common with our fellow-countrymen, that having been too demonstrative in your affection, having loved not wisely but too well, your health renders it expedient that your visit should speedily terminate. Let us hope, in the language of Lord Palmerston, that 'the early termination of your visit, and your foregoing the honours awaiting you in every town in this country, however disappointing to those who admire, may have the effect of preserving to your country a life so valuable.' In the name of his lordship in the chair, of his brethren the aldermen, and of every member of this Court, I express a fervent hope that British skill, and the invigorating air of our northern climate, may contribute strength and soundness to your enfeebled limb ; and may the unbought spontaneous love and welcome of a free people impart fresh nerve to your arm, and brace your patriotic heart for any work for Italy or for the world which Providence may yet have in store for you."

This address was much cheered, and at its close the Chamberlain said he was commissioned by the Lord Mayor to offer the right hand of fellowship to the General and his son, and accordingly shook hands with both.

General Garibaldi, still standing, amidst deep silence delivered the following reply, in earnest and thrilling tones, that awakened the sympathy of all present :—

"It is certainly impossible for me adequately to express my gratitude to you, as the representative of the glorious and great City of London, for the honour which you offer me to-day. Mr. Mayor, I am prouder of that honour certainly than of the first place in war, the false glare of war, the first honour in war, because I consider it is the greatest honour for me to be a freeman of this glorious city, the focus of the civilisation of the world. I do not exaggerate in saying that, because I have seen now that this city is the very centre of liberty. Here there are no strangers, because every foreigner is at home in England. I repeat that it would be impossible for me to express my gratitude to you and the City of London. But I return you my thanks, not for my own self or on my brothers' behalf alone, but for the sake of my country, which looks to England for any support which she can give in war. Certainly my countrymen can never be grateful enough to the English people for their support and sympathy, and for material aid in every circumstance. This is not the only occasion that I have been happy with the English people. I have been happy with them in many places in the world, and at many times—in America particularly—and under some instances it is owing to the protection of the English flag that I have been saved. In China I received from English people aid which it is impossible for me to forget, and I then said that in every part of the world my gratitude, affection, and love for the English people would be imperishable. I repeat that I am grateful to the whole of the English people, and through you I thank them on my country's behalf."

The eminent surgeon, Dr. W. Ferguson, having certified that a continuance of this work must break him down, he determined to leave this country on the 28th, and return to Caprera. The announcement disappointed many; but its propriety was evident. Although Garibaldi rose at five in the morning as usual, he had not half-an-hour to call his own; and all the scenes, addresses, and deputations were of a terribly exciting nature.

On Friday the 22nd he issued an address to the English nation from Prince's Gate, announcing his intention to depart, in the following terms :—

"I offer my heartfelt gratitude and thanks to the English nation and their Government for the reception I have met with in this free land.

"I came here with the primary object of thanking them for the sympathy for me and for my country, and this my first object is accomplished.

"I have desired to be altogether at the disposition of my English friends, and to go to every place where I might be requested to go, but I find that I cannot fulfil all these engagements of my heart.

"If I have caused some trouble and disappointment to many friends, I ask their pardon; but I cannot draw the line between where I could and where I could not go; and therefore for the present these are my thanks and farewell.

"Still, I hope, perhaps at no distant time, to return to see my friends in the domestic life of England, and to redeem some of the engagements with the generous people of this country, which, with deep regret, I feel that I cannot now fulfil.   "G. GARIBALDI."

On the day on which he received the visit of the Prince of Wales, Garibaldi wrote to Victor Hugo :—

"Prince's Gate, London, 22nd April 1864.

"Dear Victor Hugo,—To visit you in your exile was with me more than a desire—it was a duty; but many circumstances prevent me. I hope you will understand that distant or near I am never separated from you and from the noble cause you represent.—Always yours,

"G. GARIBALDI."

The following was Victor Hugo's reply :—

"Hauteville House, Guernsey, 24th April 1864.

"Dear Garibaldi,—I have not written you to come, because you would have come without that. Whatever might have been my delight to take your hand—you the true hero—whatever joy I might have had to receive you into my house, I knew that you were better occupied ; you were in the arms of a nation, and one man has not the right to take you away from a people. Guernsey salutes Caprera, and perhaps one day may visit it. In the meantime we shall love one another. At the present time the people of England are presenting a noble spectacle. To be the guest of England, after having been the Liberator of Italy, is beautiful and grand. He that is applauded is followed; and your triumph is the victory of Liberty. The Old Europe of the Holy Alliance trembles at it, because there is no great distance between these acclamations and deliverance.—Your friend, "Victor Hugo."

The disappointments at his leaving England led to remarks being made in Parliament in reply to insinuations that his leaving had been effected by a political intrigue. The General—finding that Mr. Gladstone's and Lord Palmerston's straightforward remarks in Parliament did not satisfy his friends—wrote to the Turin papers on the 22nd May:—

"I pray my friends to partake with me the deep gratitude I owe to all the Englishmen whom I have known in their noble country, from the honest sons of labour to those who preside over their Government. My friends know that I resolved to visit England to pay a sacred debt of gratitude, and I withdrew when I thought proper to do so without any instigation whatever. With regard to those from whom I received hospitality, I can never acknowledge their immense courtesy, so splendidly lavished."

CHAPTER XII.

CESSION OF VENETIA AND ROME

"Ride on, to the cries
Of ' Long live Italy !' while, near and far,
All good men's hopes bless thine investiture,
Honest king-maker of an honest king ;
And pray thy work may stand, till rooted sure,
In spite of friends that as the ivy cling
Stifling with wintry green, that shews like spring.
Ride on, Victor Emmanuel, to the throne,
From which crowned wickedness hath toppled down,
While Garibaldi, guerdonless, alone,
Takes his far higher throne and nobler crown."

GARIBALDI returned to Caprera on the 19th June 1864, accompanied by his sons and several friends, but his health had not been recovered—it had gone back ; and when he went away his voice could scarcely be heard, and he was thin, pale, and much weakened. The baths employed were absurdly unsuitable. He bore it as long as he could, and then suddenly resolved to go home the next day. He went away in the early morning, in a steamer kindly sent at a moment's notice by the municipality of Naples. He was borne to the vessel by four men in a kind of litter, which the people half-covered with roses and sweet flowers, the music playing, and the people caressing him. Waving his hand as he lay in the boat, he left the shore ; and the parting on board the steamboat left few dry eyes. But another scene had occurred before he left the courtyard. He had been doing some kindnesses while on the island, and all the poor came trudging up to have a last look at their friend. At five o'clock, quite exhausted, he was resting in his *loggia*, and hundreds of these poor wretches filled the place. "What is the noise outside?" said he. "Ah, General, it is the poor of Foria, and we tell them you are exhausted; and they say if you will appear at the window they will bless you and go away." "Let them all come in," he replied. So one by one the poor creatures passed through his chamber. He lay back too exhausted to shake hands, but smiling and blessing them all. At length there was a pause, and—"No, no, impossible; you cannot enter," the guard was saying. "What is the matter?" cried Garibaldi. "Oh, General, it is old Beppo; he is half-witted, and very dirty and miserable; we tell him he can't come in." "Come in, my brother, come in; you are not too dirty and miserable for me"—and the General took the hand of the poor sobbing old creature before them all.

When he got home his health forthwith began to recover. In another month he would have been off to Hungary to aid those people, but the king heard of it, and so plied him with arguments, that he reluctantly abandoned a project which would have killed him outright, and the sacrifice would have been of no avail. Happily he was persuaded to remain in Caprera, where he devoted himself to agricultural pursuits, away from excitement, and taking no part in the arrangements for the transfer of the capital to Turin. Thus, before Christmas, he became as sound in body as he had all along remained in mind.

As Garibaldi more and more recovered his strength, he plainly perceived that a new crisis in the national progress was at hand. The people had never ceased to execrate the unworthy compromise which left Venice enslaved when Lombardy was wrested from Austria; and the Italian Government constantly and patiently awaited an opportunity of redeeming the fault of 1860. That opportunity came at length in the Austro-Prussian war; for it was impossible that Italy should see her old enemy attacked upon the north without seizing the moment and turning it to her own advantage.   Garibaldi perceived that an alliance with Prussia must inevitably be formed ; and he no longer hesitated to prepare himself and his volunteers for a renewal of their patriotic struggles.   The enthusiasm of the Peninsula rose higher and higher during the close of 1865 and the spring of 1866 ; whilst the Government shewed its hand to Austria in a manner which the latter power could not misunderstand.   The freedom of Venetia, which France had refused to effect when it was in her power, was destined to be gained through the aid of Prussia ; and this was no doubt a wound to the self-esteem of Napoleon, which had its due share in urging him to his fate some fours years later.

The year 1866 was the red-letter day of Venice, as 1862 had been for Naples.   The king sent for Garibaldi, and the people made demonstrations requesting that the General be entrusted with special powers.   On the 8th of May the king issued a decree ordering the formation of a corps of Italian volunteers of twenty battalions, under the command of General Garibaldi, for one year's service.   This announcement produced a change in the Ministry, and Garibaldi's friend Crispi secured a place.   The General was urged to make conditions before accepting the position which the king requested of him ; but his reply was : " I will hear nothing of conditions, I make none ; for with the Austrians before us no Italian can make any.   I, you, they ; we all go to fight them."   He accepted the office.   The twenty battalions made ten regiments, each having forty-two officers and fourteen hundred and forty-six men.

On the 19th of June war was declared on the part of Italy.   Garibaldi with his forces took the line towards the Tyrol, and then went himself to Bergamo and Basua to inspect the volunteers.   He established his headquarters at

Lonato, a town standing on the southern declivity of a hill, and surrounded by an ancient wall. His camp was on the hills behind the town, from Lake Garda towards Solferino, and his outposts extending to Rivoltella, within three miles of the Austrian stronghold; so that the whole range assumed a most picturesque aspect from the multitude of red shirts all along the line, and through the dales, and on the hills all about Lonato. Suddenly the general ordered all to march to Salo, on Lake Garda; but his stay did not extend over a couple of days, when he resumed his position at Lonato, and established a camp at Cappucini.

This marching about, apparently with no settled or known design, culminated in the General's resolution to invade the Tyrol at Cattaro. He told off a brigade of two regiments, under Corte, for that purpose; and after a fatiguing march of twenty-five miles they reached San Antonio in an exhausted condition, faint, and drenched with the heavy rain.

Garibaldi had become impatient, and determined to strike a blow that very afternoon instead of letting the men, or rather boys, have food and a night's rest. The enemy had a strong position. The sharpshooters, who were to come over the mountains, had not arrived; indeed there had not been time for them to do so. The field of battle was on the steep side of a mountain nearly fifteen hundred feet high, sloping down to Lake Idro, and bisected by an exposed upper road leading to Bagolino. The whole face is clothed with underwood; a good cover for Tyrolese, but a hindrance to those not used to it. Presently the grey uniforms of the *Bersaglieri* come in sight, and at a given signal—the firing of a gun on the lake, which had an immediate response from the enemy—the conflict began.

"From 3.30," says an eye-witness, "when the first shot was fired, till 5.40, when the Garibaldians were in full retreat towards San Antonio, the fire of the enemy was

20

terribly lively and well directed, while that of the Garibaldians was in general exceedingly wild, and mostly—except the riflemen—not directed at all. Orders to charge with the bayonet were repeatedly given, but never responded to, except one instance—namely, those commanded by Captain de Verenda, who received a bad elbow wound. At the most critical moment I observed the strong grey cob Garibaldi uses in the mountains being led riderless to the front, and a few minutes later saw Garibaldi himself suddenly appear fifty yards ahead of those on foot, as if he had risen from the road. Mounting his cob, the General rode quietly towards a small body of his men, who were crouching fearfully by the roadside, and tried to encourage them to advance. Poor fellow, he could not stimulate them more; for he himself was faint from loss of blood, having received a flesh wound in the thigh, which later on compelled him to leave the field.

" By 5.30 the upper road, so exposed to a galling fire, would have been taken but for its crooked form. It presented a horrid spectacle, being completely lined with the dead and dying. Over these prostrate bodies the Garibaldians stumbled in their retreat in wild confusion, and would have been panic-stricken had not the artillery interfered, and by cannon-shot swept the advancing *Kbiser-Jäger*, doing them terrible mischief, and causing them to retreat. At six our men were completely done up ; no more could be induced to go to the front, and the fight really ended, for the enemy did not advance."

At nightfall the volunteers abandoned their position, and retired on Anfo to re-form the regiments, battalions, and companies. Garibaldi left for Salo and Briscea, to obtain better surgical advice and attention, and much dispirited at the day's disappointment. But the Austrians had received enough. Victor Emmanuel, although he lost at Verona, or at least did not gain, had convinced Austria that he would prove victorious ; and on the 5th she proposed an armistice, offering to cede the Venetian territory to the Emperor of the French as mediator, in order that she might use her army in pursuing the war for supremacy in the Germanic Confederation.

We should be travelling too far out of our course if we were to follow in detail the circumstances of the short decisive war which resulted in the overthrow of Austria at Sadowa, or even of that phase of it which led to the definite cession of Venetia. The Austro-Italian campaign was by no means decisively favourable to Italy, whilst at sea, in particular, the latter country suffered great reverses. Garibaldi's share in the operations by land did not extend much beyond what we have recorded ; and, even if he could have pushed further his successes against the highly-trained armies of Austria, the need was removed by the acquisition of Venice.

The Convention between Italy and France, signed on the 15th of September 1864, pledged the French Government to withdraw its troops from Rome within two years ; but the term was subsequently extended for another year. September 1867 arrived, but France had not fulfilled her part of the agreement ; whilst the Italian Government had been faithful to its promise to restrain all attacks upon the temporal Government of the Pope in Rome. Garibaldi and his friends vigorously repudiated the Convention ; and they represented the will and force of the nation, if not its legalised Government. The Pope expressed himself dissatisfied with the agreement entered upon by Napoleon and Victor Emmanuel, and had refused to sanction it. Thus on every ground it is manifest that Italy found herself, at the end of September 1867, completely absolved from all restrictions upon her action ; and Garibaldi in particular was in a position to give rein to the enthusiasm of his followers with a clear conscience.

The fact was that the French Government found the evacuation of Rome a very difficult matter to carry out. The opposition to such a step was very strong, not only in France but in other countries. Many French statesmen desired it—Benedette, La Valette, Prince Napoleon amongst them ; but the most that the Government could be prevailed upon to do was to wink at the attempt of the Garibaldians in 1867. At the time of the attack of the volunteers, M. de Sartiges, the French Ambassador, was absent from his post ; and his second in command, M. Armand, was a Catholic of no small ability and energy, whose attachment to the Holy Father led him to do all in his power to checkmate the Garibaldians. It was probably owing as much as anything to Armand's decision and obstinate partisanship that the designed laxity of the French Government was of no avail, and that Pio Nono secured a respite of another three years.

Enlistments of men and distributions of arms were carried on throughout Italy and in the capital under the very eyes, with the connivance and, indeed, the co-operation of the Government. Volunteers gathered on the borders of the shrunken Pontifical State under the command of Garibaldi's son Menotti. Garibaldi landed at Genoa, travelled about the country, came to Florence, and addressed the multitude in language of which the Government affected to condemn the violence, and which led to the farce of the General's arrest at Sinalunga and his removal to Caprera, where his movements were watched by royal cruisers, which, however, he was allowed to evade, when the great blow was to be struck and his assistance was needed. Garibaldi again landed at Leghorn, and at the head of five thousand volunteers marched upon Rome.

" On 26th October, Garibaldi, at the head of six thousand men, attacked Monte Rotondo, in which there was a garrison of three hundred men, who were obliged to yield.

"On the 3rd of November, at four o'clock in the morning, a column of five thousand men, composed of three thousand Pontifical troops and two thousand French, left Rome, under the orders of General Kanzler, in order to retake Monte Rotondo, and to finish with the Garibaldian army, which continued to hold positions on this side of the Teverone. The Pontifical Zouaves, who formed the vanguard of the army, having arrived towards half-past twelve, at a distance of four kilometres in front of the village of Mentana, were attacked in a hollow road by the Garibaldians, who were in ambush on the wooded slopes by the line of route. Towards three the Pontificals had already gained more than two kilometres of ground in the direction of Mentana, when General de Polhês observed that the battalion of foreign chesseurs had advanced too far in front, and was on the point of being surrounded by strong Garibaldian columns; it was then that the French were called on to take part in the action, and under the orders of General de Polhês, Colonel Fremont, of the first regiment of the line, hastened to disengage the Pontifical battalion of foreign chesseurs, while at the same time Colonel Saussier, of the 29th, made a movement of attack on the left. At half-past five all the Garibaldians were driven back into Mentana, of which the first houses were occupied by the Commandant Fouchon, of the 59th regiment of the line, and by the Pontifical Zouaves. The field of battle was gained, and Mentana completely invested.

"Such was the state of affairs on the evening of the 3rd. Kanzler, from that time certain of success, proposed to carry, on the morning of the 4th, the strong position of the Castle of Mentana, when Polhés, who is an old African, recollecting that at Saatcha the French army was stopped for forty days by a paltry town, prevailed on him to accept his very wise advice, and to demand fresh tooops from Rome, and particularly artillery, in order to spare his men. General Dumont, commanding the division in Rome, received this demand at midnight. He mustered all the French soldiers he had disposable, and started for Mentana, where he arrived on the 4th, at seven o'clock in the morning, just in time to receive at headquarters the Garibaldian envoy, who came on purpose to the surrender of Mentana."

Garibaldi escaped unwounded from the battlefield, but while making his way to Caprera was arrested at Figline and carried to the fortress of Varignano, near Spezzia. He protested against his incarceration on the ground of his being an Italian deputy and an American citizen. Finally he was set at liberty, and allowed to return to his island home.

In Caprera Garibaldi remained till 1870, leading the life which he seems to have in his heart loved better than anything else. He was beset not a little by travellers from various parts, particularly, it is to be feared, from Great Britain, to whom he was invariably kind, and to whom he largely talked what can hardly be described otherwise than the visions of an enthusiast.

The Franco-German war of 1870 and the downfall of Napoleon III. enabled King Victor Emmanuel to enter Rome after an insignificant resistance. In this triumph Garibaldi had no share, but a few months later his zeal in the cause of peoples against monarchs induced him to raise a corps of volunteers and offer his services to the French Republican Government against the Prussians. He led about twenty thousand men, who fought well and gained some successes over the Germans, but provoked a strong feeling of dislike among the French rural population by their want of discipline and the outrages they committed on the Catholic clergy. At the end of the war Garibaldi was elected a member of the French Assembly, but speedily resigned his seat and went back to Caprera.

CHAPTER XIII.

LAST YEARS AND DEATH.

" Now safe returned, of wandering tired,
No more my little home I'll leave ;
And many a tale of what I've seen
Shall wile away the winter's eve."
—KIRKE WHITE.

WE are now approaching the end of our story. The capture of Rome, and restoration to its historical position as capital of Italy, crowned the glorious work of Garibaldi, and the few closing scenes of his life which it remains for us to describe speak only of the activities of one to whose nature sloth was entirely alien—of a man who, fairly satisfied with the success by which his labours have been crowned, either devotes himself exclusively to the arts of peace, or at most reveals his inextinguishable enthusiasm in hearty sympathy with oppressed and unde-livered nationalities.

With the campaign of 1870 Garibaldi's active life in the service of humanity ended. The malady, which all knew in the end must prove fatal, though ever and anon kept at bay by his iron will, had made steady inroads through a consti-tution never of the most robust. The solitude of Caprera, and the pleasure he derived from his young family, gilded the last years of his life with a personal joy, which the changeful events of his stormy career had prevented him ever before from tasting. Regard for his family led Gari-baldi at last, in 1876, to accept the national gift of a million of francs, with an additional life pension of 50,000 francs annually. In 1875 he went to Rome with his young family

and their mother—to Rome which he had defended so nobly
in 1849, and had not since revisited.　The enthusiasm with
which he was welcomed baffles all description.　King Victor,
whose repugnance to inhabit Rome was a very sore point
with the Romans, had never excited any enthusiasm.　The
Moderates were at the height of their unpopularity; had
Garibaldi pronounced the magic word "Republic" it is
difficult to predict the consequences.　Instead of this, his
first words were a prayer for order and absence of all agitation.　His first act was to take the oath in the Chamber of
Deputies, an act most natural in itself, as he had never once
given sign of hauling down the flag he had unfurled in 1859.
Nevertheless, the Moderates were beside themselves with
astonished delight.　Now their demonstrations outshone
those of the Radicals, and when the General went in
seriously for what we may style his Tiber campaign, the
House, on Minghetti's proposition, voted sixty thousand
millions, handicapping the vote, however, with a proviso,
"when the funds shall be forthcoming."　Garibaldi, as was
his fashion, went in most seriously for the Tiber business.
Every day, in company with engineers, surveyors, specu-
lators of every description, he would visit the banks of the
Tiber, ôr go down to Fiumicino, there to trace out the future
port of Rome, and the Ministry, only too thankful that he
kept clear of politics, favoured his plans in every possible
way.　He was bent on clearing away the pestilential swamp
known as the Agro Romano, the exhalations from which
made the city of Rome at certain seasons very unhealthy.
Besides this he proposed to raise the banks of the Tiber, to
prevent the periodic floods from its overflow, and consequent
malaria entailed thereby on the subsidence of the waters.
This work involved also the partial change of the course of
the river, besides giving a better water-way to the Eternal
City, and was linked with the construction of a combined
port and harbour of refuge.　Finally, acting on the advice

VICTOR EMMANUEL

of the engineer, Temenza, whom he had called in, he settled upon Fiumicino as the spot where the Port of Rome should be, this being also the place Julius Cæsar had selected as the best adapted for that purpose.

Nor was the project very foreign to his previous experience, for his seafaring life would lead him to see that facilities for shipment and arrival of merchandise were those best calculated to consolidate the young kingdom and to stimulate that industry without which liberty is an empty sound, for that country is happiest

> "Where a man is a man if he's willing to toil,
> If he's willing to gather the fruits of the soil."

And his efforts to lead in this direction shew that, contrary to the nature of most men of martial leanings, he looked on fighting as but a means to an end, that end being the happiness of the people. In this relation a quotation from an address he delivered to the working men of Rome bears out this characteristic bent of his mind, or rather, we should say, of his life. He began by advising them to put their sons to some handicraft, so that they might find happiness in an honest and laborious occupation, and he concluded with the following high compliment to this nation :—"Be as the Romans, your forefathers, were—steady, undaunted, unflinching, persevering. Imitate the English of modern days, and particularly in the serious purpose they throw into all they do—in what they call 'steadiness.' In my opinion, the English bear a greater resemblance to the ancient Romans than any other modern people. Nothing daunts them ; whatever they desire to accomplish they set about with an earnest steady will, which seldom fails in obtaining its end. They are never beaten down by misfortune. Follow in their footsteps. This is the advice that I have to give you as your friend and brother."

But the scheme of the great Cæsar taken up by Garibaldi has, through political exigencies, and the jealousy of less favoured towns, fallen through, and the good work remains to be done by some future benefactor.

Whilst in Rome his health was very indifferent; his old wounds troubled him, and he was obliged to walk with crutches. He therefore thought it best to resign his position in the Italian Parliament, which he did in the following letter to his constituents: "My dear Friends,— I was in hopes of being able to be of use to you. I was mistaken. My health has become so bad that I am absolutely unfit for work. I heartily thank you for the confidence you have shewn me, which will be a pleasant recollection for the rest of my life."

In reply to earnest entreaties from his friends, and under the influence of a little royal and ministerial pressure, he shortly afterwards withdrew his resignation. On the Continent he was greeted in every town he passed through with tumultuous enthusiasm. At Viterbo a monument had been raised to the patriots who died in the war of liberation, and Garibaldi attended the inaugurating ceremony, where he met with an enthusiastic greeting. At Orte bands played, and there were triumphal arches. The populace accompanied the carriage for miles. There was an enormous cavalcade of carriages, horsemen, and carts, thirty-seven societies with their bands and banners. Twenty-seven mayors and twenty thousand people—the entire population—joined in the triumphal procession. Garibaldi was on crutches. He addressed the people, and afterwards renewed acquaintance with many old comrades.

It was during this short absence from Caprera that Garibaldi, in reply to a ridiculous charge of having betrayed the cause of the Republic for a "mess of pottage," wrote the following laconic letter :—"I never belonged to the party of liars. I have fought for the Republics of fact, and so far as that cause is concerned I have never betrayed it."

ın the year 1878 Victor Emmanuel died. The following extract from the *Times* sums up very ably his great life-work :—

"More than once he was struck by severe illness as well as by domestic afflictions, and in every such moment the emissaries of the priesthood were at hand to work upon those religious apprehensions to which he was by no means insensible. But the king never wavered, and no spiritual terrors could affect his resolution to be true to his oath to the constitution of his kingdom, and to his beloved people. Gradually, around this central pillar of the State, were the fortunes of Piedmont built up. Patient economy and good administration enabled the king to send seventeen thousand good troops to join the Anglo-French forces before Sebastopol, and to assert for his country an independent place among the European Powers. The reputation thus laboriously achieved rendered Victor Emmanuel and his country the natural and obvious centre of the national aspirations when the Emperor Napoleon forcibly overthrew Austrian predominance in the Peninsula. It had been made plain that there was a king in Italy who could be trusted, and who commanded the service of statesmen who could be followed. It was no usurpation in the ordinary sense of that word which made Victor Emmanuel king of Italy after 1860. It was simply the recognition of a fact. Every other kingdom, every other civil and military authority had vanished like a phantom. Victor Emmanuel, with his trustworthy character, his proved administrative and military power, stood alone erect amid fallen thrones, disbanded armies, and general disorganisation. He seized the reins of government because they had fallen from all other hands, and the people allowed him to take them because he had proved that he could be trusted.

"It is this which will always remain the grand achievement of Victor Emmanuel's career. Very powerful influences were, through the greater part of his reign, at work in Italy which were hostile to Monarchy. A very religion of Republicanism was preached by ardent enthusiasts, and the most powerful of these anti-monarchical leaders had rendered incalculable services, both by the pen and by the sword, to the cause of Italian unity. That which founded the Monarchy and founded a staple organisation for the new kingdom, was that Victor Emmanuel was the most trusted man in Italy."

Nor while we are referring to those whose lifework has left its mark upon a regenerated Italy, must we forget Giuseppe Mazzini, whose tall gaunt form and long serious face was probably more familiar to many in London than to his fellow-countrymen   It may be said that Mazzini was the sower and Garibaldi the reaper of the splendid harvest garnered for Victor Emmanuel. Early in life he set to work to scatter Liberal doctrines, founded on the idea of Italy united under one crown. However pronounced his Republicanism became, his first address was to the father of Victor Emmanuel regarding this project, but failed to meet with a ready response. He then gave rein to the Republican idea, pure and simple, as afterwards displayed on his banners, " God and the people," and abjured all kingcraft and kings : and as the father had not responded to his call, so he denounced the son as one who would ultimately betray his beloved country.

The reply to his address or letter was a sentence of perpetual banishment, upon receipt of which he set to work in the formation of the society of " Young Italy," with a breadth of aim to embrace the peoples of all and every civilised State ; and in the conducting of the correspondence connected with this movement he organised such an intelligence department in his own hands as enabled him to understand all the devious moves of the leaders of the political arena. But the very powers of his mind which enabled him so incisively to lay open the wrongs of Italy, and the means of remedy, prevented him seeing the need for a consideration for others who were engaged in the same work, but whose methods were not so sweeping as he could wish. Thus it was that, after all the noble work he bestowed in furtherance of Italian unity, he was not trusted to co-operate with Garibaldi in the Neapolitan liberation which his master-mind had, by its subtle appreciation of the course of events, acquired by his excellent corresponding powers, enabled him to see only required organisation to be successful. In this concentration he materially assisted, while courage in the breach was supplied by Garibaldi.

Latterly his failing health kept him from actively entering upon revolutionary work, although early in the spring of 1872 he was reported to be on the way down from Switzerland on an insurrectionary incursion into Italy, but the telegraphic news of Tuesday, 12th March, brought word that one of the great figures in the drama of Italian liberty had departed this life, that Giuseppe Mazzini had ceased to trouble the crowned heads of Europe, having died on the previous Sunday at Pisa.

Poor Mazzini! He who had sweethearted poor, distracted, dismembered Italy into a state ripe for union, so far from taking the place of bridegroom, for which his wisdom, energy, and moderation during the brief and troubled Republic in Rome in 1849 shewed he was not unfitted, was not even allowed to play the part of the bridegroom's friend, but from afar he was compelled to witness the consummation of that union which had been his life-thought and life-labour.

And so one by one the Saviours of Italy passed away from the scenes of their mighty labours. All of them with great faults—if men are to be judged by those alone, they were all very imperfect; and our hero, because the strongest and greatest, the most imperfect of all.

But we have only to look at what Italy *was*, and what through their joint labours Italy *now is*, to see that they were all great and noble men in the true sense of the words. Cavour, Mazzini, and Victor Emmanuel, they rest from their labours and their works do follow them,—while Garibaldi, "the last of the Romans," was left for a few years longer to help the world along, if not by new acts, at least by his presence, with its memories of the grand past.

Of course Garibaldi felt the most undisguised sympathy with the gallant struggle of the Servians and other Turkish vassals and subjects to throw off the yoke of their oppressors. It was a struggle similar in many respects to the one which he had himself brought to a successful issue ; and he wrote many letters to the newspapers and to his friends advocating the cause of the Sclavs.   We will quote some of the most noticeable of these.   One of the first was to Earl Russell, in the following terms :—

"Caprera, 17th September 1875.

"My illustrious Friend,—In associating your great name with the benefactors of the Christians oppressed by the Turkish Government, you have added a most precious jewel to the humanitarian crown which encircles your noble brow. In 1860 your sublime and powerful voice was heard throughout Europe in favour of the Italian Rayahs, and Italy is no longer a geographical expression.   To-day you plead the cause of the Turkish Rayahs, who are still more unfortunate. It is a cause which will triumph like the former, and God will bless your declining years.   I shall undertake to do whatever you wish.   I cordially salute your much-esteemed wife, and am, while I live, your devoted   G. GARIBALDI."

A few days later Garibaldi sent the following spirited appeal to the Herzegovinian insurgents and to their fellow Sclavs in Turkey :—

"Caprera, 6th October 1875.

" To my brothers of the Herzegovina and to the oppressed

of Eastern Europe,—The Turk must go away to Broussa. He descended like a wolf, passing the Bosphorus, devastating, murdering, and violating those populations who gave us the Pelasgi ; who were, perhaps, the first civilisers of Europe. He must no longer tread upon that part of the world kept by him in misery. At Broussa, with his vices, depredations, and cruelties, he will find enough people of Asia Minor to torment and plunge into desolation. Rise, then, heroic sons of Montenegro, Herzegovina, Bosnia, Servia, Therapia, Macedonia, Greece, Epirus, Albania, Bulgaria, and Roumania ! All of you have a most splendid history. Among you were born Leonidas, Achilles, Alexander, Scanderbeg, and Spartacus. And to-day, even among your robust populations, you will still find a Spartacus and a Leonidas. Do not trust Diplomacy. That old woman without a heart certainly deceives you. But with you are all the men of heart throughout the world. England herself, till to-day favourable to the Turks, has manifested to you by means of the *obolus* and sympathy of one of her great men, that she ought to prefer the alliance of and gratitude of a confederation of free peoples to the decrepit confederation of the Empire of the Crescent. Then to Broussa with the Turk ! Only thus can you make yourselves independent and free. On this side of the Bosphorus the fierce Ottoman will always be under the stimulant of eternal war, and you will never obtain the sacred rights of man.   G. GARIBALDI."

In November 1880 Garibaldi visited the Continent for the express purpose of inaugurating the monument erected to the memory of the vanquished at Mentana by the Milanese Democrats, as an off-set to the monument erected by the Milanese Moderates to Louis Napoleon.

His advancing years, and the infirmities due to his wounds and confirmed rheumatism, might well have excused him the ordeal of a public appearance ; but he whose courage never failed him in the breach was not to be deterred by mere

aches and pains, and so we find him present to unveil the
Memorial, but in a state to excite the utmost pity at his
sufferings and admiration at his courage.   Propped on a
mattress, on which he had to be borne to his carriage, he
was driven through the densely-crowded streets, in which
every balcony and every window was filled with enthusiastic
spectators, vieing with their fellows in the street in the
heartiness of their reception of the great Italian.   The
plaudits, no less than the overwhelming crowds, shewed
that Garibaldi was still a living force in the land of his birth.
Yet, what a sight!   There he lay, unable to move, save one
arm a little, and with that he feebly shewed his appreciation
of the reception.   He smiled, however, while his poor
shrunken face shewed the low ebb to which his vitality was
fallen ; yet the fire of his eye was unquenched as the spirit
within.   Arrived at length in the Piazza Santa Marta, the
horses were detached from the carriage, which was then
hauled up an incline to the platform erected alongside
the Memorial, designed and executed by Belli of Turin,
which, being unveiled, was seen to consist of a female figure
standing erect and representing Italy, holding a wreath or
immortelle in her hand, standing on a massive square
pedestal, bearing a bas-relief on each of its four sides, one
representing the resistance at Mentana, another the defence
of Monte Rotondo, the third the Capitoline Wolf nursing
the founders of Rome, while the fourth bears an inscription
by Cavalotte "to the memory of the fallen of Mentana."
An address from Garibaldi was read on his behalf by
General Canzio.   In it he described Mentana as a moral
victory obtained over the temporal power and the Empire
of Napoleon III.

Contrary to general belief Garibaldi lived latterly a very
retired life.   His sole companions were his wife Francesca,
his children Manlio and Clelia, their governess (a Milanese
lady), and two or three intimate friends.   His physicians had

enjoined him complete repose, and his wife was all vigilance to see the injunction carried out. She intercepted all telegrams and letters addressed to him, and communicated to him those only which were of a pleasant kind. His life was as regular as the clock; he rose early, and, weather permitting, took a drive in his curricle to the sea-shore. Then he would go and superintend the operations connected with the farm; and in spite of his advanced age and the gouty bronchitis from which he suffered chronically, his voice was clear, high, and ringing as in his best days. He would salute a passing countryman, and converse with him cheerily for several minutes, to the wonder of all who knew how his frame had been shattered by privation, wounds, and disease. At eleven A.M. he returned home to breakfast. This was a meal of Spartan frugality. He ate with relish certain cakes made of meal, onions, and tomatoes. When he had appetite he would take a little butcher meat, of which his attendants brought him a large slice, and this he would throw on the fire. In a few minutes they would take and cool it, and cut off the cooked bits, which the General ate, throwing anew on the fire the half-cooked remainder, which was again taken off when ready cooked, and eaten as before. When this eccentric mode of doing a beefsteak was remarked, the General replied, "I cannot eat it otherwise. I was habituated to this way when fighting in South America, where I had neither cooks, nor kitchen, nor utensils, and where it was a bit of supreme good luck when we could fell a buffalo and appease our hunger off him." After dinner the General and his family retired into a room next the dining-room—a spacious apartment commanding a view of the sea-shore and the island of Maddalena. His wife Francesca had a new window opened in the wall so as to admit of his seeing the entire seaboard without exposure to sun or wind. When the weather was good, however, he preferred to perambulate the island in his curricle, which was pushed by Vincenzo, a robust Piedmontese, a relative of Francesca's.

After his visit to Milan, and a short sojourn in Asti, his wife's native town, he returned to Caprera, resolving never again to leave it. There to the last, when not in intense pain, he thoroughly enjoyed his life, reading daily all the newspapers that were sent to him, dictating his memoirs, or scraps of novels, and, in his own fashion, educating his young son Manlio, whom he literally idolised. In the month of January 1882, while watching the lad fishing, he was upset out of his invalid carriage and rendered insensible by a blow on his head from some rough stones. When he returned to consciousness the boy was hanging over him, shrinking with fright and terror. As though nothing had happened to him, he said quietly, " What, you, who mean to be a brave soldier, cry at the sight of a couple of drops of blood !" Though the wounds were not severe, the shock to the system was great, and followed as it was by a sharp attack of bronchitis, his family and the doctors urged the necessity of passing the winter in a milder climate, and Dosilipo was fixed upon. It may be said without exaggeration that all Naples thronged to the shore to welcome the Liberator; even the Moderate papers affirmed that two hundred thousand people watched the *Exploratore* round the promontory, and with breathless anxiety watched the litter hoisted up from the commander's own cabin, which he had unroofed to make the invalid comfortable.

Too weak to be exposed to excitement or fatigue, only the Syndic was allowed to express the heartfelt joy of the Neapolitans to have him once more in their midst. A consultation of physicians was held, and with the exception of inhaling turpentine and ordering the strictest attention to be paid to the temperature, perfect quiet and freedom from excitement was the remedy from which any hope remained.

Never perhaps has any other sufferer been as patient. Grateful for any attempts to alleviate his pain, he was never peevish or impatient. Silence and solitude were his great resources; only Manlio's noise never seemed to disturb him, nor would he ever allow him to be checked. When in too much agony to speak his eyes still rested with a caress upon the boy, and when at ease he would narrate the wonderful events of his life, the prowess of his comrades, and of his first wife Anita. Often in the last months of his life he referred with tenderness to his mother, whose picture always hung at the head of his bed at Caprera, and to whom he said he owed all that was good in him, especially thoughtfulness for others. Garibaldi's last public act was to visit Sicily on the occasion of the rejoicings over the sexcentenary of the Sicilian Vespers. He was, however, unable to appear in public, and it was painfully evident that suffering had brought his long and splendid career very near indeed to its close.

On the 24th May 1882, Dr. Sirletti, the distinguished Roman dental surgeon, who had been called to prescribe for Garibaldi, observed to Manlio that the General had stayed out longer than usual, and that on his return his expression was sad. It then turned out that he had been to the east of the island, about half-a-mile from the house. There, almost on the shore, is a little enclosure containing two graves. They are those of Rosa and Anita, two young daughters of his. As a rule, however, the General was cheerful—particularly in these later days. In the evening, after the most modest of suppers, he would enjoy the conversation of his family, a few friends, and Dr. Albanese. Naturally the topics were his early adventures and his more recent exploits in the Italian wars of Independence. He would answer his eager interrogators with a smile, and concentrate the talk on the companions of his enterprises rather than on himself. Sometimes in the animation of narrative his voice would rise and his eye would flash as if the turmoil and din of combat were before him. But a sudden gesture like the attempt to raise his arm would remind him that he was a rheumatic cripple, and his manner then became subdued and melancholy. But if his body was weak his mind was clear and energetic. It only sufficed but to mention a name which had once, however long ago, interested him, and he would recall every incident connected with it down to the most minute details. He was one evening talking of rifle practice, and the name of Domencio Corrazzi was pronounced. "Corrazzi! Corrazzi!" he exclaimed, "I knew him; he was one of my best soldiers," and he forthwith proceeded to tell of Corrazzi's exploits, and dictated a letter which be begged Dr. Sirletti to deliver to Major Corrazzi on his return to Rome. This was the last letter signed by Garibaldi.

On the 24th May Drs. Sirletti and Albanese decided to leave Caprera, and their departure was fixed for the morrow. Garibaldi manifested great regret at this. They had scarcely parted from him, and gone some paces from his door, when he called them back, saying: "Don't leave a poor old man. Who knows when I shall see you again—if I ever see you again!" The renewed farewell was painful. Garibaldi had his curricle pushed down to the sea-shore, and before Drs. Sirletti and Albanese got on board the steam launch, he again called to them, and said: "It is small pleasure to kiss an old man's cheeks. Kiss me on the forehead." Then turning to Sirletti, he said, "Salute my dear Rome for me." He looked as if he would have said more, but could only murmur, "Go, go quickly," and with a tear in his eye he turned away. Then when the steamship *Lombardia* stood out seawards with his friends on board, he waved them farewell with his pocket handkerchief so long as the vessel was in sight. Then he was conveyed home, and shortly after took to bed, from which he never rose.

The end was indeed near at hand. A week after this he was so much worse that telegrams were sent summoning his son Menotti from Rome, and recalling Dr. Albanese from Palermo. He gradually sunk, and on the night of Friday, 2nd June 1882, at half-past eight o'clock, the end came, and the last Hero of the heroic age of New Italy passed away. He died with the window of his room wide open, while the sun was setting behind Corsica. Before the last agony began, a bird alighted, twittering on the window-sill. Garibaldi saw it and stammered, "Quanto o allegro" ("How joyful it is").

As the dark tidings of his death became known, great was the grief of all Italy. At Rome the news fell like a thunderbolt. All the theatres suspended their representations. At the *Valle* the comic actor forced tears instead of smiles from the audience by his cry, "Garibaldi is dead." On the news being instantly conveyed to the king by the Secretary-General of the Interior, Signor Lovito, his Majesty, overcome with grief for the loss of one who had ever been his father's firm and sincere friend, and had invariably, in the most solemn moments of his life, repeated the words "Italy and Victor Emmanuel," sat down and with his own hand wrote the following telegram :—"The grief which I feel for the death of your illustrious father is proportioned to the bereavement of the nation. My father taught me from my early youth to honour in the General the virtues of the citizen and of the soldier. Afterwards a witness of his glorious deeds, I had a deep affection for him, and still greater gratitude and admiration. These sentiments, and the remembrance of those displayed by the brave General towards my family, cause me to feel doubly the gravity of our irreparable loss. Participating in the supreme sorrow of the Italian people, and in the mourning of the deceased's family, I pray you to be interpreter to them of my condolence, which is shared by the whole nation. HUMBERT."

A newspaper correspondent in Milan gives the following graphic account of the reception of the news of his death in the North of Italy :—

"Never, I verily believe, has the sun looked out on anguished grief such as now bows down the Italian people of every class and creed, high and low, rich and poor, from the snow-clad Alps to sunny, sad Palermo, for the death of their beloved chief. The news came to me in the early dawn, in a small town nestled among the Mincian hills, undisturbed by tram or railway, where only the diligence plying between Mantua and Brescia twice a-day breaks the peaceful monotony of daily life. It was market day, and a busy one, as the silkworm campaign is nearly over, and the keenest anxiety prevailed as to the price of the cocoons. Meanwhile, the office boy who brought my telegram had spread the news : Garibaldi is dead ! A hush fell over all, then the countrywomen, bearing back their produce of poultry, returned weeping to their homes, feeling each that the head of each household was no more. As we drove to the nearest station, four miles off, every shop was closed, on each was written or scrawled, '*per lutto nazionale,*' or '*Garibaldi é morto,*' all who possessed a flag had hung it out with a crape veil or a black rag. From Desenzano to Milan the people lingered about the stations hoping against hope that the news was not true, or to glean particulars of the catastrophe. At each station veterans or younger *reduci* of the *patria battaglie* entered the train, bent on reaching Caprera by some means or other; if no steamers go there will be the coasting vessels, wanting these, fishing boats. With us was Major Carriolati, one of Garibaldi's favourite officers wounded at Calatafimi, who asked us if we remembered how Garibaldi, in 1867, had alighted from the train to visit his old, blind mother. Arriving at Milan the city seemed deserted, it might have been that the pestilence had swept over it, one could have well imagined that as in the days described by Manzoni in the *Promessi Sposi*, only the Lazzaretto, which still exists, was peopled. A manifesto signed by twenty-eight different associations had summoned the populace to the monumental cemetery, where Garibaldi's portrait, draped in black, was borne in procession.

"'Strange,' said an incomer from one of the smallest towns in the Venetian territory, 'here in this great commercial city, this centre of the material life of Italy, the outward signs of grief are the same as in my little native town, shops closed, all ordinary occupations suspended, one would think that the telegraph had issued a common order: '*per lutto nazionale.*' And in truth the national grief is the individual grief in this case, each household is mourning for his chief, refusing to be comforted because Garibaldi is not.

"This morning (Monday) the bright sun looks out on the same scene of desolation—flags crape-veiled, shops closed, every one dressed in black. From the royal palace, from the municipality and other public edifices the tricolour hangs desolate in the sultry summer air half-mast high. On the Corso Garibaldi all the balconies are draped in black; Garibaldi's portrait is there, surrounded with ever-renovated freshest flowers; on the facade of the Fossati Theatre his picture is almost hidden by ever-renewed garlands. The only trade plied is that of newspapers, all issued with black borders, the vendors with crape upon their arms.

"I must add one characteristic episode. In Milan, as in the other chief cities of Italy, all the Government and Communal schools are closed; but in one private female school, where priests predominate, the classes were kept open this morning, and the parents piously inclined sent their children. The young maidens thus harangued their mistress :—'When you want to commemorate the feast day of Santa Maria, Santa Teresa, or Santa Luca you close the schools and take us to mass; well, now we close it for Saint Garibaldi,' and up they turned the table on its legs and home they go."

And not in Italy alone was the grief felt; in England, France, and Germany the press expressed the deep feelings of admiration and appreciation which the passing away of Garibaldi called forth. Even from Austria, and from Papal organs in Rome, came encomiums on his pure patriotism, his bravery, and his unselfishness of character.

Garibaldi is dead, and

> "From the dawn it seemed there came, but faint
> As from beyond the limit of this world
> Like the last echo born of a great cry,
> Sounds, as if some fair city were one voice
> Around a king returning from his wars."

Printed by WALTER SCOTT, "The Kenilworth Press," Felling, Newcastl.

IBSEN'S PROSE DRAMAS

EDITED BY WILLIAM ARCHER.

IN FIVE VOLUMES.

CROWN 8vo, CLOTH, PRICE 3s. 6d. PER VOLUME.

VOL. I.

"A DOLL'S HOUSE," "THE LEAGUE OF YOUTH," and "THE PILLARS OF SOCIETY."

VOL. II.

"GHOSTS," "AN ENEMY OF THE PEOPLE," and "THE WILD DUCK."

VOL. III.

"LADY INGER OF ÖSTRÅT," "THE VIKINGS AT HELGELAND," "THE PRETENDERS."

VOL. IV.

"EMPEROR AND GALILEAN." With an Introductory Note by WILLIAM ARCHER.

THE FIFTH VOLUME IN PREPARATION.

London: WALTER SCOTT, 24 Warwick Lane, Paternoster Row.